THE CANDIDATE

"This man Widdell has a special computer system that enables him to know exactly what the voter wants," Pomarev explained.

"You mean to say that Widdell could make anyone president?" the Chairman asked.

"Almost anyone," Pomarev said, and smiled. "You've met with the man who's been twice elected president of the United States. What do you think?"

"Tell me the rest."

"We could ensure that his successor was ours."

"A Russian in the American presidential elections?" The chairman laughed and shook his head. "I don't think even this man Widdell's system is good enough for that."

Pomarev smiled. "Who's talking about a Russian?" he asked.

THE KGB
CANDIDATE

Owen Sela

BANTAM BOOKS
TORONTO · NEW YORK · LONDON · SYDNEY · AUCKLAND

THE KGB CANDIDATE

A Bantam Book / August 1988

ISBN 0-553-27400-7

Published simultaneously in the United States and Canada

Bantam Books are published by Bantam Books, a division of
Bantam Doubleday Dell Publishing Group, Inc. Its trademark,
consisting of the words "Bantam Books" and the portrayal of a
rooster, is Registered in U.S. Patent and Trademark Office and
in other countries. Marca Registrada. Bantam Books, 666 Fifth
Avenue, New York, New York 10103.

PRINTED IN THE UNITED STATES OF AMERICA

O   0 9 8 7 6 5 4 3 2 1

for
Jim Farbon & Alison Sanders,
fellow marathoners,
marathon friends!

THE KGB CANDIDATE

1

October 30, 1984

Huddled into his threadbare overcoat, Drew Ellis stood on the dimly lit platform feeling the cement floor tremble under his feet as the trains thundered into the Friedrichstrasse station. It was a dim, depressing place, with a thin line of shuffling, shabbily dressed East German pensioners outside the brown, duty-free shop, waiting to buy cheap presents to take to the expensive West, or a week's worth of cheap tobacco and alcohol to consume at home.

The shop was narrow and long, a boarded-up cupboard on one side, cartons of cigarettes pressed against windows on the other, an aisle in between, where a man and woman worked with the patience of primitive robots. Posters in front of the waiting room advertised holidays in the Harz mountains and the cultural delights of the Pergammon. A trio of East German Vopos, their drab green uniforms reminiscent of WWII films, walked in suspicious phalanx down the broad flight of steps at the far end, which led to the crossing point and the East.

Ellis huddled against the wall. The station was western territory, and technically speaking he was safe there. But East Germany was only two flights of stairs away, and as a senior intelligence officer, he should not have come; not alone, anyway.

But he'd had no alternative. He had to meet Emma. He'd lived without her for eight days, and those days had seemed like an eternity. Besides, he wanted to be sure Emma was safe.

Emma was Czech, and as a sturdy six-year-old, had walked across the border with her family during that Prague

spring of sixteen years ago. The family had been settled in
Germany, and Emma had inherited a tradition of anti-Communist
activity. She'd been part of the Lotus network when Ellis had
taken it over, and he'd used her to run contacts, to forward
instructions and bring back reports; used her for a while even
after he'd fallen in love with her and they were living
together in an apartment on the Schonhauer Strasse.

But experience had shown him that the law of averages
could be pushed only so far, and despite her protests, he had
made her hand everything over to Putzi and pulled her out of
the network. Emma had been furious about it, he remembered, and at the time he'd felt enormously guilty at his
disloyalty to her and to his country. But he'd believed that he
couldn't live without her, and had known she was more
important to him than his job or his network or his country.
There had been a fifteen year difference in their ages, and he
had often prayed that he would grow old slowly so he could
enjoy her more.

Then Karl had been betrayed, and Willi and Putzi and
Heller, and Emma had insisted she return to East Berlin.
"What kind of a person are you, Ellis?" She had always called
him Ellis when she was angry. "These people are our friends!
Don't you want to know if they are alive or dead?" No, he
had thought, not if it means exposing you to any danger. But
he hadn't been able to convince her, and she'd threatened to
leave him anyway unless he let her go. Emma had been
particularly close to Putzi, and had wanted to find out what
happened to her.

"Putzi is finished," Ellis had said. "The network's finished. There is nothing you or I can do about that."

"I can find out who," she'd said fiercely, and gone.

He hadn't heard from her for eight days, eight days
during which he'd jumped six feet every time the phone rang
and grown gray in the face, and haggard, and lost four
pounds. Then a message had come from the East. She'd been
lucky, she said. Emma had never believed she was a good
spy. Always, she had told him, I am lucky. Now her message
said the betrayal had been from the inside, that she'd found
out who and how, and that she was coming out.

Having made the usual report, Ellis had come to meet
her. Of course, he shouldn't have done it. It exposed her, and
more important, exposed him. But that didn't make any

difference now with the network blown, and in any case he'd wanted to bring her home.

Emma's message had said she'd be using the Friedrichstrasse U-Bahn station. She was late. Foolish to have come on time, Ellis reflected, Emma was always late. She'd frequently told him that however long she took, he shouldn't worry: "Worry never changes anything, sweetheart, believe me it doesn't."

His heart leapt as he saw her tripping down the steeply angled steps at the East German end of the platform, fawn boots twinkling, hurrying thighs kicking away the hem of her beige skirt. Her cream-colored blouse was open at the neck and she was carrying a neat, brown attaché case, looking as beautifully and as coolly efficient as she had the first day he'd seen her. His body ached for her. In the dim lighting her cornflower-blue eyes were dark. She smiled as she saw him and began to move even faster, her flaxen hair streaming behind her as she'd bounded down the last of the steps—

Then she stopped, cowering with fear.

Too late Ellis saw the man on the farther side of the platform, who despite the austerity of his surroundings was swaddled in an ankle-length fur coat. Together with a fur-covered astrakhan, it made him look like some primitive animal. The man had a drooping moustache, and a crescent-shaped scar beneath his lower lip, and as he ran toward Emma, the gun in his hand was like an extra black claw.

Ellis moved. He ran as he'd never run before, meanwhile reaching under his jacket for the Beretta he wasn't authorized to carry. He shouted, "Don't!" Voice hysterical, he cried "Emma!"

But Emma wasn't looking at him. Her whole attention, her whole being, was focused on her advancing murderer, as if she knew she was going to die, and wanted to savor the last precious moments of existence.

In slow motion Ellis saw the man reach for her, saw his thick hand rest on her flaxen hair. He saw Emma turn obediently, her head lowered; saw the man place the gun against the back of her neck, heard him fire.

Emma! Emma!

The echo of the shot mingled with the reverberation of an oncoming train as Emma flung her head jerkily forward and fell with her arms held stiffly by her sides.

Ellis felt his body hurtle through the air, arms outstretched, gun extended. He saw Emma's killer turn, felt the pressure of the trigger against his finger while still airborne. Then he fired.

An expression of shock and surprise crossed the man's face as he pitched forward. Then, still falling, he raised his gun and fired, too.

There was a sharp, burning, knifing pain in Ellis's brain. In the murk that enveloped him, he felt his body spin helplessly before it crashed into the platform. He opened his eyes at the shock. Blood gouted down the side of his face. There was shouting and the hurried patter of feet; and in front of his darkening eyes Emma, her hair spread over the cement like a fragile pillow, her eyes looking at him—no longer cornflower-blue, but opaque and sightless.

And then Ellis, too, died.

2

November 4, 1984

All that day, while the nation went to the polls, Steve Widdell, the president's campaign director, remained closeted in his offices on North Capitol Street. He was watching the commentary and preliminary reports on the old black-and-white portable television he brought to his office during elections, making occasional entries into the computer terminal on his desk.

When the results began coming in that evening, he wasn't surprised. The president was winning, handsomely; winning, in fact, by the largest majority since Roosevelt's second term. Widdell stood up and walked to the window. For him the excitement ended after the initial reports had corresponded to his forecast pattern. His Political Data System not only worked, but had been refined to the point where it was almost infallible.

He pressed his forehead to the cool glass of the pane.

Praise the Lord! Now that the results were known, he felt the fatigue of the last few hectic campaign days, when he'd flown with the president, barnstorming the country in a carefully devised wrap-up campaign intended to remind the country just how much hope and goodness they had.

President Donnelly was a good man. The best man available. And it was his essential goodness that had first attracted Widdell to him, back in the days when, having lost the party nomination, he was considered a has-been by everyone. Widdell had then begun his project of emphasizing the president's attributes and diminishing his negatives. Even then his comparatively primitive PDS system had been accurate enough to find out what the people wanted. And in Jack Donnelly he had given them just that.

A president who led. A president who cared. A president who was God-fearing and who symbolized the essential spirit of middle-class America. A president whose courage and farsightedness had lifted his people from the uncertainty of the Carter years to a new hope and belief in themselves.

Praise the Lord, Widdell thought. The Lord had used him to bring a good man to the presidency. Head pressed to the glass, Widdell prayed silently for help in choosing the next president four years from now, since the constitutional amendment of 1951 forbade Donnelly from running a third time.

3

March 16, 1985

Ellis stared out of the fifth-floor hospital window with hollowed eyes. The window overlooked a dried-out ravine, and it seemed to Ellis that if he threw himself out of the window, he would float straight down the side of the building and be wafted out along the steeply angled slope of the ravine till he crashed onto its bed in a silent shower of soft, dead leaves. There were no visible signs of spring from the win-

dow, but inside the centrally heated, dehumidified hospital
room, Ellis could feel a stirring of the heart and blood in
synchronicity with rising sap. Which he told himself was a
strange thing for a dead man to feel.

That afternoon on the Friedrichstrasse he had died with
Emma and now he sat by the hospital window, a lifeless
dummy, paralyzed and unable to move from his wheelchair,
connected to a semblance of life by tubes. No one knew the
cause of his paralysis and whether its origin was physical or
psychological. The bullet from Emma's killer had lodged near
his brain, and in Berlin they'd had to operate on him twice
before flying him back to Washington. There, after the third
operation, they'd told him that he was home and Emma was
dead.

Spring! Renewal! Rebirth! Death!

Ellis turned his head and looked at the contraption of
tubes and glass bottles which, mounted on a dolly, accompanied him everywhere. At night or when he rested, it stood by
the head of his bed. When he was moved to the window or
taken down the corridor for massage or physiotherapy, it
trundled behind his wheelchair like a space creature from a
science fiction film. It had occurred to him that the tubes
could be disconnected with a simple toss of the head or a
spasmodic jerk of his arm and soft, sweet, thick blood set
flowing. Ellis looked steadily at his arm. He could literally
pull the plug out, lose consciousness and die. He could
drown in his own blood and go to Emma. He told himself
again that he should have died.

Emma had been young and vibrant, beautiful and healthy.
She'd paid her dues and had all her life to look forward to.
Her death had been as purposeless and casual as a flash of
lightning. Here, today, gone!

Emma!

As he'd told the investigatory board which had convened
round his bed, the network had been lost, Karl, Willi, Heller,
and Putzi all dead or jailed, and Emma's visit a pointless
attempt to discover how the network had been betrayed.
She'd found out how, but hadn't been able to tell him. Jim
Colson, who had trained with him at Camp Peary and, like
him, afterward worked in TCAGE, the Agency's counterterrorist
effort in Europe, had said, "I'm sorry, Drew. It should never
have happened."

Ellis had worked with Colson in Rome and again in Paris, and then both had transferred to counterespionage, working out of Germany. Now Colson was a deputy director of the OCI, a post they had both been rivals for before Ellis had been shot. Ellis had looked directly into Colson's still boyish face and found nothing there except sympathy. Colson had no reason to have known about him and Emma, but afterward Ellis had wondered if he'd been talking about them or the shooting.

There was no reason why he should live and Emma die. No reason at all. Life was unreasonable. Life was meaningless.

If he died now, he asked himself, who would avenge Emma? Who would hunt down her killers and find out why she died? Knowing why would at least give her death meaning; hunting her killers would at least give his life a purpose.

Behind him a door opened. The nurse caroled, "Time to see—Mr. Ellis! You're standing!" There was a rush of footsteps behind him and the support of a hand around his waist. He glimpsed a familiar young girl's face, the blue eyes wide open, the cheeks turning the color of damask. In a voice that wavered from excitement, the nurse asked, "Mr. Ellis, just what the hell are you grinning at?"

4

November 14, 1985

On his ninth day at work Ellis stayed at his desk through the lunch hour. Everyone had been exceptionally kind to him, and on his first day back Theo Goddard's outer office had been decorated with streamers and large, hand-drawn WELCOME posters. The boys from the German desk had sent him a case of Veuve Cliquot, and Theo had made a short welcoming speech. But though the office had done everything possible to make him feel wanted, Ellis still felt alone. The empty hollowness was there like a cancer, and despite the assurances he'd given Theo, Ellis was determined to do something about it.

Ellis nervously drew a chair up to one of the computer terminals, keyed in his access code, and requested the file on Lotus. The screen blanked out for a moment while his authority was scanned. Then a message appeared: SEARCHING! SEARCHING!

The last time he'd worked at Langley had been six years ago, when between assignments he'd found himself under the control of Theo's newly created Office of Counter Intelligence. At that time Theo had needed bodies—no matter if they were more useful with guns than files—and Ellis had sat in this very room as an administrative assistant and kept the whole Middle East section going while the office was reorganized around him.

Much had changed since then. The office had grown larger, its operations more complicated and expensive. Counterintelligence was heavily dependent now on electronic surveillance, computer scans, electronic interception, and satellite taps. These days the field agent was more isolated and much more the rough end of the trade. It was the computer analysts who were the glory boys, and any day now, Ellis thought, all a spy would have to do was sit in a room like this and direct his computer terminal at suspects.

As the office had grown larger and more prestigious, its decor had changed, too. Gone were the patterned wallpaper, solid wood desks, and uncomfortable chrome-and-cloth typist's chairs. The whole office was sleeker now, glossier, with pastel-colored walls, modular furniture, desks studded with computer terminals now called work stations, static-free gray carpeting, and chairs designed to make you feel you were sitting at home. Goddard's outer office now looked more like the office of someone specializing in selling expensive cars.

The file appeared on the computer screen with a little click. Ellis scanned the index and pulled up the investigator's report on the shooting. The investigator had been Jim Colson, and since both matters were linked, he had investigated both the shooting and the break-up of the Lotus network.

Colson had found no external reason for the exposure and destruction of Lotus. His conclusion was that Karl, the first one arrested, had somehow been tagged and then blown the others.

That was the standard conclusion, Ellis thought, the

no-other-alternative option that assumed the first one arrested had blown the rest. But Ellis had known Karl well. Karl's father, one of the early East German trade union leaders, had been killed by the Russians, and since Karl's escape across the Wall in the early sixties, he had devoted his life to fighting the Russians and their East German Communist cohorts. A bull of a man, full of a passionate hatred, Karl would have died before being broken. Once at the Café Kanzler he had shown Ellis the cyanide capsule he always carried beneath a loose filling in his teeth. "Much better than sodium amytal," he'd said hoarsely. Ellis also remembered that Karl had not known the existence of Heller, the second man arrested.

He turned to the report of the shooting. Couched in official bureaucratese and radiant in green and black lettering, it seemed a distant experience devoid of soul and substance, archaic and stilted as a long-ago newspaper report. The report said that Emma Czazowicz, the last known surviving agent of the Lotus network, had been returning from the East when she had been spotted and killed. Colson had not known what her mission was, since she hadn't been able to make any reports, but according to her controlling officer, she'd been attempting to find out how the Lotus network had been betrayed.

Colson made no comment on the propriety of that, Ellis noted, and read how he, the head of Lotus, had contravened regulations and gone to meet her because no one else had been available. Colson had known about him and Emma, Ellis now realized, and Colson had been kind. He read the description of how he'd been shot and the details of his injuries: "The intervention of Agent Ellis was not sufficient to save Czazowicz, who was shot and killed instantaneously." Emma's killer had been a former Department 13 KGB agent on loan to the KGB's Service A. The killer's name was Arkady Zoyheddin, and his code name, given at a time when Department 13 was using the names of winds, was Zonda.

Ellis heard the sound of opening doors and Theo's familiar drawl from the next office. Quickly he hit the escape key. The screen went blank.

5

Ellis did not get another opportunity to use the computer till the following Monday. This time he called up the KGB personnel file and extracted the data on Arkady Zoyheddin, code named Zonda.

Zonda had been born in a village outside Simbirsk, the third son of a farmer, and had grown up with a wicked eye for a target and a blind courage that bordered on stupidity. At sixteen he joined his local militia, and soon got a reputation of being handy with his fists and lethal with a gun. Officially he became the district's interdepartmental shooting champion, and unofficially, the organizer of the most exciting and dangerous bear hunts.

In frequent trouble because of his recklessness, Zonda had been jailed and dismissed from the militia after he'd crashed a police car into that of a visiting inspector general. After serving two years of a sentence for manslaughter, Zonda was spirited out of jail and invited to join the KGB's lethal squad of professional killers.

Zonda was a man about Ellis's own age, and like Ellis, the high point of his active career had been during the tumultuous seventies and early eighties, when the Red Brigades had stormed all over Italy and the Baader Meinhof gang and their imitators across France, Germany, and central Europe. In his time Zonda was suspected of having taken out an OPEC head, a Middle Eastern prime minister, an American ambassador, a German finance minister, and a deputy CIC in NATO.

Ellis wondered how easily the peasant from Simbirsk had fitted into the lifestyle of a successful assassin. KGB killers, like all other successful killers, got nothing but the best. They flew first class, stayed in the best hotels, ate in the best restaurants, and had virtually unlimited expenses. They rented top of the range cars, and women were provided, if that was necessary, boys if it were not. He wondered how the former peasant had enjoyed the George V in Paris and if he missed it now.

Zonda's last assignment had been with KGB-SSD liaison in East Berlin, working for KGB Major Boris Pomarev of the KGB's Service A. It had been Pomarev who ordered Emma's death.

Ellis switched the computer on to graphics and pulled up a photograph of Zonda. It was the face he remembered from that afternoon in the Friedrichstrasse, the face he'd seen in numerous nightmares afterward: the eyes like abandoned tunnels, dark, impenetrable, cold; the drooping boomerang moustache; the crescent-shaped scar just below and to the right of the lower lip. Deep down he felt a spark of anger, all that remained of what had once been a searing flame. In the months of his rehabilitation the flame had cooled, become steeled with determination and hardness of will. Now Ellis had no doubt of it: he would kill Zonda!

He became aware of a presence behind him and whirled around. Theo Goddard stood there, bland-faced, close, and smelling comfortingly of baby's milk. He reached across and hit the escape button on the computer. "Come to my office, Drew," he said. "There's something I want to tell you."

Goddard had been Ellis's first father confessor, the father Ellis had never quite had. Goddard had been in charge of teaching Clandestine Operations when Ellis had gone to Camp Peary. A former member of Donovan's OSS who had worked with Dulles in Switzerland and parachuted behind German lines, Goddard had been a legend, even at Camp Peary, where for six years he'd been the course director on Clandestine Operations, and where the newly graduated Ellis had been one of his pupils.

They were both much older now, Ellis reflected. Goddard's downy hair was almost completely gray, and the ridges on his forehead seemed permanently etched. The grayness under his eyes had become perpetual shadow, but the eyes themselves were alert and keen, and there was a healthy ruddiness in his cheeks. And the old man could still creep up on someone as silently as a cat, Ellis thought.

They had both left Camp Peary at the same time,

Goddard to an administrative job in the Agency and Ellis to Vietnam. When Ellis had returned, Goddard had recruited him into his European counterterrorist outfit. Later, when Goddard had moved to counterespionage, Ellis moved with him.

It was as if they were bound by an invisible cord, Ellis thought, or had a shared karma. For nearly all his adult life Theo Goddard had been all the family he'd had.

Now Goddard shut the door and threw himself into his leather-covered director's chair. Whatever the Company designers had wanted, Goddard's only concession to the microchip age was the computer terminal on one side of his enormous leather-topped desk. He liked leather, and the visitors' chairs and sofa were upholstered in grained Morocco, which you could actually smell now that Goddard had stopped smoking. With a shock Ellis remembered that he'd stopped almost six years ago.

Now, he was sure that Theo was going to talk to him again about the impossibility of personal vengeance. In their discussions before Ellis had returned to the office, Goddard had made his position on revenge perfectly clear. There would be no attempts at revenge. None whatsoever.

"But they killed my friends," Ellis had protested. "They killed Emma!"

But Goddard had been implacable. "Death and the loss of a network is something you'll have to learn to live with," he had said. "The service has no room for personal vendettas."

"You mean you'd let them get away with it!"

"No one's getting away with anything," Goddard had replied. "We're in a state of war, and in war there are always casualties. Nevertheless we will take revenge, but it may not be an eye for an eye. Our business is much too complex for that, and your revenge will be part of our general offensive against the Russians."

"That's rubbish," Ellis had protested, and said he wanted the men who'd killed Emma.

"No one's going to deliver them to you alive," Goddard told him, "and they're no use to anyone dead." Unless he stopped wanting to pursue Emma's killers, he'd warned Ellis, he would not be allowed back into the service. Their work was dangerous enough without having an emotionally unstable agent on their hands.

Ellis realized there was no way he could find Emma's killers and survive without Agency resources, so he'd told Theo he would try to forget about revenge and then he'd see the psychiatrist Theo had recommended.

Now, Goddard took a small buff-colored folder out of his briefcase and said, "I've got bad news for you. I have here the Agency doctor's report. I'm afraid the prognosis is that you will never be fully fit again, that among other things you will be subject to stress-induced headaches for the rest of your life."

"That's nonsense, Theo!" Ellis cried. "Doctors know nothing from nothing!" He winced and stopped talking as a sharp twist of pain corkscrewed around his temple.

Behind the large, square-lensed glasses, Goddard's expression was blank. "I'm going to have to mark your file Not Fit for Operational Use," Goddard said.

"You can't do that! Theo listen to me!" Without realizing it, Ellis was crouching over Goddard's desk. "I'm perfectly fit. I tell you I can run thirteen miles in under an hour and a half, and I can swim five miles. The only thing I'm rusty on is combat training, and I promise you I'll start on that right now."

"It isn't my decision, Drew," Goddard said, and suddenly there was a pained expression in his eyes, as if a knife had entered his bowel. "The M.E. has marked you as unfit. I have no alternative but to take you off operational work."

"Operational work is all I know," Ellis said. "It's all I'm able to do."

"You can always learn new skills," Goddard replied. He looked directly at Ellis. "Face up to it, Drew. One day you'll have to."

No finding Zonda, Ellis thought, no finding out *why* Emma died. "I might as well resign," Ellis said.

Goddard looked at him levelly. "It is an option you'll have to consider."

6

It took Ellis four days to get to see the CIA director. A former under secretary of state, Maynard Turnbull had been brought into the CIA to ensure that the Agency adhered strictly to the guidelines laid down by the Church Commission. He was a soberly dressed, pale-faced man, dull and pedantic, with a fondness for precedent, procedure, detailed briefings, and lengthy interoffice memos.

He looked dyspeptically at Ellis's neatly typed statement and said, "Nothing I can do here." He reached beneath the statement and opened Ellis's medical file. "Doctor's prognosis seems accurate. No way I can overrule a medical opinion."

Ellis felt his temples throb. "Couldn't the doctor be mistaken?"

Turnbull's glance was liverish. "Get another opinion and take that opinion to Goddard."

Ellis knew another opinion was not possible. Dr. O'Donnell had treated him since he'd left the hospital, and no other doctor had sufficient experience of his case to challenge O'Donnell's opinion. He told Director Turnbull that.

"In that case, remain on administrative duty."

"I've always been operational," Ellis said.

"Everything's got to end sometime." Turnbull glanced quickly down at the file. "You've had a long run, and will be due for transfer to administration in a few years, anyway."

Ellis thought all he wanted was a few months. He said, "I'd like those years."

"Impossible," the director said. He closed Ellis's file. "Better reconcile yourself to administration. It can be very rewarding, give you an opportunity to pass on your experience." He nodded briefly and pulled a file from a stack. "At your age you should be thinking of what you can put back into the service."

After he'd gotten his revenge, Ellis thought.

At lunchtime he had access to the computer again. Once more he called up the file on Russian personnel and requested the data on Boris Pomarev. Almost immediately the screen blinked back: NOT AUTHORIZED!

Ellis watched the winking letters. His unauthorized attempt to get Pomarev's file would automatically be logged. But why was Pomarev's file restricted? Realizing that Pomarev's file couldn't be so restricted that a summary wasn't available for unrestricted use, he tapped in a request for the summary file.

The screen went blank, as if considering his request. Come on, you bitch, give out, he thought. There's nothing secret about Boris Pomarev. He's nothing but another KGB jerk. But then why was his data file restricted? The screen blurred with a rush of characters and froze. Pomarev's summary file said he had been born in Moscow on April 7, 1946, at which time his father had been a Grade V clerk attached to the Central Committee. From an early age Pomarev had shown impressive scholastic ability coupled with a capacity for hard work. A series of successive scholarships had enabled him to have his entire secondary education at the elitist Lenin Gymnasium, and this had been followed by the Brezhnev Award, which had enabled him to spend four years at Moscow University. He'd graduated with honors and prizes in English, French, German, and the History of Socialism.

Straight from university Pomarev had joined the KGB. He'd trained at the Foreign Intelligence School and then been assigned to the First Directorate, the KGB's foreign service. His first posting had been in Southeast Asia, running clandestine support for the Viet Cong. Pomarev must have done well in his two and half years there, because after a year in Moscow his next posting had been Paris. After three years in Paris he had made brief tours of Washington, London, Bonn, and Brussels, followed by three more years of short service visits to Prague, Budapest, Washington again, and Berlin.

Pomarev was obviously a high-flyer being groomed for a very senior post. In 1984 he had been in charge of KGB-SSD liaison in East Berlin and was credited with destroying the Lotus network. The destruction of Lotus had obviously served Pomarev well. Soon after Emma had been murdered, Pomarev

had been recalled to Moscow and appointed deputy director
of Service A, a position he still held.

Ellis switched to graphics and screened the file picture
of Pomarev. According to the statistics below the picture,
Pomarev was a well-built man, 175 pounds and an inch over
six feet. His hair was brown, his complexion fair, and his eyes
pale gray. The picture showed an attractive, sharp, triangular
face, which, with its delicate features and light eyes, gave
Ellis the impression of a watchful cat. Ellis absorbed every
detail of that face. Pomarev was the man he had to kill.

7

January 10, 1986

The transfer board consisted of CIA Director Turnbull, OCI
Assistant Director Jim Colson, and a polite-looking man from
Personnel called Palmer. Two weeks after Ellis had seen the
Agency-employed psychiatrist, Jim Styles of Internal Security
had told him of a vacancy for an analyst at the embassy in
Moscow. "You could do it easy, Drew," Styles had said. "You
know the language, have the embassy experience, and analysis is
a piece of cake." He had even given Ellis an application form.

Ellis had applied for the post. After examining Pomarev's
file, Ellis realized once again that if he wanted Pomarev and
Zonda, he had no alternative but to stay in the service; it was the
only way of knowing where they were. He hadn't dared plan
what he would do after he got to Moscow. Everything would
depend on what he might discover there, but basically his plan
was to find and kill Pomarev and then get out. If he could get
Zonda, too, it would be fine, but apart from noting that Zonda
had been invalided out of the service, there was no indication of
Zonda's whereabouts except that he was no longer in Moscow.

Smiling gently, the man from Personnel looked up from a
file and said, "Mr. Ellis, I see you have spent the greater part
of your career in Europe countering Russian efforts in terror-
ism and espionage. Bearing in mind that in the course of your

duties you had to invalidate and sometimes terminate personnel loyal to Moscow, don't you think you are tempting providence by requesting a transfer there?"

Invalidate, terminate, Ellis thought. It made you feel that people died without bleeding. He wondered if on one of Pomarev's files Emma had been marked off as terminated. He said, "As I will not be operational, it shouldn't be a problem."

"But how will the Russians know you're not operational?" Palmer had a high, squeaky voice, which now rose to a minute crescendo of triumph.

"They'll figure that out from the fact that if I were operational, I would not be openly assigned to the embassy. They'd also pick it up from my behavior."

"Will that be enough?" Palmer asked, not bothering to keep the incredulity out of his voice.

"If it isn't, we could tell them."

A cool silence descended over the room. Ellis stared at the paneled wall decorated with reproductions of the insignia at the main entrance to the building. THE TRUTH SHALL MAKE YOU FREE. Director Maynard Turnbull asked, "Just why do you want to go to Russia, Mr. Ellis?"

Ellis paused with a great show of hesitation. After two apparent false starts, he said, "It came about after my meeting with you. You told me I should reconcile myself to administration, that I should put something back."

"Russia would seem a little extreme," Turnbull replied. "Even for someone taking my advice."

"I've always believed in total commitment," Ellis said, and watched the three men eye each other.

They whispered among themselves for a while and pointed at files. Then Jim Colson asked, "Would you be wanting to go to Moscow, Drew, because Boris Pomarev is there?"

"Boris . . ."

"You know," Colson snapped. "You accessed his file."

"I was merely updating myself on what had happened since Berlin."

Colson looked at him steadily. Ellis thought there was a hint of sadness in his childlike blue eyes. Colson said, "We also have here a psychiatric report from Dr. Larry Adcock. According to Dr. Adcock, you are obsessed with the idea of taking revenge on the people you feel were responsible for the death of Emma

Czazowicz." He looked up from the file at Ellis. "Someone like Dr. Adcock doesn't use words like obsession lightly."

"No," Ellis agreed. "Sometimes he uses words like sublimate." He could feel his head begin to throb.

The three board members exchanged puzzled glances. Then Palmer asked, "What would you do if you met Boris Pomarev on a Moscow street?"

Ellis could feel his hand start to tremble. He put it underneath his thigh. "Why. . . I don't know. Nothing, I suppose. He'd probably have other KGB men with him and—"

"How would you recognize Pomarev?" Director Turnbull asked.

"Well. . . you see, that is the point. How would I recognize Pomarev?"

"From the file you accessed and the photograph you looked at," Colson said dryly.

"And what about Zonda?" Palmer asked. "What would you do if you saw him?"

"Zonda was only the mechanic," Ellis snapped. The ache behind his eyes was almost blinding now. "It was Pomarev who wanted her dead."

"And you want Pomarev?"

That was Colson. Ellis wasn't sure he was hearing or seeing right. There was a tumultuous pounding in his chest, a repeated flash of lightning before his eyes. "Yes—no—well, shouldn't we do something about Pomarev? Are we going to sit back and allow him to destroy an entire network, to arrange the killing of—"

"Drew! Shut up!" That was Colson again.

"No, I won't shut up. There are things that need to be said and things that need to be done. We need to show the Pomarevs of this world that—"

Palmer, the man from Personnel was shouting, "And you mean to show him, is that it?"

Ellis wondered why Palmer was shouting, then realized that everyone was shouting and that his voice was loudest of all. "Yes, that's exactly it! I'm going to kill the bastard!"

The silence that followed was deafening.

8

From the window of his rented apartment Ellis stared at the clouds pressed low against the buildings of east Washington, gray and ominous and full of snow. Below him snowbanks covered the pavement and people walked, huddled against the cold and the driving wind, dark smudges against the pale gray background. Ellis was thankful he did not have to go out in that wind and cold. He had nowhere to go. Today was his first day of freedom.

His severance from the Agency the day before had been clinical in its ease. A single meeting with a man from Personnel, a series of signings—acknowledgment of his severance check, a waiver of claims against the Agency, an agreement that he would not unlawfully disclose Agency matters—was followed by the surrender of his authorization cards, the cancellation of his ID, the receipt of a separate check for his last salary payment, and a final handshake. It was over; nearly half a lifetime of work, service, and travail was finished. The man from Personnel had accompanied him to the parking lot as if he might secret himself inside the building. As he'd left the lot, the attendant had taken away his permit.

Just before he'd gone to Personnel, Ellis had looked in on Theo. Their farewell had been almost formal. "Keep in touch. Let me know if you need anything. Of course, we'll see each other. Take care. Look after yourself. Always take good care."

He was alone, Ellis thought, exactly as he'd always been. His father had been a surgeon, a man traumatized by his own brilliance. At nine Ellis was sent away to boarding school, to become a little man. The only role models he'd had were the priests at St Michael's and the remote, unemotional figure of his father. He'd chosen a bit of both and become withdrawn, reclusive, and emotionally self-reliant. He'd taught himself not to need people. Theo had been a symbol for what he'd never had, but Theo had not been a father, only someone who looked and occasionally behaved like one. In all his life the only person he'd cared about and relied on had been Emma. And now Emma was dead and he was more alone than before, severed from his father symbol and the only family he'd had.

He looked at the checks on his dresser. In the last year his salary had accumulated because he'd been too ill to spend much of it, and that together with his severance pay came to over a hundred thousand dollars. Fuck working, he thought. He'd never had so much money in his life before, which made him feel strangely excited.

There was a lot he could do with a hundred thousand dollars. Like wait for something interesting to turn up. He did not want to end up in security or private investigations, like most ex-Agents, and with his record, he could forget about the FBI and the police. If he were lucky, maybe he could join someone's private army. Or sign up as a mercenary.

Or buy a ticket to Moscow.

That afternoon he went out and bought all the maps and guidebooks on Moscow he could find. He spent the next few days poring over them and memorizing locations, street names, and buildings. In the evenings he began showing up at the bars where men from the Russian desk drank. Four days later he found the headquarter's address of the KGB's Service A.

9

January 28, 1986

Abe Makram stood in front of Fra Filippo Lippi's *Adoration of the Magi*, observing neither the sensuous lines of the ex-friar's painting nor sensing the joy the lusty friar had had from painting actual Florentine women. Brow furrowed with worry, Makram did not notice the careful detail with which the landscape had been observed or the carefully defined and colored costumes. Abe Makram had no interest in medieval Italian art. The only reason he was standing in front of the Lippi painting in the Early Italian section of the Washington National Gallery was that was where he'd been ordered to make his *treff*.

Makram was a heavily built man in his late thirties, the points made by his sharp nose and gently receding chin blunted by the fullness of his cheeks and the droop of his lower lip. To take his mind off why he had come, he tried to think about the machine code of his computer. Makram loved computers, and his dream was to actually see a computer go out of the door with his name on it. For the present, however, he could not work in a place that designed computers. For now he was required to concern himself with the application of computers. But he had a right to dream. And to work in his spare time. He stared the length of the gallery and wondered why they had demanded another meeting so soon.

The last meeting had been six weeks ago, and normally they only wanted a meeting every six to eight months. Without doubt something had gone wrong, something very serious, otherwise they would not have risked another meeting so soon. Makram felt his heart beat wildly against his ribcage. With a growing sense of apprehension and despair, he concluded that he'd been discovered.

If he had, he would have to flee, and for a moment he thought he wouldn't mind that. The Center would organize his departure, and it would be nice to go home. Then another terrifying thought: what if the Center couldn't organize his flight? What if they decided to abandon him?

He told himself the Center didn't do things like that unless they were compelled to. The Center looked after its own. It repaid loyalty with loyalty, and he'd always been loyal.

He scanned the gallery. There weren't many visitors on a Tuesday morning: a student earnestly sketching a da Vinci; a middle-aged couple from out-of-town staring blankly at the paintings; a slim, balding man in a Gandhi top and baggy cotton pants darting from painting to painting with the nervous excitement of a gun dog. If he had to return home, Makram wondered, would he be able to take his new Compaq computer with him?

He turned to stare at the painting. Why couldn't they have chosen something more modern, something with a nude or a car? Fra Filippo Lippi! The Center must be infiltrated by Christians. A soft voice behind him said, "Josef."

Instinctively Makram started to turn, stopped, then turned more slowly. He had been born Josef Vyssorian Markovich, but no one had used that name for fifteen years, for at the Center the use of a previous identity once an agent was introduced into his new surroundings was definitely verboten.

Out of the corner of his eye Makram glimpsed the handsome triangular face and smiling light gray eyes of Boris Pomarev. He whirled, thrusting out his hands, opening his arms in the beginnings of a great big Russian bear hug.

Pomarev moved quickly, stepping away from Makram's reaching arms. "Not here, fool." He smiled and quickly shook Makram's hand. "Josef, *priyatel*, how are you?"

"I am well, Boris. Only you must call me Abe."

"Of course. Of course."

Eyes wandering inquisitively over the pictures, Pomarev began to walk out of the gallery. If anything, Makram thought, Boris had gotten slimmer and dressed smarter. If you saw him on the street, you would take him for a European, a successful German businessman, perhaps, or a French nuclear physicist. At the university, and afterward at Foreign Intelligence School, Makram and Boris Pomarev had been the closest of friends. In the years he'd spent in America, Makram had heard vague rumors of Boris's swift rise within the KGB. Pomarev stopped and examined the da Vinci. He looked as if he understood painting. Makram waited patiently till they could move outside.

They ate caviar and blinis in a cloistered booth at Ziggy's, and drank genuine Stolichnaya vodka. "You must tell me everything you've been doing from the first day you got here," Boris cried enthusiastically. "Leave nothing out."

Makram laughed. "That would take another fifteen years."

"Fifteen years," Pomarev mused. "That long. I thought of looking you up when I was here two years ago, but there was too much to do. But this visit," he grinned triumphantly, "I made the time."

Makram looked at his friend in admiration. Not only his clothes and the expensive restaurant, but the fact that he could arrange a meeting with a "sleeper" meant that his friend was very powerful within the KGB. "What do you do now?" he asked.

"I am a deputy director of Service A."

Almost on top of the heap, Makram thought. And Boris hadn't forgotten him. Boris had sought him out here in Washington. He felt his insides melt with gratitude.

Pomarev smiled and said, "Now tell me what you have been doing with yourself. What did you do when you first got here?"

Makram was flattered by the interest in Boris's eyes, and began to tell him that soon after he'd arrived in America he enrolled in a post-graduate course in computer studies at the University of Florida and obtained a masters degree; that while at the university he had devised a system for forecasting election results, and how the system had been used by the Democratic Party in local county elections.

"Brilliant, Josef!" Pomarev cried warmly. "Brilliant! I always knew you had the makings of a genius in you."

Makram told him that since leaving the university he had worked for Gallup and then for former president Jimmy Carter in 1976 and 1980. He told Pomarev the experience had taught him what America was really about.

"Carter lost in 1980," Pomarev said. "Isn't the American experience about winning?"

Makram laughed. "I changed sides." The vodka was making him feel very relaxed and slightly light-headed. "I worked for Steve Widdell and the opposition, and we won."

"Yes," Pomarev said, suddenly abstracted.

He was losing his friend's interest, Makram thought. Wanting to keep Boris interested, he said, "I still work for Widdell. The man is a genius. It was his system and nothing else that got Donnelly elected. With Widdell's system anyone can become president." Makram became aware of Boris looking at him as if from a distance, the eyes like faraway searchlights, the face set in an expression of total concentration.

"How did Widdell do that?" Pomarev asked.

"It's highly technical," Makram said. "And there isn't time."

"You have all the time in the world," Pomarev said. And in a much harsher tone added, "Start now."

10

The Paradise Bar was dark, its windows perpetually boarded against the garish illumination of the street outside. It consisted of two rooms, one of which had red-check tablecloths and pretensions to a restaurant, the other dominated by a large bar and a series of bare wooden tables filling an area the size of a small dance floor. In a kitchen somewhere in the back the owner's wife produced steak and pasta.

The bar was owned by a Chinese, Lee Fong, who made almost perfect martinis and whose surliness kept most customers away. Which was why the group of coordinators, cryptanalysts, and analysts, attached to various CIA Russian desks met there most Friday nights. Habitués of Russian desks found that while they were obsessed with Russia and all things Russian, there were few people away from the desks who shared that obsession or whom they could safely talk to. So they tended to hang out together most Friday nights to share information, discuss social events, talk about Russia, and give and receive background, and the bar they met in most frequently was Lee Fong's.

For the past three weeks Ellis had drunk regularly at Lee Fong's. He had by now come to know most of the men from the Russian desks by sight, just as they had come to accept him as a regular bar fixture. The fact that he was Agency made that acceptance easier, and through the occasional shared conversation, he'd managed to get across to them that he was trying to find out as much as he could about Russia and exactly where Zonda and Pomarev were.

Last week an analyst called Briggs told him he knew someone who'd seen a cipher message that showed Zonda's latest posting. Briggs had said if Ellis were interested, he could arrange for him to meet the man.

24

Which was why shortly before six that evening Ellis had turned up at the Paradise. Now he sipped a beer and looked around wondering why Briggs was late.

Half an hour later Briggs entered from the back room and placed his empty glass on the bar near Ellis.

"Want a refill?" Ellis asked.

Briggs shook his head. "My friend's waiting in the back."

Ellis felt a small thrill of anticipation, and kept his gaze on Lee Fong muscularly polishing glasses. "Has he got a copy of the message?"

"What? Yeah . . . sure." Briggs gestured with his head toward the back room. "He's waiting for you there."

Ellis swung off the bar stool. Lee Fong glowered. The men at the tables looked studiously away. Ellis walked beside Briggs to the restaurant.

"My friend's in there," Briggs muttered, again pointing with his head, this time to a room beside the toilets. "He can't be seen talking to you, in case anything happens afterward."

Briggs jerked open the door of the room and motioned Ellis to precede him. Ellis glimpsed boarded-up windows, dim yellow lighting, a total absence of furniture, and five men standing in a loose circle in the middle of the room, looking expectantly at him. He recognized the man in the center as Calloway, the senior controller at the Russian desk. Calloway was the last person to tell him anything about anything. Then he recognized the four men with Calloway as Internal Security bulldogs and stiffened, realizing that Briggs had led him into a trap.

As if rehearsing for a ballet, the four men moved neatly away from Calloway to greet him. A vicious blow caught him on the side of his head and sent him spinning. Vainly Ellis raised his arms, struggled to regain his balance and keep from falling. Their fists came at him from all sides, short, vicious blows, pile driving into his stomach, kidneys, face, and shoulders. Two men moved in front and a little to the right, the other two to the back and the left, their blows alternatively knocking him off balance and knocking him upright.

Ellis gasped and staggered. His lips smashed against his teeth. His mouth filled with the tangy taste of blood. He swung back at the men, tried to move in and wrestle one of them, but his assailant expected that and skipped away while the other men pounded at his back and neck and shoulders.

"Asshole!"

He was barely conscious as fingers gripped his hair and pulled his head up. He stared into Calloway's face. "I hear you're looking for someone called Zonda," Calloway said, holding his head by the hair.

Ellis choked.

"I take it that means yes. Well, don't look for Zonda here. We're not interested in what he did to your network in Berlin. That's history. We're not interested in you!" He shook Ellis's head. The pain brought tears to Ellis's eyes. "We don't want you hanging around our bars scrounging information. Do you understand that?"

Ellis closed his eyes in submission and tried to nod.

"We don't give a shit if you've been severed or if your severance and this whole Zonda business is just a cover to infiltrate us. We don't like infiltrators. We don't like the OCI. Got that?" He tugged Ellis's head savagely.

Ellis gasped assent.

"We don't want you around us. Got that?"

Again the savage tug. Again the gasped assent.

"Now get the hell out of here. And don't ever come back. The next time we won't be this kind." Calloway allowed Ellis's head to sink back on his chest.

Ellis slumped against the men holding him. His scalp seemed full of burning needles, his body a single mass of pain, and his swollen tongue filled his dry throat. He heard Calloway say, "Take him away."

He tried to make his legs move but there was no life in them. He heard his feet drag as the men pulled him out of the room. His eyes hurt at the lights from the restaurant and his head sagged. Once again he tried to walk and nearly fell. The men dragged him through the bar. As if through a mist Ellis saw men look curiously at him and heard a few loud sniggers. Near the front door someone threw his coat over his shoulders. A blast of cold air hit him as they went outside, and it made his bruises ache until he thought he might faint. Then the men were fumbling in his coat pocket for the keys to his car and he was being bundled into the driver's seat. He saw a hand place the key in the ignition, heard a voice say, "Get the hell out and don't even think of coming back," then heard the car door slam and the sound of receding footsteps.

Numbly he turned the ignition key. The engine caught

and fired. His body aching, and tears of anger, frustration, and humiliation rolling down his face, Ellis lurched out of the parking lot.

11

February 13, 1986

Makram waited, hunched over his computer terminal, staring unseeingly at the amber and black screen. He had begun to sweat slightly, and the coffee he'd drunk was filling his bladder. Either that or he was piss scared.

He listened carefully to the sounds outside his cubicle. Someone pecking at a keyboard, someone else scrunching paper. A third person was walking between the cubicles on the far side of the floor. He looked at his watch and waited for the footsteps to cease. It was a quarter after eleven, the quietest time on the night shift, when people dozed, sent out for pizzas, or worked at their own computer schemes. He heard the murmur of low-pitched conversation from the cubicle across the floor, then the sound of footsteps returning their owner to his seat. Someone coughed. The keyboard clicked. Makram reached behind his computer screen and switched off his terminal.

The sudden blankness was like a hat being pulled over his head. He felt momentarily cut off from the outside world and the rest of Widdell's office. He pulled the terminal toward him and snapped open the outer casing, waited with a tripping heart to see if anyone else had heard the noise and would come to see what he was doing.

He heard voices again, nearer this time but remaining fixed in a cubicle diagonally across the corridor from him, where he also heard the shuffle of paper and a rattle of keyboards. His hand, holding open the casing cover, was slimy with sweat. Quietly Makram lifted the cover and placed it on the desk beside him. The inside of the terminal was green, with white lines like road markings. It was surprisingly spacious, and with its metallic brown rectangles and neat rows of brown and gold auxiliary slots, looked like a scale model of a railway siding. There were circuit cards stuck into some of the slots. After a moment's thought, Makram removed one of them and replaced it with a card he had designed. Grimly, he thought: who said there was no pleasure in working for Boris Pomarev?

Over lunch at Ziggy's Boris had made Makram tell him everything about his work at Widdell's, and now Boris wanted documentary information about the last presidential campaign. Makram couldn't imagine what use Boris would make of the information, but it was a necessary favor for a very influential and powerful friend. Makram hoped that when the time came, Boris would remember the exceptional risk he had run and the highly complex computer skills he'd applied.

Makram replaced the casing of the terminal and paused, his finger on the power switch. He had checked the circuit card numerous times on his terminal at home, but this was the crucial test. Would the card bypass Widdell's code system and give him access to the 1984 campaign files? Would it delude the computer into believing it was simply passing the information to another screen? He switched on the terminal and booted the system. There was a fierce whirring from his disk drive. The screen came alive with a bright amber glow. So far so good. He typed in SYSTEM LINKER and waited. For a moment nothing happened. Then the screen confirmed, SYSTEM LINKED. WHAT SYSTEM DO YOU WANT?

Makram typed: GET DIR CAMPAIGN 84.

Immediately there scrolled up on his monitor a list of the subdirectories on the file. He stopped the scrolling at SUM STRAT and pulled up the file. The file came on screen: SUMMARY OF CAMPAIGN STRATEGY 84. He typed in an instruction to open the file, inserted a blank diskette into his drive, and typed in EXECUTE.

The screen went blank.

Makram waited, staring at the screen like a rabbit transfixed by oncoming headlights. If he'd got his program wrong, the shit would hit the fan *now*!

The soft whir of the disk drive made him almost jump from his chair. The glowing red light on the drive casing seemed as bright as a beacon. He pressed his hands to his ears and waited. No alarms. No startled cries. Nothing.

Hunched over the terminal, he waited till the transmission was finished. Then he took out the disk, carefully opened its paper envelope, removed the soft interior disk of mylar on which the information had been recorded, and inserted it into a penlight from which he had removed the batteries. Then switching off the terminal and sticking the penlight into the front of his damp shirt, he waddled to the washroom, hurrying to get there before his bladder burst.

12

February 28, 1986

In the weeks that followed his beating, Ellis found himself alternating between profound despair and violently ordered activity. The maps of Moscow and the Russian guidebooks lay unused on his desk, while unwashed crockery accumulated in his sink. He didn't shave for days on end and would often wander the streets, eating only when he remembered to, changing his clothes when they seemed ready to fall off his body, walking continuously until, finally exhausted, he would crawl back to his apartment and sleep.

Whatever his mood, he always thought of killing himself. More than once, sitting before a soundless television, he'd put his Beretta 92F to his mouth. More than once, sitting alone at dinner, he'd picked up the gun and stared longingly down that tiny black tunnel to eternity.

There was nowhere for him to go and nothing for him to do except muse on the impossibility of getting to Zonda and Pomarev. He had wild thoughts of returning to Langley and, under threat of sabotaging their precious computers, forcing them to reveal the Russians' whereabouts. But reality always intervened. Langley was too well-guarded for him to even get inside the place, let alone get in with an unauthorized weapon.

He began to think about flying to Moscow as a tourist and making plans when he got there. But his passport wasn't valid for Russia, and when he'd applied for an extension, it

had come back with a refusal. So he had nothing left to do, no
hope of getting Pomarev or Zonda, unless either or both of
them left Russia and he learned about it.

That Friday evening was one of his better ones. After a
workout at Masimoto's Dojo he'd had dinner at Yorkies on
First Street and was walking home to his rented apartment
four blocks away. The rain had stopped and there was just a
hint of warmth in the night air, which might have been the
first indicator of spring or the precursor of a thunderstorm.
He saw the men as he approached the alley on O Street
leading to the side entrance of the high school; two blacks
with woolen caps pulled tightly over their skulls, lithe bodies
identically clad in windbreakers, skin-tight jeans, and running shoes. They were pointing knives at a third man,
conventionally dressed in a dark blue suit with a white
mackinaw draped over his shoulders, the victim backing away
from the knives and into the alley.

Fool, Ellis thought, feeling a peculiar, predatory light-
ness come over his body. Go back in there and they'll both
rob you and mark you for life. He approached the entrance to
the alley on cat feet.

"Give us the money, motherfucker!"

"Give us the money or I'll draw a subway map on your
face!"

Ellis saw the solidly built, middle-aged white man, hand
over his wallet.

One of the muggers opened it and spat. "You fucking
bastard!" He snatched the contents of the wallet and threw it
in the victim's face, following the throw with two rapid slaps
that sent the victim's head rocking from side to side. Ellis saw
cheeks redden, and a thin trickle of nosebleed.

The second mugger cried, "Come on honky, give."

"I've given you what I have to give." The man's voice
was strangely calm. "Take it and go."

"Give us the money you hid in case you got mugged!"

The muggers were crazy, either addicts desperate for as
much cash as they could get or sadistic bullies. Their victim
repeated, "I've told you, I've given you all I have to give."

"Don't hold out on us, man, unless you want this." One
of the attackers pricked the point of the knife into the victim's
neck. A little pimple of blood darkened the blade.

Ellis swung his bag over his shoulder and hurled it at the

attacker. The bag caught the man on the head and slugged him away from the victim, who didn't move. Too petrified, Ellis thought as he turned to face the second black, advancing on him, his knife blade glinting eerily in the dim light. Ellis feinted to the left, moved to the right, grasped the man's wrist and slammed it down onto his rigid, upraised knee.

There was a sharp crack. The knife clattered onto the road as the man screamed. Ellis moved in fast and low, pulling the man up and over his hip. Ellis held him upright for a moment before letting him go.

The man made a clumsy half turn in the air, cried out in fear and surprise, and landed uncomfortably on his face. Ellis turned back to the other assailant, who was smaller, slimmer, meaner. He'd gotten rid of his knife and had pulled out a small nickel-plated gun. "Stay away from me, whitey, or I'll fucking drill you full of holes!"

Ellis stared at a crazed face, a close-cropped head shiny with sweat, eyes wild and staring. A skiving addict, Ellis thought. The man said, "Now, give us your money, smartass!"

Ellis looked quickly from the man to his companion, still sprawled on the pavement, and felt a sudden surge of anger and wild excitement. "No," he said. "You want my money, you come and get it."

"Fuck you, asshole, I've got the gun!"

Behind him he heard the second mugger get to his feet. "Use the fucking gun!" Ellis shouted. "Let's see what kind of a man you are." The excitement was making him shake.

The whites of the man's eyes totally encircled the eyeball. A froth of white spittle trickled from the corner of his mouth. Ellis determined to smash his fist into that mouth.

"Don't needle him," the victim called. "It isn't worth it."

Ellis ignored him and kept his eyes on the mugger. "Come on, creep, come and take my money." He stepped toward the man, beckoning.

"You come any closer and I'll shoot." The man's voice was breaking.

Ellis took another step forward. The mugger backed away, obviously scared. Ellis felt the wonderful triumph of conquest. Because he didn't care to live, he was invulnerable. "You know something, asshole?" he said. "I don't give a shit if you pull that trigger or not. So go on, shoot me and do me a favor. Because that's the only fucking way you'll stop me."

"You're crazy!" the mugger cried. "Don't you fucking move!"

"Give him your money," the victim ordered. "For heaven's sake give him your money."

"Go fuck yourselves!" Ellis cried at both of them. The mugger's fear heightened his excitement. Right now he wanted that mugger more than he'd wanted anything in the world. He was going to take that gun from him and ram it down his glistening throat.

"Look man, I'm going, right. Let's not have any trouble, okay."

Ellis kept moving forward. "You've already got trouble, brother. You've already got a whole lot of trouble."

The mugger tried to put the gun away, then brought it out and up again. "Asshole! Stay away from me or I'll shoot."

"Go ahead and shoot, then. Pull the fucking trigger. Go on. Pull the fucking trigger!" Losing control, Ellis jumped the mugger. The mugger tried to back away. Ellis snatched the gun, wrenching it free from a suddenly lifeless hand. The mugger weaved, ducked, and ran past Ellis. Too late Ellis got a foot out and tripped him. The mugger lurched and staggered, recovered his balance and started to sprint down the alleyway.

Ellis turned. The second man was right in front of him, the knife in his left hand scything through the air in a vicious, upwardly cleaving thrust at Ellis's stomach. He tried to twist, tried to bring his hands down, knowing instinctively it was too late. He heard the knife's hiss, braced himself for the savage, tearing slash.

There was a thump of leather meeting bone. A shoe kicked away the man's knife hand. Ellis heard the man cry out with pain as the knife tore free and sailed through the air. From the corner of his eye Ellis glimpsed the mugger's victim standing by them in the ready to attack position, feet splayed apart, arms thrust forward hip high, ready to grab or strike or strangle.

The mugger gave them one frightened look, turned and sprinted for the road. Ellis started after him, but the victim grabbed his jacket. "No point in that! He's only got the five dollars I carry when I expect to get mugged."

Ellis turned to stare at the man. He could see now that the intended victim was a couple of inches taller and fifteen pounds heavier than him, a man with a strong, hard body just starting to turn to fat. "Why did you back off?" he asked. "Why did you allow them to push you in here?"

"They needed the money," the victim said. "I thought if I went through the motions, they would just take it and go."

"Don't get clever with muggers," Ellis said. "Muggers kill."

"May God save them from such a sin."

Jesus H. Christ, Ellis thought, bending down to pick up his bag, a fucking sky pilot.

"Thank you for getting involved," the victim said. "God bless you for caring."

Ellis straightened up slowly and brought his face close to the victim's, embarrassed at having intervened and by the man's thanks. "You a nutcase or something? You go around looking to get beaten up?" He stared into the man's face. The man had a good strong face, square and regular, with deep-set, dark eyes, bright with attentiveness and candor.

"I'm not a masochist," the victim said. "I'm a priest." The cut in his nose had stopped bleeding.

Ellis saw the man wasn't wearing a dog collar, and recalled the kick that had sent the mugger's knife flying. "Where did you learn to look after yourself?"

"Special Forces. Vietnam."

"Special Forces! Holy shit, man! You could have taken those assholes blindfolded and with one hand tied behind your back."

"An exaggeration, perhaps, but yes, I reckon I could have taken those two."

"And you were prepared to let them beat you up?"

The priest laughed. "I'm not as Christian as all that. Let's say I was prepared to allow them to take liberties up to a point."

"You're crazy," Ellis said. They walked to the bottom of the alley and stopped hesitantly on O Street.

"You're crazy too," the priest said. "What was all that about pull the fucking trigger? Did you really want that man to pull the trigger? Or were you just acting crazy to scare him?"

"I wanted him to pull the trigger," Ellis said. "I didn't care if he killed me or not."

"Why do you want to die?" the priest asked. "You're young, you're fit and strong, you have the best part of your life ahead of you. Remember Deuteronomy? This day I call

heaven and earth as witnesses against you, that I have set
before you life and death, blessing and curses. Now choose
life, that both you and your children might live."

"I don't wish to live," Ellis said, "and I have lost the
courage to kill myself."

"Once I felt like that, too," the priest said as they began
to walk along O Street. "That is the most terrible thing that
you can feel." The priest spoke softly, without affectation. "It
happened while I was on my way home from 'Nam. My
parents and fiancée met me in London. It was a kind of
holiday for all of us, and we were going to spend a week there
before returning to America. We had three glorious days.
Even the English weather was perfect." The priest's voice
shook momentarily. "On the fourth day I'd arranged to visit
some English friends I'd met at Harvard before meeting my
girl friend and parents at a restaurant in Knightsbridge. I
couldn't get a taxi and was fifteen minutes late. When I got
there, the street was cordoned off and there were ambu-
lances, fire engines, and police cars everywhere." The priest
stopped and looked Ellis full in the face. "The restaurant had
been bombed by terrorists. Both my parents died instantly.
What was left of my fiancée died forty-eight hours afterward."
The priest turned and walked on.

Ellis didn't know what to say. He thought: You're unhap-
py because you have no shoes, and you find a man with no feet.
He asked, "Is that when you decided to become a priest?"

His companion threw him a small smile. "No. That came
later. After God gave me hope."

"And didn't you want to take revenge? Didn't you want
to find those terrorists and kill them?"

"Of course I wanted to do that. But then I learned it was
the wrong thing for me to do. It is not for you or me or any of
us to take revenge. In doing so we debase ourselves and risk
our immortal souls."

They stopped outside a small house. "My name's Patrick
Morell," the priest said. "I'm the pastor at Cherokee Falls,
and I'm down here visiting an old Vietnam buddy. Come in if
you like and talk. You sound as if you need to talk to someone
other than yourself."

Damn you for being right, Ellis thought, and said, "No
thanks."

"Whatever you tell me," Morell said, "will go no further.

And I need never know who you are." He smiled. "It would be like talking to a stranger on a train. When the journey's over, you each go your separate ways."

"I don't have anything to talk about," Ellis said.

The priest continued to smile. "Tell me why you want to die." He paused, looking down at Ellis for a moment, a peculiar, comfortable brightness in his eyes. "You came to my aid. Now let me come to yours. Do you realize, my friend, that if that man had shot you, you would have been condemned to eternal torment—not, I think, the old-fashioned torment of hell fire, but the torment of being deprived, of missing someone you love deeply and knowing that you will miss them forever and ever." With a toss of his head, he asked, "You ever miss someone that much?"

"I do now," Ellis said tightly.

"Tell me about it," Father Morell said. "It can't do you any harm."

Why the hell not? Ellis thought.

13

March 4, 1986

Four days later Ellis drove out to Cherokee Falls. It took fourteen hours and cost him two speeding tickets. He reached the town shortly after seven, found the church and drove up to the two-room wooden bungalow beside it. Hearing the sound of the car, Father Morell came onto the porch. "I'll throw another potato in for dinner," he called cheerily. "How long are you staying?"

The night of the mugging, Ellis had talked to Father Morell till five in the morning, telling him about his life right up to the death of Emma. He'd told Father Morell that he would not rest until he'd found the men who'd killed her.

"I felt like that too," Patrick Morell had said. "But one day you have to ask yourself why you lived when others died. One day you have to decide if the circumstances that led to

your being alive and unhurt were determined or fortuitous."
Morell had paused and smiled. "Then you have to find out if
you control the most important aspects of your life or if it is
controlled by some greater force. You have to discover that
force and find its purpose. You have to find out for yourself if
the purpose of that greater force goes beyond the mere
exaction of vengeance." Morell's wide, candid, brown eyes
had been fixed on Ellis as he'd said, "When you think about
it, you'll find that revenge is a wasted emotion."

Ellis remembered he had shifted uncomfortably beneath
Morell's gaze, not wanting to disappoint the man by telling
him that revenge was the only thing in his life that mattered.

"You don't believe me?" Morell had smiled. "All right. I
want you to close your eyes, take deep breaths, and imagine
you've found Zonda. Imagine you've found Pomarev. Imagine
you have them right here in front of you, cowering before you
and your gun. Listen to them beg for mercy, listen to them
plead that the murder of Emma was a dreadful bureaucratic
mistake. Imagine yourself shooting them." Morell clapped his
hands twice in a simulation of gunshots. "They're both dead.
How do you feel now?"

"Satisfied," Ellis said. "Relieved."

"And one with Emma? You feel like a man?"

"That's right," Ellis agreed.

"Okay, now imagine afterward. Imagine a year afterward.
How do you live after the purpose you live for has been
achieved?"

"I don't know. . . I'll—"

"Think about it," Patrick Morell had said. "Think about
it very carefully. There is no point in killing them only to kill
yourself afterward."

"How did you survive?" Ellis asked.

"I looked for and found the reason why I had to choose
life."

"And what reason was that?"

"You'll have to find your own reason," Patrick Morell had
said. "I can only help point out the way."

14

Steve Widdell fought to control his impatience as he dealt with Jonathan Bradley's stream of questions. No detail seemed too small for Bradley's earnest curiosity. He wanted to know everything from the size of the computers to the brand of tapes they used, and as he reeled out answer after boring answer, Widdell could feel his heart race and his head grow tight. His doctor had warned him of the effects of stress and all kinds of impatience, and he reminded himself that it was not Christian to be selfish with one's time. Besides, Widdell told himself there were advantages in satisfying Bradley's curiosity.

Dr. Jonathan Bradley was research director of the Bildeberg Institute, a geopolitical research organization and think-tank which Widdell believed was attached to Georgetown University and which Widdell knew advised large industrial corporations and governments. Bildeberg needed organizations like Widdell's to carry out market surveys and polling research.

The growth of his company, Widdell told himself now, meant he needed a lot more extra work between presidential elections to keep his team together. Behind the cover of his hand he slipped a pill into his mouth. Almost instantly he could feel the pounding of his heart slow.

"The political work never really stops," he said, thankful that Bradley seemed to be drifting into broader areas of inquiry. Because of his slim body, Afro curls, and contact lenses, Bradley looked fifteen years younger than him instead of ten, Widdell thought. He determined to start on a diet. According to his doctor, he was thirty pounds overweight, which was putting an unnecessary strain on his heart. He said, "The presidential election is the big event, but in between there are congressional and senate elections."

"How much time will you devote to political research this year?"

"It's difficult to say," Widdell replied. "In one sense we are always concerned with political research because we need regular surveys to keep our data bases up to date. Then, of course..." Widdell wondered if the point of Bradley's question was to ascertain how much spare capacity he had. He said, "In a nonelection year political research occupies some thirty-five to forty percent of our resources."

Bradley nodded encouragingly and smiled as if that were the answer he wanted. "What do you do with the spare capacity?"

"Theoretically we have no spare capacity," Widdell said. "But then theoretically also, our spare capacity is limitless." He explained that the limitations on the size of his organization were the amount of unused capacity in his computers and the number of staff he had available. "Right now," he went on, "we have lots of spare computer capacity but very little extra staff. However, if we got a big new job, we could staff up in a couple of weeks. Polling staff is easily recruited and easily trained. We could take on a medium-sized job in three weeks and something like a presidential campaign in three months."

"That's amazing." Bradley smiled. "How do you manage in nonelection years."

"We have a constant series of industrial surveys."

"Remarkable," Bradley said, and directed his attention to detail again. He asked Widdell what kind of back-up systems he had and where they were stored. He asked how they were transported and what security arrangements were in force. Then he asked to see the computers again.

With a suppressed sigh of relief, Widdell called the computer room supervisor and asked him to give Dr. Bradley yet another tour of the machines.

15

Unlike his Creator, Pastor Patrick Morell did not rest on the sabbath but on Monday, and that Monday morning, taking a packed lunch that his visiting housekeeper had prepared, he and Ellis went walking in the hills above the falls. The path was steep and rocky, much of it slippery with spray and the residue of Saturday's rain. They climbed in silence most of the morning, each engrossed in his own thoughts and the difficulty of the terrain. Later, when they spoke, it was without conscious effort, each commenting on whatever subject was foremost in their minds: the need for a church organ, how Ellis had once escaped from Italy to Switzerland over the mountains near Chiasso, how Patrick had never been able to play his fiancée's collection of Beatle records, of fragments during that brief eight-month period with Emma in West Berlin when Ellis had had a place he'd thought of as home.

Ellis had been in Cherokee Falls five days, and for the first time since Berlin, felt rested and content. He'd slept well, the torture of the nightmares gone; he no longer walked down tunnels in his dreams. That evening, sitting with Patrick before the fire in the small living room, he realized that it had nearly been a whole week since he'd put a gun to his mouth.

Shadows danced on the boarded walls, making the large oil painting and the small altar in the corner of the room look ghostly. Ellis's legs and back felt stiff and heavy, his body full of the pleasant ache and blessed tiredness that came with healthy effort. They had eaten the spaghetti Bolognese Patrick had cooked and drunk most of the wine Ellis had bought. Ellis stared into the fire, seeing shapes and dreaming.

Patrick placed a bible on his lap. "You have to make your

mind up," he said. "Is this the word of God or not, and if it is, what are you going to do about it?"

16

March 25, 1986

Abe Makram waited in front of the Fra Filippo Lippi, his nervousness making him irritable. He couldn't understand why Boris wanted so much detail concerning the history, background, and organization of Widdell's corporation, and so much information regarding the last presidential campaign. Even when Makram had protested that the information required was so voluminous it necessitated risking his cover and meeting every week, Boris had insisted he do it. And with the way Boris's supplementary questions were going, Makram thought glumly, he'd soon be meeting every day.

It also concerned Makram that his information was being conveyed to Boris directly, bypassing his own section head. But Boris had insisted on the personal meetings, so the resultant plan could be quickly finalized and rushed with equal directness to the chairman of the Politburo. Boris had intimated he had a private relationship with the chairman, and that if his plan based on the information Makram was providing worked, the directorship of Service A was a certainty and the directorship of the entire KGB a possibility.

And Makram would not be forgotten, of course. Makram well knew that a man needed friends in high places, just as a man in a high place needed friends—friends whose loyalty had been proved. Friends of people in high places had their own cars, shopping privileges, access to *beriozkas*, special holiday facilities, and the use of weekend dachas near Moscow. Life in Moscow even as an assistant to the director of Service A would be very much better than that of an illegal sleeper. You wouldn't always have to watch your back and worry about arrest, Boris had said. Boris hadn't told him anything about it, but Makram had been able to imagine the consequences if he had refused to do a favor for such a powerful friend.

He sighed and looked around the gallery. As always, Boris's contact, a spindly, nervous-looking man called Nikayevich, was late. Makram suspected that Nikayevich was also working for two masters, and unused to field work, made checks of the rendezvous at the appointed time before revealing himself. He'd have to get Boris to change his contact, Makram thought, and the meeting place. He was developing a passionate hatred for the painting of Fra Lippi.

17

April 8, 1986

"Why did Emma die?" Ellis asked.

"God didn't kill Emma. A man called Zonda did."

"But why did God allow Emma to die? Surely He could have stopped Zonda from killing her?"

"Of course He could have. But He had to leave Zonda free to shoot her or not. For the sake of Zonda's immortal soul."

"Never mind Zonda's soul. What about Emma's life? She was so young. She had all her life stretched out before her."

"Exactly. And what fate awaited her in that life? Can you be sure that she would have been happy and fulfilled, that she would have died a better person?" He paused and added, "Emma made her choices, too, when she left you, Drew, when she went to East Berlin, when she found out whatever it was she did."

"Who betrayed the Lotus network. That's what she found out."

"Right. And her actions weren't your responsibility. You cannot hold yourself responsible for her death. Was she religious?"

"Emma was a Catholic. She believed in God."

"Was she reconciled with Him before she died?"

Ellis recalled the way she had bowed her head and

waited for Zonda to kill her. Now he realized what she had been doing. She'd been praying. In those last fleeting moments she had realized she was going to die and had prayed. "I think so," he said. "I certainly hope so."

"In that case she is happier now than you could ever have made her," Patrick said. He put his arm around Ellis's shoulder. "God, you see, is more considerate than we imagine."

18

April 12, 1986

As the days blended smoothly into weeks, Ellis fell into the routine of Patrick's parish work, helping out with the family night on Wednesdays, taking the basketball team on Thursdays, accompanying Patrick on visits to parishioners, helping put together a newsletter and prepare the church for midweek and Sunday services. In between he read and thought, and every morning he and Patrick ran.

Running was good for the soul, Patrick said. It stilled the mind and encouraged concentration. It was nonaggressive and made one aware of the wonder of the body. On some days, Patrick said, running was all the evidence one needed for the existence of God.

Standing on the porch doing their cooling down stretches, he asked, "Now that you've accepted Christ, how do you feel about killing Zonda and Pomarev?"

"As I've always felt," Ellis said. "Murder is wrong, and having a reason for murder doesn't make it right. But the fact that it is wrong for me to kill Zonda and Pomarev still leaves me feeling wounded and outraged. I still feel they ought to be punished."

"And they will be," Patrick said. "What would be wrong is for you to punish them. Their punishment must be left to God."

"I wish it were not so."

"Have you thought that in killing them you may be doing

them a favor?" Patrick asked. "Have you thought that death might release them from a situation they find intolerable right now?" He smiled and added, "That is why these things are best left to the Lord."

19

April 27, 1986

Six weeks after Ellis had so impulsively left Washington and driven the fourteen hours to see Patrick Morell, he drove back. He hadn't wanted to leave Cherokee Falls, but Patrick had made it quite clear he wanted to be no man's crutch. It was time, he said, for Ellis to go back into the world and practice flying on reconditioned wings.

There were times during those weeks that Ellis had felt he wanted to become a priest. But Patrick had told him it was purely an emotional reaction and that he should concentrate on rebuilding his life doing something else. "Try writing," Patrick had said. "Try telling people the story of your accident and recovery. Your descriptions to me were pretty darned dramatic."

In those six weeks he had not only been renewed, Ellis thought as he watched the hood of the car float over the undulations on the freeway, he'd become a new man. Now he not only felt confident, he had inner strength, and there was something positive he wanted to do. The more he thought about it, the more he felt Patrick's idea was a good one. The book was already taking shape in his mind, and he was excited about it.

He looked away from the undulating road to the fields stretching flatly to the horizon. He was now able to handle Emma's death, and somewhere out there, in the wide open spaces of America, there was one person who loved him like a brother!

20

PRIMARY POLITICS

Why we have more candidates campaigning harder

With five months and six million campaign miles to go before the first primary of 1988, ten candidates have already committed themselves to campaign for the presidency of the United States. Already campaign teams have been recruited and support organizations formed, fund-raising events have been organized and moneys raised from friends, relatives, well-wishers, industry, special interests, and supporters of every kind. Already canvassers are out on the streets taking preliminary surveys and public relations specialists are advising on techniques of image building and presentation; advertising agencies are creating campaign slogans and millions upon millions of buttons, flags, and pins are being ordered. Five months before the first vote will be cast, the noisily flamboyant, frequently raucous, multimillion dollar bandwagon of electoral politicking has started to roll.

What has made the politicking bandwagon start to roll so early and so expensively is the change in the structure of presidential nomination. Whereas formerly presidential nominees were selected at conventions, today most delegates to those conventions are committed to the winners of their state primaries.

Primaries are unique to American politics. In no other country are voters, taking part in what are essentially local elections, called upon to express their views on the selection of a presidential candidate. In the quadrennial presidential primaries that is what happens.

However, it was not always so. Originally presidential nominees were determined by party members in Congress. Then, in 1830, the Anti-Masons introduced nationwide conventions, and this was followed by the Democrats in 1832 and the Republicans in 1854. At the turn of the century progressives, dissatisfied at the way party bosses manipulated the conventions to nominate their favorite candidates, insisted that delegates to the national conventions be picked by open vote at primaries.

In 1904 Florida became the first state to run a primary, followed by Wisconsin in 1905. By 1916 there were twenty-six states holding primaries, but they had little effect on the selection of delegates. The party bosses still controlled the local political machinery, which enabled them to pick primary delegates just as easily as they had previously picked convention delegates. So, for nearly half a century after the First World War, the primary remained nothing more than one of the gravestones of liberal idealism in American politics.

Then came 1968 and Chicago. By 1968 the number of states holding primaries had dropped to fifteen, and in that year Hubert Humphrey secured the Democratic nomination without contesting a single primary. But 1968 was a year of restlessness, of change, growing social awareness and responsibility; the year when a combination of flower children, Radcliffe girls, innocents, and crazies attempted to wrest control of the party from its power brokers.

The causes of 1968 were many: Vietnam, black rights, student unrest, equality for women, and a demand for more democratic political parties. Confronted with such highly publicized violence, the Democrats had no choice but to reform. One of the consequences of that reform was to reinstitute the importance of the primary by ensuring that more delegates were elected by that method. The revolution of 1968 found its echoes among the Republicans, and by 1976 not only had the number of

primaries almost doubled, but over 75% Democratic
and 66% of Republican delegates were chosen at
primaries.

At the same time two other factors served to
encourage the importance and the permanence of
the primary. The first was the media, which simply
by paying more attention to primaries increased
their importance and that of the participating candidates. The second was the new finance laws, which
by restricting the capacity of the candidate to raise
private finance, and committing federal funds to
those candidates who could show a measure of
electoral support, encouraged more candidates to
seek office while at the same time compelling more
candidates to undertake primary campaigns in order
to qualify for election funds.

The consequence of all this is that there are
now more primaries. And more candidates, who
start their campaigns earlier, work harder, and
cover a great deal more territory than any previous
group. And every one of them is playing against the
odds.

Of all the presidential candidates, only two will
become their party's nominees, and only one will
become president. Nevertheless, the politicking bandwagon continues to roll. . . .

—JAY EMERSON III
© Time Inc.

21

October 29, 1987

The room was vast. Along one side tall windows overlooked
Red Square. To the left French doors opened onto a balcony
and lush Oriental rugs were scattered over the floor. To the

right a sofa and armchairs in green leather were arranged before an ornate Italian fireplace.

Sitting in one of the armchairs, Boris Pomarev tried to keep his gaze from wandering over the room. Though it was not the first time he had visited this room, he was still staggered by its vastness, by the richness of its furnishings and the intricacy of its carved paneling. He was overwhelmed by the fact that he, the son of a Grade V clerk to the Central Committee, was actually sitting here. The power centered in this room excited him, power that reached out from the Arctic to . . . well, almost the borders of Pakistan; power that spread from the Chinese border to the middle of Europe and dominated half the world. Controlling that power and its symbols was one man: Politburo chairman Anatoly Kyrelin, his friend.

Four months ago a young captain in the Sluzbha, Mikhail Droznin had told Pomarev he had uncovered a ring of young louts who bought jeans, records, cassette players, and western currency from tourists and sold them at enormous profit on the thriving black market. Droznin's problem was that the group was headed by a student at Moscow University, the chairman's nephew.

Pomarev had acted with speed, discretion, and, he thought, a degree of compassion. First of all he had spared Droznin the embarrassing responsibility of his knowledge and taken over the case himself. Then he had visited with the chairman's nephew. A series of mistakes had been made, mistakes that Pomarev understood. He, too, had once been young and attended this very same university. But they were mistakes nevertheless, and serious enough that enemies could use them to wreck the chairman's plan to rid Russia of moral and economic corruption, use them even to destroy the chairman. Now, if the chairman's nephew would agree to immediate recruitment by the KGB, his training need not be arduous nor his career prospects any worse than in the diplomatic service. If the chairman's nephew liked, Pomarev could arrange training at the KGB's school in Havana, where there was magnificent weather, brilliant beaches, and tempestuous Cuban women, according to interesting stories Pomarev had heard.

The chairman's nephew had liked this, and a month later Pomarev met with the chairman for the first time. He had been promoted to the rank of lieutenant colonel and invited him to join the chairman's Political Security Unit, with special responsibility for investigating opponents to the chairman's plans for the modernization of Russia.

While helping the chairman circumscribe the powers of a rival who led the Leningrad Communist Party, Pomarev had come to know the chairman well. Younger than any of his predecessors, Kyrelin was fifty-three, twelve years older than Pomarev. He was the first Soviet leader not to have participated directly in the Great Fascist War, and more importantly, the first Soviet leader not dominated by the presence of leading figures of party history, most of whom were now dead.

As a consequence Kyrelin was able to give his extremely forward thinking and liberal sentiments full scope. He made no secret of the fact that he believed the future of Russia lay not in head-to-head confrontation with the Western powers, but in the development of a strong economy which would one day wrest economic superiority from the Americans. Kyrelin believed that for too long rigid party ideology had condemned Russia to remain a nation of peasants. He was determined to transform it into a strong economic power whose citizens would have as high a standard of living as the West. Russia would become a showpiece, living proof that communism worked.

Pomarev shared the chairman's ideas. In fact, he was a little in advance of them. Three years ago in Berlin he'd formed a bond that had come close to carrying them out. He smiled abstractedly. The foundations had been laid. And it was up to him to build on those foundations now.

Seated across from Pomarev, the chairman said, "I don't understand how such a man could be leader of the . . . well, the second most powerful country in the world."

The chairman had recently returned from a meeting with the American President at Reykjavik at which he'd once again failed to divert his counterpart from proceeding with his Strategic Defense Initiative. If Soviet Russia were to keep up, it would have to spend billions of dollars in research, billions of dollars it didn't have; and if he did, Kyrelin would rather have spent it on improving the living standards of his people.

The consequences of Star Wars were therefore great.

Not only would it neutralize Russia's expensive nuclear arsenal, but it would commit Russia to an expensive research program it couldn't afford and which, whether it succeeded or failed, would smash all hope of Russian economic growth, thereby permanently restricting Russia to the economic status of a second-rate power. "I simply don't understand it," the chairman repeated. "Jack Donnelly is the stupidest man I know. How could he have become president of the United States?"

Pomarev let his breath out slowly. He knew the chairman's summit had been an embarrassing and humiliating failure and that already there were some in the Central Committee asking if Russian prestige could survive that failure and if Russia could afford Kyrelin's liberalism. Pomarev had a note of the detractors names and would discuss them with Kyrelin at some future time. But right now he had more important things to do. This was the moment he'd been waiting for ever since meeting with Abe Makram; this was the moment when he would start to reap the rewards of all the risks he had taken in running Makram under the noses of Section D. This was the time to strike another massive blow for Boris Pomarev and for Russia!

Pomarev said smoothly, "In a year's time the president won't be there. We can negotiate with his successor."

Seated across from him, Kyrelin shook his head. He was a big man, even for a Russian, over six feet four and very broad. He had a round, babyish face and a kiss curl in the middle of a broad and balding forehead. At times Kyrelin could look quite petulant and childlike. He said, "A year is a long time in politics. And we have no guarantee that his successor won't be Vice President Bradley Taylor, who, if anything, is more reactionary than Donnelly."

Pomarev held his breath momentarily. His hunch on Makram was starting to pay off, just as his hunch on Droznin's file had. "That can be changed," he said, exhaling slowly. "Without too much difficulty."

Kyrelin listened intently as Pomarev explained the intricacies of the American electoral system. He asked, "If they spend so much time holding elections, where do they find time to run the country? And how does anyone make anything work, when everyone knows he may be overthrown tomorrow?"

"Not overthrown," Pomarev corrected gently. "Simply not reelected."

The chairman got up from the sofa, stomped across to the samovar, and poured himself another cup of harsh black tea. "But even such a system must at times produce a wise and capable man," he said, walking back to the sofa. "A strong man, not this athlete, this actor. . . ." The chairman paused to collect his thoughts. "This cowboy!" He threw himself down on the sofa and gazed challengingly at Pomarev over the rim of his cup.

Pomarev told himself to proceed carefully. If he presented his case diligently, he could obtain the chairman's support for the scheme he had worked out, a scheme that would not only bring the bold new future the chairman wanted within his grasp, but could make him, Boris Pomarev, the second most powerful man in Russia. He said, "The presence of an actor in the White House is the logical conclusion of democracy."

"Talk Ukranian," the chairman snapped. "I'm surrounded by Central Committee philosophers every working day."

Pomarev explained. "The essence of democracy is that every few years the people are able to choose who they want to rule them. And people being what they are, they want that choice made as easy as possible. You know how difficult it is to choose between two candidates for the chairmanship of some local committee. You know how much you have to learn about their family history, their academic backgrounds, their work patterns, the philosophies they endorse, their character—"

"Get to the point," Kyrelin said.

"The American people do not choose their leaders like that," Pomarev said. "They do not have the time or inclination to examine alternatives closely. Those who do usually make no choice at all. Like all of us here in Russia, they are the party activists and will vote for the man chosen by the party. But unlike here, these party devotees do not control the result. There aren't enough of them to do so. The result is controlled by the person they call the floating voter, the man who is what he is because his interest in politics is slight. So the major challenge for American political parties is to nominate and portray a candidate who will capture the attention of the nonpolitical people and make them vote for him."

"I can tell you what not to do," Kyrelin grinned. "You

don't give such people detailed economic or philosophical arguments, or anything too complex or boring."

"Right. What the candidate must do is present himself in the friendliest possible way and keep his arguments simple and short. But the question is: what arguments does he use? And how does he know what issues interest this floating non-political voter? What policies will ensure that he will be elected?"

"You know about America," the chairman said defensively. "You tell me. That is why I asked you here."

Pomarev nodded acknowledgment. "Every American politician has what is called a market researcher, a person who, through a combination of polling and statistics, tries to determine the kind of policies and the sort of candidate the electorate will support. The object of the market researcher is to first find out what the electorate wants and then to package the candidate so the electorate believes it is getting what it wants."

"So you get an actor instead of a politician."

"In democracies few perceive the difference." Pomarev smiled and saw an accompanying glint of amusement in the chairman's eyes. "The best market researcher in America right now is a man called Steve Widdell. It is because of Widdell that this cowboy president was elected twice."

"This man Widdell must be a genius," the chairman said.

"He probably is. What he has is a special computer system that enables him to know exactly what the voter wants. And he is able to use that knowledge to transform the candidate into—"

"I knew there had to be a reason," the chairman interrupted. "You mean to say that this man Widdell could make anyone president?"

"Almost anyone," Pomarev said, and smiled. "You've met with the man who's been twice elected president of the United States. What do you think?"

The chairman busied himself with a piece of fluff that had appeared on his trouser leg. He grunted, "Tell me the rest."

Pomarev said, "From what I hear in America, Widdell's system is not only the best, it's nearly infallible. Anyone using it is sure to win."

"Are you suggesting we persuade this man Widdell to make the president lose?"

Pomarev had thought of that and rejected it as being too limited. He said, "The president will not be running again. But if we wanted to, we could ensure his successor was ours."

"The next president of the United States," the chairman mused. He leaned back on the sofa and stroked his chin thoughtfully before suddenly leaning forward and asking, "How would you do it?"

Pomarev suppressed a smile. This was what he'd been waiting for. "We start with Widdell," he said. "Or to be more precise, with Widdell's system. If we had his system, we could run it. We could run our own candidate."

"A Russian in the American presidential elections!" The chairman laughed and shook his head. "I don't think even this man Widdell's system is good enough for that."

Pomarev smiled. "Who's talking about a Russian?" he asked.

22

October 30, 1987

The wintry sun slanting through the leafless branches gave little heat. Compared to the rest of his body, encased in the pale gold track suit, Drew Ellis's face felt chilled. He breasted the hill and loped down the trail that meandered through the woods. At the picket fence it would be four miles. A mile and a half to home.

He ran easily, without strain, his breath floating through his partly opened mouth, the sheen of sweat beneath his headband the only indication of effort. He watched the ground ahead of his feet, watched his feet pad over the brown earth. Winter. Autumn. He'd never really known the seasons till he'd come to Fairmont, never really watched a single tree grow alternately barren and fruitful.

Three years ago today Emma had died, and this morning

he had picked the hardy remnants of wild flowers, plaited them into an untidy wreath and placed them before her photograph in the house. He had prayed for her soul and had talked with his friend Patrick Morell, now pastor to a church in Chesterbrook, not far from Washington. Deep down the pain was still there, but with God's help it was bearable. Since coming to Fairmont he had not once put a gun to his mouth.

His book, published three months ago, had been a success. He'd spent two weeks on the road, being interviewed by radio reporters and the hosts of talk shows, before getting bored with the whole process and returning to Fairmont. Nevertheless his publishers had given him a contract for a second book, and that morning his agent had called saying his publishers wanted to know how he was getting on with the sequel. Drew's eyes crinkled with amusement. In fact he wasn't getting on with any sequel. He was beginning to realize there wasn't a sequel to a cure. Once Lazarus had told the story of what it was like to take up his bed and walk, that was it, unless he fell ill again, or was cured again, or died.

Where the fence ended, the trail turned sharply right, uphill. He braced himself for it, felt his legs stretch easily, his arms drop into a natural pumping motion. This morning's run had been good. He would come out again in the evening and do the same circuit, running ten miles a day, as he had every day for the past year.

If anyone asked him why he ran, he would say it kept him fit. But no one ever asked him, because he lived alone and saw no one. Drew preferred it that way. He raised his hand to his head. Through the thin glove he could feel the lump at the side of his head and the ridge that ran above his ear. He reminded himself he could have been blinded from the shot. Or paralyzed. He thought about the way his legs moved over the earth, the way his lungs took in air and his heart pumped blood. He thought if the bullet had hit his skull at a fractionally different angle, he could have been dead.

But he was alive! As on each day when he felt lonely, as on each day when he felt the emptiness, he reminded himself that he was alive. Which was why he ran. Twice a day. Every day. As Patrick Morell had said, when you ran, you sometimes felt God.

23

December 13, 1987

In Moscow Boris Pomarev dutifully finished making love to his wife. As a schoolgirl Natalya Pomareva had entertained ambitions of dancing with the Bolshoi, and if her failure to do so had subsequently disappointed him, Boris Pomarev had never revealed it. His large and buxom wife was the daughter of the Moscow party chairman, a connection ensuring that Pomarev had received the promotions he'd earned. Even in Leninist Russia well-connected marriages had their advantages.

Pomarev lay back and thought that by this time tomorrow he'd be in Washington, getting Red-One under way. Red-One, he thought, fighting back his excitement; the code name for the plan that would take him to the top of the Russian *nomenklatura*.

Kyrelin had taken four weeks to approve the plan. He'd thought its concept too daring and had reservations about the excellence of Widdell's system. Pomarev smiled as he recalled how he'd explained the elements of computing to the most powerful man in the world. Praise all the revolutionary saints that he'd had the foresight to get so much detailed information from Makram. Kyrelin had learned fast, and once convinced, had become almost impossible to stop.

The chairman had put his authority behind Pomarev's requisitions and given him the power to virtually commandeer any Russian facility abroad, short of a nuclear submarine. Best of all, Pomarev thought, Kyrelin had agreed that it would be between the two of them—that he'd report only to Kyrelin, who would tell no one in the Politburo, Central Committee, or KGB about it.

The only other person who knew about Red-One, Pomarev thought, was Vladimir Yefimovich. Yefimovich was one of Kyrelin's confidential secretaries, and the chairman had insisted he should be present at their last meeting, yesterday. Pomarev and Kyrelin had gone over the entire structure of Red-One. Once a bureaucrat always a bureaucrat, Pomarev reflected, knowing Kyrelin wanted a witnessed record of Red-One in case Pomarev stepped out of line or anything went wrong. Which meant he had to deal with Yefimovich.

Pomarev phoned Major Mikhail Droznin, who owed him for his handling of the chairman's son, and told Droznin to initiate a discreet surveillance of Yefimovich. The link man would be a Kremlin secretary named Sergei Kamarov, who worked with Yefimovich and, like Yefimovich, was divorced. Major Droznin was to remind Kamarov of the occasion shortly before his divorce, when he'd been found blind drunk in a worker's bar near Kuntsevo and was only prevented from being assaulted and robbed through the intervention of the local militia, who at Pomarev's request had not made a report to the Kremlin. Pomarev asked Major Droznin to ensure that Kamarov reported to him scrupulously at least three times a week, and Droznin assured Pomarev he would do everything he could to control Yefimovich. When Pomarev put the phone down, he was smiling.

Still smiling, he looked across at his wife, catching the glint of her still open eyes. Her hand touched his. "Will you be safe, my darling?" she asked. She always asked him that the night before he left on a mission.

And as always Pomarev replied, "Of course. What could harm me?" He'd even told her that the night before he'd left for two years in the jungles of Vietnam.

"And you will succeed."

That was what he liked about Natalya. His success was the closest thing to her heart. "Have I ever failed?"

She brushed his cheek with her lips. "No. And you will not fail this time. Now you must sleep, my love. You have a long day tomorrow."

Pomarev closed his eyes. He felt like a medieval knight going to war. He would return a hero or not at all, and if he succeeded, the kingdom, or more correctly, a large part of it, would be his.

24

December 16, 1987

Vladimir Simenon, deputy director general of the KGB, lit another of his ubiquitous *papyrosi* as he looked at his hastily scribbled record of Boris Pomarev's visits to the Kremlin. In the last six weeks Pomarev had visited Kyrelin eight times. The shortest visit had been for seventy-five minutes; the longest, which had been attended by a single stenographer, Vladimir Yefimovich, four-and-a-half hours.

What had Kyrelin found to talk to Pomarev about for four-and-a-half hours? Simenon briefly contemplated bringing Yefimovich in for interrogation, and immediately decided against it. Yefimovich was a Kremlin clerk, and any apprehension, arrest, or interrogation would require first notifying the Kremlin. Once Kyrelin heard of it, he'd soon ascertain the reason for the arrest, and then good-bye Simenon.

So what was he to do? Simenon had never liked or trusted Pomarev. He'd always thought him a fancy boy, with his American-styled suits, Rolex watch, and silk ties. He'd known Pomarev to be a wily, experienced, ambitious bastard who'd never made any secret of his ambition to get to the very top, to become the youngest KGB director ever. At forty-two director of the KGB, at forty-three, member of the Politburo, and at fifty chairman! Never, Simenon thought, not if he could help it. Not if he, Vladimir Petrovich Simenon, had blood around his bones and not water.

He put away the notes, the result of many secret conversations with an informant inside the Kremlin, lit another cigarette and wondered what Pomarev was up to. His contacts in the Politburo knew of no special plans and could give him no reason why Pomarev had abandoned his search for enemies of Kyrelin and left for Washington. Surely Kyrelin, the least paranoid of Soviet leaders, did not believe he would be overthrown from there, and even if he were, that Pomarev could stop it.

Then Simenon remembered that if not for circumstance, he'd have had Pomarev in Berlin three years ago. In Berlin Pomarev had been dallying with the Americans, and now Pomarev had not gone to Washington to suppress a coup, but to pursue that dalliance. That was the only theory that made sense, Simenon thought with quiet triumph. Both Pomarev and the chairman were fancy boys with impractical ideas of coexistence and détente. They had lunatic dreams of a consumer-oriented society financed by the diversion of resources from the army and the KGB. Simenon fought to control his anger. These betrayers of the revolution, these inheritors of Brezhnev, had to be brought under control! Pomarev and the chairman had to be stopped.

25

December 22, 1987

At first sight the pale cream, four-story building looked part of Georgetown University. But it wasn't. The words BILDEBERG INSTITUTE carved into the stone pediment across its colonnaded entrance gave the impression it was a Germanic historical society. It wasn't. The five men meeting in the executive chamber on the fourth floor were the Institute's patrons. However, only the names of two of them appeared on the tasteful notepaper and in the glossy brochures that went out to wealthy industrial corporations and prominent members of governments throughout the world. The brochures described in vivid detail the services the Institute provided—political and economic intelligence of unsurpassed quality, introductions to highly placed contacts, facilities for the creation, negotiation, and servicing of lucrative contracts—all of which were only some of the functions of Bildeberg and only part of the reason for its existence.

The man seated at the head of the green baize table was

popularly thought to have founded Bildeberg, which was the impression he liked to give, because he believed people felt safer with legends who were alive. But that, too, was only part of the truth. Former Ambassador Whillan Courtney had not founded Bildeberg. He had succeeded to it. Everything he was, everything he had been, he owed to the men of Bildeberg. And because he was the only survivor of the old guard, he was today the person most commonly associated with Bildeberg.

Thirty-five years ago, with the help of Bildeberg, State Department career eagle Whillan Courtney had almost become secretary of state, and there were many who believed that the world would have been a better place if he had. But Bildeberg had finally decided that Courtney's experience, diplomatic skills, integrity, and discretion were best directed to a position of similar importance requiring a much lower profile. It was always the policy of Bildeberg to work secretly. In his capacity as diplomatic counsel, Whillan Courtney had served four presidents, and in the last twenty-five years there had not been a single foreign policy crisis in which Whillan Courtney had not participated or advised upon, either as a servant of the state or, more recently, as the head of Bildeberg, which not only obtained the finest intelligence, but had an uncanny capacity for reaching people and sources the government frequently could not.

Soon, Whillan Courtney thought, looking at the four men seated two and two on either side of the green baize table, he would have to ensure that the Bildeberg tradition of selfless and anonymous public service would be passed on. Soon he would have to nominate a successor, and he couldn't help wondering what effect such a nomination would have. These newer members of Bildeberg were more vociferous and self-confident, more nakedly ambitious, less tolerant and more self-seeking than the men he had known. His choice would not be accepted as blindly as all previous Bildeberg nominations had been. These new men would demand a vote and get it. Courtney hoped they would not fall out among themselves and would remember that the objectives of Bildeberg were immeasurably more important than any personal ambition or reward.

Courtney diverted his attention to Dr. Jonathan Bradley, the Institute's thirty-six-year-old research director, who was telling the group about his examination of Steve Widdell's computer system. "I have been studying Widdell's operation for nearly a year," he was saying, "and I have absolutely no doubt that PDS—Widdell's computer system—was the raison d'être for the president's last two overwhelming election victories." Bradley had a doctorate in Political Economy and a masters in Cybernetics, had studied at Cornell, the Harvard Business School, and Cambridge University. He read both Plato and computer manuals with equal facility, and was fluent in French and German. His soft, well-modulated voice had a ringing quality to it, as if he were addressing a classroom. Courtney remembered that Bradley had been a lecturer in Computer Sciences when he'd been recruited to Bildeberg.

Too young to lead Bildeberg and too much of an egghead, Courtney thought. He repressed a smile at the old-fashioned phrase and looked at each of the other men: Jim Colson, Senator Kevin Anderson, and Cas Hardinger.

Colson was a deputy director of the CIA's Office of Counter Intelligence, in charge of his own department and an alternative member of the National Security Council. A brilliant career officer, he had distinguished himself in the field, in Vietnam and Europe, before being transferred to Langley, where he'd used those same qualities of astuteness, intelligence, and mild paranoia to triumph over internal political maneuvering and orchestrate some of the most brilliant counterespionage campaigns in the history of the Agency. Already many people believed Colson would be the next director of the Agency. An ideal choice for Bildeberg, too, Courtney mused, recalling that Colson's father had been a member of Bildeberg, except... Courtney couldn't enunciate his reservation precisely. He fumbled for thought. There was something distant about Colson, something dispassionate, as if he were always observing and never feeling. That was it, Courtney concluded. Colson lacked emotion.

Unlike Senator Kevin Anderson, who had been one of the brightest architects of the Kennedy years and was respected now in his own right for his uncompromising stands on civil rights, government extravagance, and the welfare of the less fortunate. A temperate man used to leading, a political moderate with a public record of compassion, the senator would make an ideal successor. Except that with the help of

Widdell's Political Data System, Senator Anderson was going to be the next president of the United States!

Cas Hardinger sat opposite Anderson, thin and balding, with the same sharp eyes and aquiline features of his father, who had made his fortune through Bildeberg and then walked out of the organization. Hardinger was every spare inch his father's son, and in more than looks. He had in fifteen years quintupled the fortune he had inherited and was now the funding force behind Bildeberg. But though Hardinger gave generously, what he gave was measured and recorded to the last cent, as if someday there would be a reckoning. On that day, Courtney thought grimly, Hardinger's true nature would emerge.

He turned his attention back to Jonathan Bradley. Bradley's report was of the greatest importance. What the men of Bildeberg did with it could alter the whole future of the United States. Bradley was saying, "Essentially, Widdell's system consists of massive data bases, the first and most important of which contains the historical voting records of every county in the United States for the past four elections. This is linked to another equally large data base containing complete demographic information on every county in the United States. The third strand of Widdell's system are his surveys which continually update the information he already holds and enables him to check various issues against the voting patterns of the electorate.

"All this information is stored in two VAX computers here in Washington, with spare capacity and back-up facilities in Falls Point. What is significant about Widdell's system is the way he makes this huge mass of information work for him. He has constructed a mathematical model into which all the information from the computer, demographic statistics, surveys, opinions, and questions are fed, and"—Bradley snapped his fingers—"the computer produces the electorate's reaction, county by county." He smiled and added, "As you can see, Widdell's system is so sophisticated it goes way beyond the simple forecasting of a vote. It can predict how any part of the country will react to any issue.

"For instance, if the candidate is due to speak on abortion in two different counties, he can, using Widdell's system, check not only how the voters of those counties felt about the issue, but how they feel now. Which means he can tailor his message accordingly." Bradley smiled and finished. "Quite simply, Widdell's system can ensure the public gets the candidate it wants."

"How accurate is all this?" Hardinger rasped.

"Frighteningly so," Bradley replied. "In the last two congressional and senatorial elections Widdell's margin of error was zero point two five percent." Bradley threw back his head as if dealing with a gifted but truculent student. "That's as near as you can get to being infallible."

Courtney leaned forward. "Is it your conclusion that anyone using Widdell's system could win any election?"

"Yes, if the system were run correctly." Bradley looked at his colleagues. "Widdell's system only works if it is applied correctly. First of all, the proper procedures have to be applied to the system. Then the appropriate codes have to be obtained to get into the more complicated parts of the program. Without the codes, no one can operate Widdell's system."

"Who has the codes?" Hardinger asked.

"Right now," Bradley replied thoughtfully, "I believe only Steve Widdell."

"What if Widdell meets with an accident?" Colson asked.

"I don't know. Up to last year Widdell shared the codes with his chief associates, Lucas Amory, and then after Amory's retirement, Dick Schaffer."

Hardinger said, "If what you say is true, this system is too dangerous to be left to whoever can grab hold of it. If the system is as powerful as you say, it must be controlled by us."

"How do we do that?" Courtney asked.

"Simple," Hardinger snapped. "We buy it." He flung the pen he was holding across the pad in front of him. For Hardinger price settled everything.

"That may not be so easy," Colson said, seemingly selecting each word like someone picking chocolates from a box. "As I understand it, Widdell is a man with little need of money. He is in his late forties, married, with no children. He is a workaholic and has few interests outside his business. Whatever you offered him, he'd want to go on working."

"Everyone has a price," Hardinger said.

"You might find Widdell's unacceptably high."

"All that means is that we will have to pay a little more

for it." The tiny muscles of Hardinger's jaw flickered as he threw everyone in the room a tight smile.

Colson said, "I think we should discuss alternatives should Widdell not want to sell. We should talk about other means of getting the system." He turned to Bradley. "Where are Widdell's tapes stored? Does he have a back-up facility? What do you know about his security arrangements?"

"The tapes are stored in his office," Bradley replied. "And the back-ups at a computer facility in Falls Point. His security arrangements are carried out by a private firm."

"I insist you stop this line of questioning at once," Courtney cried. "We will either acquire this system legitimately or not at all!"

The others looked embarrassedly away. Colson was the first to speak. "If we don't take the system," he said, reasonably, "someone else will." He smiled and waved a hand around the room. "Do you want me to put it to the vote?"

Courtney looked from Colson to the others. Only Anderson looked uncertain enough to support him. Wearily he said, "No, let's not take a vote."

26

January 21, 1988

Steve Widdell savored yet another massive spoonful of fettucini Alfredo before swallowing it. Ruggeiro's was his favorite restaurant, and Tony Ruggeiro made the best Alfredo he'd ever tasted, creamy and smooth, light and rich, subtle hints of garlic, nutmeg, and pepper caressing the palate before sliding down with deceptive ease. Widdell swallowed and nodded politely as Cas Hardinger finished his story about the time he'd been offered an ambassadorship to Chile and declined. "I was right," Hardinger said. "They started shooting the very next year."

Hardinger was a small, balding, sharp-featured man, with eyes that had the hardness and glitter of polished gemstones. He owned the Hardlan store chain, Mantel Airways, and Hardinger Oil. Widdell had been surprised to receive an invitation to dine with him. When people like Hardinger needed market research, they normally had managers fix it for them, and if Hardinger needed a political favor, the size of his political contributions ensured that he would be attended by far more politically influential people than Widdell. The only way to find out what Hardinger wanted, Widdell decided, was to accept Hardinger's invitation. He was glad he had, since Hardinger had suggested Ruggeiro's.

Hardinger didn't eat much. His Alfredo went nearly untasted, and Widdell wondered if Hardinger would mind if he finished it.

The businessman asked him about his family, and Widdell replied there was only his wife Sara, and that they had no children. He thought he saw a shadow of disappointment cross Hardinger's face.

Widdell gestured across the table. "Don't you want that?"

"What . . . oh, no. It's nice. But go on, help yourself."

Widdell reached across and spooned Hardinger's Alfredo onto his plate. They were in a private room supervised by Tony Ruggeiro himself. Bottles of Pinot Grigio and Fontana Candida reposed in an ice bucket, while on the table a recently opened bottle of Barolo breathed. Whatever people said about Cas Hardinger, Widdell thought, he was an excellent host.

The waiters removed the fettucini and brought in veal escalopes, Milanese for Widdell, grilled with a sprinkling of lemon juice for Hardinger. If he continued to eat like that, Hardinger thought, eyeing the crisp, brown coating of the Milanese, Widdell wasn't going to be around long enough to spend the money he was about to receive. Hardinger poured some of the red wine. "To our future." He smiled.

Widdell hesitated a moment before he raised his glass. "The future." He wondered what future Hardinger was alluding to.

Hardinger began to talk as soon as Widdell had sliced his escalope. "We're interested in buying your company, Mr. Widdell," he said. "That's why I've asked you here."

Widdell chewed slowly, swallowed and put down his fork. Since people had got to know that his system had put

Jack Donnelly into the White House for a second term, he'd
had twelve offers to buy it. "Who exactly is we?" he asked.

"Myself and some associates. Does it really matter who
we are? I would have thought that you would be more
concerned with the terms and the price."

"It matters," Widdell said, still not eating. His business
was more serious and more important than food.

Hardinger picked at his plate. "We are the Hardinger
Group, which is controlled by a private company, Hardinger
Associates, which is controlled by me."

Widdell ate. "So if I sell out, I'll be working for you?"

"That's correct."

"What are your terms?"

"Eight million dollars cash, four million payable on signature of contract, four million upon evaluation and certifica-
tion that we have what we want—your entire computer
system, Mr. Widdell."

Widdell put down his fork again. Jeydell Industries had
offered him as much, and Telecomp Data a little less. "The
system's not for sale, Mr. Hardinger," Widdell said.

Hardinger smiled. "Not even if we say you will continue
to run Widdell Associates and the price will be ten million
dollars?" He pushed away his plate. "Part of the deal will be
the retention of your services for a period of ten years,
together with share and profit participation. You're going to
end up a very rich man, Mr. Widdell."

Widdell smiled. "I'm already that."

Hardinger frowned. His research had shown that Widdell's
net worth was only about six hundred thousand dollars. "You
are rich enough to walk away from ten million dollars?" He
made no effort to keep the surprise out of his voice.

Widdell nodded. "Let me explain. Neither Sara nor I
would know what to do with ten million dollars. Sure,
sometimes I think we need another computer, or a newer car,
but those things are given to us when they're needed. So ten
million dollars we don't need."

"What *do* you need, Mr. Widdell?"

"For the purpose of this exercise, my work. I need that."

"And you shall have it, plus the ten million dollars. Just
think, the interest on your capital would give you more
than enough to live on, and you will never need to work
for money again. Any work you do will be of your own

choosing. You'll only do the work you want to do. You will be a truly fortunate man."

"You make it sound mighty interesting, Mr. Hardinger, but the answer's still no. You see, I like the feeling of running my own business. And I couldn't do that if you owned it."

"You'll still be running it," Hardinger protested. "I certainly won't have time to get involved in telling you how to run what you know best."

"Then why do you want to buy it?" Widdell asked.

"Because I think that with an injection of capital, the commercial aspect of your business can be expanded. Because many of the businesses I own need the kind of research you provide, and it would be more economical to have all their work put through the one organization and to share in that organization's profits."

"Then I take it you're not interested in the political side?"

"We are interested in your entire business, Mr. Widdell, including the political side."

Widdell pushed away his plate and poured himself more wine. His system worked better on industrial surveys than political ones, but everyone wanted the political system. "Would you be wanting to nominate the candidates who use our services?" he asked.

"We would want to approve the candidates, yes."

"And if we disagreed on who those candidates should be?"

"Mr. Widdell, the purpose of our association is not to disagree, but for us to cooperate to maximize our mutual profits and our contribution to society."

"You sure about that?"

"I am sure that any disagreement we may have can be satisfactorily resolved." Hardinger smiled. "After all, without you we could not run the system or the business."

Widdell's smile was wary. "Weasel words, Mr. Hardinger, if you don't mind my saying so. You realize that my computer skills are a gift from God and that I have a duty to use those gifts for the spiritual benefit of my country. Now, while I'm happy to make a living from the talents I've been given, to allow others to control those talents is not something I can do. It is essential that I use whatever gifts I have been given wisely and well, and therefore, Mr. Hardinger, an unalterable condition of our agreement must be that I and I alone will decide which political candidates will be allowed to use my system."

"Please be reasonable, Steve." Still smiling, Hardinger twisted his head. "We are, as they say, setting you up for life. We are paying you a substantial sum of money." He enunciated the words slowly, "Ten million dollars. You can't expect us to give you that for nothing."

"No," Widdell replied. "It is a lot of money. It may be that we'll both be happier if you kept it."

"You don't mean that," Hardinger said. He leaned forward and filled Widdell's glass with wine. "Let's see if we can handle this another way. Let's say we increase our offer to twelve million dollars and give you the right..."

Widdell pushed his plate away. He was no longer hungry.

27

January 28, 1988

Giant yellow eye of traffic light blinking, Abe Makram bounced the service truck onto the curb and stopped outside Steve Widdell's office on North Capitol Street. Traffic hissed by, throwing icy shards of spray. As soon as he switched off the engine, the temperature in the cab fell noticeably and a thin film of ice misted over the windshield. Makram looked in the rearview mirror and stared at his face in the muted glow of the streetlight.

Since he'd left Widdell on Pomarev's orders nearly six months ago, Abe had put on fifteen pounds—again on Pomarev's orders—cropped his hair short, and sprouted a virulent moustache. No doubt about it, he looked different, and no one would expect him to appear at Widdell wearing white overalls and a cap and carrying the fitted tool kit of a service mechanic. He'd been a senior analyst at Widdell, and people only recognized what was familiar. No one at Widdell would ever imagine that Abe Makram would return as a service engineer.

So he was safe—if he didn't run into anyone with a good memory for faces or anyone who'd seen him recently. He'd told Boris this was the weakest part of the plan, but Boris had said there was no other way. Makram was the only person who knew enough about computers, the only one who knew exactly what they wanted and how to get it. There was no alternative but to send him in.

Makram decided to enter the building before one of the security people wondered what a service truck was doing parked outside with its driver preening himself in the mirror. He yanked open the door and dropped onto the pavement. The chill wind bit through his jacket like a knife exposing bone. Bent double and twisting to one side with the weight of the tool kit, he ran lopsidedly across the snow-grimed pavement and shouldered his way into the warmth of the entrance lobby. Lenin preserve me, he thought.

The warmth misted his glasses. The gleaming cement floor was soiled by a fading trail of damp mud from the entrance doors. Giant potted plants, the large counter with its raised partition running the width of the lobby, and the two uniformed guards seated on either side of it were exactly as he remembered it. Except he didn't recognize either of the security guards. Nothing to worry about there, he told himself. As a matter of routine, Widdell changed his security firm every nine months, which was a hidden blessing. An alert security guard who been there for a couple of years might have recognized him.

Makram walked over to the older guard. More experienced guards had nothing to prove and were less likely to be aggressive. "I hear you've got a problem," he said. He rubbed his glasses with his sleeve, pulled open his jacket and leaned forward so the guard could examine the plastic card and photograph on his lapel.

"Didn't know we had a call out today," the guard said. "You hear anything about a call out today, Andy?"

"No," the second guard replied, and went back to his comic book.

"We had a call about five," Makram said. "Sorry we only just made it. It's a skating rink out there, and we're short-handed. A lot of our people are down with the flu."

"Hasn't hit us yet." The guard sniffed and looked from the picture on Makram's lapel to his face. "Haven't seen you before. You're new?"

Makram felt his heart hammering in his chest. "I normally work Arlington." His voice was suddenly guttural and his accent harsh. He stopped talking. In moments of stress he reverted to his native Russian, a habit that he'd been warned would one day lead to his execution. He forced himself to look directly into the guard's face. "As I said, we're running shorthanded today." He spoke slowly, having to translate the sentence from Russian.

The guard looked at him closely. "Yeah. The flu." He got to his feet and waved Makram around the counter. "Guess I'd better take you downstairs."

The guard inserted a key into the panel beside the elevator and rode with Makram to the basement, the short, downward plunge giving Makram time to recover some mental poise. In the basement the guard led him to a metal framed door enclosing wired glass panels. Makram's mouth began to go dry. *Gypak!* A year ago he'd worked down here in Maintenance and Systems. He saw Pat Cleary, one of the supervisors, appear on the other side of the threaded glass. The guard spoke quietly into an intercom by the door. Cleary opened it.

This was it, Makram thought frantically. When he'd first joined Widdell, they'd sent him down here to learn how the machines functioned and he'd worked with Cleary. His former colleague was now looking at a thick leather-bound book on a stand near the door. *Fucking revolution!*

"Didn't know we'd had a callout," Cleary said. "Everything's been functioning normally."

Makram's chest felt about to cave in. He had personally arranged for the data to be tampered with and for the service call to be made. If Greg Vassilos had simply taken the ten thousand and disappeared, Pomarev's operation was fucked, and Abe Makram was well and truly fucked. He said, "We had a call around five," relieved to find himself thinking again in English. "That's why I'm here. The problem was described as urgent. Sorry we couldn't get here before. It's a skating rink outside, and half our people have caught the flu."

Cleary riffed through a couple of pages. He was a pale, red-haired man with clouded blue eyes set a trifle too close together. "Ah, yes, here it is. There was a call around five." Cleary seemed mildly surprised. "Vassilos was having trouble with his readouts."

Suppressing a sigh of relief, Makram reached over and looked at the log. "This here says your operator was having difficulty in getting the computer to read *and* write." He frowned worriedly at Cleary. "That's a nasty one for this time of the night." He returned the log book to Cleary.

Cleary said, "No one else has complained."

"Maybe no one else noticed."

Cleary stared at him for a moment, then turned and inserted a card into a slot and led Makram through another door and into the computer room.

When Makram saw the familiar hulk of the VAX computer, he felt his heartbeat ease and the tremor in his stomach fade. He put his tool kit down by the machine and stared at it. Now that he was about to actually start work, he felt calm. "Failure to read/write could be disastrous," he said. "You've been keeping the computers operational since this report was made?"

"Sure. We don't stop the computers unless we have to."

Makram took out a diagnostic tape from the tool kit and inserted it. "It could be a major fault," he said. "If it's what I think it is, you could be in a whole lot of trouble." He stared closely at the machine.

"A whole lot of trouble is just what I don't need," Cleary said, peering closely at him.

Makram felt his heartbeat accelerate. A warm, acrid taste tickled the back of his throat. He pulled his cap lower on his forehead. "Anything wrong?"

Cleary colored. "No, no. It's just that you remind me of someone. I can't think—"

"You drink around Arlington?"

Hurriedly Cleary shook his head. "I'm not a drinking man."

"In that case, we're unlikely to have met." Keeping the cap low over his forehead, Makram crouched and peered closely at the computer. He took a screwdriver and unfastened a part of the casing. "This'll take me a while," he said. "I'll shout if I need anything."

"Right," Cleary said. "Sure. There's a coffee machine down the corridor to your left."

Just in time Makram stopped himself from saying, "I know." He focused his attention on the computer. The thing now was to take time, to create an impression of worried activity. He spread his tools out and inserted a circuit break-er. Lights glowed. He told himself everything was going to be all right.

Red-One, as Boris had told him the operation was called, had to be the biggest KGB operation going. It was certainly the biggest Makram had ever been involved in. There was no shortage of money, and everything he'd asked for had been delivered without question and on the double. And when it had come to bribing Vassilos and the mechanic who'd provid-ed them with the van, uniform, and service codes, Boris had been overly generous, insisting that the job be done quickly and well rather than cheaply. A real turnaround for the KGB, Makram thought.

He looked at his watch. In an hour he would start to escalate the crisis, and as a precaution he ensured that the machine wouldn't read/write anyway. He worked directly for Boris now and had no need to worry about Section D, but the operation was still being run very privately. Boris had brought in his own team, and upon arriving in Washington, had told him that all contact with the Residency had been severed and he was to say nothing about Red-One to anyone. This is our operation, Boris told him, yours and mine. When it succeeds, all the glory will be ours. *If* it succeeds, Makram thought, and turned his attention to the computer.

He worked on it for an hour and a half. At ten minutes past nine he asked for a shutdown. At 9:22 he summoned Cleary. "Your problem is the machine codes," he said. "Every so often they've been jumping a byte. I've changed the unit, but it still means that some of your data is junk."

Cleary's face paled. The data bases were the heart of Widdell's system, and if they were inaccurate . . . "Which part of the data?"

"I don't know," Makram said, "it's difficult to pinpoint." He paused and added, "And I don't know how long it'll stay fixed."

"You mean—"

"I mean I'm not sure it is the machine codes. To be certain of what's caused the problem, I'll have to download all your tapes and check the frequency of the glitch."

"Download all—Surely you can't mean—"

"It's the only way to be absolutely sure," Makram said. "If the problem recurs, you may not know till it's too late."

He watched Cleary's anguished frown; they both knew that statistical tapes with unreliable data was the worst situation of all.

Cleary said, "I'll need authority."

"Get it. And tell whoever you're talking to that without checking the tapes, I can't guarantee your present work or that the fault will not recur."

Cleary picked up a phone and checked with a second supervisor, who ran over the problem again with Makram and agreed they should start backing up the tapes and prepare the computers for downloading.

Four hours later the operation was finished. Except neither of the supervisors knew that the data bases had been downloaded not to the computers of the maintenance firm, but to a set of identical computers housed in a building in Aurora Heights.

28

January 29, 1988

CRANE BRINGS GLAMOR TO PRESIDENTIAL NOMINATION

It's a new race for VP Taylor—and a few others

With his belated campaign proclamation last week, Senator Frank Crane, Jr., became the eleventh person to announce that he would be seeking his party's nomination for the presidency. In doing so he brought both a hint of much-needed spice and challenge to what has so far proved to be an unremarkable campaign. If Crane makes it to the presidency, he will be the youngest president since John F. Kennedy, but whether Crane achieves that ambition depends on the extent to which he can sway the electorate, and in their turn, the party gurus who up to now have been religiously putting forward the candidacy of Vice President Bradley Taylor.

Taylor, Jack Donnelly's faithful Vice President for four years, has a long record of party loyalty. A former national committee chairman, he is perhaps best known for his brilliant damage control after Watergate and for structuring the Donnelly-Ford ticket that got Donnelly elected in 1980.

The contrast between Crane and Taylor could not be more striking. While Taylor is serious, withdrawn, and often described by both colleagues and opponents as "the perfect civil servant," Crane is flamboyant, charismatic, and full of an unashamed candor which in this campaign could turn out to be more help than hindrance.

Former party chairman Steve Lassakis did not think Crane's entry into the presidential stakes would divide the party. "Our whole system is based on free and open elections, and for Crane to hold back in the name of the sacred cow of party unity would seem to me to be a negation of democracy itself." Rival party coordinator Bill Hoglund echoed Chairman Lassakis's views. "Challenge is the essence of democracy, and I believe Bradley Taylor should be challenged," Senator Hoglund said. "I believe Frank Crane is the right man to make that challenge, and I do not think the presidency should be made a sinecure."

To convince the electorate and the party gurus, Crane has a formidable list of assets. Personally wealthy—at twenty-one the senator inherited a fortune of five million dollars—Crane has considerable television presence, as was evidenced in the televised hearings of the joint congressional committee investigating arms sales to Iran. Consistently identified with the progressive wing of the party, Crane can call upon numerous powerful allies for support, such as former Secretary of State Colman Jackson and Majority Leader Franklin Kemp, both of whom regard Crane as a desirable alternative to Taylor. The senator has youth on his side, good looks, and apparently limitless energy. The fact that he has a distinguished war record will also not go unnoticed. Taken prisoner in Vietnam, Crane engineered the escape of his entire platoon, and avoiding recapture and Vietnamese ambush, led his men to safety in a series of complex marches over a period of eleven days.

Crane also has a dedicated state organization and a devoted campaign team, whose key members served with him in Vietnam. "I guess we're the only campaign team that's ready to die for our candidate," Crane campaign director Luther Waverley quipped when asked if he felt the senator had begun his campaign too late. "Which means we're prepared to work harder and longer and better than anybody else, so there's no way the senator could have entered the campaign too late."

Of course, getting the party nomination is very different from becoming president. And here both Crane and Taylor must reckon with Senator Kevin Anderson, basking in the hopes of a renewed Camelot, and Governor Afram Milovan, whose track record, speeches, and attitudes are likely to bring him the votes of the underprivileged, and thus the support of the major cities.

As John Carlson wrote: "The way ahead is long and hazardous," and thanks to Senator Frank Crane, a lot more fascinating.

—JAY EMERSON III

Reported by Elaine Dominez/Washington and Richard Beatty/Boston
©Time Inc.

29

As he'd done at five o'clock almost every weekday evening for the past eight years, Vladimir Yefimovich joined the patient line of Kremlin clerks standing before the appropriately called Second Nameless Tower to be cleared for leaving the Kremlin. He kept his eyes averted as he joined the line. The pickup was going to be on the embankment between the Moskvoretsky and Usinsky bridges, so it was essential he left the Kremlin unaccompanied. The line shuffled slowly forward, taking longer than usual today. Yefimovich felt his heart squeeze up inside his chest. Did they know? Had they found the American and broken him? Were they setting a trap? He peered anxiously along the line, jostling the man in front of him as he did.

"New guards," the man grunted. "It always takes longer when they have new guards."

Yefimovich acknowledged that was true. The regular guards knew most of the Kremlin employees by sight and didn't have to check everyone's work pass. He looked to the head of the line. There wasn't a face he recognized among the guards. His heart raced uncontrollably and so loudly he felt sure his neighbor must hear it. He spoke to drown its patter. "It's good neither of us are in a hurry, comrade."

"Yes." The man took a copy of that morning's *Pravda* from his briefcase and held it up in front of his face. Yefimovich wished he'd thought of bringing a paper. Held in front of his face, it would have been all the barrier he needed. He stood with averted eyes, a tall, gangling man with a head of dark, wavy hair pressed flat under his astrakhan. Moscow was still in the thrall of winter, and everyone in the line wore heavy boots, overcoats, gloves, and hats.

One thing for sure, he wouldn't miss the Russian winter.

Yefimovich stamped his feet, smacked his gloved hands together, and wondered what winters were like in America. The one time he'd been there, it was autumn and everything had been luscious brown and red, as if the earth were being reborn instead of dying. His heart quickened at the thought of America. Hot dogs, hamburgers, Jane Fonda. Crowds of people lining outside the theaters on Broadway, with their bright colors, neon and dazzling bulbs; cars everywhere, big, small, dented, noisy, squawking, grinding; and people who walked the street as if they owned it. Best of all, no KGB. Never any KGB. He thought longingly of the shops he'd seen with their windows stacked with clothes and food, of the thousands of restaurants, Chinese, French, Creole, Indian, Turkish, even Russian. Once in America, he would have a centrally heated apartment that would never be cold and a kitchen and bathroom of his own. He would have a car, a bright yellow Camaro and two color television sets! He'd have a portable radio he could listen to in his bathroom. He would buy a Japanese stereo system and all the Elvis Presley and Jim Reeves records he could get his hands on. And he would drink cocktails, dry martinis, shaken not stirred. And there would be wom—

The guard's hand was thrust impatiently before his face. Yefimovich handed over his work pass. Inside the leather glove his hand was like ice. He was certain the guard must feel it. He fought a tremor of fear as the guard's eyes darted between the photograph on his pass and his face. Steady, steady. There was nothing wrong with his work pass or his appearance.

The guard slapped the pass into Yefimovich's palm. Fighting back a cry of relief and forcing himself to move slowly, he walked under the massive arch into the street. For a moment he stood there hesitating as traffic swept by on hissing tires. Then thrusting his head down and pulling his scarf tighter around his neck, he hurried along the Embankment, the lights from passing vehicles elongating his shadow on the pavement, making it seem he was fleeing from the giant shade of the Kremlin spreading across the street.

The black limousine slid silently past him and stopped. Its door swung open like the wing of a huge, ungainly bird. Yefimovich hurried to it and got in. Hamburgers, hot dogs, and Marilyn Monroe.

* * *

Two hundred yards behind Yefimovich, Sergei Kamarov stood frozen with shock. Like Yefimovich, he was a Kremlin stenographer and over the past three months had, on the instructions of the Political Security Unit, successfully cultivated Yefimovich. Using their common misery at the greediness of their ex-wives, he'd progressed their relationship from a visit to the Bolshoi to a regular schedule of drinks after work, movies and dinner twice a week. He'd found that Yefimovich and he had more in common than their work and grasping ex-wives, that they had a shared fondness for the films of Sonya Matsyeva, the poetry of Mandelstam, the songs of Elvis Presley, and the Yunovst bar. In a strange way Kamarov felt closer to Yefimovich than many former school friends, and he knew more about Yefimovich than almost anyone else.

When Yefimovich had stopped by his office shortly before four o'clock, he'd known something was seriously wrong. Yefimovich had looked more tense and abstracted than he'd been all week and had given no proper reason for cancelling their visit to the first film of the Matsyeva retrospective the following Saturday. And so when Yefimovich had left work, Kamarov had followed him out of the Kremlin.

He'd seen Yefimovich hurry in the opposite direction than of his home and get into an official-looking black limousine. Kamarov's oversized glasses slipped down his nose as he peered down the street, hoping to see the limousine stop, see Yefimovich get out and walk back toward him, hear Yefimovich say he'd only been dreaming.

Kamarov watched the twin red rectangles of the limousine's taillights disappear. Pressing his hat to his head, he turned and ran awkwardly back toward the Kremlin. He had to find a phone, and fast.

The limousine had darkened windows and wallowed smoothly in the rush-hour traffic as the driver cut away from the Embankment, headed toward the Inner Ring Road. It is over, Yefimovich thought. He'd left the Kremlin for the last time, walked the Embankment for the last time. He thought of the fatherly man with the square-lensed glasses who would be waiting for him in Washington, and for some reason it irked him that the last time he'd walked the Embankment it had been in the wrong direction.

But there was nothing he could do about that now. Everything was over. Everything was beginning. Hamburgers, hot dogs, and Doris Day. On the seat beside him was a small suitcase. He took off his hat, topcoat, and jacket and opened the case. Inside, exactly as the American had told him, was a suit of good quality, socks, and shoes. The shoes were of good quality, too, and had been worn enough to scar the soles and crease the uppers. In a small compartment set into the cover of the case was a small plastic container and mirror.

Yefimovich had visualized so often what he had to do, it felt as if he were reliving a previous experience. He opened the plastic container and balanced the damp little disk on the edge of his finger. This was the part he disliked, and he hoped the swaying of the car wouldn't blind him. Fitting the mirror into a slot in the partition separating him from the driver, Yefimovich brought his eye close to it and pressed the plastic disk against his eyeball. The disk stuck. His eyes—one brown, one blue—made him look like an evil clown. He inserted the second lens and his eyes teared. When that had subsided, he changed, twisting uncomfortably in the car, protected from the gaze of curious onlookers by the tinted windows. When he'd finished, he removed the documents from a zipped pocket at the back of the case and studied them. Passport, exit visa, photograph, documents. Everything seemed in order. According to the documents, he was an export cost controller on his way to London with documents for a meeting of the trade delegation. Yefimovich smiled thinly at the thought of what he was taking inside his head.

30

Fifteen minutes later Vladimir Yefimovich got off the bus outside Sheremetyevo Air Terminal and walked with the crowd of disembarking passengers into the building. Despite the briefing he had been given by the American, the interior was unfamiliar, with large electric signs everywhere and a stream of announcements floating over the public address system. He tried to hide his feelings of strangeness by walking at the same pace as the others, his eyes scanning the small battered signs over the ticket desks for one that said London.

He saw it and joined the line of passengers standing patiently in front of the desk. Halfway along the line, standing sideways to the reservations desk, he saw the American, a brown suitcase at his feet as he casually surveyed the lounge. Yefimovich smiled. The American looked past him without expression.

"Papers!"

Yefimovich nearly left his skin at the shouted demand. His heart set up a wild tattoo and his mouth felt as if it had been suddenly swabbed with blotting paper. He stared white-faced at the hand thrust out so arrogantly before him. The ticket clerk said, "Without papers and tickets, comrade, you cannot go anywhere."

An hour after the British Airways Boeing left, the controller of the Border Guards Directorate at Sheremetyevo telephoned Major Droznin. "We're still keeping a full alert," he said. "But I think your man has flown."

"You don't mean literally?"

"I'm afraid I do." The controller told Droznin how one of his men had checked out a forty-year-old auditor on his way to London with papers for a trade delegation. "The description did not quite fit Yefimovich," the controller said. "According to my officer, the suspect's eyes were a very startling blue."

"Why wasn't he stopped?" Droznin demanded.

"The officer had not received notification of your alert," the controller said. "In fact, because he was on mobile duty, he did not receive the message till ten minutes ago. According to the officer, the suspect was wearing different clothes and his papers were in order. However, we have a good description. If it is any help, comrade, the suspect boarded a flight to London."

"Do you have a passenger list?"

"It was the first thing I obtained. There is a possible shadow. An American diplomat named McKinley."

"Where is the plane?" Droznin demanded.

"It left Russian airspace ten minutes ago." He paused a moment before he added, "I am sorry, comrade. I hope the loss will be bearable."

The loss was irretrievable, Droznin thought. Not only Pomarev but the director of the Second Chief Directorate would have his guts for garters for letting someone under surveillance simply walk out of Russia. He put his head in his hands. It couldn't be true. It was impossible that someone could leave Russia that easily. Yefimovich was probably still in Moscow, drunk in some bar or indulging himself with a woman. But then he thought: what if Yefimovich had gone? Droznin reached for a phone and dialed the number Pomarev had given him in Washington.

31

February 2, 1988. Washington

Gently, almost caressingly, Boris Pomarev put the phone down. His chest was tight and the tips of his fingers chilled with tension. Droznin couldn't have given him worse news. If Yefimovich had defected, Red-One was finished. He was finished, and probably Chairman Kyrelin, too. He suppressed a spasm of rage at the injustice of it all. There would be time for rage and justification afterward, but right now he had to do something. Somehow he had to stop Yefimovich, who was already on a flight to London.

How?

The question mocked him. The KGB had no power over a British aircraft in international airspace. The plane was too far out to scramble Soviet fighters out of Sovetsk, even if that were possible. Deliberately shooting down a British aircraft over the North Sea would be a very different matter than accidentally shooting down a Korean airliner over the Sea of Okhotsk. But he had to do something! No point in silent recriminations now, no point in even thinking that he'd had warned Kyrelin that their formal ratification of the plan should be done without witnesses. Kyrelin had been too much of a bureaucrat for that, and consequently Yefimovich knew everything. Somehow Yefimovich had to be stopped before he reached London.

London? But Yefimovich was defecting to the Americans. He would not talk till he was safely in Washington. Yefimovich would lay over in London till he got a flight to Washington tomorrow, which meant that the CIA would have cleared Yefimovich's passage with the British, which meant Yefimovich could be stopped in London. If Pomarev knew where he was being taken.

Finding out what was happening in London wasn't a problem. The British, with their class consciousness and resentments, made ideal recruits, and their service was riddled with ideological fellow travelers. Risking using an open line, Pomarev called a high-ranking civil servant he'd once run out of East Berlin and whose ideological divergences were matched by sexual divergences Pomarev had ensured were fully gratified and carefully photographed on the man's last visit to Moscow.

It was four-thirty in London, and the man was just leaving for home. But a reminder of what could happen to that home if Pomarev released certain photographs, encouraged him to linger in the office and check the arrangements made for housing the defecting Yefimovich. Twenty minutes later he called Pomarev back.

Yefimovich was expected to land in London in two hours. He was being escorted by McKinley, an American operating under diplomatic cover, and would be handed over at London's Heathrow Airport to Jeff Unsworth, an agent specially sent from the Office of Counter Intelligence in Washington. Yefimovich would spend the night in a hotel near the airport and be flown out to Washington at two o'clock the next afternoon. The civil servant gave Pomarev the name of the hotel and the room number. Which was all good news, except it gave Pomarev very little time to do anything.

Getting up from the desk, Pomarev went to the stereo and put on a record of his favorite, Vivaldi. Yefimovich would have to be stopped before he made contact with the agent sent from Washington. But how? Yefimovich would be arriving in two hours, and he, Pomarev, was seven hours from London. Two hours wasn't enough to move anyone from

Europe or Russia. Which meant he'd have to use someone already in England. But who? The embassy there was run as an information-gathering agency, and rough stuff was proscribed. In fact if they ever needed to do anything nasty in London, they used the Bulgarians. So what should he do? Hire someone? Again, no time. He had to use someone on the spot, someone who could move without thought or premeditation. What he needed was an instant action man. Action Man! The phrase struck a chord. He picked up the phone and dialed the embassy in London.

Arkady Zoyheddin had been one of the stars of Department V until that terrible incident three years ago when he'd been crippled in a shootout at the Friedrichstrasse. He was in London now, recovered sufficiently to be able to walk if not run, and in the year since his convalescence, to carry out routine security duties at the embassy in London.

Pomarev was grateful that he'd kept in touch with Zoyheddin after the Friedrichstrasse incident. While Zoyheddin had been convalescing, Pomarev had sent him caviar, lemongrass vodka, and other hard-to-get Russian delicacies. He'd visited Zoyheddin twice at the rehabilitation center when the gunman had been relearning how to walk. Now, as soon as Zoyheddin's tobacco-dredged voice came on the line, Pomarev asked, "How would you like to become Zonda again?"

32

February 2, 1988. London

Two hours later OCI agent Jeff Unsworth stood at Heathrow's Terminal 1, staring at the opaque glass doors through which McKinley and Yefimovich would emerge. He had flown from Washington the previous night with orders to collect the defecting Russian agent from NSA representative Charles McKinley, take him to a hotel, and keep him there till it was time to board their flight the next morning.

At that time of the evening the emerging passengers

were mainly businessmen, with a sprinkling of tanned holiday travelers returning from spring skiing or the Mediterranean sun. He looked up at the arrivals board. The flight from Moscow had landed half an hour ago. Casually, almost boredly, Unsworth looked around. The faces of the small crowd were unerringly fixed on the doors. Behind them the car rental desks were empty and a thin line of passengers trooped down an escalator to the subway. The bookstore was still open. Passengers moved hesitantly behind luggage trolleys. On the gallery above him two young Asians leaned over the rail, immersed in conversation and looking blankly at the concourse below. Satisfied, Unsworth looked back at the doors again. No one was checking him and no one was checking the arrivals area. Unsworth wished he didn't feel so lethargic.

The evening before in Washington Theo Goddard had barely given him time to collect a change of clothes before getting him on a flight to London that had arrived at breakfast time while his body clock had been ready for sleep. He'd nodded off over breakfast in the hotel, fought the tiredness for most of the morning, then slept till it was time to collect Yefimovich. Sleeping so long had not been such a good idea. Already the initial alertness of his waking was being replaced by lassitude. And he was beginning to feel ravenously, debilitatingly hungry.

He concentrated on the doors. The dry heat of the building was accentuated by the voluminous raincoat he wore. He'd been told it always rained in England, and the raincoat was a perfect camouflage for the gun he wore. The heat was soporific and made his eyes feel as if they had pebbles in them. He'd have been better off with just the blazer over his holster, and with the blazer, the gun would have been easier to get to. Not that he really anticipated using the gun.

Unsworth fought back a yawn and watched a trio of dark-suited businessmen emerge together and hurry toward the main exit doors. Behind them came McKinley walking beside a tall, gangling man wearing a fur astrakhan and carrying only a large briefcase. Yefimovich! Unsworth pushed his way through the crowd to the open space from which they would exit. Yefimovich was younger than he'd expected and was looking around the terminal with a mixture of excitement and apprehension. McKinley introduced them quickly and said, "He's all yours."

"Thanks."

"You owe us one," McKinley said, and strode away.

Unsworth wondered if he'd attempted to debrief Yefimovich. He smiled encouragingly at the defector. "Don't worry. You're safe now. You'll be safe with me. "You speak English?"

"A little."

Unsworth walked him toward the exit. "We'll talk English for the present. We're going to a hotel." Unsworth spoke loudly, slowly and clearly. "We will stay there tonight. Tomorrow afternoon we will fly to Washington."

Yefimovich looked about him nervously. "Why tomorrow afternoon? Why not now?"

"Because there are no flights till tomorrow afternoon." Again Unsworth smiled. "But don't worry." He patted Yefimovich on the shoulder. "I'll take good care of you."

Yefimovich accepted his encouragement without expression. "We must talk quickly. There is a lot I have to tell you."

Unsworth tried another encouraging smile. "Don't worry. We have plenty of time."

"Where is Goddard?"

"He's waiting for you in Washington. He will be the first person you'll see when we get there."

That seemed to relax Yefimovich somewhat. "What I have to say is very important," he said.

It always was, Unsworth thought, and motioning Yefimovich to wait, he pushed through the swinging doors and checked the sidewalk outside. Satisfied there was nothing suspicious, he beckoned Yefimovich and bundled him into a taxi. "We can talk in the hotel," he said.

The hotel was four minutes from the airport. On the way there Yefimovich asked if he could have an apartment in New York and a yellow Camaro. "Depends," Unsworth said warily, "on how important your information is."

"It's very important," Yefimovich said. "Very, very important. Top secret. First class."

Zonda waited, huddled, his fist closed round the butt of the SIG Sauer double-action automatic, his palm lightly covered with sweat. He wished Pomarev had given him more time to plan, more time to arrange his departure. But Pomarev had insisted that the job be carried out within the hour and that he leave England immediately afterward. As it was, he'd barely had time to set everything up. He wiped his hand on his jacket and thought Pomarev must have been in a devil of a hurry to have this job done. But whatever Pomarev's reasons, Zonda was grateful to him. He was back in the service and had status and prestige, which was a whole lot better than spending his life looking through embassy wastebaskets for defector's secrets.

Yefimovich kept looking around them in surprised wonder as Unsworth walked him through the reception area of the hotel to the bank of elevators beyond the lobby. "We'll go to our room and change," Unsworth said. "Then we'll have dinner."

Yefimovich pointed at his case. "I have no clothes. In there are only documents."

Unsworth reached for the briefcase.

Yefimovich gave it to him. "Don't worry." Yefimovich smiled. "Documents are fake. For my identity to get out of Russia."

"And you don't worry about clothes," Unsworth said, measuring the Russian with his eye. He would have Resources rush something around to the hotel.

They got into the elevator and rode up. Unsworth stepped out first. The corridor outside the elevator was empty, all soft carpet, flecked wallpaper, and an air of neutral anonymity. He beckoned Yefimovich out and walked with him to the room he'd picked at the end of the corridor, far away from the elevators, where they would not be disturbed by passing guests. The room, large enough for both of them, had a picture window overlooking the front of the hotel with its flag, car park, and view of the highway.

He stopped outside the room and looked back along the corridor. It was still empty. He eased Yefimovich to one side, fumbled for the key in his raincoat pocket, inserted it into the lock.

The key stuck. Then he felt it move between his fingers, felt a draft of air as the door was yanked open. A man stood there, a big, tall, bulky man with a gun in his hand. Unsworth glimpsed his face. High cheekbones, a crescent-shaped scar below his lower lip, an untidy, drooping moustache. The man's eyes were gray, level, and bleak.

Unsworth dropped the case, his hand brushing away the

folds of the raincoat and his fingers spreading, anticipating contact with the butt of his Detective Special. The man fired. Unsworth stared in disbelieving horror as the gun belched flame. He felt his body float backward. It couldn't be, he thought. It was impossible. His hands flailed and caught his billowing raincoat. The gun belched flame again. The lights above his head spun. He cannoned into the wall and felt the pain in his chest rise in a seething wave to meet the concussion from above.

The lights went out.

The gunman turned to Yefimovich. With his left hand he reached out and drew him into the room. Numbly Yefimovich felt himself being turned around to face the door. He saw the body of the American agent sprawled in the corridor, his coat spread out around him like an untidy shroud. He felt the cold circle of the barrel press into his neck just below the hairline. He closed his eyes. Hot dogs, hamburgers, yellow Camaro . . .

When it came, the sound of the shot was deafening.

33

February 4, 1988

In the offices Boris Pomarev had rented in Aurora Heights, Abe Makram sat beside Dick Schaffer, religiously noting every combination Schaffer entered into the VAX computer. Schaffer had once been Widdell's partner, with access to the highest level of Widdell's codes. In typical American fashion Widdell and Schaffer had fallen out over money, and Schaffer had left Widdell Associates to start his own consultancy. When Pomarev had put Red-One on go status, Makram had begun a search for Schaffer and found him barely able to afford the rental of his offices in Reston. A few friendly dinners, sympathy, and offers of financial help, and Schaffer's loyalty and expertise and professional skills had been bought. But not cheaply, Makram reflected. Schaffer had finally settled for seventy thousand dollars and fifty percent of the profits he expected from the exploitation of Widdell's tapes.

Makram looked at Schaffer's long fingers darting over the keyboard, tapping out combinations with practiced precision. Schaffer was a tall, lanky, fair-haired man, a limp-looking sort of fellow with pale blue eyes and a weak, sensual mouth. If they were ever found out, Makram thought, Schaffer would be the first to crack. He wondered if Pomarev had thought of that.

"Fuck!" Schaffer exclaimed as the terminal screen demanded INSERT SYSTEM CARD! He leaned back in his chair, stared thoughtfully at the screen, then studied the figures Makram had noted. He tapped the keyboard again. "We're getting close," he said.

Scrupulously Makram entered the new combination. Widdell's codes, Makram knew, consisted of an application program built into the machine which restricted access to various levels of operator. At the lowest level, where much of the work consisted of updating the data bases, the codes were merely a mater of record, accessed by the insertion of an employees "smart" card into a terminal. At higher levels access depended not only on use of the appropriate "smart" card, but the ability of the operator to respond to the computer with further codes. Schaffer was working on building a "smart" card for the highest level from the responses he remembered the computer required.

INSERT YOUR CARD the terminal demanded.

Schaffer tapped the keys excitedly, without checking Makram's figures. "C'mon, baby," he breathed. "C'mon you little bitch—give!"

34

Februrary 7, 1988

The repeated beeping of the phone set off a sympathetic jangling in the middle of Steve Widdell's chest. He snatched the phone off the bedside table and squinted at the digital clock. Two o'clock in the morning! He pressed the phone to his ear, feeling his heart pumping wildly against his ribs. Take it easy, the doctors had said, take it easy and sleep more. "Yes," he said into the phone. Beside him Sara still slept.

It was someone from the office on North Capitol Street. Widdell did not recognize the voice, but the message was very clear. Everything had suddenly gone crazy and they'd had a shutdown. The service team was on its way, and they thought Widdell would like to know.

Goddamn right I'd like to know, Widdell thought, rolling out from under the covers. He was sure the breakdown had to do with the previous week's failure to read and write. "I'm on my way," he said, got out of bed and dressed hurriedly. As he was leaving the room, he saw Sara's eyes glinting at him from above the bedclothes. "Small problem in the office," he said. "Be back soon."

Sara sighed. "Don't forget to take your pills."

"I won't. I'll take one now." Snatching the bottle from beside his bed, he swallowed two pills and hurried downstairs. He'd gone out so often at night he had no need to turn on any lights. Pausing briefly in the corridor beside the kitchen to put on his overcoat, he opened the door to the garage.

Immediately he sensed something was wrong. The door from the corridor was unlocked. And someone was seated in the passenger seat of his Buick Riviera!

Disbelieving still, his mouth going dry with fright, he reached for the light switch beside the door. Something cold and hard snapped into the side of his neck. A gun! A voice whispered harshly, "Keep very still."

Widdell's hand stiffened. Out of the corner of his eye he glimpsed a hooded figure standing between the door and the shelves of old computer tapes and files at the front of the garage. The silence was broken by the measured click of the gun being cocked.

Widdell couldn't believe it was happening to him. Not in his own home. Not in his own garage. "Who are you?" he asked. "What do you want?"

The voice whispered, "Get into the car, behind the wheel."

The man in the passenger seat reached across and opened the door.

Widdell remained still. "You don't understand," he said, speaking quickly and softly. "I have nothing of value, and you're welcome to what I have. But you must let me go. I have to get to my office. There's been an emergency."

"Get in the car," the voice whispered. As his eyes got used to the dark, Widdell saw the man wasn't hooded but had a nylon stocking pulled over his head. Widdell thought it made him look like a burn victim, with horribly distorted lips, flattened nose, and no eyebrows.

"You don't understand," Widdell repeated. "You can take what you like from the house. If you give me five minutes, my wife and I will leave. I promise we won't call the police. Only leave me the car. And let me get to my office."

"Get in the car," the man said again, jabbing Widdell in the throat with the gun barrel.

Only after he'd gotten into the car and backed out of the garage did Widdell speak again. "I must get to my office," he said. "There's been a computer breakdown. It's urgent. We have a lot of vital work being processed."

"Don't worry, we'll take care of that," the man in the back seat said, the man beside him sniggering. He, too, was wearing a stocking mask, which made his head look like that of a massive insect. He told Widdell to drive east.

"Where are we going?" Widdell asked.

"You'll know when we get there." He directed Widdell along a deserted New Hampshire Avenue and then northeast past the park. There was little traffic. At Hollywood Park they pulled off the freeway and headed west. They directed him to a lonely house by Northwest Branch Park, whose garage door the man in the front passenger seat opened with a radio device.

The door closed automatically behind them. The man in the rear got out, walked to an entrance door and opened it. The man in the passenger seat asked Widdell to extinguish the car's lights. "Where is this?" Widdell asked. "Why have you brought me here?"

The man in the passenger seat sneered. "You'll find out."

Inside the house it was cold and musty. The men did not turn on any lights till they had led Widdell into a room on the ground floor and shut the door.

The room had no windows. Its walls were padded with a rigid foamlike substance, the kind found packed inside cartons of electrical goods. In the middle of the room there was a metal chair bolted to the floor, with heavy leather straps fixed to its arms and front legs. Opposite it was a table and two straight-backed chairs. The men sat Widdell in the metal chair and stood over him while they peeled off their masks.

Both men were in their late twenties, with craggy, muscular faces and puckered skin over their cheekbones and at the corners of their eyes. They were lighter than him and stronger and fitter. The men blinked at the light as they put away their masks. Widdell noted that the one who'd pulled the gun on him had a crew cut, and the one who'd sat in the passenger seat had a tight head of dark curls.

It was the crew-cut one who seemed to be the leader, sinister and massive in his loose-fitting uniform jacket and baggy trousers. He'd kept his gun leveled at Widdell while pulling off the mask, and now he said, "All we want you to do is make one phone call. Then we'll take you home."

The second man picked up a phone from the table and carried it to Widdell.

The crew-cut man said, "We would like you to phone your vaults in Falls Point and have them deliver all your back-up tapes to the delivery truck that will be calling on them in the next fifteen minutes."

"My back-up tapes!" Widdell cried. "No, I won't do it! What do you want with my computer tapes?"

A hand and gun crashed into the side of his face, and light exploded blindingly. Widdell's cheek flamed and his body twisted against the arms of the chair, which pressed suffocatingly against his ribs. His heart beat uncomfortably.

"Use the phone," the man said.

Widdell found he had closed his eyes. He opened them and heaved upright. His cheek stung and felt raw. He raised his hand to it and saw the blood on the front of his shirt before he felt its wetness. He told himself to be calm, to be reasonable. "There is no point phoning the vaults," he said. "They will require written authority before they hand over any tapes."

"Written authority and telephone confirmation," the dark-haired man said. "They have the written authority."

Widdell felt his body sag. The raw sting in his cheek was replaced by a steady, burning pain. He pressed his palm to the cut. It ran from the cheekbone halfway down to the jaw.

Widdell wondered if the men would let him bleed to death, if he would be permanently scarred. "Who are you?" he asked again.

"Never mind that. Just make the call."

The men were Cas Hardinger's, Widdell thought. Three weeks ago Widdell had turned down Hardinger's offer for his data system, as he'd turned down everyone else's. His system was too powerful a device to allow just anyone to control it. He had a moral duty to nurture it, and when he could no longer run it, to deliver it into safe hands. He said, "I'm not making any calls."

The crew-cut man hefted the gun threateningly. "Don't make it hard on yourself."

Hardinger had been furious when his offer had been refused. But even Cas Hardinger couldn't possibly imagine he could steal a computer system this way and get away with it.

The crew-cut man slapped the gun in his palm. Widdell winced. He didn't want the man to hit him again. He thought the tapes were only back-ups and contained only demographic information, voting records and the results of surveys. The tapes could be read but couldn't be interlinked or used constructively without the codes. He asked, "If I make the call, will you let me go home?"

"We'll take you anywhere you want" the crew-cut man replied.

"There are a lot of tapes," Widdell said. "How big a truck do you have?"

"Big enough," the crew-cut man said.

Widdell took the phone. "Who shall I say is collecting the tapes?"

"The Frederick Corporation."

Widdell said, "The vaults will need a phone number to call back. That's standard procedure."

The dark-haired man sniggered. "Give them your home number."

"But—but—"

"Don't worry," the crew-cut man said. "We'll get the call here."

Widdell dialed and told Bob Deakin, the head of the vault's night security section, what he wanted. "I'll call you right back," Deakin said. Seconds later the phone in the room rang. The crew-cut man indicated that Widdell should answer it. It was Bob Deakin. "You sure you want the tapes shipped right away, Steve?"

"Yes," Widdell said, a plan taking shape in his mind. What was it the Japanese said about using a man's strength to defeat him?

Deakin said, "It'll mean a few hours delay till we back up a second set of duplicates."

Widdell looked at the crew-cut man. "I want the tapes right away." He slipped another pill into his mouth. Deakin would know something was wrong, that no one in his right mind would order tapes that weren't backed up to be sent anywhere.

"Yes," Deakin said.

Widdell's heart sank like a stone.

Deakin said, "I'll get them ready for loading right away."

Come on, Bob, wake up. Come on, Bob, realize something is wrong. Insist I collect the tapes myself! Widdell said, "Thanks, Bob, it will be good to have the Frederick Corporation run an independent check on the lab report." That should do it. He was sure Bob Deakin had never heard of the Frederick Corporation, that he'd never heard of a laboratory wanting to run a nonurgent tape check in the small hours of the morning.

In his offices at Falls Point Bob Deakin pressed the receiver more closely to his ear. Definitely and without any doubt the voice he was listening to was Widdell's. Definitely and without any doubt the number he had called on receiving Widdell's earlier telephoned instructions was Widdell's home number. He thought Steve Widdell not only headed Widdell Associates, it was his genius that had created the company and kept it together. It was Widdell's genius that had won two presidential elections. And genius had a unique way of working, Deakin reflected. Especially at three o'clock in the morning. "That's a great idea, Steve," he said. "The tapes will be ready by the time your guys get here."

Widdell put the phone down feeling weak and helpless. The crew-cut man was smiling at him. "You did that very well." He came and stood in front of Widdell, slapping the butt of the gun lightly against his palm. "Now tell us about the source codes."

He wouldn't tell them, Widdell decided. There was no

way he would let Hardinger or anyone else take his system by theft and violence. Thinking of what they had done and were doing made him angry. He said, "The source codes are very complex. To get them you'll have to let me go to the office."

"Take twenty seconds to think about it," the crew-cut man said. "We believe those codes are in your head."

"You're wrong," Widdell said, his anger increasing now. "And you can tell Cas Hardinger he'll never get away with this."

"Cas who?" the dark-haired man asked.

"Cas Hardinger. You work for Hardinger, don't you?"

The crew-cut man cuffed Widdell lightly across the ears. Widdell felt a surge of triumph as he saw the crew-cut man raise his gun then lower it and back away. Feeling confident, Widdell lifted himself out of his chair. "If you kill me, you'll never get any source codes," he said.

As his dark-haired cohort watched, the crew-cut man came at Widdell, a smile playing at the corners of his mouth. His left hand rasped out and caught Widdell in the face, snaked out again twice in flicking jabs that stung.

Widdell backed quickly away. The man was a trained fighter. Widdell swung a wild right hook, felt it smash through the man's guard and connect with his head. Great! He swung again. Not so clean this time. And again. The sheer weight of his punch broke through the man's guard and smashed into his body.

The man shook his head and approached again. Widdell found he was panting and sweating. He backed away and swung. Missed. Swung again. Sweat trickled off his forehead into his eyes. His eyes teared. He didn't see the punch that exploded on the side of his jaw. His body went suddenly limp and his arms fell uselessly by his sides. Another punch crashed into his solar plexus. The air smashed out of him. He opened his mouth, gasped, sucked, choked, couldn't breathe. It was as if the inside of his body was a vacuum. He choked. No air rushed into his open mouth. His heart began to stutter, its irregular beat filling his ears. Through a faint gray mist he saw the man's face frozen in surprise. The mist grew thicker, filling the room with a dark cloud. He felt the cloud descending upon him. Everything was growing dark. He couldn't see the man. The darkness grew thicker. The throbbing in his ears grew louder, thumpity-thump, wilder, thump, thumpity-thump . . . thump . . . thump . . . thu—

35

February 8, 1988

In the richly paneled room in the pale cream four-story building near Georgetown University, Ambassador Whillan Courtney stared angrily along the table at the two men seated opposite. "You are disgusting!" he breathed. "Revolting! You have sullied the names and tradition of Bildeberg." The men had been provided by Colson, who, pleading important company business, had excused himself from that morning's meeting.

Tony Ulner, the crew-cut man, stared back defiantly at Courtney. "We didn't know he had a weak heart," he said. "We should have been told."

"You killed him!" Courtney gasped. "You are murderers!"

"If we are, so are all of you!" It was the dark-haired man, Mike Karowitz, who spoke. "And if we go to the chair, you'll come with us."

"There's no need to talk of anyone being executed," Cas Hardinger interposed. "We're all in this together." He looked defiantly at Courtney. "What's done is done. The question is, what we do about it now."

Senator Anderson said, "I suggest we allow these gentlemen to return to their normal business, and that we get busy with implementing Widdell's system."

Jonathan Bradley said, "Without the codes, the tapes are useless."

"Useless!" Anderson's face grew florid. "What the devil do you mean, 'useless'?"

"I mean that without the codes we cannot operate Widdell's system," Bradley said tersely. "I've explained about the codes before."

"Who else has the codes?" Hardinger asked.

"Lucas Amory and Dick Schaffer, Widdell's former partners."

"Find them," Hardinger snapped. "Get them. Make them decode the tapes."

Bradley shook his head slowly. "Amory isn't a well man. Some months ago I hinted at the possibility of his working with us and he refused. As for Schaffer, he's disappeared. He hasn't been in his office in Reston for weeks."

Anderson asked, "Isn't there someone presently working for Widdell who knew the codes?"

"No," Bradley said glumly.

Hardinger turned to Courtney. "Have Colson find Schaffer," he said, and turned back to Bradley. "Then you persuade him to decode the tapes for us."

"There's something else," Bradley said, worriedly. "The tapes we have are numbered four. I've checked, and numbers one and two are at Widdell's offices, but the tapes numbered three are missing."

"Missing," Anderson echoed.

"That's right. A complete set of tapes. I checked with the vaults, too, and it seems that someone else has got another set of tapes."

"Who?" Hardinger, Courtney, and Anderson asked together.

Bradley shrugged. "That's for Colson to find out."

The university cafeteria was as empty as it always was at eleven in the morning. Professor Loren Eastman threw her sports bag onto a chair, walked up to the counter, placed two English muffins and an apple on her tray, and poured herself a cup of coffee.

"How was your game today?" the cashier asked.

"A bit windy," Loren replied, "but great!" She'd spent the last hour playing tennis with the university coach. Her body felt nicely taut from the exercise and pleasantly warm from the shower. She looked at the figure on the cash register and gave the cashier a five dollar bill.

"You look really great from playing all that tennis," the cashier said, handing Loren her change. "You think if I started playing I'd end up looking like you?"

"Never know what you can do till you try, Mary." Loren laughed as she carried the tray to her table.

For five years Loren had been Mrs. Wallis Tredigar,

being in turn disciple, lover, secretary, wife, and mother. During that time she had borne his child, cooked his meals, washed his socks, and waited for him to come home from faculty meetings. For five years she had typed his manuscripts, corrected his proofs, filed his letters, listened for hours to his theories on history, computers, the beat generation, and modern jazz. For five years she'd attended endless faculty soirées, smiled at the right people, hosted the right dinner parties, and been the perfect Mrs. Head of History Department.

Then, two years ago, she'd discovered that her husband was having a passionate affair with a research fellow from Harvard. A divorce had followed, and when it finally came, Loren felt a great sense of release. In her five years of marriage, Loren concluded, she'd become housebound, overweight, and stupid. Her conversation had become indistinguishable from Marty's baby talk and revolved round Marty, nursery, kindergarten, other children, shopping, and birthday parties. She'd lost her looks, her sharpness, her vivacity, her intelligence. She'd become a boring nonperson. And that was going to change.

The settlement had left her with custody of Marty, a three-bedroom house near Serena Gundy Park, a year-old Volkswagen Rabbit, and maintenance of three hundred dollars a month. She had converted her part-time lecturing assignment at the university into a full-time one, had gone on a diet and had begun to exercise. She had looked for a dress she liked that was two sizes too small for her and determined to scale down to fit it.

The dress now fit. She could run ten kilometers in forty minutes, was now a professor of Computer Studies, and had never felt healthier or happier. So who needs you, Wallis Tredigar? she thought.

She reminded herself that if she was going to finish the *Globe* & *Mail* before her lecture, she had to do it now and put all thought of Wallis out of her head. Ottawa was still concerned with import duties on American corn, and the finance minister was wrestling with the problems of a balanced budget. The Russian foreign minister was saying that a more progressive American government could make the difference between world peace and a nuclear holocaust, and the French were once again supplying fighters to the Israelis and ground-to-air missiles to the Syrians. And in America the President's pollster had been killed in a car crash. . . .

Poor Steve. She stared incredulously at the photograph of an impossibly young Steve Widdell. Had he ever been that slim? The picture must have been taken ten years ago, she decided, about the time she'd begun working with him on his Political Data System. She'd refused his offer of staying with the system and exploiting it commercially, because her first love had been research. Despite Steve's pleas, she had returned to university teaching, where she'd met and married Wallis and sacrificed her career for marriage. She wondered what would have happened if she'd stayed with Steve. Would she, too, have become rich and famous and the friend of presidents?

It was hard to believe. She continued reading the news report. Steve had suffered a massive heart attack while driving, and crashed his car into the bottom of a gully near the Triadelphia Reservoir. The doctors believed he'd been dead before his car came to a stop against a tree.

Tears abruptly filled her eyes as she remembered how he'd set up his computers to play the theme music from *Casablanca*. Poor Steve, rich and famous and brilliant and dead!

36

February 11, 1988

Zonda's knee hurt. Walking across uneven ground made his foot hit the ground at varying angles, which after a while sent shooting pains along the side of his knee all the way up his thigh. During his convalescence he'd worked in the gymnasium till his muscles burned, and he still regularly carried out all the exercises prescribed by the KGB physiotherapist, but he would never walk normally again. The best he could hope for was to be able to maneuver himself from one place to the other without too much discomfort. But not for long distances. Or over uneven ground.

He reached the clump of trees and stopped, sweating though the temperature this murky February day was only a few degrees above freezing. He leaned against a tree and waited for his breathing and his pulse to return to normal. You couldn't function efficiently under strain, and he had plenty of time. The subject would not reappear for another half hour, after he'd finished his lunch. Zonda closed his eyes and concentrated on breathing in and out slowly. Characteristically, he did not wonder if the subject's last meal was a good one.

The subject was a sixty-five-year-old farmer who for the past two mornings had, together with an assistant, ploughed the field behind the house. Zonda did not know why the farmer had been made a target, and, typically, did not care. All he knew was that he had a job to do and that after lunch the farmer would return to the field and work for an hour alone.

Zonda opened the rigid-sided leather attaché case he'd brought from the car and took out the heavy metal tube clipped to the inside of the lid. He placed the tube on his lap, unscrewed the bulbous rear end, took the bottle of compressed air from the case and slipped it into the rear of the tube. Placing the rear of the tube carefully in the case, he donned a pair of gloves before taking a steel dart from the case and inserting it into the front of the tube. When he felt the dart seated firmly, he screwed everything back together, locked it tight with the special screwdriver, then took the firing mechanism from the case and screwed it into the bottom of the tube. He raised the contraption to his shoulder and sighted down the tube, centering the V of the sights on a stone about twenty yards away. The weapon felt heavy but nicely balanced. He'd only used it in practice before, and knew it was accurate up to thirty yards. He looked at the patch of unploughed earth near him and hoped the farmer would bring the tractor close enough.

Then he saw the exhaust of the tractor moving above the hedgerows, the man perched behind it seeming disembodied till the tractor turned into the opening halfway between Zonda and the farmhouse. Zonda watched the machine lurch across the uneven ground and stop at the end of the row of furrows.

The farmer was a small, wiry-looking man who wore a

dirty wool lumber jacket with red and black checks and the collar turned up against the cold. Zonda raised the gun to his shoulder and squinted along the barrel. Sixty yards, fifty. The angle was too wide. He decided to wait, weapon held to his face, and stood as motionless as the tree he was using as cover until the tractor completed its first pass and turned back again. Two more furrows and the farmer would be close enough not to miss.

The farmer turned and came toward him, a tiny figure crouched like a performing monkey behind the high, wide oval of the engine covers. A puff of blue smoke belched out of the exhaust. The engine note rose angrily. The blue smoke turned to black as the tractor swerved, throwing up clumps of mud while its engine shrilled.

What's the matter, fool? Zonda fumed. Can't you control that machine? Can't you drive a tractor? The tractor bucked. The farmer bounced in his seat. For a moment Zonda thought the farmer was going to be thrown off, that the driverless tractor would come straight at his hiding place, forcing him to limp into the open. His finger tightened on the trigger.

With a frantic roaring of the engine and much sawing at the wheel, the farmer got the tractor straightened. He slowed and came toward Zonda, looking back at the eccentric furrow he had created. Still looking back, he steered erratically, moving the tractor closer to the clump of trees.

Zonda wanted to shout stop! The farmer had passed the edge of the furrows and was heading directly for him, the beat of the engine growing louder every second. He looked through the gunsight at the spindly front tires, caked with earth and trundling remorselessly toward him. No, he told himself. He had only one shot.

The farmer was so close he couldn't miss. Zonda targeted the gunsight on the farmer's face. As the tractor jerked, he glimpsed the farmer's eyes, wide open and horrified, a split second before he caught the side of the farmer's neck in the middle of the V and fired.

The explosion of air against his shoulder flung Zonda sideways. He cannoned into the tree, staggered onto his wounded leg and fell to the ground. The noise of the tractor engine remained static. Zonda twisted around and looked.

At the last moment the farmer had turned the tractor away from Zonda's hiding place, and it was now chugging driverless across the width of the field. Ignoring the pain, Zonda forced himself to his hands and knees, crawled on all fours to the nearest tree and pulled himself upright. The farmer was lying in a multicolored heap on the dark earth. The tractor moved inexorably toward a boundary fence.

Hurriedly Zonda turned the farmer onto his back. There was a graze like a shaving cut by the jugular, and the dart itself had become embedded in the checked collar of the farmer's lumber jacket. Taking great care not to touch its tip, Zonda pulled out the dart and put it carefully away in his pocket. He pulled back the farmer's sleeve and bared the wrist, then gently inserted the needle of a syringe into a narrow blue vein and pressed the plunger. The syringe made a slight sucking noise as it discharged, and he withdrew it quickly, dabbing at the blood that flowed after it with his handkerchief.

Without bothering to look around, he limped back to the clump of trees, where he put the syringe and the dart back into the attaché case, and carrying both case and weapon, hurried to the boundary fence.

He had just reached it when he heard the tractor plunge into the ditch at the side of the field. The sound made him break into an agitated dog trot, which he kept up till he reached the car parked in the woods off the road. Tossing both weapon and attaché case into the trunk, Zonda climbed quickly into the car, not noticing in his hurry that his near-side rear tire had been penetrated by a metal spike and was almost completely flat.

37

February 12, 1988

Theo Goddard was still puzzling about the reason for the president's summons when he was ushered into the sitting room near the Oval Office. President Donnelly sat alone, waiting to meet him. The president rose from the print-covered rocker. "Thank you for coming," he began graciously, shaking hands and waving Goddard to a brown leather sofa beside the rocker. The room was cozy and intimate, its walls crowded with photographs and portraits of former presidents. On a table by the fireplace stood a picture of the first lady and photographs of the president's grandchildren.

The president's dark hair, still thick, was shot through with silver, and close up his face was more lined than was noticeable on television. Goddard had not met with him for nearly eight months, and the strain of the latest crisis in Central America had aged him. The once-champion athlete's body was still robust, however, if a trifle more solid and wedgelike, but the smile that had taken a popular football star to Hollywood and the White House was still gloriously pristine, together with the actor's charm. In his well-known, husky, honeyed voice, the president asked, "Did you know Steve Widdell?"

Goddard shook his head. He knew Widdell had been the president's pollster, but he'd never met him.

"Steve was my pollster in 1980 and my campaign director in 1984," the president said. "While driving to his office early one morning last week, Steve had a heart attack, crashed his car and died." The president pressed his lips together in an expression of controlled sadness. Then he threw back his head and gave Goddard a brave half smile. "At least that's what the medical experts and the police would have us believe."

"And you don't believe that?"

"No, Mr. Goddard, I don't. I don't believe Steve Widdell died of a heart attack, and I don't believe he died accidentally. Which is why I have invited you here." The president's gaze locked on Goddard. "I believe Steve Widdell was murdered."

Goddard looked embarrassedly at the floor. He said, "If you have evidence to support that belief, Mr. President, you should place that evidence before the FBI."

The president's face hardened momentarily, then he leaned back in his chair and smiled. "Before I do that, let me tell you a story. I want you, if you can, to take yourself back eleven years, to the primaries of 1976. Do you remember 1976, Mr. Goddard?"

Goddard nodded. In 1976, after a strong initial showing

in the primaries, the president's campaign had faltered and died.

"No one believed I would come back," the president said. "No one thought I would be heard of nationally again."

That was true. Even eleven years ago the president had been older than the majority of other candidates, and the sophisticated East Coast opinion makers had felt that whatever support he'd had would disappear with his massive defeats in the later primaries and his failure to secure the party nomination.

"They were wrong," the president said. "I came back, and I came back big." His eyes clouded. "And that was because of one man—" The President's voice broke. "Steve Widdell!"

The president lapsed into silence. Goddard decided he would not fall into the trap of breaking it. Finally Donnelly said, "I fought the '76 campaign the way most other people did, with a campaign manager, the best staff I could afford, and a political platform that combined my views with those of the party and what my campaign staff and I believed to be the views of the majority of the American people."

The president flashed Goddard a boyish grin. Careful, Goddard told himself. That grin had charmed a lot of senators and State Department officials into doing things they'd determined not to do. The president said, "We were horribly wrong, and we bombed out. In my view, rightly so. The problem in 1976 was that no one knew what the majority of the American people wanted. And by knowing, I do not mean guessing, or estimating, or gut feelings. I mean really knowing!"

Again the president lapsed into silence. When he spoke, his voice was strained. "After my defeat, I came close to quitting politics altogether. As you know, I spent the next two years as a private citizen and did not hold any political office. It was during that time that I met Steve Widdell and heard his theories on polling and the evaluation of the electorate. He showed me some early work he'd done, and I had him demonstrate his system to me during the '78 Senate elections." The president smiled. "There was no doubt Steve's system worked. No only was he able to forecast results accurately, he was able to predict how various modifications of a candidate's views affected his standing in the elections.

"Steve became my pollster for 1980," the president continued. "He used his surveys to show me how I had failed in 1976—how my image in the East was that of an aging, gun toting, irresponsible freak, far too senile to be in charge of the nuclear button. And more important than showing me what had gone wrong in 1976, Steve showed me how to win in 1980.

"Because we got our message to the people, because we turned ourselves into what the people wanted, we won in 1980 and again in '84." The president leaned forward, his face serious and sad. "And now Steve Widdell is dead. And I gather from his widow that his system is inoperative and that the essence of it might have been stolen."

"And you want the OCI to—" Goddard started to say.

"Before I get to that," Donnelly interrupted, "let me tell you something about Steve Widdell's system. It was very complex and needed computers to run it. It was also very precise, very detailed, and very, very accurate."

Placing his elbows on his knees, the president leaned forward and again studied his visitor. "The point I am making is that Steve Widdell's political data system was damn near infallible, and that anybody using that system could win any election he damn well pleased." The president sat back in the sofa, allowing that information to sink in.

Goddard asked, "Mr. President, are you suggesting that Steve Widdell was murdered because of this system?"

"I believe that to be a very real possibility. Someone wanted to stop Widdell from using his system to benefit a rival candidate, or else killed Widdell in order to get his system and become president of the United States!"

Goddard wondered if there was some truth in what the president was saying or if he were simply grandstanding. Then he remembered that the presidential campaign had already begun. "That is a very serious accusation," he said. "It impugns the reputations of many very prominent men."

"I'm aware of that," the president said. "The first primary begins in two days. In less than four weeks most of the no hopers will have dropped out and the race will be between the chosen few. One of those men will be the person who has stolen Widdell's system, and he must be stopped before he becomes too well known, before he becomes identified in the public mind as a serious candidate. Can you imagine the furor there will be if a president-elect were accused of theft and murder?"

"I could," Goddard replied. "But first of all, the accusations you make should have a little more evidence to support them."

"Let me tell you about that little more evidence," Donnelly said. "Widdell's system was very valuable. In order to prevent unauthorized use of it, it was protected by certain computer codes. I won't pretend to know how those codes worked, but I understand that anyone attempting to use the system without using the appropriate codes would only receive garbage.

"The codes that made the system operate were known to Steve and two other people—Lucas Amory, who helped found Widdell Associates with Steve, and Dick Schaffer, who replaced Amory when he retired." The president looked balefully at his visitor. "Yesterday Lucas Amory was found dead on his farm in Vermont. And Dick Schaffer has not been seen at his office in Reston for over two weeks!"

"Sweet Jes—" Just in time Goddard remembered the president did not like swearing. He whistled softly and said, "Mr. President, I believe this is a matter for the FBI." There were eleven men running for the presidency. Investigating all of them could tie up his staff forever. Also, it was illegal for the Agency to be involved in domestic affairs.

The president nodded and said, "I agree. That would be the right thing to do under normal circumstances." Abruptly the president's voice hardened. "But these are not normal circumstances, Mr. Goddard. In the first place, it is not politic that the public should know the extent to which a pollster can influence the outcome of a presidential election. In the second place, I do not want this investigation hampered by allegations that I am investigating my successors.

"As you are aware, there is a lobby calling for a repeal of the constitutional amendment of 1951, which prevents a president standing for election more than twice. For that reason alone, my involvement in an investigation of my successors will arouse suspicion and controversy—suspicion and controversy that will prevent anyone finding out who killed Steve Widdell and Lucas Amory."

"There need be no controversy if you distanced yourself from the investigation," Goddard said.

"What I do, and what the media thinks I do, are not always the same thing," the president replied. "Any controversy over Steve Widdell's death would be embarrassing for the administration, the party, and to me. I think we owe it to the nation to settle this matter discreetly."

"Which is why you have come to me?" Goddard asked despondently.

"Yes," answered the president.

Goddard realized that the most likely consequence of his undertaking an investigation such as the president suggested would be political suicide. He asked, "Is that an order, Mr. President?"

The president smiled. "Of course not, my dear fellow. I am merely suggesting that suspicious enough circumstances exist to warrant you mounting a very low-key, very discreet inquiry into the all the circumstances surrounding these deaths. If you discover they were murdered, we can conclude it was because someone wanted Widdell's system for himself, and that someone is going to use that system to become the next president. You must find that man and stop him. *A murderer should not become president of the United States!*"

38

February 14, 1988

A Rand McNally Atlas spread on the seat beside him, Theo Goddard drove the old Cadillac southwest along Route 81, his car radio tuned to the BBC World Service.

In the Mid-Atlantic accent so commonly affected by foreign journalists dealing with American affairs, Alistair Collins of the BBC said, "With the Puerto Rico primary this Sunday, the 1988 presidential campaign officially turns into a race. Today the preliminaries of the past three years are over and all the presidential contenders face the first of the real contests. The strange thing about Puerto Rico, however, is that few of the candidates and none of the leading contenders will be there today.

"Each of the leading candidates has a good reason for this," Alistair Collins continued. "According to Vice President Bradley Taylor"—Taylor's clipped tones replaced Collins's mellifluous voice—"In not going to Puerto Rico, I have placed the interest of my country before my own. Campaigning must take second place to affairs of state which, I am afraid, require my presence here in Washington."

What a boring, pompous ass Goddard thought. Bradley Taylor had support now because of his long record of party loyalty. Goddard doubted if he could sustain that support through a long and arduous campaign. Good thing, too, he thought. Taylor would be a very dull and dangerous president.

Senator Kevin Anderson's broad accents filled the car. "Puerto Rico is a very important primary, Mr. Collins. Let's make no mistake about that. The reason why I am not going is that I have no reason to. We have an excellent party organization in Puerto Rico, and here in America we vote for a party and a program, not for a personality."

Sheer political balderdash, Goddard thought. The real reason Kevin Anderson was not going to Puerto Rico was that it was too far away to matter.

Alistair Collins asked, "Governor Milovan, why won't you be in Puerto Rico today?"

"Because I don't have the money." Governor Milovan's accent, cruelly amplified by the microphone, made him sound as if he'd just cleared Ellis Island.

Alistair Collins said, "Senator Crane, you obviously have no problem with money. Will you be going to Puerto Rico on Sunday?"

"Quite candidly, Alistair, I will not. I believe we have too many primaries these days, and to put a hundred percent effort behind each one is counterproductive. I believe it to be the duty of a candidate to concentrate on those primaries which will best enable him to present his views to the largest number of people and thereby achieve his goal. This is no reflection on the people of Puerto Rico. The unfortunate fact is that how people vote in Puerto Rico today will not have the slightest effect on how people vote on the mainland over the next few months."

Very well said, sir, Theo Goddard thought. A shade too frank, but never mind. He liked Senator Crane and thought him young enough to learn from experience. He had no doubt Crane would make an excellent president.

"So there you have the views of the leading candidates in the presidential primaries that start today," Alistair Collins concluded. "My own view is that no candidate is going to Puerto Rico because no candidate wants to be photographed against palm trees in February while voters back home are worrying about heating bills, struggling with cut power lines, icy roads, and the problems of getting to work through arctic winds and falling snow."

An announcer interrupted. "You have been listening to Alistair Collins's 'Report from America.' There now follows a review of the week's sports..."

Goddard turned down the sound and thought of his decision to personally investigate the deaths of Lucas Amory and Steve Widdell. Were Amory and Widdell murdered as the president believed? He'd decided to begin his inquiries with Amory because Widdell was too high profile, and the faintest whisper that someone was investigating his death could attract all kinds of unnecessary attention. Which was why he was driving in his own car to Nine Forks, the hamlet to which Amory had retired from public life to become a farmer.

Past Staunton he turned off Route 81. If the president was right, he had until the Illinois primary in the middle of March to find and stop the rogue candidate. Almost a month, he thought. Barely enough time.

Nine Forks was three streets of wood-framed houses, a tiny main street with fire and gas stations, grocery and hardware stores, a small bakery, two restaurants, and half a dozen souvenir shops. The police station had a single chimney sending up a trickle of pale smoke which seemed to hang almost vertically in the still air.

The police officer on duty was a young man impressed enough by someone down from Washington on a Sunday to telephone Captain Harmer right away. Goddard listened to the station radio softly burbling a religious service until Harmer arrived ten minutes later, skidding a squad car on the gravel before the station.

"Go on, Cyrus, get us some coffee," he cried, marching up to Goddard and extending his hand. "Nick Harmer." He took Goddard's ID and studied it carefully as Goddard studied him—a big, round-shouldered man who seemed shorter than he was because of his girth, his stubby forearms sticking out from under the uniform shirt. "Office of Counter Intelligence," he murmured, returning Goddard's ID. "What will they think of next?" He led Goddard into a small untidy office with a desk, a chair, and a wall full of box files. Cyrus brought in coffee.

Goddard placed his elbows on the desk and said, "We're interested in Lucas Amory's death."

"Far as we know, Lucas Amory died of natural causes," Harmer said. "He had stomach ulcers. Lots of them. One of them burst." Harmer scratched his ear abstractedly.

"You absolutely sure?" Goddard locked his eyes on Harmer's round blue pupils.

Harmer said "Yes," then colored under Goddard's stare, shrugged, and added, "Hell, I'm no expert. That's what his doctor said. That's what the autopsy said. Natural causes. Ruptured ulcer."

Goddard asked to see the autopsy report and Harmer rummaged in one of the box files and gave it to him. Lucas Amory had been found in a field near his house with the engine of his ditched tractor still running. He'd been lying on his side, curled into a ball, hands pressed against his stomach. The autopsy revealed that Amory had died from a perforated ulcer, that the stomach contents had been analyzed and found to contain no harmful or unusual substances. The body was unmarked except for a sting at the side of the neck and scrapes and contusions consistent with his falling off the seat of the tractor.

Goddard phoned the doctor. It wasn't exactly a sting, the doctor said, but it was the nearest he had come to accounting for it. The wound was more like a puncture.

Goddard asked if he'd probed the wound.

"There was no reason to do that," the doctor said.

Only if you were very suspicious, Goddard thought. A puncture indicated a needle; and a needle, poison. He remembered how some years ago in London an exiled Bulgarian journalist had been murdered with the poisoned tip of an umbrella. But how would someone stick a poisoned dart into the neck of a man driving a tractor? He decided to go out to the farm and examine the area where Amory had been killed.

"Were there any other marks or wounds on the body?" he asked the doctor.

"No," the doctor said. "Nothing at all."

39

An hour later, having spoken to Amory's widow, Goddard
drove to the farm. Mrs. Amory was a sturdy woman in her
sixties, with thick-lensed glasses and small, splayed, protruding front teeth. Her hair, more white than brown, was pulled
back in a bun.

She saw Goddard in a rustic lounge containing a dusty,
boarded floor, wooden furniture, curtains and covers of naturally spun fabric. The Amorys were very much into the
natural and primitive. The kitchen had a wood-burning stove,
and Goddard wondered how Mrs. Amory would manage now
that her husband wasn't there. He told her he was from the
Department of Justice and wanted to check a few details
concerning her husband's death.

"Go ahead," she said, sitting down on an austerely erect
sofa covered with a pattern of sunflowers.

Goddard sat opposite her on a straight-backed armchair.
He asked, "How long did your husband have ulcers?"

"As far as I know, all his life. He certainly had them when
I married him. It's why he stopped teaching, you know. He
was a professor of Cybernetics at MIT." She sighed and a
faraway look came into her eyes.

Goddard asked, "What did he do when he stopped
teaching?"

"He concentrated on research." Her eyes brightened.
"On pure research. That way he didn't have to compete for
promotion or recognition. He didn't need to fight to have his
papers published or read." She blinked back tears and forced
a smile.

Goddard asked, "And he did all this at MIT?"

"Yes. He stayed at MIT until he joined Steve Widdell."

"And when was that?"

"About ten years ago, I guess. As I recall, Steve wrote to
him at MIT with the outlines of a computerized analysis and

108

forecasting system. Luke liked the system and he liked Steve. According to Luke, he ironed out a few of the bugs and helped Steve refine the system. Then Steve very kindly invited Luke to join him at Widdell Associates—the company Steve formed to exploit the system. It was very kind of Steve, but I didn't like it."

"Why was that?"

"I didn't think Luke could take the strain. He was a habitual worrier, you know. He worried about everything— money, work, health, even his habit of worrying."

"Did your husband worry about his work at Widdell's?" Goddard asked.

"Not at first. At the beginning he was all caught up in he excitement of a new project and the miracle of seeing his theories put to practical use. Then—I think it was halfway through the first presidential election—it all started again. He and Steve were working all the hours God gave them, and Luke began worrying about money, about what would happen if they made a mistake, if the system had any unresolved bugs or glitches. . . ." She looked down at her large hands, firmly ensconced in her lap. "In the end we decided he should get out, and after the 1980 elections, he did."

"Did that cause any problems with Widdell?"

"Steve didn't want to let Luke go, but he realized that Luke was not a well man. Steve was very kind to us. He paid Luke more than market value for his shares, and kept him on a retainer for two years afterward."

"And you moved here?"

"Yes. And it was the best thing for Luke. For the first time in all the years I'd known him, he couldn't find anything to worry about. He enjoyed farming. He put on some weight and for once was able to eat more or less what he liked. He was a well man when he died, Mr. Goddard. Something caused that ulcer to burst. I don't know what, but something did."

Goddard asked if he could see the spot where Lucas Amory was found.

Mrs. Amory put on a woolen jacket and drove him to the field in a high-sided AMC Wrangler. "Was it you who found him?" Goddard asked.

"I found him over there," she replied, pointing to a spot

near a clump of trees two thirds of the way across the field. "He was lying on his side, and the tractor was in a ditch—" She stopped the Wrangler and pressed her forehead against the steering wheel, tears streaming down her face. Her body shook with sobs.

Goddard crouched beside her with embarrassment and stared across the field. There was nothing he could say, and he did not know Mrs. Amory well enough to put an arm around her and draw her sobbing body to him.

A while later she stopped and lifted her head away from the steering wheel. "Its engine was still running," she said brokenly, and pointed to a corner of the field.

"Was your husband alive when you got to him?" Goddard asked, anxious not to provoke another bout of tears.

She blew her nose, wiped her face, and turned toward him. "Luke was dead when I got to him." Her face twisted, and for a moment Goddard thought she was going to cry again. With an effort she regained control. "I turned him on his back and beat at his chest to pound his heart into life. I gave him mouth-to-mouth resuscitation. But it was useless. He was already dead."

She drove the jeep near where Luke Amory had fallen, and stopped, staring white-faced through the windshield. The engine thumped monotonously. Goddard said, "Think carefully, Mrs. Amory. Did you see any marks or anything unusual on or near your husband's body?"

She stared vacantly at the spot where she'd found her husband. Speaking softly and distantly, she said, "I remember there was a little prickle of blood on the inside of his elbow, as if he'd had an injection. It was a very tiny spot. When I saw it, I wondered why Luke had been taking injections, since Dr. Keegan had said he was getting on so well. Then, afterward, I forgot to ask Dr. Keegan about it. But I can tell you one thing. By the time we brought Luke back to the house, the mark was no longer there."

A dart followed by an injection, Goddard thought. The dart could have been tipped with a powerful soporific, the injection loaded with a swift-acting poison that caused ulcers to rupture and left no trace in the body afterward. Goddard climbed down from the Wrangler. It was fresh outside, with a brisk wind. The earth folded over his shoes. Mrs. Amory came and stood by him. "Luke died over there," she said, walking over the roughened earth to a faint patch of oil.

Goddard stared at the spot and leaving Mrs. Amory behind, walked quickly to a clump of trees. Beyond them he stopped. Around the foot of one tree the grass had been trampled, as if someone had stood there for a long time. And a small white strip where the bark had been torn and something heavy had rested against the tree.

Goddard turned and looked back at the field. He had an excellent view of Mrs. Amory and the Wrangler, and from where he stood, even a man on a tractor would be an easy target. But what weapon would he use if he wanted to fire a dart and not a bullet?

A blowgun of course! Not one of those simple aluminium pipe affairs, but one of the more sophisticated types the Agency weapons coordinator had shown him, with a stock, a trigger mechanism, and a canister of compressed air. Goddard looked back at the Wrangler and thought, with a blowgun like that, I could put a dart through one of the buttons on Mrs. Amory's coat. So how much easier to shoot someone driving a tractor? He looked down at the stripped bark. The weapons coordinator had told him the new blowguns were quite heavy and long. With his hand Goddard measured the height of the white strip in the bark. Yes, a blowgun like the coordinator had described could have rested there. He turned and returned to the Wrangler.

40

Back at the police station he asked Captain Harmer if any strangers had been seen near Lucas Amory's farm the day he'd died.

"Funny you should ask that," Harmer replied. "Cyrus and I were just talking about it this very minute." He told Goddard on the day Luke Amory had died, Cyrus had helped a stranger change a tire, not near Luke Amory's farm, but about six miles away. He leaned toward the outer office and shouted, "It was near Ed Gilmore's farm that you saw the guy, wasn't it, Cyrus?"

Cyrus shouted, "Yep!"

Harmer turned back to Goddard and continued in a normal voice, "From what Cyrus said, it seems as if this stranger had driven some way on the rim." Harmer shouted to Cyrus to come into the office.

Cyrus came in, scratching his head and looking shyly at Goddard. "Man had been driving a while on the rim," he confirmed. "You could see marks on the road for nearly a mile, and the tire was completely shredded off."

Goddard felt his palms tingle with excitement. "What did the man look like?"

"He was foreign and spoke English with a thick accent," Cyrus said, "like someone recently arrived in America."

"Did you get a good look at the man?"

"Sure did." Cyrus closed his eyes and pursed his lips with the effort of recalling what the man had looked like. "He was a big guy, and he had a thick moustache that drooped. His eyes were a kind of slate gray, and when they fixed themselves on you, they stayed fixed."

"And you'd never seen him before?"

Cyrus shook his head. "He was not from these parts."

"Anything else you recall about him?" Goddard asked.

"Sure," Cyrus said. "Guy had a crescent-shaped scar beneath his lower lip."

Fighting to keep his voice even and still the excitement jangling through him like a ball of loose wire, Goddard asked, "Did you happen to see the man walk? Did he have a limp."

"Yep," Cyrus announced. "He sure did."

Moustache, scar, gray eyes, and limp—it had to be Zonda, Goddard thought. But what could a pensioned-off Russian assassin be doing here in Virginia? He felt a sudden chill. Zonda had killed Yefimovich and Unsworth in London and was now here in America killing again. If Zonda had killed Lucas Amory—who'd worked with Steve Widdell and knew his codes—it probably meant the Russians were involved in the theft of Widdell's system. Which meant the president was more right than he'd imagined.

41

All that evening Goddard sat pondering what to do. Not only had Amory been murdered, but he'd been murdered by the Russians. Not only had a presidential candidate stolen Widdell's electoral system, but it was likely that the candidate was working with the Russians. If the thief was not found and stopped, the next president of the United States could be a candidate set up by the KGB!

A revolting, impossible idea! But it had more than a vestige of probability. And it could become reality, Goddard thought, unless he did something about it. He had to find some safe way of exposing the guilty without outraging the innocent, some way of stopping the rogue candidate and protecting the office he had so carefully created and whose demise would be a triumph for the opposition and the forces of evil.

So what was he to do?

The television newscaster was silently mouthing the results of the Puerto Rico primary. Goddard turned up the sound. As expected, Vice President Bradley Taylor had won comfortably, but Senator Kevin Anderson had lost. To everyone's surprise, Anderson had been soundly defeated by Governor Afram Milovan, who'd had little in the way of money and even less in the way of support from the local party machine.

So how had Milovan done it? Did Milovan have Widdell's system? Milovan was of Russian background. Had he not gone down to Puerto Rico because with Widdell's system he was certain of victory?

Governor Milovan appeared on the screen saying his victory was the consequence of the underprivileged staying together. He was followed by Senator Anderson saying the real battle for the party nomination would be fought on the mainland. Goddard turned off the television and wrenched his mind back to his immediate problem. Even if Milovan was the KGB candidate, how was he going to stop him? And what if Milovan's success was pure coincidence, or as Milovan had said, simply the result of underdog voters voting for an underdog?

Goddard knew he had to find some way of discovering what the Russians were doing. Which meant finding Zonda . . . and if Zonda was in America, Pomarev.

Even though it was after midnight, he called the office and had someone make a couple of checks. Ten minutes later the office called him back. Boris Pomarev had arrived in America the previous December, and though he was on the diplomatic list, had not been observed at any diplomatic gathering, or for that matter, at the Soviet embassy.

Zonda, he thought . . . Pomarev, and then by association, Drew Ellis. Pomarev had destroyed Ellis's Lotus network. Zonda had killed Ellis's lover, Emma Czazowicz. Ellis had been discharged from the service because of his obsession with revenging himself on Pomarev and Zonda. Now, Goddard thought the sensible thing to do was turn Ellis loose on Zonda and Pomarev.

Ellis had extensive experience of anti-Soviet operations. He was tough, imaginative, shrewd, and determined. He was used to working alone. And he had a motive!

But Ellis was no longer in service.

Which made the problem simply one of getting him back and keeping him under control afterward. Goddard stretched out his length on the sofa. It was an interesting problem.

42

February 15, 1988

Unlike other visiting dignitaries, Vladimir Simenon, deputy director of the KGB, wore a suit from the GUM department store and a black overcoat that was heavy and functional. His eyes, raking the office of the KGB's London resident, had all the emotion of gray metal disks. "Tell me again exactly what happened," he said, his voice roughened with black tobacco.

Podgornin, the London resident, suppressed his tiredness and launched into his story for the fifth time. Two weeks ago last Tuesday Boris Pomarev had telephoned using a Kremlin priority code and requested—no, demanded—the immediate release of Arkady Zoyheddin, the retired KGB gunman formerly code named Zonda. Pomarev had not stated why he required Zonda's services, and while they were speaking, Podgornin's secretary had brought in a thermo fax of Pomarev's Special Authority, signed on behalf of the Politburo by the chairman himself. Podgornin touched the document on the desk as if it were an exhibit in a courtroom. Simenon's gaze followed Podgornin's hand. He stared belligerently at the document.

The document required all Soviet citizens and authorities to aid, assist, and accept the legitimate directions of Lieutenant Colonel Boris Pomarev, deputy director of the Kremlin's Political Security Unit, as if they emanated from the Politburo itself! In all his forty years of service Simenon had only heard of such authority being given once before, and then it had been given to no less august a personage than Yuri Andropov. Once in forty years, he thought disgustedly, and the authority had been given to Pomarev! What was Pomarev doing that required such an authority? And if it was that important, why did no one else in the Politburo or the KGB know anything about it?

Podgornin was saying, "He did not tell me why he wanted Zonda. And he must have already spoken to Zonda, because no sooner had I finished talking to Pomarev than Zonda limped into my room, looking tense, which was unusual for him. He muttered something about needing more time to set up a proper job." Podgornin looked across at Simenon and shrugged helplessly. "Then he gave me written instructions for the transfer of his personal effects and left."

"To kill Yefimovich and Unsworth. Were those his orders, do you know?"

The resident said, "Pomarev briefed Zonda directly. All I had to do was sign his release papers, pay him, and arrange his air ticket."

"First class to Paris and then the next day's Concorde to

Washington," Simenon mused aloud. Not even the blowing up of Congress merited such extravagance. "Was that Pomarev's order too?"

Podgornin nodded. He was hoping the director would not count him among Pomarev's supporters.

Simenon summarized what he knew. Over the past few months Pomarev had become increasingly close to the chairman, and a few weeks ago Yefimovich had been the only witness to a lengthy meeting between them. Yefimovich had then defected, and Pomarev had pulled Zonda out of retirement to kill him and his American shepherd. Obviously it was Yefimovich's knowledge of what had happened at the meeting between Pomarev and the chairman that had led to his death. In fact, Yefimovich's death had been so necessary that Pomarev had pulled Zonda out of retirement to accomplish it. And then he had ordered Zonda to America. Pomarev also was in America, and Yefimovich had been trying to get to America. So it was reasonable to surmise that whatever Pomarev and the chairman were doing had to do with America. Simenon decided he would return to Russia and then go to America and find out.

43

February 18, 1988

Ellis ran. That morning he'd had an idea about how to write the sequel. In the *Therapy of Motion* he had advocated a purging of mind and body through action. Now he would go a step further. He would write how the purged body could be energized and revitalized through the mind. Once again his writing would be a reflection of his life, but this time he would have to create the experiences that shaped his work. He would have to leave Fairmont and the security he had achieved through isolation and go out into the world. It was necessary, he told himself, not only for the book, but for himself. Until he'd exposed himself to the outside world, he would never know if he was whole or not.

Please God, give me the strength, he prayed, as he came over the hill. He decided that afternoon when he went into Fairmont to collect his groceries and the new pair of running shoes he had ordered, he would stock up with paper and ribbons. When he'd finished the outline, he would have his agent invite some people to dinner. If that went well, he could call up friends from the old days.

He was over Emma's death—or as over as anyone could ever expect to be. He would always miss her, but the emptiness she'd left in his life was no longer total. He had his work, his exercise, his prayer and contemplation. And he believed that in the weeks he'd been unconscious in the hospital, when he'd been able to choose between life and death, God had helped him choose life for a purpose. And that simply by living he fulfilled that purpose.

That afternoon he drove cheerfully into town. His Thursday shopping days had become something of a routine, and increasingly he found himself looking forward to them, looking forward to being back again with people. More and more he was finding he needed to hear other voices, to watch the activity of a town, to make human contact, even if on the most superficial level.

He bought his groceries and writing supplies, had his hair cut and ate lunch. Surrounded by people, his solitary life seemed distant and a little crazy. But that life was real, he told himself, just as this life was real. Once he finished his book, he would think about the way his life needed altering. He thought he needed a home and a friend in addition to Patrick.

At the sporting goods store the salesman showed him a pair of new running shoes. "Kinetic wedge," he said. "Very interesting." He flexed the soles before putting them back in their box. "Let me know what you think of them." Ellis promised he would, bought a copy of *Runner's World*, and left.

He saw the Russian as he crossed the parking lot. There was no mistaking the ill-fitting, bright brown suit or the dented black Chrysler the man was leaning against. No mistaking the flat Slavic cheeks or the thick chestnut-brown hair cut to military shortness. As he grinned at Ellis, the Russian flashed a glittering bridge of stainless steel teeth.

Ellis felt a shiver of fear. He recognized the face but

could not put a name to it. He knew the man was Russian, and that for some reason the man frightened him, as if at their last meeting something terrible had happened. Irritation mingled with his fear. Time and lack of use had eroded his reactions and his ability for association. He turned away from the Russian and inserted the key into the lock of the car door.

A mistake! *Never* turn your back on a hostile agent. He felt his back prickle with the sensation of the expected bullet, and whirled. Another mistake! God, how rusty he was! He stared at the Russian.

The Russian's grin widened. The steel teeth glinted. Slowly the Russian extended his hand, the index and second finger pointed at Ellis like a make-believe gun. Still grinning, he raised and lowered his hand rapidly in the simulated motion of a man firing a pistol.

What the hell! Ellis put down his groceries and rushed past the line of cars at the Russian. The Russian slipped behind the wheel of his Chrysler. He'd kept the engine running, and without bothering to fasten his seat belt, gunned the car engine.

Ellis turned and shouted after him. The Chrysler zoomed out of the lot, racing furiously toward town. Ellis turned and ran back to his car, then decided that by the time he loaded his purchases, the Russian could have gone anywhere. In any case, he thought, if the Russian was looking for him, sooner or later they'd meet. He loaded the car, climbed in and drove off.

What was a Russian doing in Fairmont, threatening to kill him? Ellis had no doubt that that had been the significance of the shooting gesture. But why? The Russians knew he was retired. Could it have something to do with his past before Berlin? Unlikely. All his work against the Russians had been professional, and the Russians were professionals too. They did not use up their luck or talent on revenge. Perhaps the Russian's gesture had not been a threat but a greeting. Perhaps he had been in Fairmont on another mission and recognized him.

Trying to think of something that would make the Russians want to kill him, Ellis reviewed his past assignments and associations, but could come up with nothing.

When he'd been in the service he'd had a trained

memory for faces and names. So why couldn't he remember
this Russian? The failure irritated him. Why had he looked so
familiar? And how had the Russian recognized him? His
memory, he knew, had not been impaired by the shooting. Or
had it? If it hadn't, why was he struggling to remember
where and when he'd seen the Russian before?

Then he remembered. The shock was so startling, he
swerved the car along the road. The pain in his head was
suddenly intense and he felt unable to breathe. He'd both
seen the Russian and not seen him! The Russian had been at
the Friedrichstrasse the afternoon of the shooting, and Ellis
had not recollected seeing him before he was shot, but had
identified him afterward from photographs. His name was
Fyodor Petrovich, and he'd been the KGB's observer.

Ellis's sweaty palms slipped on the steering wheel. The
road undulated. He jammed a trembling foot on the brake
pedal. He couldn't see. He couldn't move. He couldn't
breathe. He felt as if he were dying.

Emma!

He found he was parked at an angle to the edge of the
road and sobbing uncontrollably. The pain inside his head
was still there, knifing his skull. The engine had stalled and
the red ignition light was glowing angrily. He restarted the
car and drove slowly home. Opening the car door, he nearly
fell out of the seat. He opened the rear doors, took out the
bags and packages, and walked slouch-footed to the front of
the house—

And stopped.

He would have sworn he'd locked the front door before
he'd left. Now it was ajar.

44

It was the Russian. The Russian had raced back to the
house, and now it was too late. Cursing himself for not being
more alert, Ellis looked around slowly. Wherever the Russian
was, he must have seen him. The front of the house was

surrounded by a circle of trees. To his left was a tree-covered hill, a perfect hiding place for a sniper, but no one there now, or else he would have fired by now. So the Russian had to be inside the house. But then why hadn't he done something?

Ellis studied the earth and noticed that the grass on the edge of the lawn was crushed and yellow from the passage of tires. But he wasn't expert enough to distinguish the tread of his own tires from a stranger's. There was no trail of footprints going up the steps, no movement in the foyer or living room. Deciding to go in, he held the sack of groceries in front of him and ran up to the front door. Eyes fixed on the windows for the first flash of fire, he was ready at any moment to hurl himself to the ground.

But there was no gun flash and no sound of a shot. No one called out to him. No one fired. He stopped abruptly before the open door and in the same movement hurled the sack of groceries through it. There was a clatter of cans and the sound of heavy objects skidding about the wooden floor. Good-bye eggs, avocado, and fruitcake, Ellis thought, and rushed into the foyer, flinging himself against the wall next to the living room.

Nothing moved. Slowly he edged along the wall. If someone was in there, perhaps he was experienced enough to have expected that the groceries would be thrown first, before Ellis sidled along the wall. There seemed nothing to do but go in, so Ellis pivoted on his heel and fell through the door, sliding on the small Bokhara carpet toward the fireplace. His hand reached for the poker and his shoulder hit the side of the hearth. He stopped and looked.

The room was empty. But someone had been there. Cushions from the sofa and armchairs were scattered on the floor. Gripping the poker, he rose cautiously to his feet. No one. But someone had searched his house! What for? He wasn't an agent any longer!

Rubbing his aching shoulder, he went into the dining room. Drawers had been pulled open, cutlery examined. In the kitchen all the cupboards were open, their contents spread along the counters and over the kitchen table. He picked up a long-bladed kitchen knife and went upstairs.

So far as he could tell, though everything had been disturbed, nothing had been taken or damaged. He couldn't understand it. A strange robbery, if it was a robbery. It seemed the kind of mess intelligence people made when they were looking for something. Or wanted you to think they were looking for something.

But what did they think he had? The Americans *knew* he had nothing. The Russians should have known that too. So why had the Russians sent a man after him? And why had they searched his home?

He was standing by his desk when he saw a glint out of the corner of his eye, a vivid, bright circular flash like the reflection of the sun off the metal body of a car. Only the glint was much sharper, and fiercer. Not like the body of a car, he thought, more likely a small mirror.

Instinctively he dropped to the floor and crawled out of a direct sight line to the window. He waited, staring up at the glass. Then he saw it again. A quick, blinding flash. And this time, behind the flash he saw movement. A man moving among the trees on the mound. Ellis crawled to the side of the window and watched. He could see the man clearly now. He had built himself a cover and was lying on top of it with the sun glinting off an attachment to his gun barrel.

Quietly Ellis crawled to the door. Turning the other cheek did not mean he had to stay there and be killed. He crept to the landing outside. Hidden from the observer, he put on a pair of running shoes, a pale gold-brown top, and olive-green pants. Ideally he would have liked a camouflage shirt and trousers, but he had to make do with what he had. Slipping the knife into his pocket, he went out the kitchen door, giving the man no more than a split second to realize he was out of the house, to take aim and fire, before he lost himself in the clump of trees beyond the house.

Ellis ran into the undergrowth, turned and waited. From where he crouched, he had a view of the mound, but he couldn't see the Russian. Ellis set his stop watch and waited. Nothing moved. After ten minutes he crawled through the undergrowth onto the trail. He ran quickly, circling behind the house, heading in an arc that would bring him behind the Russian.

He was a good three quarters of a mile away from the house now and had to hurry. If the Russian had been properly briefed on his habits, he would be expecting Ellis back within the hour. Ellis moved quickly, smashing through the undergrowth. The noise didn't matter unless the Russian had suspected what he was doing, in which case the noise mattered even less. A man with a knife was only a match for a man with a gun if he were close enough.

He had an advantage over the Russian, though. He knew every part of the territory, where the land rose and fell, where the trees thinned and the thickets were impenetrable. Keeping to the fence, he skirted the hill and then climbed slowly up it from the rear.

At the brow of the hill he lay flat. Slowly he raised his head and peered. The Russian was still there, gun resting by his right arm, his gaze fixed on the house, his hand covering the mirrored gunsight that had caused the reflection.

Ellis waited, recovering his breath, resting his muscles, mentally preparing himself for the final attack. When he felt he was ready, he dragged himself over the crest of the hill and slipped softly down through a patch of undergrowth on his right. The Russian turned on his side and stretched. Ellis froze. Almost casually the Russian looked behind him. For a moment his gaze lingered on the patch of undergrowth where Ellis hid, and Ellis was sure he'd been spotted. But after a moment the Russian turned his attention back to the house. Ellis breathed out softly and quickly slid down another three feet.

Ellis moved into a crouch and sprinted the last twenty feet. The Russian heard him and turned, twisting the gun and trying to point it at Ellis, who stopped, swerved, and jumped at the Russian from the side. One of his feet hit the rifle; the other pounded into the Russian's stomach. The Russian gasped and twisted. Ellis dropped on him, pressing his body down against the rifle, bringing the knife over the rifle and against the Russian's throat.

He moved the knife quickly, cutting, drawing blood, and held the bloodstained blade against the Russian's face. The Russian twisted his head away and his arms went limp. Ellis sat across the Russian's body, placed the knife against the Russian's jugular, and angled his body over it, so that if the man moved, the knife would plunge through the vein. "Who are you?" Ellis asked hoarsely. "And why are you trying to kill me?"

45

The Russian took his hands away from the gun and spread them on the ground. "Fyodor Petrovich," he ground out. "That is my name."

Ellis jabbed him under the jawbone with the point of the knife. "Why me? I'm retired."

"That is what I was told," Petrovich said. "But they insisted I carry out my orders. You are to be killed."

"Who's they? And why? The past is over."

"For you, maybe. But not for some."

"For who?"

The man took a breath. "Zonda and Pomarev."

Ellis jabbed him with the knife. "You lie! Zonda's crippled and Pomarev is in Moscow!"

Petrovich tried to twist his head away. "You're wrong, my friend. Zonda and Pomarev are both in America. And they are worried about you. There were rumors you were seriously ill after Zonda shot you, and that afterward you were dismissed from the Agency because you were unstable. It was said you were destabilized by your emotions and were planning to kill them."

So the Russians had a good source in the office, Ellis thought. He asked, "Even if that was true, why do Pomarev and Zonda want me killed now?"

"Because they fear you could reach them here in America."

Ellis felt a shiver run through him—whether of excitement, fear, or anticipation, he wasn't sure. "Where are they?"

"I don't know. They contact me through the embassy and set up meetings at various places. All our contacts are sterile. You see, they are doing something very big and important in America, something so big that if it succeeds, it could change your country's entire future." He grinned wryly and added, "And make Pomarev director of the KGB."

So to kill Pomarev now would rid the world of a greater

evil, Ellis thought, feeling the anger burn again. But it was not for him to judge, he told himself, not for him to take vengeance. He asked Petrovich, "What are they doing?"

"I don't know. All I do know is that they are spending millions of rubles, that Zonda has already killed three men, and that the operation is so important they cannot risk sending Zonda after you."

"And so they sent you?"

Petrovich swallowed and nodded. "They have a contact in your office. They know everything about you. About this place. About your book."

"Are you the only one they sent?"

"I'm the only one I know about."

"Who has Zonda killed?"

"A Kremlin clerk called Yefimovich who was defecting to you, and his shepherd, an agent called Unsworth."

"Jeff Unsworth!"

"That's right. And here in America he's killed a man named Lucas Amory."

Ellis felt the knife in his hand waver. He'd known Unsworth. In Rome, once, Unsworth had been his courier. He remembered a tall, fair-haired man with an amiable expression. Theo should know about this, Ellis thought. Something had to be done about Pomarev. He reached beneath Petrovich's jacket and took out a Colt .38. He cocked it and allowed Petrovich to sit up. "Why are you telling me all this?"

"In the hope you will let me go."

"And what will you tell Pomarev?"

"That I couldn't make the hit."

"How do I know you are telling me the truth?"

"You can easily check. You can call Unsworth's wife. You can call the Agency and check Amory."

Ellis got to his feet. According to the rules, he should kill Petrovich, but even in the old days he couldn't have done that. He told Petrovich, "Get up."

For a moment Petrovich hesitated. Then he did as he was ordered.

"Turn around and raise your hands," Ellis ordered. When Petrovich had done that, he said, "Okay, now walk slowly and carefully in front of me to the house."

46

As soon as he got Petrovich back to the house, Ellis tied him to a kitchen chair. He pulled Petrovich's jacket off his shoulders, wrenched his sleeves up above the elbow, and set a pan of water to boil.

"What are you doing?" Petrovich asked nervously.

Ellis ignored him as he stood before the kitchen window, staring into the forest. Petrovich had talked too easily, he thought, almost as if he'd been sent to deliver a message, not to kill. But why send a message that Zonda and Pomarev wanted him dead? Why send a message telling him of Pomarev's plans? If Pomarev was running an important mission in America, the last thing he would do was set up a confrontation. Which meant that Petrovich could possibly be telling the truth.

Or a large part of the truth. Ellis glanced out of the corner of his eye at Petrovich, staring glumly at the kitchen floor. Because of the powerful drugs available to intelligence agencies these days, controllers attempted to limit the damage a captured agent could cause by limiting the information given rather than training the agent to withstand torture. These days agents were told to talk if they were captured. Ellis wondered if that was how Petrovich had been trained. He heard the water boil, picked up the pan and advanced toward Petrovich. He would soon find out.

Petrovich frowned worriedly, his gaze fixed on the steaming pan. "What are you doing?" he asked thickly.

"I am going to pour this over your arms, drop by drop," Ellis said. Torture was something he'd never felt easy with, even before he'd met Patrick Morell. Now he told himself his life depended on making a show of it.

Petrovich stood up, pulling the chair with him.

Ellis pushed him back. "If you move around, you'll only make me spill it all over you." Ellis brought the pan to

Petrovich's face so he could feel its heat. Petrovich began to sweat.

"Tell me, who sent you and why?"

"I've already told you. Pomarev sent me. Pomarev is in America on an important mission. Pomarev thinks you might try to kill him. So he wanted me to kill you."

"Why you and not Zonda?"

"I don't know. Honestly I don't know." Petrovich pulled at his bonds. His forehead and neck gleamed with sweat.

Ellis sloshed the water around the pan.

Petrovich cringed. "I swear to you that's all I know."

"Who has Zonda killed?"

"I told you: Yefimovich, Unsworth, Amory."

"Who else?" He touched the side of the pan to Petrovich's face.

Petrovich hesitated. Then he said, "I think he killed Steve Widdell."

Ellis kept the pan pressed to Petrovich's cheek. He had no doubt now that Petrovich was telling the whole truth.

"I think what Zonda and Pomarev are doing has something to do with Widdell," Petrovich continued.

"What?"

"I don't know."

Never mind. Ellis knew that Steve Widdell was the president's pollster and had been killed in a car accident a few days before. "Why would Zonda and Pomarev want Widdell killed?"

"I don't know. I swear to you, I don't know."

Ellis thought he could easily check into how Steve Widdell died. He looked at Petrovich's clammy, terrified face. He's got nothing more to give, he thought, and replaced the pan of water on the stove. He pulled Petrovich's sleeve down and his jacket over his shoulders. Petrovich slumped in the chair.

Ellis left the room and called Patrick Morell. As a great favor, he asked the pastor to meet him near the railway crossing at Fern Creek. He went back to the kitchen and asked Petrovich where his car was. Then, keeping the Russian's hands still bound and the gun stuck in his back, Ellis walked Petrovich to the car and made him climb into the trunk.

He parked Petrovich's car in a field past the railway crossing, walked back and waited for Patrick. On the way back to Fairmont he had Patrick stop at a phone booth, and called Theo's office, and told them where Petrovich could be collected. Then he told Patrick everything that had happened and what he planned to do.

"This is none of your business," Patrick replied. "You're no longer operational. You should leave everything to the OCI."

"That way I could end up dead," Ellis said. He told Patrick the OCI's main concern was not protecting his life but in finding out what Pomarev and Zonda were doing in America. "And in order to do that, they'd have no hesitation in using me as bait."

"But Theo Goddard's your friend!"

"Theo Goddard did nothing to stop me being booted out of the OCI."

"You can't run this kind of investigation on your own," Patrick protested. "You're just one man—"

"If I can find out what happened to Steve Widdell," Ellis interrupted. "I'll be one man who will be too valuable to lose."

47

February 19, 1988

At ten o'clock the next morning Ellis stood with Captain Cord Rogers on the Brighton Dam police at the spot Steve Widdell's car had gone off the road. It was an innocuous enough place—an unfenced bend in a single-lane road running high over the lake and an escarpment studded with trees. The route Widdell's car had taken was still visible, twin tracks of flattened grass running from the edge of the road down the escarpment, white wounds of stripped bark on gouged trees, and thirty feet below, the glitter of broken glass and an oil stain by a wall of rock.

"It ran headfirst into the rocks," Captain Rogers said. "Lucky it didn't catch fire."

Ellis wondered what difference that would have made if
Widdell was already dead when he hit the rocks. He walked
with Rogers down the escarpment. Rogers was tall and lean,
and young for a police captain, and kept most of his face
obscured by a pair of outsize aviator's sunglasses. Ellis had
called on him earlier that morning using an old Department
of Justice ID, and Rogers had told him that his men had
found Widdell's car "off-road," as the police report had it, at
7:32 in the morning of February 7. His officers had scrambled
down the gully and found Widdell slumped behind the
wheel, with an arm that had been hanging outside the
window cruelly mangled and almost torn off. Widdell had
been the only occupant, and he was already dead.

"I tell you it weren't a pretty sight," Rogers said. "The
face was blue. The eyes were open. And the seat belt had
held him so the steering wheel got him right in the chest.
His ribs were sticking through his shirt."

Ellis tried to visualize it as they stood among the fragments of glass near the rocks. According to the authopsy,
Widdell had died sometime between three and six in the
morning and the cause of death was a massive coronary
occlusion.

"How can you be sure the heart attack occurred before
the accident and not after?" Ellis asked.

"Stands to reason, don't it?" Rogers replied, looking back
up at the road. "If he didn't have a heart attack, he wouldn't
have driven off the road."

They started to climb back up the escarpment. The
autopsy report had stated that while traces of a heart stimu-
lant had been found in the body, there were no traces of
alcohol or other drugs. Ellis recalled his phone conversation
with the doctor. He'd asked why it had been concluded that
Widdell had suffered his heart attack before the accident and
not after.

"Simple," the doctor had said. "The deceased suffered
other injuries, bruising and cuts to the face, a massive injury
to the chest and sternum, numerous injuries to the left arm
which had been thrust through the open window. If these
injuries had occured before death, there would have been
much more bleeding than there was. In fact, the interior of
the car was surprisingly free of blood, indicating that the
victim died before the accident."

Or died elsewhere, Ellis thought.

"Secondly," the doctor had said, "the victim's arm remained outside the vehicle throughout the duration of the accident, indicating that the victim was dead or unconscious for all or part of the time the accident was occurring."

"Makes sense," Ellis said, but he didn't think so. If Widdell had died before the accident, the injuries and the lack of blood in the car would be the same. He asked the doctor how he'd arrived at the time of death.

"From the condition of the body when I saw it."

"What time was that?"

"At ten-fifteen in the morning." The doctor had lectured Ellis about the rate at which dead flesh cooled, the time rigor mortis took to set in and disappear, the rate at which food was digested, and the contents of the dead man's stomach. "Even with all that data, we can only approximate the time of death," he said. "The body was in the open air, so it would have cooled faster, but precisely how much faster, I couldn't say. The faster rate of cooling would have brought on rigor mortis slightly earlier, but again, exactly how much earlier I couldn't say. The victim's dinner was only partly digested, which meant that he could have eaten within four hours of the accident, or had a slow digestive system, or eaten a lot of food more than four hours prior to the accident."

"So that's why you say death occurred some time between three and six in the morning?"

"That's right," the doctor said.

"Did death occur nearer to three or six?"

"Quite honestly, I couldn't answer that."

"Could death have occurred before three?"

"If it did, not much before then," the doctor replied.

They reached the top of the escarpment and got back into Rogers's car. Between three and six was a long time. It could cover Widdell being killed elsewhere, put into his car, and pushed into the gully. Ellis asked the captain if the car had been checked for fingerprints.

"Sure we took fingerprints," Rogers replied. "Car was covered with them. You know how many hundred fingerprints you get on a car, from pump attendants, garage mechanics, friends, relations, hitchhikers, and family? The only prints we identified positively were Widdell's. We gave the best copies of the others to the FBI. But so far nothing."

Which meant the FBI hadn't yet gotten around to checking the prints, or that none of the prints were those of a wanted or convicted criminal or a Russian assassin known as Zonda.

Ellis asked if Widdell was known to anyone in the area, or if he or his car had been seen in the area before.

"Not that I know of," Rogers replied. "The frst time *I* saw the deceased was on the slab in the morgue."

"I was wondering what he was doing here at that time of the morning," Ellis said. "I was wondering if he knew anyone, if he was visiting someone."

"If so, nobody's stood up and said so," Rogers said. "If you're asking me, I don't think he knew anyone around here." He looked challengingly at Ellis. "And I know everything that goes on here. If this man had a girlfriend or visited regularly, I would have known about it by now."

48

The battered metal sign dangling over the wide gateway said: JED ATKINS—CRASH REPAIRS. Ellis parked by the service area, stepped round a pile of used tires and walked up to the man under the hydraulic lift. Captain Rogers had said Jed Atkins had towed Widdell's car out of the gully and that the car was still at Atkins's garage.

"You Jed Atkins?"

The wiry figure beneath the ancient Chevrolet wiped a spanner on greasy overalls and squinted sideways at Ellis. "That's what it says on the sign up front." Atkins was a perky, slope-shouldered little man in his mid-forties. He wore a cap that said STP, a three-day growth of gray-flecked stubble, and blue grease-stained overalls.

"Cap'n Rogers sent me," Ellis said.

"Yeah, he said I should expect you."

"The captain tells me you're the one who towed the wreck back."

"Sure did. Right sonofabitch it was too. Nearly burned out both my clutches dragging that heap of metal up that gully."

"Pretty stupid thing to do," Ellis said, "drive off a gentle corner like that."

"It happens," Atkins said. "I hear the guy had a heart attack before he crashed."

Ellis appeared to consider that for a while. "There were no brake marks where he went off," he finally remarked.

"Maybe the guy didn't know he was going off."

"You reckon he had his heart attack and drove into the gully."

"That's what they say." Atkins reached up with his wrench and let out a viscous black stream of oil from the car above his head. "I thought there was something funny about the car, though. When I got there, the shift was already in neutral."

"How do you mean?"

"If the guy had driven down the hill, the shift would have been in drive."

"Could someone checking the car afterward have moved the shift into neutral? Or could Widdell have moved it in the accident?"

Atkins shrugged. "Who can tell?"

Ellis asked to look at the car, and Atkins led him to a crumpled heap of blue metal behind the lubrication area. The steering wheel was mashed into the roof, the hood almost pushed through the windshield. "Hit those rocks head on," Atkins said. "Poor guy didn't have a chance."

Ellis walked around the car. There were clumps of grass stuck between the flattened tires, and the wheel rims and the impact had made the car sag in the middle. The rear bumper was smashed too. Ellis looked closely. The marks were fresh, and beneath the bumper he saw scratches of green paint, as if the car had recently been hit or, Ellis thought, pushed. He showed it to Atkins. "What d'you think caused this?"

Atkins shoved his cap to the back of his head while he studied it. "He either reversed into something, or someone drove into him, or some kind soul gave him a push start."

Or, Ellis thought, a push.

49

Sara Widdell was a trim woman in her late forties. Her dark swept-back hair was covered with wings of gray, and her eyes were dark and bright, and her cheeks hollowed. She looked attentively at Goddard's ID and listened carefully while Goddard told her the purpose of his visit.

"If what you're doing is checking up on the police, it's no good talking to me," she said. "Steve died in Brighton Dam. You should be talking to the police there."

"We're checking everything," Goddard said. Sara Widdell didn't look as if she believed him. "Could you tell me what happened the night your husband died?"

"It was a Saturday," she said, then, as if suddenly reminded of the fact, "Two week ago. Steve got home from the office around seven. We had dinner that evening with some friends and got back here about half past ten. I went straight to bed. Steven had some work to do, and he came up around eleven-thirty. At two he was woken by a call from the office. . . ." Her voice trailed off. "You know the rest."

Goddard decided to spare her the strain of going over it again. He asked, "Did you know Lucas Amory, Mrs. Widdell?"

"Yes. We knew both Luke and his wife Grace quite well. It seems strange, Luke dying so soon after Steve. He helped Steve set up PDS, you know. He was a lovely man, quiet, kind, always helpful. . . ."

"Did you know Dick Schaffer?"

Her expression hardened. "Yes. But I thought he was an opportunist. I thought Steve made a mistake by employing him. Dick Schaffer was too selfish, too ambitious, and too concerned with money. And in the end Steve agreed with me and had to get rid of him. Schaffer wanted money to be the only arbiter of who the company worked for. He wanted to open the company up to the highest bidder."

"And you and your husband didn't agree with that?"

"No, Mr. Goddard, we did not. Steve felt he had a God-given talent and an enormous power. He had a moral duty to see it was not abused, that it was used to help the majority of the people."

"I see. Do you know where Dick Schaffer is?"

"No." She shook her head. "We had no reason to keep in touch after he left. I haven't seen him since then."

Goddard said, "My office doesn't believe that your husband or Lucas Amory died naturally. In fact, we believe that both of them might have been murdered."

"Murdered!" Sara Widdell's hand flew to her mouth. "But why?"

"That's what I was hoping you would be able to tell me, Mrs. Widdell. What was the one thing common to your husband and Lucas Amory?"

"They founded Widdell Associates and worked there. They worked together on the president's 1980 campaign, but I guess you've already thought of that. They developed PDS."

"Your husband and Lucas Amory were partners, is that right?"

"Why, yes, of course. And after Luke retired, Dick Schaffer was a partner."

"Is there anything they would have known that no one else did—because they were partners."

"Well, I don't know. There's noth—Of course! The codes! Steve, Lucas, and Dick Schaffer were the only people who knew the codes that made the PDS system work!"

"The only people? Didn't you know the codes, Mrs. Widdell?"

Sara Widdell smiled sadly and shook her head. "No. I know nothing about computers."

"Are you sure no one apart from your husband, Lucas Amory, and Dick Schaffer knew of the codes?"

She shook her head slowly. "I don't think so."

"Didn't your husband keep a copy of the codes anywhere?"

Again Mrs. Widdell shook her head. "No," she said.

"So the only person alive now who knows those codes is Dick Schaffer?"

Mrs. Widdell pinched her brows together in a thoughtful frown. "I suppose so."

"And you don't know where Dick Schaffer is?"

"No."

Goddard asked, "Do you know if any attempt had been made to interfere with your husband's business. To steal his computer data, for instance?"

"According to what Pat Cleary told me, there was some interference with the computer tapes," she said. "Apparently, about a week before Steve died, a maintenance man came into the office and downloaded all the tapes. After Steve's death, when Cleary was collecting all the copies of the tapes, the maintenance company denied taking copies or sending the maintenance man." She paused and looked hopefully at Goddard. "Also, the night Steve died, a batch of tapes were collected from the vault in Falls Point. Bob Deakin, who was on duty that night, swears Steve authorized the collection and that he spoke with Steve at home around three o'clock. But I can't think how. You see, Steve left home shortly after two o'clock, an hour before Deakin says they spoke."

"Couldn't Steve have called him from elsewhere?"

"He could have. But before Deakin could release the tapes, he would have had to make a call to Steve either at home or at the office."

"And Deakin says he called Steve at home?"

"Yes." Sara Widdell nodded vehemently. "At about three o'clock."

Goddard made a mental note to talk with Deakin and Pat Cleary. He asked. "Did anyone ever attempt to buy your husband's system?"

Sara Widdell nodded with pleasure. "Oh, yes, many times. The last time was at the end of January, when he was offered twelve million dollars."

"Twelve million," Goddard repeated softly.

She went on. "Steve told me about it a few days afterward. Apparently, they'd had this magnificent dinner which he hadn't been able to finish because he turned the man down."

"Turned down nearly twelve million dollars?" Goddard said in surprise. "Do you happen to know who this man was?"

"I wish I did." Mrs. Widdell shook her head sadly. "Steve never told me."

"Twelve million dollars is a lot of money," Goddard said. "Had your husband received similiar or larger offers before?"

"Not larger offers," Sara Widdell said.

"So why did he turn down this offer?"

"Quite simply, Mr. Goddard, because Steve loved his work and running his own business. To Steve it was much more than a means of earning money. It was what he lived for. And no sum of money was big enough to separate him from his computers."

"When did your husband first install codes into his system?" Goddard asked.

"Oh, right at the beginning. I think afterward the codes became something of a joke, because Steve and Loren put them into the software, and so..." Sara Widdell stared at Goddard as if she'd seen a ghost. "They... couldn't be changed!"

"Mrs. Widdell, what's wrong? What's so significant about the codes not being changed?"

Without warning, she began to sob. "It's not the codes," she cried. "It's Loren. Steve and Loren."

"I see. Your husband's friend in Brighton Dam?"

"Don't be ridiculous, Mr. Goddard! My husband wasn't that kind of man! Loren," Sara Widdell said, recovering her composure, "is Loren Eastman. She worked with Steve right at the beginning, when he was developing PDS. It was Loren and Steve who programmed the codes into the software."

"So this Loren Eastman would know the codes?"

"Yes."

"And if your husband's system was stolen, she would be able to recognize it?"

"I—I think so."

"And where is Loren Eastman?"

"I—I don't know," Sara Widdell replied. "I know she left Steve to go into research and joined some university."

"Which university? UCLA, Harvard, Princeton—"

"It wasn't an American university," Mrs. Widdell said. "She went to Canada. To a university in Toronto."

And with a bit of luck she'd still be there, Goddard thought grimly.

50

Zonda edged the Buick Skylark slowly up the suburban street. A nice, quiet neighborhood, he thought; respectable. At three o'clock in the afternoon the houses appeared to be dozing, menfolk out at work, womenfolk working, shopping, collecting children from school, and doing whatever women did when their husbands were away. The main thing was that the street was quiet.

Zonda stopped by 4601, checked the name on the mailbox, and hesitated a moment before turning the car up the drive. Pomarev had assured him that the subject would be at work all day and wouldn't return home till after five.

Zonda stopped the car in front of the garage. What if the subject had been taken ill? Or had changed his mind? "Then we'll know," Pomarev had said, "and we'll tell you." Zonda remembered how Pomarev had looked when he'd said that, studying his face closely, as if it would show if Zonda had lost his nerve or not. Now Zonda stared at his face in the rearview mirror. The heavy moustache obscured all expression, and the eyes, pale gray and cold, were a little frightened. But not dead, he told himself, not dead.

Not dead, he repeated as he opened the car door and climbed out. The only way to find out what was behind a door was to open it. Rubbing his upper arm against the holstered .38 for comfort, he walked up to the door, trying to disguise his limp in case anyone was watching.

Berlin had been his mistake, Zonda thought. Pomarev couldn't have known that the girl would be met, that the agent who came to meet her would be her lover and would be armed. Zonda knew he should have anticipated that. Make your plans and then expect the unexpected. That's what he'd been taught. Yet the last thing Zonda had expected that day in the Friedrichstrasse was a man leaping at him across the station platform with a blazing gun.

It had been the first time he'd been shot, and afterward he'd had time to think. Which was why, he supposed, they had taken him off the active roster; not because of his leg—he didn't shoot with his leg—but because of his brain.

It was a common truth in the business that a killer who thinks about his job is only half effective. That's why it was better not to think, but to do one's job, to believe one was simply a public hangman and go home afterward. As he had done. Until Berlin.

He had never liked Pomarev or trusted him totally. Pomarev was a perfectly rounded man without any apparent hard edges, a meticulous man, hard driving and ambitious. In his early forties he was already a director of the Political Security Unity, and somehow too perfect and aloof. Pomarev's aloofness, Zonda thought, would make him the perfect killer.

He wasn't paid to think, Zonda told himself now, inserting the key Pomarev had given him into the lock. See what thinking had got him—a permanent limp and a job holding coats for diplomats. He opened the front door.

Just as Pomarev had said, there was an immediate angry humming from the coat closet to the right of the door. Zonda hurried to it. He had to work fast. In twenty seconds the alarm would go off. A pair of red and green lights glowed at him. He removed a screwdriver from his pocket and quickly unfastened the four screws that secured the front of the white box. Behind it was a maze of circuits and boards. Pomarev and Abe Makram had briefed him carefully about what he had to do and made him rehearse the routine on a dummy box numerous times. Fingers flying, Zonda disconnected the circuits. The alarm shrieked.

Zonda jumped and nearly dropped his tools. The scream of the siren above his head was deafening, drowning out the clanging of the bells. Outside and upstairs, he knew, lights were flashing on and off. He forced himself to concentrate on the circuits. All he needed to do was isolate three. Fingers slippery with sweat, he fitted the insulators Makram had made for him. The siren beat at his ears. His heart pounded. Sweat prickled down his back and across his forehead and temples.

The siren and the bells stopped, everything going so silent that Zonda thought he'd gone deaf. Using only two of the screws, he refastened the front of the box. Then, ears buzzing, he walked to the front door and looked.

Though it had seemed endless, the disturbance had only lasted seconds. There was no sign outside of racing police cars or inquiring neighbors. Across the road a curtain flickered. Zonda glimpsed a head being rapidly withdrawn before the curtain blanked his view. He sighed and limped down the hill toward the house.

51

As soon as he got back to his office, Goddard ordered a trace on Loren Eastman, then reread his notes on the debriefing of Petrovich. No doubt Petrovich had done exactly what he'd been told. He had frightened Ellis, had pretended to ambush Ellis and been captured by him. He had told Ellis about Zonda and Pomarev, had told Ellis about the deaths of Yefimovich, Unsworth, Amory, and Widdell. So why hadn't Ellis done something yet? Had Ellis seen through their stratagem? Had his delivery of Petrovich been a sign of rejection? Or was Ellis simply taking time to decide what to do next? Ellis had always been thoughtful, careful. Or was he doing something independent of the OCI? Goddard wondered if the psychiatrist had been right when he'd said Ellis could be triggered by a forcible recollection of the past. Goddard wondered what he should do now. Act or wait? Call Ellis? Mount surveillance on Ellis? He told himself there was no alternative but to wait. Contacting Ellis now or mounting surveillance woud give the game away. So he would wait. If Ellis didn't take the bait, Goddard decided, he couldn't be used anyway.

52

Later that evening Dick Schaffer drove home to Reston a happy man. And soon, he told himself, a rich one. His inner coat pocket sagged comfortably with the contract Abe Makram had given him together with a check for $50,000. Schaffer had spent the last two weeks working with Makram, decoding the tapes that Makram had somehow obtained from Steve Widdell. He felt no remorse, no sense of guilt or betrayal for what he had done. It was all Steve's fault. Steve had never listened to him, never cared about what he'd wanted.

Together, he and Steve could have made millions. But Steve had only been interested in computer systems and had suffered from a growing messianic complex. It is essential that we support the right candidate, not merely the richest! And the right candidate, according to Widdell, had been Jerry Pressler, a heavily committed right-wing Republican from North Carolina, with a lot of support in the Bible belt and not a lot of cash.

Who had Steve thought he was, deciding who would be the next president of the United States? Schaffer wondered. American democracy demanded that the best candidate should be president, and the best candidate was the one who was best able to buy the support his candidacy needed. He sighed. If only Steve had agreed to offer the system to the candidate who would pay the most for it.

Between now and November, Schaffer thought, he and Abe Makram would clean up, and afterward, when they were known as the men who had elected the president of the United States, there was no end to the opportunities that would come their way. Half a million dollars a year was not too much to dream about, and, Schaffer mused, a new Mercedes, instead of his rusting two-year-old heap.

He shook his head. After he'd left Widdell, it had hurt to realize that people wanted Widdell and not someone who'd worked with him, not even someone who'd been in partnership with Steve Widdell and knew how the Political Data System worked. After he'd left PDS, it had hurt to have his phone calls go unanswered, to find all the cozy consultancies he'd been offered crumble because he was no longer with Widdell. He'd felt bitter about the small office he'd had to rent in Reston afterward, and that he'd had to pretend to former colleagues and business contacts that he worked more intensively and creatively away from the bustle of Washington. No more, he thought, no more. Dick Schaffer was back on top again, where he belonged. And he would show everyone that he didn't need Steve Widdell.

Schaffer avoiding thinking of how Makram had obtained Widdell's system. That was none of his business, and in any case, he was certain that Steve's death had nothing to do with Makram. Steve had died two weeks after Makram had got the system. He wondered if he should have attended Steve's funeral, and decided he'd been right not to. Steve's widow Sara and everyone else at Widdell's knew he'd quarreled with Steve and been booted out of the company. Why be a hypocrite, he thought, when one could use that time to work and make money.

He decided that as soon as the shock of Widdell's death faded, he and Makram would offer Widdell's system around. There were enough people who knew of the magic of the system to want it, even with dubious provenance and under another name. Schaffer turned into his driveway. His house, programmed by computer, was ablaze with lights, the curtains drawn. He flicked a switch on his dashboard and drove into the garage.

When he'd begun the job, Makram had paid him $20,000. Together with the $50,000 he had in his pocket, it was enough to buy himself out of the trouble Steve Widdell had gotten him into. That was poetic justice, he thought. Who'd ever heard of a partner being fired like an office boy?

The garage door closed automatically behind him. Schaffer switched off the engine and then the car's lights, got out and reached for the wall switch. He sensed rather than heard the brief rustle of movement. A split second later a hand was flung across his throat and something cold and round and hard was pressed into the side of his neck.

Schaffer went still, petrified, as the hand wandered down the inside of his jacket and removed the contract and the check. "No—" he started to say, when something very hard crashed against his head, the force of the impact mingling briefly with a red flash of pain that turned slowly black.

53

February 20, 1988

That Saturday morning Goddard was again summoned to the White House, but this time he was met in the private sitting room beside the Oval Office by a tall, smooth-faced individual with a quiff of silvery gray hair, rimless glasses, finely manicured nails, and a charcoal-gray business suit. The man said his name was Sid Rayburn and that he was the president's attorney.

"You have no doubt heard of Rowglass, Harcourt, and Rayburn, Mr. Goddard," he said smoothly. "We are one of the oldest firms in Washington, and that makes us very old. Theodore Roosevelt was a friend of the first Mr. Rowglass." With a delicate flick at his razor-edged creases, Rayburn lowered himself into a chair and crossed his knees. The brightly polished toe of his right foot pointed unmovingly at a spot forty-five degrees away.

"President Donnelly has told me of his previous discussion with you," Rayburn continued, "and I asked you here to discuss the constitutional implications arising from that discussion."

"Of the president employing the OCI for domestic purposes?" Goddard asked.

"No, not quite." Rayburn managed a polite, braying laugh. "The constitutional implications of Steve Widdell's system becoming publicly known. I'm sure you appreciate,

Mr. Goddard, that the concept that a pollster can elect a president is one that radically alters the fundamentals of democracy. Were the public to learn how easily they could be manipulated, how little power they actually have, I am afraid we would see the collapse of all our major political institutions. And without those institutions, Mr. Goddard, we will not survive because we having nothing with which to replace them."

"What are you asking me to do?" Goddard inquired.

"I am, on behalf of President Donnelly, requesting you to exert a great deal of care in your investigation, Mr. Goddard. I am requesting that you remember the special emphasis we place on the constitutional and political implications of your discoveries. We cannot have the public alerted to the truth. We cannot have them know the real reason Steve Widdell was murdered."

"My investigations so far have been very low-key and discreet." Goddard did not bother to keep the irritation out of his voice.

"I'm sure they have." Rayburn's smile was bland as gelatin. "Except yesterday a Mr. Drew Ellis, who used to work for your office, was in Brighton Dam inquiring into how Steve Widdell died."

Goddard fought to suppress the mixture of triumph and protest that surged to his throat. Ellis was doing something. Ellis was hooked. Ellis was coming on board. He said, "I'm sure Drew Ellis will be most discreet."

"I'm sure he will. But as you know, these things have a way of building up momentum. I'm sure you and your officers take special care to be discreet, but the sad fact is that you cannot conduct any investigation without talking to people who are not intelligence officers and whom you do not control. There is nothing you can do to prevent those people talking among themselves and to outsiders, any more than you can prevent birds flying. And before you know it, you have a newspaper reporter or a television journalist publicly asking if there's an investigation into Steve Widdell's death, and if so, why."

Rayburn held out smooth palms toward Goddard and continued. "Once those questions start being asked, Mr. Goddard, it is too late. The juggernaut gathers momentum, and all that can be done is delay the inevitable." Rayburn paused to look suitably grave. "And so we request you, Mr. Goddard, to please be very careful." He brought his palms together and asked, "Is there any way you can obtain the same results without too detailed an investigation into the death of Steve Widdell?"

Goddard told Rayburn about Loren Eastman. "If we can locate her," he finished, "we could use her to find who has Widdell's system, and that way we can leave Widdell's death alone."

"Then find her, Mr. Goddard," Rayburn said urgently. "Use every resource you have."

54

Finding Loren Eastman proved a lot easier than Goddard expected. When he got back to the office, he discovered that she was a professor of Computer Studies at an affiliate college of Toronto University. In her work she had access to computer networks shared with NORAD and the Pentagon, so she was on file and subject to regular security checks, the last of which had been completed two months ago. In order to avoid raising any alarms, Goddard decided to wait until after the weekend before he collected her file. Meanwhile, he thought, there was no harm in making a few routine checks himself.

He'd just finished briefing Agent Peters in Toronto when the fourth phone on his desk rang. It was a friend in the FBI Missing Person Bureau whom he'd asked for help in tracing Dick Schaffer. "Thought you'd like to know, Dick Schaffer's dead," the contact said. "He was found shot in his garage last night. The Reston police think it was suicide."

Or murder, Goddard thought. Apart from Loren Eastman, Dick Schaffer had been the only other person alive who knew Widdell's codes. It was time, Goddard thought, to bring Ellis into the game.

55

Ellis jogged slowly up to Theo's Cadillac, parked at the curb in front of his house. Drowsily listening to the radio, Theo started and pulled his head away from the window at Ellis's sharp rap on the glass. He climbed out sheepishly, the precise tones of the BBC World Service following him as he drew himself erect and stretched. "I came to thank you for Petrovich," he said, "and to find out what protection you needed. I came as soon as I could."

On a Saturday, too, Ellis thought, as he led Theo through the house and into the kitchen. Theo looked older, grayer, and more tired than he'd been eighteen months ago. The job was finally wearing him down, Ellis thought. He put on water for coffee and changed into a dry warm-up suit.

Theo smiled archly. "More important than Petrovich, is what we're going to do about you." He looked carefully around the kitchen and peered into the living room. "It'll take an army to protect you here. Looks like we'll have to move you to Washington."

Ellis placed his palms flat against the kitchen wall, thrust his legs straight out behind him and stretched his calf muscles. "I won't leave here," he said, staring at the wall. "And I don't want protection."

"And I don't want you dead." Goddard moved to the single armless chair by the china cupboard and perched on it.

Ellis said, "You know as well as I do that protection doesn't always work. The best and safest way to save me from Zonda and Pomarev is to stop them before they stop me." He finished stretching and poured a cup of instant coffee for Theo.

Theo studied the coffee closely, as if his future lay in the cup. "I'll go along with that," he said. "I'll give you whatever help you need."

Ellis threw him a sharp glance. Goddard seemed to want

him to go after Pomarev and Zonda, though he'd been forced out of the Agency for just that desire. "Why?" Ellis asked.

Theo said, "I'd like you back, Drew." His face, suspended over the coffee cup, creased into an embarrassed smile. "Drew, I need you."

And where were you when I needed you? Ellis thought. He knew that deep down Theo was a bureaucrat, that all Theo lived for now was the service he had created. And Theo wasn't going to endanger that service by re-employing former agents without very good reason. "Why?" he asked for the second time.

Theo sipped his coffee. "Because of Petrovich. What did Petrovich tell you?"

"That Pomarev sent him to kill me. That Pomarev was running a very important operation in the U.S. and was frightened that I might kill him."

"He told us the same thing. And we believe it's true. Zonda's already killed three people."

"Zonda's not operational! Zonda's a cripple! The KGB doesn't use blown, combat-fatigued agents!"

Goddard put down his coffee cup and patted his pockets as if searching for a cigarette, then placed his hands on his knees and leaned forward, his tired eyes fixed unwaveringly on Ellis. "I know for a fact that Zonda killed Jeff Unsworth and Vladimir Yefimovich," he said earnestly. "I also know that Zonda killed Lucas Amory, who used to work in partnership with Steve Widdell."

So there was a connection between Zonda and Widdell, Ellis thought, struggling to keep his face blank. He was going to investigate Zonda and Pomarev in his own time, and he wasn't going to be suckered into investigating them by Theo.

Goddard said, "When Jeff Unsworth was killed, he was bringing Yefimovich to me . . . and Yefimovich was bringing the details of a KGB conspiracy that would radically alter the face of America. It is, I believe, the same conspiracy Pomarev is now running, the conspiracy which, if it succeeds, will make Pomarev the next head of the KGB."

Ellis suppressed his disgust at the thought. "What conspiracy?" he asked.

"I was hoping you'd help us find that out."

"Why me? I was discharged from the service, remember?"

"Maybe that was a mistake," Goddard conceded. He

looked speculatively at Ellis and added, "I could arrange to take you back if you wanted."

"Why should I want that?" Ellis asked. He gestured broadly at the kitchen. "There's nothing I need."

"You need your life," Goddard said harshly. "You know as well as I do that no form of protection can guarantee you safety from Zonda and Pomarev. As you said earlier, the only way to keep them from killing you is to get to them first."

Ellis carried a glass of water back to the kitchen table and sat down. "I'm not into killing anymore, Theo," he said softly. "I'm not looking for revenge."

"Who's talking revenge? I'm talking survival!" Goddard leaned forward. "Don't you see, Drew. If you do nothing, they'll kill you. You have to stop them!"

"Why are you so anxious to save my life by sending me after Pomarev and Zonda?"

"Because . . . firstly because I think it is the only sure way of saving yourself. Secondly, because I need you working for us. You'll be better able to go after Pomarev and Zonda if we work together than if you work alone."

Ellis gave Theo a thin smile and shook his head. "What's in it for you, Theo? Why aren't you going after Zonda and Pomarev?"

The lines of Theo's face deepened. His face sagged. "There's no way I can have the OCI stop Zonda and Pomarev, Drew. You've got to believe that. The OCI has been penetrated!"

"Penetrated! Who by? How do you know?"

Goddard closed his eyes as if suppressing a secret pain. "How do you think they were able to kill Unsworth and Yefimovich? How do you think they know you wanted to go after Pomarev and Zonda?"

Ellis felt the sweat break out along his forehead and the back of his neck. Theo was right. There was a mole in the OCI. "What are you doing about it?" he asked.

"Inquiring patiently and carefully, without very much success." Goddard tilted his chair against the wall. "You know how it is, Drew, you know how long these things can take. . . ."

Ellis knew looking for a mole could sometimes take forever. Then he thought: If what Theo said was true, there was no way the OCI could stop Pomarev and Zonda, which meant he would have to do it himself. "Are you leveling with me, Theo?" he asked.

Again Goddard's face held an expression of secret pain. "Do you think I would have killed Unsworth and Yefimovich to provide you with a reason?"

"No," Ellis said softly. There was no way Theo would have done that. Theo was wily, cantankerous, bloody-minded and stubborn, but he was always totally loyal to his agents. "So you want us to go after Pomarev and Zonda together?" he asked.

"Yes." Goddard looked directly at Ellis. "I want you to find out who they're working with and exactly what they are doing. I want you to scare the life out of them and panic them into revealing their operation and their accomplices."

"And if I refuse?"

Goddard reached out a hand and touched Ellis's shoulder. "You know the answer to that better than I do. If no one does anything, Zonda and Pomarev will surely kill you." Goddard took his hand away. "You probably know more about Zonda and Pomarev than anyone at Langley. You know how they think, how they react . . . I can arrange to take you back into the service."

"And that happens when I find them?"

"That depends," Goddard said, and moved his chair closer. "Everything I'm going to tell you now is classified. What do you know of Steve Widdell?"

Petrovich had suggested that Steve Widdell had been murdered and Ellis's inquiries at Brighton Dam had supported that theory. Now he wondered if Goddard knew of his inquiries. He said, "He was President Donnelly's pollster, wasn't he?"

"He was the man who put Jack Donnelly into the White House—twice." Goddard told Ellis about Steve Widdell's system. "Just imagine it, a system that could virtually guarantee anyone the presidency. . . ."

Did the Russians kill Widdell for that? Ellis wondered, and asked, "Are you saying Pomarev's plan is to run a KGB candidate for president?"

"That's what I suspect. And that's what I want you to stop."

"But that's a massive job! There are . . . God knows—ten, fifteen candidates."

"There's only one Pomarev and one Zonda," Goddard said. "Stop them and you stop everything." He got to his feet. "What do you say, why don't we both take a ride to Langley and look at some files?"

56

At Langley Theo arranged authorization codes, entry permits, and a parking allotment. He gave Ellis a freelance contract to read over, sign, and return. He assigned a corner of his private office to Ellis, and gave Ellis the Agency file on Steve Widdell and his own reports on the deaths of Yefimovich, Unsworth, and Amory. Ellis spent the afternoon reading.

Steve Widdell had been a late developer. He'd had an undistinguished scholastic record, and after he'd left Columbia, had worked with Harris and Gallup and then with a succession of smaller polling agencies. In 1969 he'd married Sara Lomas, the daughter of a banker, and used her father's money to set up his own market research business.

Widdell's overpowering interest, however, had been politics, and he'd immediately canvassed for work among congressmen and senators. When he'd conducted a brilliant campaign for a little-known senator in Minnesota, he struck paydirt. The senator went on to become chairman of the National Committee, and in gratitude introduced Widdell to the hierarchy of the party. From then on Widdell's political contacts grew, and though short of money, he began to devote more time to election campaigns.

The campaigns provided a basis for the extensive data base system Widdell had been working on and which he hoped would be the best and most accurate election guide ever created. Hindered at first by the limitations of computers, he'd only started to make progress around 1974, when faster and more flexible computers became more readily available. He completed the system around 1976, and in 1978 demonstrated it to Senator Donnelly, who had been badly defeated in the 1976 presidential primaries. In 1980 he successfully computed Donnelly's campaign for president, and he did it again in 1984. His company had grown prosper-

ous, and there was now an aura of infallibility about Widdell's
system.

Two weeks ago, driving to the office very early one
morning, Widdell had suffered a heart attack, crashed his car
and died. He had no children, and was survived by his
widow.

Ellis turned to Goddard's reports on the deaths of
Yefimovich, Unsworth, and Amory. The reports confirmed
much of what he'd already been told, and the descriptions
given by the British hotel clerk and the policeman in Nine
Forks tallied, and described Zonda right down to the limp.

Ellis wondered where and how he should begin his
search. It wasn't enough to seek and destroy Zonda and
Pomarev. It was necessary to force them into the open and
compel them to leave a trail that would reveal the entire
conspiracy.

A gigantic task, Ellis thought, especially since he had no
idea where to begin and an all-out search for the Russians
might make them panic and disappear. It made more sense to
try and anticipate what they would do next. A near to
impossible task. Ellis was thinking about that when Jim
Colson walked into the office. "Drew," he called out softly,
"good to see you, man. What are you doing here?"

Ellis pushed away his papers. "I'm back. Working for
Theo."

Colson's smile was replaced by a puzzled frown. "But—
but there hasn't been—"

"It's unofficial," Ellis said.

Colson's face momentarily clouded. Then his eyes twin-
kled. "That's good. That's real good. It's nice to have you
back, even though it's unofficial." He looked pointedly away
from Ellis's desk. "What's the crisis? Yefimovich, the
mole . . . Widdell?"

"Widdell," Ellis said. "It looks like as if he could have
been murdered. And Theo wants an outside look at the
problem."

"You're sure that's wise?" Colson asked. "I mean, wise
for you. If Widdell was murdered, it's something that should
be handled in-house. There's no reason to bring in outsiders,
and no reason for you to get involved." Colson stood away
from the desk. "Unless Theo's looking for deniability."

"There's more to it than that," Ellis said heatedly.

"I'm sure there is," Colson replied. "But be careful, Drew. Theo is a shrewd old bastard, and if there's any trouble over this, you're the one who's going to carry the can." He smiled gently and added, "The nut case who was obsessed with Zonda."

"Zonda's part of—" Ellis started to say, when Theo Goddard appeared, moving with the same stealth he had once used against the Nazis. "Hello, Jim, what brings you in here on a Saturday?"

"I wanted to have a word with you. I looked in here and saw Drew."

"Drew's going to be working for us for a while," Goddard said.

"Yes, he's told me." Putting a finger to his lips, Colson backed out of the room. "Mum's the word." He stopped at the door and looked at Goddard. "Give me a call when you're free. We need to agree on a position on the latest arms-sales inquiry before Monday."

"I'll do that," Goddard said, and waited for Colson to close the door before he turned back to Ellis. "I've just heard that Dick Schaffer, who used to work with Steve Widdell, was found dead in his garage yesterday."

"Dick Schaffer?"

"The third man who knew Widdell's codes," Goddard said solemnly. "It seems he committed suicide."

"But you don't think so?"

"I certainly don't."

"And you'd like me to look into it?"

"First thing tomorrow morning, I've arranged for you to see Detective Mahoney of the Reston police."

"You think Zonda might have killed Schaffer?"

"I think it's worth knowing how Schaffer died."

57

Whether it was because they worked harder or drank harder on Saturday nights, Ellis didn't know, but he'd always found cops more bilious on Sunday mornings than any other morning of the week. Detective Sergeant Pat Mahoney of the Reston police was no exception. He sat in a frosted-glass cubicle in a squad room that smelled of stale sweat, disinfectant, and coffee.

Mahoney slapped Ellis's ID on a desk that was as battered as his face and said, "Tell you something, boyo, I don't like fancy documents from Washington. And I don't like fancy boys from Washington busting in on my cases. What do you want to know about Schaffer's death?"

"How it happened."

"He shot himself." Mahoney looked up and glared at Ellis. "He came home one evening after work, drove into his garage, put a Colt Detective Special right up against his earhole, and pulled the trigger."

"Just like that?"

"Just like that."

"Why?"

"Schaffer was in debt up to his eyeballs, that's why." With great satisfaction Mahoney told him the coroner had returned a verdict of suicide.

"Did he leave a suicide note?" Ellis asked.

"No such note has been found." Mahoney sounded as if he were testifying under oath.

"Don't suicides usually leave notes? Don't they want the world to know why they've killed themselves?"

"Not always," Mahoney said. "And not in Schaffer's case."

"Whose gun did he use? His own?"

151

"Schaffer didn't own a gun. But that doesn't mean a thing. In this country anyone who wants a gun can usually get one."

True, Ellis thought, but was Schaffer the kind of man to point a gun at his head and shoot himself? According to what Goddard had told him, Schaffer was a computer expert, someone uninterested in physical things—a man who, if he were going to commit suicide, would be more likely to do it with sleeping pills than a gun. "Was anything taken from the house?"

"Absolutely nothing." Mahoney seemed to enjoy Ellis's discomfort.

"Any witnesses?"

"No." Mahoney smiled.

Ellis said, "I'd like to take a look at the place where he killed himself."

Mahoney stopped smiling. He summoned his assistant, Detective Constable Lawrence, and asked him to drive Ellis to Schaffer's house.

It was one in a row of houses set back from a comfortable suburban street. A short, graveled drive led from the road to the garage. Lawrence was a slim, dark-haired man in his late twenties. He parked the car and they went up the drive. "That's where he did it," Lawrence said, pointing to the garage. "Everything is computerized," the policeman explained. "The garage doors, the drapes, the lights in the house. I was on duty here after the shooting, and it was eerie to watch those lights going on and off and hear the radio and TV coming on."

Lawrence opened the garage. Schaffer's car, a two-year-old Plymouth sedan, stood among rows of neatly arranged tools, its body covered with a fine dusting of white powder. A stain that looked like rust was on the front passenger seat.

"That's where he did it," Lawrence said. "Bled all over the front seats."

Ellis looked from the dried bloodstains to the dusting of powder. "Anything show up on fingerprints?"

Lawrence threw him an amused glance. "Nothing except a very clear set of Schaffer's prints."

Just as one would expect. "What other prints were there?" Ellis asked.

"Hundreds. Nothing identifiable, though."

"Of course." What little hope he'd had, died.

"What's your interest in the case?" Lawrence asked.

"Schaffer once worked on a Pentagon contract. We're checking to see that he hadn't gone over to the other side."

The policeman smiled. "If he had, it's a bit late for you to do anything about it."

"True," Ellis agreed. "Very true." He asked Lawrence if he could take a look around the house.

"Don't suppose Schaffer will mind," Lawrence said, and led him out of the garage and up the drive to the front door. From the house on the opposite side of the street, Ellis saw a curtain flicker.

It was dusty and dark inside. "We had the computers turned off," Lawrence said. "The neighbors complained it was too ghostly, all those lights going on and off after everyone knew Schaffer was dead." He asked, "Anywhere special you want to look?"

"His office."

Lawrence led him to a room to the left of the foyer where a cluttered desk was flanked by three computer terminals, piles of manuals, and boxes of disks. Lawrence handed Ellis a box file. "If it's bills you're looking for, take your pick."

Ellis opened the file. It was stuffed, and a spike on the desk held another wedge of bills.

"The guy was in so much trouble, he was dead long before he shot himself," Lawrence said.

Ellis sat behind the desk, riffled through the bills. He added them up in his head. Schaffer had had about $11,000 of unpaid bills in his house and probably twice as much as that in his office. There was no doubt that he'd had big money troubles, Ellis thought. Which was perhaps the reason why he'd agreed to decode Widdell's tapes. But if he had decoded Widdell's tapes, he would have been well paid. And if he'd been paid enough, what reason did he have for killing himself?

Ellis stood up and walked to the window. In the house directly opposite, the curtain flickered again.

58

Loren Eastman nosed the Volkswagen by the chicken wire of the tennis court and watched little Marty hit a two-fisted backhand cross court. Larry, the coach, made an exaggerated lunge at it and allowed the ball to pass him. "Great shot!" he shouted, lowering his racket and leaning on the net. "We'll stop on that. Remember, keep your knees bent and your eyes on the ball." He picked up Marty's sweatshirt from beside the net and helped him into it.

Marty dressed quickly, said good-bye and ran lopsidedly to the car.

"Got a right-hand Jimmy Connors there," Larry called after him. "Keep him at it and we'll soon have a champion."

Loren stepped out of the car to greet the running figure. Marty was small and wiry like his father and had his father's tight curls and large eyes. But he had her mouth and her nature, Loren told herself as she gathered him to her.

Marty allowed himself to be kissed, wriggled his head away and said, "Mommy, Larry says he wants me to come to tennis camp with him. Bruce and Mike we'll be there too. I'd like to go."

"Let me think about it."

"Jeremy's going, too, Mom. I want to go."

Loren stared past the coach at the car on the opposite side of the court. She was certain it was the same car that had been parked outside the university when she'd left to collect Marty, the same car she'd seen in the nearly empty parking lot outside the movie house yesterday. She knelt down, hugged Marty, and looked at the car from over his shoulder. No doubt about it. It was the same car and the same driver, a thin-faced man wearing the same off-white panama hat.

"Get into the car."

154

She felt Marty's shock at the unaccustomed firmness in her voice. Without a word he climbed into the back. Loren started driving. As she pulled up at the four-way stop sign down the road, she looked in her mirror and saw the Dodge lurch out of the park and settle comfortably behind her.

She tried to tell herself it was a routine surveillance because of her access to computer networks linked to the American defense establishment. But she knew that wasn't right. Her last check had only been two months ago, and the intelligence agencies were especially careful about intrusions on privacy when dealing with foreign residents.

Loren moved away from the stop sign. The Dodge followed. She knew she hadn't been involved in anything remotely radical in the last two months. Hell, the last radical thing she'd done had been to divorce Wallis. She wondered if someone had discovered she'd once attended an end the Vietnam war rally in Washington. But she'd been only sixteen then, and her whole life since had been a model of conservative virtue. Or had there been a mistake?

She turned into her driveway, rolled the car into the garage, and waited with the garage door open. A minute later the Dodge drove slowly past.

59

The woman who opened the door to Ellis was small and spinsterly, with a shock of silver-gray curls and bright inquisitive eyes. "Young man," she said sternly, "I don't buy encyclopedias, subscribe to magazines, read religious tracts, or particularly want to help people through college." This young man, she thought, looked painfully thin.

"I'm not selling anything," Ellis said. "I'm looking for information." He flashed a card before her face. "Information concerning your former neighbor, Dick Schaffer."

Mrs. Harris looked over Ellis's shoulder to the Schaffer house. She suppressed a shudder. "What's your interest in Dick Schaffer?" she asked. "Are you some kind of reporter or—"

"I'm a lawyer with the Justice Department. We are inquiring into the circumstances of Dick Schaffer's death."

How exciting, Mrs. Harris thought. She said, "I think you'd better step inside. Would you like some coffee?" Her visitor looked too young to be a lawyer, but then, Mrs. Harris reflected, everyone was looking younger these days.

Ellis asked, "Do you have any decaffeinated?"

"Of course." Mrs. Harris led him along the corridor between the living room and the stairs to the kitchen. He stood politely while she put water, a filter, and a Brazilian medium roast into the percolator for herself and Sanka into a mug for him. "If poor Mr. Schaffer killed himself," she asked, "why are you still investigating?"

"That's normal procedure," Ellis said. He climbed up onto a stool by the dinette. "Do you remember the day it happened?"

"Of course, last Friday. There were police vehicles everywhere jamming up the street, and people from the newspapers and television. I couldn't get my car out of my garage for over an hour. And people kept ringing my door bell and asking—"

Ellis smiled sympathetically. "What do you usually do Fridays?"

The young man had such soft brown eyes, Mrs. Harris thought. They looked so . . . so vulnerable. She said, "On Fridays I usually give the house a good clean. That's what I did the Friday Mr. Schaffer died. That was the day Mr. Schaffer's burglar alarm went off."

"Burglar alarm, eh? What time was that?"

"In the afternoon. Around three. I remember I was in the front parlor. I pulled back the drapes and looked."

"And?"

"A few minutes—no it couldn't have been minutes, it must have been seconds—a short while later, anyway, a man came out of Mr. Schaffer's front door—"

"Running?"

"No, he didn't run at all. He just shut the door behind him and the alarm stopped."

"And this man wasn't Mr. Schaffer?"

"No, it wasn't. I'd seen Mr. Schaffer leaving for work at seven-thirty that morning when I went to the porch for my newspaper."

"What did this man do after the alarm stopped ringing?"

"He stood outside the house for a while, looking up and down the street. Then he came across and rang my door bell. He was terribly nice, and told me he'd seen me looking through the curtains and hoped the alarm hadn't disturbed me. He told me he was from the burglar-alarm company and was servicing the system. He said he would try to make as little noise as possible and told me not to be worried about anything, and that Mr. Schaffer had given him keys to enter the house."

"Have you told anyone else about this?" Ellis asked.

"No." Mrs. Harris sounded nervous. "Should I have?"

"Not even the police when they came around?"

"No," she said. "It was silly of me, but with all the excitement of Mr. Schaffer's death, it went clean out of my mind. Anyway, they only asked me if I'd seen Mr. Schaffer coming home, or going to his garage, things like that."

"Did you see Mr. Schaffer returning home the day he died?"

"No," she said.

"What did the man do after he'd spoken with you?"

"He went back to the house. I saw him let himself in. The alarm did not go off."

"Did it go off again that day?"

Mrs. Harris shook her head.

"Can you describe the man?"

"He was about your age, with brown hair cut short. He had a moustache, and a scar below his lower lip shaped like a bird's beak."

Ellis felt his breath catch. "How big was he?"

"Oh, bigger than you, a couple of inches taller, too, I'd say. I remember his eyes were gray and they never moved all the time he was speaking with me."

"Speaking with you," Ellis repeated, feeling he wanted to run, to scream. "Did he have an accent?"

"The man was foreign," Mrs. Harris said, "He spoke with a strong accent."

Ellis reached into his pocket and took out the photograph of Zonda Goddard had given him. "Did he look anything like that?"

Mrs. Harris took the photograph and looked at it. "Why, bless my soul. That is the very man."

60

That evening Ellis saw Goddard in the small Arlington apartment where he had lived since his wife's death eight years ago. As he followed Goddard into the living room, he remembered Margaret Goddard, a cheerful, buxom woman who had died of cancer. After her death Theo sold everything, keeping only the Cadillac Eldorado, the last car he and Margaret had bought, and which he'd once told Ellis Margaret had enjoyed so much that even near the end she'd wanted to be taken for drives.

Goddard was at the open roll-top desk, his reading glasses pushed to the top of his head. He gestured at the papers on the desk and said, "I've been reading your reports. I see you've lost none of your writing flair."

"It's gotten better since I've had to make a living from it." Ellis sat on one of the chairs and turned it to face Goddard.

"Your investigation's been first class," Goddard said. "There's very little doubt that Amory, Schaffer, and Widdell were all murdered and their deaths covered up enough to stop immediate investigations."

Ellis felt a little quiver of suspicion run through him. Theo was being unusually vague. He said, "There's no doubt Zonda was at Schaffer's the afternoon of Schaffer's death. I want an FBI alert on him. And I want a forensic report on Widdell's car."

Goddard sat hunched forward, elbow balanced on top of crossed knees. He said, "For the present I want you to put both those requests on hold. Zonda and Pomarev are our only leads to the conspiracy. If we scare them off and lose them, we may never find who else is involved or if the conspiracy worked without them." Goddard shook his head. "We've got too much to lose to risk scaring them." He stared thoughtfully at Ellis. "As for Steve Widdell, I want the investigation of Widdell's death left to the police."

158

"To the Brighton Dam police! That's crazy! Cord Rogers is already convinced that Widdell died in an accident!"

"Then leave him in his ignorance," Goddard said. "Our job is not to find who killed Steve Widdell, but who stole Widdell's system."

"The same people—"

"And in order to do that, we don't have to find Widdell's killer. In fact, finding Widdell's killer might well be to our detriment."

"How so? Widdell's killer will lead us to whoever has Widdell's system."

"It will also draw public attention to Widdell's system. Which would be even more dangerous than letting Widdell's killers go unpunished." Goddard twisted his body so that he could lean against the desk. "We're not going to cause waves by announcing that Widdell was killed for his Political Data System, which as I understand it enables whoever controls it to elect whomever he likes as president. What I want you to do is go after that system and get it back."

"Finding the system doesn't help me get rid of Pomarev and Zonda."

"It will," Goddard said confidently. "Getting that system and using it is Pomarev's mission. If we take that system away, Pomarev's bound to come after it, together with his accomplices. Get the system, you get Pomarev, Zonda, and everything."

"I wouldn't recognize that system if it fell on my foot," Ellis protested.

"Right. So you will work with someone who knows Widdell's system, someone who helped develop it."

"Work with? I know nothing about computers."

"You don't need to. Your function will be to give support, familiarize her with our techniques and resources, and give her protection from Zonda."

"Her?"

Goddard held out Loren Eastman's photograph. "Professor Loren Eastman of Toronto University. I want you to come to Toronto with me Thursday and help collect her."

"I'm not going to be a bodyguard!" Ellis protested. "You've got dozens of bodyguards in the office. Take two."

"But I want you," Goddard said. "The moment that system is tagged, someone's going to have to handle Zonda

and the others who will come after it. You've the best person
for the job."

"But—but—" Ellis felt alternating shivers and hot flushes
run through his body. "But—"

"Don't worry, Drew," Goddard said softly. "You won't
lose her. And someday you'll have to face the fact that you
didn't lose Emma."

61

Goddard asked Ellis to stay and watch the results of the
New Hampshire primary. "The winner could be the next
president of the United States," he said.

And the KGB candidate, Ellis thought. He sipped tea
and watched the screen while Goddard mused about the
illogical preponderance of New Hampshire. "The state's only
got a quarter of a million registered party voters," Goddard
said, "forty conference delegates and four electoral votes. As
a state it is small and prosperous, it has low unemployment,
no sales or state income tax, and a commuter population that
works in Boston. In other words, New Hampshire is totally
unrepresentative of the nation as a whole, yet it holds one of
the most important primaries."

"Why's that?" Ellis asked.

"Simply because of where it comes in the calendar. And
the politicans of New Hampshire know it. They use that
primary to drive some hard bargains." He stretched his legs out
toward the television. "Tell you an interesting fact. Since 1952
no one has become president without winning New Hampshire."

"Is that so!" Ellis turned his attention to the screen
where results were being announced with brief clips of the
candidates. Vice President Bradley Taylor was pictured shaking hands with supporters and smiling thinly.

Taylor's chief rival, Senator Frank Crane, was easy with
people, smiling readily, pumping hands, grinning warmly at
the camera. He was a good-looking man with a thatch of
unruly blond hair and a heart-warming grin.

Kevin Anderson was demanding the nation turn from selfishness to compassion, from amassing private wealth to sharing. He'd been trumpeting the same message for twenty years.

He looked sympathetically at Milovan, handicapped by his small stature and wisp of a moustache. Someone should tell him to shave off that moustache, Ellis thought.

The pictures suddenly faded and were replaced by shots of excited crowds and then the projected final result. Vice President Taylor had won and his party, Senator Kevin Anderson in his. Neither, however, had won comfortably.

"You think one of them's the KGB candidate?" Ellis asked.

"It's hard to believe," Goddard replied, "but one of them has to be." He paused and shook his head tiredly. "Damned if I could tell which one, though."

"We'll have to," Ellis said.

"Yes," Goddard said. "Before Illinois."

62

February 25, 1988

Ellis climbed out of the brown Dodge and followed Peters, the thin-faced man in the white panama hat who had met him at the Toronto airport. "She works out with her tennis coach two mornings a week." Peters spoke hoarsely over his shoulder as he led Ellis from the car lot past a vast hangarlike building. "Then she lectures at eleven, lunches in the cafeteria, does tutorials till three, and collects her boy from school."

They walked along a narrow cemented path between high wire fences. Ellis wished there had been some way other than involving Loren Eastman. He'd read the Agency files on her and did not want the responsibility of shepherding a mother and woman of thirty-three to death. But Theo had been adamant. Any other way would risk a seriously damaging public outcry over Widdell's death. This way, his way, was more discreet.

A game of doubles was in progress on an end court, and a vicious singles match on a middle court. On a single court in an adjacent row a pro was hitting balls to a young woman, calling to her to hit her ground strokes deep and with more topspin.

"That's her," Peters said. "Court eleven."

She was slimmer in tennis clothes than in the photograph Goddard had shown him. Nice figure, Ellis noted, nice mover, good legs. She had a good forehand and an erratic backhand, and because of her slimness, looked more like a student than a professor. Her forehand wavered as she caught sight of them, and she hit two successive balls into the back netting.

The coach called, "Keep your head down, Loren! Keep your eyes on the ball."

Ellis asked Peters why he wore the hat.

"Gives them something to recognize," Peters said. "Helps get them off balance." Peters gave him a twisted smile. "She's all yours."

Ellis didn't say anything. His breathing felt tight and there was a clamminess in his palms.

From beside him Peters asked, "You all right?"

"Sure. Let's go and wait for Theo."

63

Despite the hard workout, Loren still felt a cramping knot of tension as she walked into the cafeteria. The man with the panama hat was back again, and this time he'd brought a friend. By now he must know everything she did, from the time she woke up to the time she dropped Marty off at school.

"Good morning's tennis?" Mary the cashier, asked.

"Yes," Loren replied abstractedly. White Hat's companion had been young-looking and dark-haired, with very dark eyes. Why did they need two men to follow her? Was the second man a replacement? She caught Mary's frown, smiled mechanically and added, "It really feels like spring at last."

"That's good." Mary looked at Loren's tray with its English muffin, pot of tea, and newspaper. "That'll be one seventy-five." Loren gave her the money. "Oh," Mary said, "there was someone looking for you from the dean's office. They wanted you there right away."

"Before I've had my muffin?"

"They said it was important."

"Nothing's more important than my muffin." Loren carried the tray to a table. What could Dean Stockwell want that was so important six weeks before the end of term? she wondered as she ate. Her work was on schedule, her reports were all filed, her students well-disciplined, unpregnant, and not overly into drugs. She finished eating, and after taking a last swallow of tea, walked over to the administration building.

"He's expecting you, Professor Eastman," the dean's secretary said. "Go right in."

Harvey Stockwell was a ebullient, career-oriented man in his mid-fifties. Stocky and well set, he had the friendly aggression of a boxer pup, qualities he used unashamedly in his fund-raising. "Nice to see you, Loren," he caroled, coming forward to shake hands. "Did you have a good game this morning?" Behind Stockwell a lean, elderly man rose from the worn leather sofa opposite Stockwell's desk.

"Yes," she replied, studying the visitor.

He had a pale, care-worn face, and wore old-fashioned, thick-rimmed glasses. "This is Theo Goddard," Dean Stockwell said. "He works for the U.S. State Department and would like to talk to you."

"The State Department?" Loren repeated. "You wouldn't by any chance be responsible for the men who have been following me around?"

Goddard's expression was blank, but she had an impression of being studied very carefully from behind the thick glasses. "Yes, I'm afraid we have," he replied apologetically.

"You have a nerve!" Loren said angrily. "I was checked out and cleared two months ago. Why do you need to check me out again?"

"This has nothing to do with your security clearance or

your access to intergovernmental networks," Goddard said slowly. "It has to do with the death of Steve Widdell."

"Steve Wid—What's Widdell's death got to do with your watching me?"

"Everything." Goddard gave her a rueful smile. "You see, we need your help. We don't believe Steve Widdell died in a car accident, but was murdered by someone one wanted his Political Data System."

"Murdered!" Loren cried, horrified. This was crazy! People did not go running about Washington murdering important men like Widdell. She said, "I don't believe you, Mr. Goddard."

Goddard's face remained fixed in a rigid pose of blandness. "We also believe the person who murdered Widdell has his system and is using it now. And that is why we need your help, Mrs. . . ."

"Eastman. It's not unusual for divorced women to revert to their former names."

Goddard nodded acknowledgment. "We know you worked with Steve Widdell and helped him create certain codes, which we believe you can use to identify the system."

"Me!" Loren said, surprised. "I last worked with Steve ten years ago!"

"But the system hasn't changed. It's simply gotten bigger."

Loren nodded hesitantly. "That may well be true."

"And you are familiar with his system and his codes."

"Steve may have changed the codes. I mean, it's been ten years. . . ."

"I've been told such changes were impossible."

"Things have changed," Loren said. "What was impossible ten years ago is possible now."

"We need you to help us find that out too," Goddard said. "You are our only hope."

"Wouldn't it make more sense if you concentrated on finding Widdell's murderer?" Loren asked.

"Our problem is that we cannot mount a large-scale investigation into Steve Widdell's death. For one thing, it's not within our jurisdiction. For another, eleven presidential candidates are involved, and there isn't one of them who's going to like being investigated."

"But this is a question of murder, Mr. Goddard. If you believe Steve was murdered, surely you or someone in the government must find who killed him. As for politicians, you cannot allow yourself to be influenced by their likes and dislikes."

"Unfortunately, the likes and dislikes of politicians rule our lives," Goddard replied. "One of those politicians is going to be the most powerful man in the world."

"There is another aspect," Dean Stockwell said, interrupting. "How good was Steve Widdell's system, Loren?"

Loren looked at him in surprise. She said slowly, "Steve's system was pretty damn good. It's elected one president already—two times."

Goddard said, "That's why we must not leave it in the wrong hands. We need you to help us find it, Mrs. Eastman."

Loren shook her head. "I wish I could help, but my first loyalty is here, to the university. I have classes, seminars—I can't take myself away for an indefinite time."

"The period won't be indefinite," Goddard said. "Whoever has this system must be found and stopped before the Illinois primary. By then, within the next month—three weeks—the surviving candidates will have had so much public exposure that forcing them to withdraw could not be done without a devastating public scandal... which we're trying to avoid at all costs."

"I sympathize with your problem," Loren said, "but you'll have to find some other way of resolving it. It's not possible for me to make myself available to you for three weeks. I have work here at his university, examinations. . . ."

Stockwell said, "It is the American government that has asked us for help, Loren. America, our friend and neighbor. I believe university examinations must take second place to a problem of this magnitude."

Perhaps Stockwell got funds from the American government, Loren thought. "I have a seven-year-old son," she said desperately. "I cannot leave him."

"I'm sure Wallis would love to have the boy for a few weeks," Stockwell replied.

Loren shot him a glance of pure hatred. "I'd rather he didn't." She turned to Goddard. "Marty is at the age when he needs me. For him three weeks would feel like eternity."

"Children are more resilient than we imagine," Stockwell countered.

"I'd like you to think very carefully about helping us,"

Goddard said gently. "A lot, the future of America, could
depend on your cooperation."

"You flatter me," Loren said. "There are other computer
experts, people more up-to-date than I am."

"You're the only one who knows Widdell's system,"
Goddard replied.

"Speaking for the university," Stockwell boomed, facing
Loren, "we think you should accept. We must show solidarity
in a crisis such as the one Mr. Goddard cites. The university
will keep you on full pay for the entire period, and I believe
that in addition, Mr. Goddard has a sizable gratuity in
mind."

Thanks, but no thanks, Loren thought. She wanted to
stay in Toronto, stay with her work, her home, and her son.
"I'd like to help in any way that doesn't require my spending
so much time away from home," she told Goddard.

"I understand," Goddard said sympathetically. "I'll see
what I can do. But meanwhile, could you please think about
our offer tonight and meet me here tomorrow with a list of
your objections. We bureaucratic curmudgeons have ways of
accommodating people."

Loren hesitated. The right thing to do was refuse out-
right, but in the face of Goddard's reasonableness, that would
be churlish. "Allright," she said. "But I won't promise anything."

"Don't," Goddard said. "Until you've thought about it."

He was too damned reasonable, Loren thought.

64

Loren left the administration building and took a deep
breath to quell her irritation. From behind her Goddard
asked, "Mind if I walk with you, Professor? If you won't help
us, I'd like to at least pick your brains."

Goddard's smile was placating and there was a curve of
supplication about his angular frame. She told herself he was
simply an old man trying to do his job, and that she had a
duty to help. "All right," she said.

"Tell me about your time with Widdell," Goddard said, moving down the steps with her.

"It was about ten years ago," Loren replied. "At that time Steve, like most of us, was simply a computer junkie with machine codes instead of brain cells and programming language instead of corpuscles. We worked out of a basement on New York's west side, and the computer continually kept breaking down because of dampness and pollution.

"But they were good days. We were young and adventurous, and I thought Steve's concepts were fantastic and was proud and happy to work with him on it."

"How many of you were there?"

They reached the foot of the library steps. "Just four of us. Two researchers, Steve, and myself. The researchers ran the polling side of Steve's operation, which kept us in funds. I was the entire development division, and Steve divided himself as much as he could between us."

"So you were with Widdell at a crucial point in his career? You helped create his Political Data System?"

"I suppose—yes, I did."

"So why didn't you stay on and become rich and famous?"

"Because I didn't want to spend the rest of my life as a pollster. I've always been fascinated by research, but when a job's done, I feel a need to move on to something else."

"But the money," Goddard probed.

"Was the result of Steve's ideas," Loren said firmly. "I only helped Steve develop those ideas. I wasn't entitled to the rewards."

Goddard asked, "Has anyone else talked to you about Widdell recently?"

"Steve's name does come up in seminars and group discussions. His techniques are—were—unique."

"I meant a direct approach, something outside normal academic discussion."

"No," Loren said.

"You're sure?"

"Very sure."

"I want you to let me know if anyone approaches you about Widdell. Please treat this request seriously, Professor. Your life could depend on it."

Loren turned to look at him. Goddard was watching her, his gaze steady and serious. "I'll let you know—" she started to say, when she heard the roar of an engine, the slap of metal moving rapidly through the air. She saw Goddard's head tilt and his eyes widen. She felt his hands grab her and wheel her around behind him.

With a thumping of wheels, a black Oldsmobile raced over the grass toward them. Loren felt her heart plug her throat, her body lock in a gigantic frozen shudder. The wheels of the Oldsmobile jigged over the grass like bowling pins. A rear window slid down. A hand carrying a gun protruded.

"Down!" Goddard's hands on her shoulders were like bags of cement. Instinctively she resisted, then let herself go, kneeling first, then curling sideways on the grass. The gun spat flame. Sharp cracks snapped at her. She saw Goddard's already falling body jerk as if tugged by a terrier. Then he slumped down beside her, blood spurting from his chest.

Tires gouging chunks of grass, the car sped past and veered around in a wide U-turn that left thick black streaks of rubber on the pathway. Loren stared in wide-eyed silence as it raced back toward her, the guns in the back aiming down now, framing her. She stared into the black barrels, too numb to move, too petrified to think. Little moans escaped her barely parted lips. Tears rolled down her cheeks. Marty! Who would look after Marty? She tried to gather herself up, to stand, to run.

Two shots crashed out from behind her, louder than those from the car. The car's windshield shattered, and Loren saw four tight, set faces. Then the car was swerving away, bouncing over the edge of the lawn, racing for the gap between the buildings as the thin, hollow-cheeked man she'd seen watching her from above the tennis court flung himself down beside her. The gun in his outstretched hand barked twice more, deafeningly. The gleaming back of the Oldsmobile edged between the buildings and disappeared.

The man rose to a crouch, one hand on Loren's neck, pushing her to the ground. He looked around, then pulled out a small radio. "Attack," he snapped. "Four men in a black G-bodied Olds Cutlass Supreme with Ontario plates. Car leaving the campus about now. The chief's been hit. I've got the subject." He looked down neutrally at Loren. "Subject appears unhurt." He put away the radio and looked angrily around before leaning over Goddard.

Putting the gun down by Goddard's head he turned the older man over on his back. Loren saw him bring his cheek close to Goddard's mouth, saw him feel for the pulse at the throat. When he pulled away from Goddard, there were tears in his eyes.

"You," he cried, looking at Loren and reaching for the gun. "On your feet! Move!"

Startled by the anger and urgency in his voice, Loren stood up. A second man ran up. There was a brief exchange of words, then the hollow-cheeked man was prodding her with the gun. "You got a car here?"

"Yes."

"Okay, then let's go."

"What . . . where . . . put that—"

"Move lady, before they come back to finish you off."

65

The man kept his gun in his pocket and a firm grip on Loren's arm as they jogged raggedly to the staff parking lot. He stood by impatiently while she opened the door. "Where are we going?"

"To your place."

"What . . . why—"

"We'd better check to see if your boy's okay."

"But he's in school."

"Your place is where he's coming back to."

"Oh, my God!" Loren got in and drove. She didn't speak till she reached the highway. "Who are you?"

"My name's Ellis."

"You worked with—"

"Yes." The interruption was as brutal as the shots he'd fired. "Is there any place you can leave your boy?"

There was nowhere she would leave Marty, not with this shooting and killing. "No. As I was telling Mr. Goddard, Marty needs a mother. He needs attention and care—"

"Which he won't get if you're dead."

The words flicked across her like the tipped lash of a whip. "Dead? What do you mean?"

"Whoever killed Theo was after you," Ellis said flatly. "You know things they'd rather you didn't."

"But knowledge—"

"You aren't dealing with professors who'll slap you on the wrist," Ellis said. "These people use real guns and real bullets. And you've seen them kill."

"But why should I come with you?"

"Because it's better than staying where they know you are. Because its better than waiting for them to kill you."

Loren stared through the windshield. "This is ridiculous!" she shouted. "What am I doing here, driving away with you from a crime? We should be going to the police. The police will resolve everything."

"Not this time," Ellis said, his tone expressionless. "This could be too big for the police. Theo Goddard was a very important figure in American intelligence. If they killed him, what chance do you think you'll have?"

"You—You're just trying to scare me."

"I don't have to try. The facts are scary enough." There was a tight, ugly look about Ellis's face. "Do you know why Theo came all the way here to talk to you about computer codes? Because Dick Schaffer and Lucas Amory, the only two other people who knew of Widdell's codes, have both been killed—murdered."

"You mean—"

"I mean that whoever has the system will go to any lengths to keep it, and to keep themselves from being identified. We found out about you quite easily, Mrs. Eastman. So can anyone else. What's more, the men who killed Theo will go to any length to stop you—which means they'll take out the boy, too, if you make them."

"Marty! No! Marty's not involved."

"Neither were you, Mrs. Eastman." Ellis turned away as if bored by the conversation.

Loren drove for a while in silence. She turned off the freeway and headed along Eglinton. "What do you want me to do?"

"Leave the boy with his father. We'll arrange protection for him through our people here. Then come with me to

Washington and help me find the people who stole Widdell's system. Until they're found, you'll never be safe."

66

Loren switched off the ignition and, leaving the key in the lock, went into the house three doors down from her own. The street was empty, Loren's the only car parked on it. A sharp February sun presaged the advent of spring.

Someone had known Goddard was coming to Toronto that day, Ellis thought, and had arranged to kill him and Loren Eastman. Who? Because of the effect publicity would have on the nature of the presidency, Goddard had kept their investigation very low-key. Only he and Ellis knew everything, and Jim Colson, who'd been kept on a strictly need-to-know basis. So how had anyone learned where Goddard would be with sufficient precision to arrange his murder? Ellis had no doubt that the office had been penetrated by Russians.

He felt a moment's sympathy as Loren came out of the house and walked toward him, her face pale and drawn tight. It must all be a terrible shock for her, too, he thought. He had to get her moving while she could still move, while she was still in a state of confusion and dependency. The important thing was to get her safely to Washington and into hiding.

"Wallis will take Marty," she said, getting into the car. "But I don't want him staying with Wallis and Jeannete for too long, and—"

"We'll be back as soon as this is over, Mrs. Eastman," Ellis said. "Not more than a week." In a week, he thought, it would be over or they'd both be dead. Then he recalled Theo saying, "Don't worry Drew, you won't lose her! You didn't lose Emma." He felt as if Theo had just spoken the words. "Damned right, I won't." His hand tightened on the gun.

Loren asked, "Did you say something?"

He turned, startled. "Sorry, just thinking out loud."

While she went upstairs in her own house and began packing, Ellis thought about who might have betrayed Theo. The only way anyone could have known what Theo was doing was from the files, which meant he had to put a seal on Theo's files. But he had no authority within OCI. Should he ask Colson for authority? No, the explanation would take too long. Better get someone who would believe him. Theo's senior assistant, Tom Graydon, he thought, and dialed.

Upstairs while Loren packed, she tried to make sense of what was happening to her. A man who had been talking to her less than an hour ago had been shot dead. Downstairs another man sat with a gun, and she was preparing to go to Washington with him to help find out who killed Steve Widdell. She was leaving Marty with Wallis, she was leaving her classes, she didn't know when she would be back—it was crazy, it was goddamn unreal, it couldn't really be happening!

It was!

"Director's office," Tom Graydon said.

"Drew Ellis," Ellis said. "Can you patch a scrambler on to this line?"

"Sure. Give me a minute."

A few moments later he heard Graydon's faintly distorted voice say, "You're patched now. How's every—"

"Not good," Ellis said. "I've been doing a QT job for the chief outside, and came here to Toronto this morning with him."

"I know," Graydon said.

"The chief's been shot," Ellis said. He heard Graydon's exclamation, drove it out of his mind and said, "I'm afraid he's dead. Peters will be talking to Colson about it, but meanwhile I want you to put a stop on all the chief's files."

"That'll be done anyway, Drew, soon as we get official notification."

Ellis said, "I don't want anyone checking those files. Not even Colson."

"That'll be tough, Drew. Jim's next in command."

"Stall him. I'll see you soon as I get back to Washington."

"Drew—you're no longer official!"

"Till tonight," Drew said. "Theo was set up by someone in the office. And I'm coming back to get him." Abruptly Ellis put the phone down.

Upstairs, Loren pulled the case shut and locked it.

Silently she prayed, Please God, keep me safe, bring me back to my son and this house. She wondered if she should call down to Ellis and tell him she wouldn't go, then remembered what he had said about Marty, went to the closet to get her coat . . . and screamed as the window shattered and a bullet smashed into the wall above her head.

Ellis heard Loren's scream and the tinkling glass, heard the sound of footsteps by the side of the house. "Keep down!" he shouted, running in a crouch to the wide picture window at the front of the foyer as he drew the gun from beneath his jacket.

The black Oldsmobile was in front of the house, its occupants' shadowed forms behind the raised windows. He looked across the neat lawn and flowerbed to the fence. No cover at all there. Ridiculous place to start a shootout, unless—

As he heard Loren's footsteps on the stairs, the door bell rang, its sudden, piercing, insistent sound making them both jump. There were simultaneous explosions in front and back accompanied by a brief metallic clatter.

"Ellis!"

The front door swung open and a man stood there, his gun pointing at Loren, halfway down the stairs.

Ellis fired, saw the puff of plaster as the bullet winged the wall, saw the man pull back in surprise, hesitate, then turn and sprint down the path.

Crack!

Ellis turned, dropped, and heard the whine of a ricochet follow the angry snap of the bullet. He saw a second man crouched in the doorway between the kitchen and the living room, gun wavering indecisively between him and Loren. Hitting the carpet with his elbow, Ellis fired, pumping the trigger rapidly, spraying the area of the kitchen door.

The intruder hurled himself sideways behind the dividing wall. Ellis rolled behind a sofa, moved to get a better aim, saw the man dart across the rear of the kitchen, heard the rear door open and the sound of running footsteps. He got to his feet, ran toward the kitchen, realized the front was uncovered, stopped, turned, and stood on the landing beneath the stairs, head turning this way and that, uncertain about what to do next.

There was a time when he would have known, he thought,

and a moment later heard the tinny sound of a car door slamming, then the startled yelp of tires. He ran to the front door. Stupid, he told himself—they could have a man waiting. He ran outside, stopping too late on the paved stone driveway outside.

The Oldsmobile was gone, and they didn't have a man waiting outside. Ellis turned and returned to the house, heart pounding, legs like wet twine.

Loren came white-faced down the stairs, eyes wide, mouth open. He put his arms round her and held her till the panic subsided and she was able to cry.

67

Two hours later Peters had arranged for protection. Loren's house had been secured by a hastily summoned locksmith, and she'd visited Marty's school and made a tearful farewell. Now she and Ellis were on an airplane on its way to Washington.

Ellis told her what she needed to know: the Russian plan to steal Widdell's tapes, and Theo Goddard's conclusion that there was a KGB candidate in the presidential election; Steve Widdell, Lucas Amory, and Dick Schaffer had all been murdered, Amory and Schaffer surely by the Russians; Goddard's reluctance to pursue a direct investigation into Widdell's death. From the beginning their investigation had been very discreet, but somehow it had been penetrated and someone had known when Goddard would be in Toronto and why.

"So what am I doing provoking them!" Loren cried. She was on her second gin and tonic and wishing she'd had the sense to stop after the first. "The safest and most sensible thing to do is to go back to Toronto and show them I'm not interested in their computer system, that I'm doing nothing to interfere with them."

"It's too late for that," Ellis said. "And what happens if they don't believe you?"

I could reason with them, Loren thought to say, then

realized how naive it would sound. There was no reasoning with men who were beyond morality. Not wanting Ellis to think she was drunk or weak, she fought back tears of helpless anger.

Ellis told her it wouldn't be safe for either of them to report back to or work with the OCI. He had a place outside Washington known only to a few friends, and they would stay there for now.

For now, Loren thought despairingly. What about the future? And where was this place? How safe? She asked Ellis.

He told her.

God, it was worse than she'd expected. An isolated cottage with no one for miles around and Ellis her only protector. She felt tremulous and weepy. She pushed away her drink. Getting sloshed wasn't going to help anyone. Ellis, she noticed, was drinking only orange juice.

Her companion, she noted, was a lean man, gaunt almost, with the darkest, most intense eyes she could remember. There was a coppery glow to his skin, as if he'd spent time outdoors through the winter. His black hair was curly, unfashionably long, and slightly unkempt. There was a sense of hardness about him, but also a great vulnerability. This, she thought, was the man she was trusting with her life—had to trust with her life.

When he'd begun to tell her about the OCI, he'd said he was Goddard's assistant and had known Goddard for many years. Loren recalled the sheen of tears immediately after the shooting. A glimpse of emotion, of heart? Now he sat tightly controlled, remote. She remembered that moment in the house when he'd taken her into his arms and eased her panic, remembered how strong and wonderfully comforting his body had felt. . . .

She thrust the recollection from her mind. She was going to Washington on a job that could end in her death. For Marty's sake and her own, she should focus all her energies on that job, getting it over with as soon as possible, returning home as soon as she could. She took out her notebook and with pencil poised, asked, "How do you propose to run this investigation?"

Ellis turned and looked at her. "You don't need that," he said, folding her palm around the notebook. "First I'm going to get you safely to Fairmont. Then I'm going to have a look at Theo's files. Then we'll see." He looked past her, at the plane window, ending the conversation.

In fact, Ellis didn't know what to do with Loren Eastman. He'd brought her because he suspected that Petrovich had been working for Theo, so no one else probably knew of his Brighton Dam home. And because she'd been marked in Toronto; leaving her there would have been tantamount to sentencing her to death. He had no idea how Theo had intended to infiltrate her among the candidate's computer systems, nor how he'd planned to use her. He would have to keep her and use her as best as he could, Ellis thought. Until he'd found Zonda and the men who'd stolen Widdell's tapes and killed Amory, Schaffer, Widdell, and Theo.

68

An hour after leaving Washington's National Airport, Ellis turned the Porsche off a side road onto an unmade track. It led to a clearing where a small, simple, two-story wood-frame house stood.

There were bare, shady porches in back and front, a rusting white table and garden furniture on the unmown front lawn, tightly shut windows, and timber frames painted a deep brown and white paint burnt pale yellow flaking off the planks.

"Ellis, it's charming!" Unkept but charming, she thought, and noted his fleeting smile as he took her suitcase from the trunk of the Porsche.

"Glad you like it."

He carried the case up the front porch steps and fumbled with keys. The interior was dark, and smelled of old wood and log fires. When he opened the screens, dust played in shafts of late-afternoon sunlight. He showed her up to one of the bedrooms, most of it taken up by a long, wide bed and a rustic closet.

"I hope you'll be comfortable."

"I'm sure I will. Anyway, it's not going to be long, is it?"

A pensive glance. "No. I'll go down and make you some coffee. The bathroom's at the end of the corridor. Come down when you're ready."

After unpacking, she went downstairs. Crammed with old furniture and a grandfather clock, it had a natural charm. On a table and over the mantlepiece were photographs of a beautiful, bony-faced girl with bright, straight flaxen hair, gorgeous eyes, and a brilliant toothy smile. In one photograph she and Ellis were holding hands, looking at each other. Loren could never have imagined him looking so tender.

"I've brought your coffee."

She turned, startled. His face looked strained, a white half circle round his mouth. She asked, "Is that your girlfriend?"

He put the tray down with a clatter. "That's Emma."

"Is she—" He was staring angrily at her. "I'm sorry if I shouldn't have—"

He seemed to control himself with great effort. "She's dead."

"I'm sorry."

Ellis's face was tight and hard, as it had been that morning when Goddard was killed. "It wasn't your fault. She was working for me on an assignment in Berlin when she was shot and killed."

"Oh, Ellis! How terrible!"

He stared at her blank-eyed, then poured her coffee.

Loren took the cup and sipped it. So that was why he was at once so hard and so vulnerable, she thought, wanting to reach out and take him in her arms.

69

Shortly after seven, warning Loren not to leave the house and telling her there was a gun in the second drawer of the table in his study, Ellis drove back to Washington. Tom Graydon was waiting for him in a motel off the Beltway, his cheeks covered with a day's growth of dark stubble.

"What happened to Theo?" he asked, his voice high with emotion.

Briefly, Ellis told him, then asked, "Have you got the files?"

Graydon hefted a combination-locked briefcase onto the table between them. "I've got everything you wanted," he said, and told Ellis he'd opened the private safe Theo kept in one of his desk drawers and had brought the file he'd found there. Despite the coolness of a February evening, sweat gleamed in the dark wrinkles of his forehead. "Fortunately, Colson's been too busy handling the Canadian reaction to Theo's death to bother about this just yet. But by tomorrow morning he will." He opened the case.

Inside was a single file, the index tab marked in Theo's handwriting: *KGB Candidate?* "Anyone else been wanting this?" Ellis asked.

Graydon shook his head. There was no reference on the file, Ellis noted, which meant Theo had not passed it through Central Records; it was still a private operation. Ellis opened the file and read. Theo had been to the White House twice, the first time to meet with the president and be briefed on Widdell's death, the second to be warned not to investigate it. Which Ellis supposed was why the investigation was still private.

Next were his reports on the killings of Schaffer and Widdell and Theo's own report on the death of Lucas Amory. Ellis read through the notes of Theo's meeting with Sara Widdell. That was where Theo had learned about Loren Eastman, he thought. Theo had met a Pat Cleary, who worked for Widdell and told him about computer codes. There was a two-page summary concerning Widdell, culled from various files, together with photographs and a short biography of Loren Eastman, also with photographs.

Loren had been born in 1954. An honors graduate in Computer Sciences from MIT, she had refused lucrative offers from industry in order to work with Widdell. After three years with him, she'd taken a research appointment at Scarborough College, a satellite campus of the University of Toronto. She'd married Wallis Tredigar there, given up teaching, and become a wife and mother. After her divorce she returned to teaching and earned a professorship in three years. Not bad for someone only thirty-three, Ellis thought, and closed the file.

Stuck to the inside of the file cover was a Department of Justice ID for Loren and a special phone number for the president. Ellis pocketed the ID and stared thoughtfully at the White House number. If he called that number, would he get through to the president? And would the president accept him as Theo's successor, or would he—alarmed at the possible repercussions of Theo's murder—hand everything over to the Secret Service with instructions to bury it. Bury him, too, Ellis thought. And Loren. Going to the president at this stage, he decided, was no guarantee that he would be given the green light to stop Zonda.

70

Loren waited nervously in the house. Unused to being surrounded by trees and forest, every sound was unusual, and every unusual sound made her cringe with fear. This was ridiculous, she scolded herself. No one knew where she was. No one could find her. She called Toronto and spoke to Marty, who sounded resentful at being disturbed. Afterward, when she spoke to Wallis, she asked him to make sure Marty didn't watch too much television, stay up too late, or miss his Friday tennis lesson.

"When are you coming back?" Wallis asked.

She felt a momentary spasm of panic. "Why? Is there anything wrong? Is Marty—"

"Marty's fine," Tredigar said. "I was simply curious, that's all. Marty can stay here as long as he wants to."

She put down the phone and walked around the cottage. It was comfortable, but like Ellis himself, remote, not the sort of place that invited you to kick your shoes off, flop down on the rug and watch television. She went up to his study. On the bookshelf facing the desk were fifteen hardback copies of a book Ellis appeared to have written, *The Therapy of Motion*. Curious, she removed a copy. Was Ellis a psychiatrist, or did he have someone else write under his name?

The book was easy to read, and began with an account of

the gunshot wounds Ellis had suffered. Fascinated, she read
on. About a third of the way through, a review from *The New
York Times* dropped out from between the pages. Ellis was
not only a writer, but a successful writer. So what was all this
with the OCI and guns?

A sound like a shot sent her leaping from her chair. She
found herself by the desk and scrabbling to open the second
left-hand drawer. The gun lay there, shiny blue metal in the
lamplight, seeming deadly and lethal, and smelling faintly of
oil. She could not bring herself to touch it. Hearing no more
noises, she went to the window and looked out. There was
nothing. No one knew where she was. No one could find her.
The false alarms were only imagination, nothing more. To
take her mind off it, she decided to occupy herself, like doing
something about why she'd come to Washington, something
to find Widdell's murderer and the KGB candidate. In a
corner beneath the bookshelves she found six months back
issues of *Time*. She carried them to Ellis's desk and began to
work.

71

It was nearly eleven when Ellis got home. The light
washing over the stairs flashed a momentary caution before
he remembered Loren was staying there. He went slowly
upstairs. She was seated at his desk, writing, her hair down
to her shoulders, her face soft in the muted glow of the desk
lamp. She looked far more relaxed than when he'd left, Ellis
thought. She saw him, looked up and smiled.

"I've got something to show you," she said. "I've listed
the key presidential candidates and their political positions.
Here, take a look."

He stood over her and read the list.

| Bradley Taylor | Vice-President | Strong association with the right. Prime mover of Soviet Olympic boy- |

		cott; advocate of trade & other sanctions.
Kevin Anderson	Senate Leader	Political liberal. Key role in Salt talks. Advocate of greater American presence in Europe. Highly regarded by Pentagon.
Frank Crane, Jr.	Senator, Virginia	Wealthy background. Moderate. Campaigns on understanding & dialogue. No clear position on foreign affairs.
Afram Milovan	Governor	Russian emigré background. Strong liberal activist. Grass-roots support. Strong condemnation of Russian excesses. Calls for dialogue as a prelude to confrontation.
Jerry Pressler	N. Carolina	Strong association with right. "Born again" Christian.

"Which one do you think it is?" Loren asked.

"Could be one or all of them."

"So what do we do? Start with Taylor and work our way down the list?"

Ellis walked around the desk and sat opposite her. "That would take up to next year, even if we had all the resources of the office. We'll have to find a simpler way."

"Sure," Loren said. "What?"

Ellis shrugged. "If I knew it, I'd do it."

They looked glumly at each other, and then for no reason, smiled.

72

February 26, 1988

When Loren came downstairs the next morning, Ellis was in the kitchen, toweling off after his run. There was a welcoming smell of fresh coffee, and she thought he looked quite boyish, with his hair tousled and his body so lean. "Didn't want to disturb you," he said, attempting to put his track top back on.

Noting his embarrassment, it occurred to Loren that Emma hadn't lived here and Ellis hadn't lived with a woman for a long time. She said, "Don't dress up just for me." Ignoring his embarrassment she went to the refrigerator and took out eggs and bacon. "How do you like your eggs?" she asked.

"There's no need—" he started to say, then, "Boiled for three minutes."

Over breakfast he told her what he thought they should do. He felt that they had the choice of finding out who killed Widdell, or who stole his tapes. Since the president had proscribed looking into Widdell's death, they were left with the tapes.

Loren laughed. "Pretty damn logical."

They drove to Widdell's offices after breakfast. There was an air of abandonment about the place, with only one security guard in the lobby, two empty floors with empty cubicles, and a pale-faced, red-haired man with tired eyes in Widdell's top-floor office who said his name was Pat Cleary. Ellis showed him his ID and said he worked with Theo Goddard, who'd met Cleary previously.

Loren asked, "What's not happening here?"

"We have to shut down," Cleary said, and told them everyone else had left. He'd stayed to clear up a few loose ends and would be starting a new job in two weeks. Cleary looked despondent and tired, and glad of someone to talk to. "Want some coffee?" he asked, looking toward an electric coffee pot in a corner of the room.

Both Loren and Ellis said they would.

"Why is Widdell Associates closing down?" Ellis asked.

"Do you know anything about the codes?" Cleary asked.

"Only what you told Theo Goddard," Ellis replied.

"That's enough," Cleary said with a hint of bitterness. "Without the codes we couldn't service our clients. And in a nutshell, that's it."

"Couldn't you keep going till the codes were deciphered?"

Cleary shook his head. "It seems Steve didn't have the financial reserves. As you can imagine, the bulk of our work was political, and we were supporting Jerry Pressler in the primaries."

"Jerry Pressler," Loren breathed. "Why he's—"

Cleary raised an impatient hand. "I know. But he was Steve's choice for president."

Widdell must have had delusions of grandeur, Loren thought, picking a virtual unknown and hoping to make a president of him. Then she remembered that was exactly what Widdell's system was programmed to do.

"We've been supporting Pressler for six months," Cleary continued, "and Pressler's problem was he didn't have a whole lot of cash. So Steve agreed that we'd get paid only after Pressler got elected."

"Where's Pressler now?" Ellis asked.

"He did the obvious thing when he found we couldn't support him. He got himself another pollster."

Ellis said, "A week before Widdell died, I understand you had a fake service call. Is that right?"

"Too right," Cleary said. "They downloaded all our tapes. Mind you, whoever it was couldn't have got much out of them without the codes. But the darndest thing about it all is that the face of the service engineer looked so familiar."

Loren asked, "Someone you met in a bar, perhaps, or someone you see on your way home from work?"

Cleary shook his head. "It's someone I know. I wish to hell I could think how."

"The service company honest?" Ellis asked.

"Their whole livelihood depends on it. Besides, they knew the tapes were useless without the codes."

"Could the service engineer have been fake?"

"He had all the right ID," Cleary said, "and he knew all about the machines."

Loren asked if she could see the service log book.

"Sure." Cleary rummaged in a carton and handed it to her. "There, you see, a service call was made on the twenty-eighth of January."

Loren looked at it carefully. "Failure to read and write," she said. "That's unusual. And it was noticed by only one man. What's happened to Vassilos?"

"Oh, he's left."

"With the others?"

"No. Before the others." Cleary laughed uncomfortably. "As a matter of fact Vassilos didn't return to work after the twenty-eighth, the day he made that entry in the service log."

"You have his address?"

"More than that. I have his last pay check."

"You tried calling him or checking out his address?"

"I tried calling him," Cleary said. "His landlord told me Vassilos moved and he didn't know where he'd gone." He gave them the address and phone number.

"So where were the tapes loaded down to?" Loren asked.

"The telephone company's traced the number," Cleary said. "It's a computer agency in Aurora Heights."

An hour later, on the opposite side of Washington, Ellis and Loren stared at another abandoned office. "Moved out without any notice," the janitor said. "Mind you, they paid six months in advance, so the boss didn't care."

"Paid?" Ellis asked. "How?"

"Certified check for deposit, rent, insurance, everything." The janitor smiled and added, "You know a funny thing? They haven't asked for the return of their deposit." He led them up the stairs to his office on the ground floor. "I suppose you'll be wanting to know what he looked like. Well, you're lucky. I have a good memory for faces. Used to be with the Washington PD once, and you never lose the habit."

The janitor flaunced behind the desk and said, "The man who paid the rest was white, about five ten, 175 pounds, very pale eyes, spiky hair, triangular face, pleasant, regular features. I'd say he was a naturalized American. His English was accented."

Triangular face, light eyes, spiky hair. The janitor was describing Pomarev! Ellis could feel his pulse race. So the Russians had rented an office, arranged a fake service call, and downloaded all of Widdell's tapes. But how had they gotten the tapes decoded?

"There were never very many people using the office," the janitor was saying. "Even after they put the computers in. The head guy was American, white, about 190 pounds, I'd say, and short, with a heavy moustache and overgrown, greasy hair. In the last few weeks he came in every day with a man about his own age, mid to late thirties, blond, short hair, blue eyes, about six feet and around 185. They were here, let's see, till last Friday. And then on Monday the moving vans came and took the computers and furniture away—"

"You know where they went?"

"The furniture and the computers went back to the leasing company. Where the men went, I have no idea."

"Did you get references?" Ellis asked.

"No. The boss didn't need them. He'd got his rent in advance and he wanted a short-term rental without any fuss. He's thinking of selling the building, you see, so he didn't want tenants on long rentals sitting around."

"You have the rental agreement?"

"Sure." The janitor reached back for one of the box files and took out a printed form at the bottom of which was scrawled a signature that looked like: Nicholas Pillich. Ellis made a note of the address.

"What have these guys done?" the janitor asked. "The old teeming and lading scam?"

"Stolen computer data," Ellis said.

"Well, I'll certainly recognize them again," the janitor said. "Drop by anytime you've got their mug shots."

It took them an hour to get to Falls Point, where Bob Deakin, the supervisor who'd spoken to Widdell, showed them in to a thickly carpeted basement room with a glass-sided wall through which one could see rows of computers with slowly revolving tapes.

Deakin was in his mid-thirties, with neatly cut hair, rimless eyeglasses, and a houndstooth sport jacket over an open-necked shirt. "It was a Saturday night nearly three weeks ago," he said. "I was on the morgue shift." He reached for a log book, looked at it, and continued. "At 2:46 I received a call from Steve Widdell asking me to arrange immediate delivery of a complete set of backup tapes. As we're required to do, I called Steve back."

"At the number he gave you?"

"No. At his home. I dialed the number myself. Steve answered after two rings and confirmed his instructions." Deakin looked again at the log book. "That was at 2:48."

"You're sure it was Widdell?" Ellis asked.

"It sounded like him. And it was his home number that I'd dialed."

And if Deakin had misdialed, it would be a hell of a coincidence to get Widdell, Ellis mused. "How precisely did he confirm his original order?" he asked.

Deakin scratched his head. "He said something like, 'I want the tapes right away.' I remember thinking that was a bit unusual. Usually people like us to back up tapes before sending them anywhere."

"Did he say anything else?" Ellis asked.

"Yes. Something about having a lab run a check on them. I knew there'd been a shutdown the previous week and assumed the check had to do with that."

"Wasn't it an unusual time to run a lab check?" Loren asked.

"Yeah, sure it was. But I didn't know if there'd been some kind of crisis, or if Steve was trying something new. Anyway, I'd gone through the check procedures and I had no reason not to deliver the tapes."

"How did Widdell sound?"

"Well, normal, I guess." Deakin shrugged. "As normal as anyone can sound at three o'clock in the morning."

"What happened after that?"

"I got the tapes ready and forty-seven minutes later a truck arrived and I handed them over." He showed Ellis the receipt. It was signed by a trucking company on behalf of Widdell Associates. The trucking company's address was in Agoura, California.

"A long way from Washington," Ellis said, "and a perfect dead end."

73

It was ten o'clock in the evening when Jim Colson let himself into his Watergate apartment. Goddard's death had rocked the office and kept everyone busy. Toronto had had to be sanitized, the Royal Canadian MP kept sweet, liaison established, diplomatic interference curtailed, arrangements made to attend inquests and ship bodies. It had been a long and nerve-wracking day, and Colson was thinking of a shower, a drink, and a late supper with Tracy, his woman of two months.

Colson hadn't wanted Goddard killed. But Goddard hadn't heeded any warnings, and when he'd begun to move too fast over Widdell's death and brought Ellis in on a private arrangement, Colson saw no alternative. There was too much at stake to allow the investigation to succeed. He wasn't worried that Ellis and the Eastman woman had disappeared. Neither of them could get far without Goddard, and sooner rather than later they would have to come out of hiding, and then—
Strrp!

Colson gasped as the thin noose flicked and tightened around his neck, the pressure pulling him upward and back onto his heels. But even as his hands flew to his throat, he realized that the pressure was not firm enough to cut or kill, and the man was using a wide swath of silk, not wire or strong, thin rope. A light came on. Hands quickly caressed his pockets. The pressure on his neck eased and his heels touched the floor. Standing in the foyer across from Colson, his face back lit by the flashlight he was carrying, was Boris Pomarev.

Pomarev said, "It's very nice to see you again, *priyatel*. Won't you offer me and my friend a drink."

Colson looked angrily from Pomarev to the man who'd garotted him so gently. Zonda stood close to him, stolid and impassive, hands stroking the silk scarf as if it were a neck he was crushing. Colson moved and saw Zonda's hand drop to his gun. More protective than a German shepherd, he thought, and walked past Pomarev into the living room. He opened his cocktail cabinet and poured out a Chivas Regal for Pomarev and a gin for himself. "I thought you'd got over childish games by now, Boris," he said. "What does your minder drink?"

"He doesn't."

Probably doesn't eat, and craps bullets, Colson thought, handing the Chivas to Pomarev.

Pomarev smiled. "Thank you. How thoughtful of you to remember." He raised his glass.

Colson walked to one of the chairs opposite the sofa and sat. "How the fuck did you get in here?"

"Simple. I told them I was the person you were expecting."

"And they let you in?"

"Of course they did, my dear fellow. You called earlier this afternoon and told them, remember."

"I did nothing—" Colson stopped himself. Boris's peculiar sense of humor would always be an irritant, but it was best he learned to live with it. He forced a smile. "Good for you, Boris. I see you've lost none of your cunning."

Boris lifted his glass higher. "To our glorious past and even more illustrious future." He drank, sipping gently.

Colson took a long pull at his gin. "What do you want?"

"To talk to you, to recapture memories of days gone by." Pomarev looked appreciatively at his whiskey and sighed. "Ah, Berlin, Berlin." Abruptly he leaned forward. "We were friends in Berlin, remember? Very good friends."

"Such close friends that I saved your neck by sacrificing the Lotus network to protect you from Simenon."

"For which I now bring you fourfold returns," Pomarev said softly. "In Berlin four years ago we were both committed to rapprochement. I was leading a group of dissident KGB officers, just as you were concerned with a group of loyal Americans who above all were looking to an end to the cold war and a lasting peace with Russia."

"Times have changed," Colson said. Two years ago, when he'd met Boris in Prague, he'd told him of the hardening of American public opinion and the support President Donnelly was getting for his hard-line foreign policy. "We will soon have the first part of Star Wars in operation. We don't need rapprochement as much as you do."

"Perhaps not military rapprochement," Pomarev said. "But we both need economic rapprochement, America now more than ever. The giant American industrial machine is being choked to death, far more than even four years ago. America's traditional foreign markets have been undercut by cheap, foreign competition, and its domestic base has been eroded by a ceaseless flood of cheap imports. To survive, America needs new industrial bases and new markets. It needs virgin territory into which to export its capital, to produce its goods and sell its high-cost wares. Together we can provide that territory. Together we can provide a whole new market of two hundred fifty million people waiting eagerly for capital, for technology, for any kind of consumer product."

Pomarev leaned forward and patted Colson on the knee. "The plans we discussed four years ago need little revision. Our commitment to a lasting peace and prosperity for both our countries remains unchanged." Pomarev's smile grew wider. "As do the benefits for me and for you."

Colson put down his drink. His rapprochement with Boris had not been an exercise but a commitment. And he was just as committed now as he'd been then, because what was true then was even more true now. "Cut the crap about Berlin, Boris," he said. "Tell me, what are you doing in Washington and what is it you want?"

The smile faded from Pomarev's eyes and his face became set and serious. He said, "I've come to tell you we have Widdell's Political Data System. We have it decoded, and we have it up and running. That is what I have been doing in Washington."

"Shee-it!" Colson exclaimed softly. Suddenly everything, the second theft of Widdell's tapes, the deaths of Amory and Schaffer, all fell into place. "You bastard!" he exclaimed. "You shrewd, calculating, brilliant, little bastard! You're the one who lifted the other set of tapes! And you took care of Schaffer and Amory so you could shut us out."

Pomarev smiled. "As our neighbors the Chinese say, No tickee, no laundry. No codes, no system."

Colson looked at Zonda, seated like a giant Buddha between them and the door. The perfect killing machine, the magnificent, programmable robot that had taken out Schaffer and Amory. He smiled approvingly at Zonda. Zonda stared back.

Almost swelling with pride, Pomarev said, "We can run the system for you, anytime you want to."

"That's great." Colson put away his drink and asked, "So why come here and tell me about it? You've got the system. You're in the driver's seat."

Pomarev leaned forward, hands on knees, eyes locked on Colson. "I'm looking for a trade-off, my friend. I want a deal with Bildeberg."

"With Bildeberg? What kind of deal?"

"A partnership. I put up the system and you put up two million dollars through a bearer bank draft, in Switzerland."

Colson suppressed a smile. What he liked about Boris was his unashamed capitalist virtue. "Getting the system was that expensive?"

"It's cheap at the price. Cas Hardinger tells me you were prepared to pay Widdell twelve million dollars for it."

Cas Hardinger talked too much, Colson thought. He held up his hand in a mock salute. "No offense, captain. I was only teasing." He lowered his hand. "You didn't go to all this trouble getting the system merely to sell it. Why are you offering it to us?"

"Because the object of the exercise," Pomarev replied, "is not to win an election but to control the president. And the fact of the matter is, apart from myself and perhaps six people in the Soviet-American Institute, there is no one else in Russia who knows how the American presidency actually works. So, we look for help from people we trust and with whom we share common objectives. Bildeberg!"

"I don't believe the objectives of Bildeberg are the same as the Soviet government," Colson said cautiously.

"They aren't. But if the man who controls the American president is, say, a senior and respected member of the Politburo, they can be."

And, Colson thought, the man who was the source of that Politburo member's control would have even more power and influence than the Politburo member. He asked, "How do you propose we continue?"

"Simple. We give you the system and we work together to support our candidate."

Colson frowned. "I don't see Bildeberg buying that. Bildeberg already has its own candidate."

"Had," Pomarev said pointedly. "The only way we can let you control the advisors is if we have the man at the top."

"That'll be a tough one to run past the committee."

"Cas Hardinger's already agreed," Pomarev said. "Also, I think you?"

Colson nodded. "But there's Courtney..."

"Tell him it is an unalterable condition," Pomarev said. "Remind him if he rejects it, Bildeberg has nothing. Remind him of the objectives of our partnership and the fact that our alliance is the only way of achieving them."

"Courtney's stubborn," Colson said. "And subject to fits at morality."

Pomarev's smile was tight. "Persuade him," he said. "Or kill him."

74

February 27, 1988

Vassilos had lived in a converted brownstone in northeast Washington, not far from the office. The landlord who lived on the premises was a balding flower child, with John Lennon glasses, patched denims, and an array of Peace buttons. "The place is already rented," he announced as soon as he opened the door to Ellis and Loren. "A nice couple, just like you."

"Actually, we're friends of Greg's," Ellis said. "From the office." He held up a small brown envelope. "We've brought his paycheck."

"Greg's not here," the landlord said. "All he told me was that he'd got a fantastic new job in Houston and would write when he got there. He hasn't written."

"I wonder if we might look around?" Ellis asked. "He may have left some indication of where he was going among his papers." He held up the brown envelope again. "There's a whole month's money in here."

"He took all his things when he left," the landlord said. "And the new people have already moved in."

"Sure," Ellis replied placatingly. "I understand. Sure." He turned as if to leave and then turned back. "Has he had any mail?"

The landlord shook his head. "No letters. Just a few circulars and a computer magazine."

"What magazine?"

The landlord reached back to a table by the door and showed him.

Ellis thanked him and left.

From a phone booth in the street Ellis called the magazine. Though it was Saturday, the subscription department was open. Not the most prosperous of times for computer magazines, Ellis thought, and said, "My name is Vassilos." He gave the subscription number he'd glimpsed on the magazine's wrapper. "I gave instructions for my subscription to be changed. Why hasn't it been done?"

"Just a moment," a woman replied. "Let me look." She came back on the line a few seconds later. "We have a record here of an address change as of the fifth of February, Mr. Vassilos. Your last issue of *Computer Scan* was mailed to your new address on the twelfth."

"You sure you got the right address?" Ellis asked.

"I have what you wrote, Mr. Vassilos." The girl sighed and read the address aloud. Porter Street in Cleveland Park.

"That's right," Ellis said gracelessly. "If it isn't your fault, it must be the damn post office." He hung up, turned to Loren and smiled. "Got him."

"Where did you learn all these things?" she asked as they walked back to the car.

"Page three of the training manual. How to find an absconder. Read page four and you could set up as a bounty hunter."

She said, "You didn't tell me you're a writer."

"No. One book doesn't make a writer, just as one swallow doesn't make a summer." They reached the car. He opened a door for her.

She looked up at him. "I read part of your book," she said. "It's good enough for you to call yourself a writer."

He smiled.

Vassilos's new building was almost a ringer for the old, a

modish conversion, the street lined with hardware stores. Ellis rang the door bell.

The intercom squawked. "Who is it?"

"Registered letter for Vassilos."

"Coming down."

Moments later the door opened. A stocky, dark-haired man in a warm-up suit blinked bleary-eyed at the street, didn't see a mailman, saw Ellis and Loren, and moved to shut the door. But Ellis was too quick for him. One foot already wedged into the jamb, he shoulder-charged the door, knocking Vassilos backward. Vassilos gave a little yelp of pain and surprise, turned and sprinted across the vestibule and up the stairs. Ellis caught him on the first landing, swung him against the wall, and punched him hard in the stomach.

Vassilos doubled over. Loren stared with a mixture of horror and surprise as she saw Ellis grab Vassilos by the front of his warm-up suit, bring his head close to Vassilos's and say, "I want to talk to you, punk. Where's your room?"

Still bending over, Vassilos led them to a studio apartment on the second floor. The bed was unmade, the curtains still drawn. Ellis pushed him into the middle of the room and kicked the door shut behind him. "Okay," he said. "Now tell me why you left Widdell Associates?"

Vassilos stared at him, his fear replaced by truculence. "I got another job, that's why. Anyway, what the fuck has it to do with you?"

Ellis said, "I want to know how the serviceman who answered your call on the twenty-eighth of January stole Widdell's tapes."

"So why don't you talk to him?"

Ellis cuffed him again.

"Drew, stop that!" Loren's voice was shrill, her face flushed and taut.

Ellis turned back to Vassilos and held a clenched fist in front of his face. "The good news, punk, is that the lady likes you. The bad news is, I don't. So tell me about the service engineer."

"I don't know anything about that. I worked in Records, not Maintenance."

"It was your call that got the engineer."

"So? The computer doesn't work, and I call the engineer. Is that a crime?"

"Why haven't you been back to work since?"

"I was ill. Then I got another job."

"Where?"

"None of your business."

Ellis hit him.

"Stop it!" Loren threw herself between Ellis and Vassilos. Vassilos twisted on his toes, dodged around Ellis, and sprinted for the door.

Ellis turned to go after him and cannoned into Loren. By the time he regained his balance, pulled her upright, and raced through the open door, Vassilos was already leaving the building. Ellis ran after him.

Nearing the end of the block, Vassilos began to slow down. His body started to weave, his head roll from side to side. He slowed to a walk and at the intersection, stopped, panting. Ellis laid a hand on one sweaty shoulder. "Vassilos, I only want to talk—"

With a startled scream, Vassilos leaped off the pavement. The speeding van slammed into his side, knocking him onto the street. Brakes shrieked. The van veered, one wheel bouncing over Vassilos as it stopped. A metal door crunched back and a white-faced driver got out.

Ellis saw him bend over Vassilos's prone body. Vassilos didn't move. He felt a press of gawkers push him off the curb as the driver stood up. "Shit! The guy must have been crazy! The guy just jumped!" Ellis pressed back into the throng.

A man said, "Hey, weren't you running after him?"

Ellis shouldered his way past the man and ran back down the street.

"If you hadn't hit him, he wouldn't have run," Loren cried.

"And if you hadn't interfered, he wouldn't have gotten away!"

They were in a diner near Logan Circle. "You had no business hitting him in the first place," Loren said. "The man had rights."

Ellis shrugged tiredly. "I know. But I had to make him talk and talk quickly."

"Was that the only way?"

"You know any others?" Ellis paused in his eating and looked directly at her. "It was the only way I could think of, taking into account that we've got people on our tail looking to kill us, and that some of them killed Theo." He sipped some water. "Believe me, I've thought a lot about ends not justifying means. But whatever you decide, whatever you believe, you get a situation like this—when to hold onto a principle becomes unrealistic, when you have to commit a venial sin in order to save a life..." He sighed. "At those times I console myself with the thought that the law was made for man, not the reverse."

Loren stared at him across the table. "I'm sorry I interfered." She fidgeted with her fork. "If I hadn't, perhaps..."

He leaned across the table and waved a finger in her face. "Whatever happens, you must never think like that. That kind of thinking won't bring Vassilos back, won't change anything."

His eyes blazed with a fierce intensity. She took his admonishing finger and placed it on the table. "You're a strange man, Drew Ellis. I wish I understood you."

"I feel that way myself. Especially when I have to do things like today."

She kept her hand on his. "You must do the best you can." She forced a smile. "Especially when it comes to looking after us."

75

KGB Deputy Director Vladimir Simenon looked at the blanket of soggy late-morning mist hovering over the Potomac and wished he was back in Moscow. For the fourth time— Simenon was of the old school, and believed in running the same questions over and over again—he asked Nikolai Malevich, the Washington KGB resident, to tell him about Pomarev.

The story got no less depressing with repetition. Pomarev had arrived in America two months ago, armed with a Special Authority signed by the chairman himself, which he had used to commandeer vehicles, cash, coded telex machines, type-writers, and other equipment which he'd had shipped to an address in Aurora Heights. He had brought in his own cryptanalysts, communications experts, and telephone engineers, and had no contact with the embassy after the last of the equipment was delivered. All his communications were now beamed directly to Moscow, and for the past month no funds had come to the embassy for onward transmission. In Malevich's opinion, Pomarev was running an independent operation linked directly to Moscow, and Malevich assured Simenon he didn't like it either.

"How much money did you give him?" Simenon asked.

"Half a million dollars."

Simenon whistled quietly. Pomarev's operation was not only independent, it was very expensive. "And you cooperated in all this?"

Malevich nodded mournfully. "Insofar as it was necessary." He cleared his throat and added, "I must point out, Comrade Director, that I had no alternative. Pomarev's authority was signed by the chairman of the Politburo himself."

"I know that." The thought of that authority made Simenon's wish he could stub out one of his *papyrosi* on Pomarev's face. He asked, "You have made no attempt to find out where Pomarev is or what he was doing?"

Malevich shook his head. "It is not for me to spy on those who have the full confidence of the Politburo."

Or some of the Politburo, Simenon thought. "That's going to be changed," he announced. "From now on we are going to keep tabs on Comrade Pomarev. Comrade Pomarev is young and ambitious and sometimes prone to impetuousness." Simenon remembered that if not for that business of the Lotus network, he'd have caught Pomarev in Berlin with his pants down and his dick exposed. He said, "It is good that some of us more experienced people should be available, in the event of unforseen troubles." He lit another *papyrosi* and hissed the smoke into his lungs. "I want you to mount a search for Arkady Zoyheddin," he said, "also known as Zonda. He is here in Washington with Pomarev. I want him found and brought to me. Urge your men to take the greatest care. Zonda is an expert killer."

76

After dinner they sat before the log fire Ellis had built, Loren sipping brandy and coffee, and Ellis a Japanese tea made from twigs which had no caffeine or tannin. Loren was surprised at the precision and delicacy with which Ellis had cooked the meal. His lasagne filled with chopped vegetables and dressed with an oil, lemon, and garlic sauce, was a revelation, as was his breast of chicken cooked in white wine and flavored with cheese. He told her he'd learned to cook in Rome.

He'd told her too much about Rome, Ellis thought, too much about his past. It came from living alone too long and the fact that she was such a receptive listener.

Loren had told him her life hadn't been all that easy. Her mother had died when she was nine, and she'd been brought up in an exclusively male household of a father and two brothers. She'd fought to get to university, fought against an early marriage, ultimately married a selfish, opinionated prig, fought to make that marriage work, fought the envy and resentment of male colleagues to establish herself in the arcane field of computer research.

Loren thought: that day, with not much to do, they had begun to behave less like strangers thrown together by some disaster. For the first time they'd talked about things other than the events which had brought them together.

For his part, Ellis liked the way Loren had accepted the essential abnormality of what they were doing and how they had come together.

Running together that afternoon she had said that she thought she should talk to Pat Cleary again. A company Widdell's size would have kept security records of its employees, complete with photographs. If Cleary went through the photographs, perhaps he would recognize the serviceman who had stolen the tapes.

197

Ellis had told her he believed their only way forward was to reopen the inquiry into Widdell's death, and that afternoon they had driven into Washington and had copies made of Widdell's photographs in Goddard's file. The photographs would be ready on Monday, and he intended to return to Brighton Dam then and see if anyone remembered seeing Steve Widdell there.

Loren had enjoyed running with Ellis. He'd slowed down somewhat for her and showed her his favorite trail. He'd looked calm and relaxed as they'd run, and afterward she'd felt as cleansed as she did after four sets of tennis.

Staring at the fire now, Ellis thought it was inevitable they would sleep together. They were both physically active, reasonably attractive people thrust into an idyllic setting and with time on their hands. He found the possibility very pleasant.

Loren thought it would be nice if they made love. She thought Ellis was a fascinating man. She liked his self-possessed silences, liked the leanness and the hardness of his body, the narrowness of his chest and shoulders, and the way his muscles were defined. She felt his hand on her arm and turned. His eyes were dark and intense and said everything they were feeling. She leaned into him, tilting her head back, allowing his mouth to press against hers, opening her lips.

He could feel the trembling in her body as she leaned against him. She wanted the expression of love as desperately as he did.

"I don't want to go upstairs," she whispered, her breath coming rapidly against his mouth, her fingers digging into his back.

"We won't," he answered softly, reaching for the buttons of her blouse.

She turned partially and in one gesture tore the blouse away; with a second she opened his shirt. Their flesh met.

He was aroused in a way he had not been since Emma. He leaned over her and gently unhooked her brassiere. It fell away revealing soft, sloping breasts, the nipples taut, awakened. As his mouth roamed over her skin, her fingers fumbled with the buckle of his belt and the top of his jeans.

His hands moved, unhooking the demure skirt and pulling it off her, lifting her lower body and rolling the thin panties down her thighs. The cool, silky smoothness of her skin inflamed him. Impatiently he kicked off the jeans as she coiled an ankle out of the panties and lay tremulous below him, abandoned, willing, legs slightly parted, her body delightfully open.

Flesh met flesh. Her eyelids fluttered as she looked into his face. She pulled his head down to hers. He began to kiss her, covering her cheeks and brow with light little touches. She moaned and he felt her tongue on his chin and throat. He ran his hands beneath her, along the smooth indentations of her spine, the curve of her buttocks, the backs of her thighs. Her legs were smooth and firm, and he felt indescribably lustful. He pressed her body against his and felt the moist center of her.

She cried out and writhed against him, hands reaching down to take him into her. Her sex felt like a furnace. She arched her back and pulled him down as he went deep into her, thrusting up to the hilt, and they both cried out with the magic of it, wrapping their arms around each other, moving in ragged unision.

77

February 28, 1988

As Boris Pomarev stepped into the richly paneled room where the executive committee of Bildeberg met, his gaze darted from the lavish furnishings to the men seated around the table. Colson and Hardinger he already knew. Ambassador Whillan Courtney and Senator Kevin Anderson he recognized from photographs and television news clips. He deduced that the young man seated to Courtney's right was the computer scientist Jim Colson had told him about, Dr. Jonathan Bradley.

Pomarev went directly up to the place that had been set for him at the foot of the table. The mere fact that he had been admitted to the committee room meant that in principle Bildeberg had accepted his offer. He addressed his opening remark to Courtney and Anderson. "Thank you, gentlemen, for allowing me to attend your deliberations." Courtney's face was flushed and angry, as if he'd been on the losing end of an argument, and Anderson looked sullen and thoughtful. Pomarev added, "I look forward to working closely with you all."

"There is one problem," Courtney said, rubbing his fingers together as he tried to control his irritation. Colson and Hardinger must have been mad to have brought an outsider into Bildeberg he thought. And not just any outsider but one with reported KGB affiliations. He stared at Pomarev. This was not the way it should have been; this was not what Bildeberg was created for. But then, as Colson had pointed out, what alternatives were there? Courtney said, "Your offer is accepted except for one point."

Pomarev smiled at him. "The money?"

"No. The candidate."

Pomarev's face appeared set in stone, and when he spoke, only his lips moved. He said, "As I hoped was made clear from the very beginning, our choice of candidate is not negotiable." Abruptly, Pomarev stood, as if to leave the room.

"Wait," Colson cried.

Fool, Courtney thought. Colson should have let Pomarev go. Pomarev needed them as much as he needed the system, and he had nowhere to go but them. Sooner or later Pomarev would be back, and they could then fashion a compromise.

Pomarev looked inquiringly at Colson.

"Let's talk about the candidate." Colson said. Kevin, here, has been a trusted member of Bildeberg for many years. He has..."

Don't talk about it, Courtney thought. Let the man go!

Pomarev turned away and walked toward the door. "The candidate will be ours," he called over his shoulder. "And through him we will both attain our objectives." He stopped and turned back. "With our candidate we will save both Russia and America. That, gentlemen, is the opportunity you are being offered. Not the selfish aggrandizement of any individual."

"Who is your candidate?" Courtney asked.

"I am prepared to reveal that only after the principle has been formally accepted," Pomarev replied, and took several steps toward the table. "I believe, gentlemen, according to your rules, it is customary at this time to call a vote."

"Now look here," Anderson began. "I'm not standing down simply because—"

"There will be no vote!" Courtney declared. "The matter has already been decided. The only candidate we will support is Kevin Anderson."

Cas Hardinger said, "I vote that we accept Boris's proposal without any variation."

"I second that," Colson said.

Anderson looked angrily across the table at his colleagues. His face was flushed, and he swallowed angrily before saying, "Naturally, I am opposed."

"And me," Courtney said.

Everyone's eyes turned to Jonathan Bradley. Bradley looked from Courtney to Hardinger and back again. Then, looking away from Anderson, he said in a low voice, "I vote to accept."

"Then we are agreed," Pomarev said, sitting down. "Now there is the question of my fee." He avoided looking at Courtney as he spoke.

78

February 29, 1988

Early that morning Ellis collected copies of Widdell's photograph and drove to Jed Atkins's garage in Brighton Dam, where he shot two rolls of Polaroid pictures of Widdell's car. Then he drove slowly around the town and its outskirts, showing the photographs to as many people as he could, asking them if they recognized the car or the man.

He was convinced that reopening the investigation into Widdell's death was the right way to go. It had left too many question marks. Widdell was the only person not obviously killed by the Russians. Sara Widdell had said her husband had left home around two o'clock on the morning of his death. Yet according to Bob Deakin's log, Widdell had been at home as late as 2:48 A.M. and had initiated the phone call authorizing the transfer of the tapes.

Sara Widdell had also said that her husband hadn't made any phone calls but had received one call, which had been from the office and not Deakin. Of course, Steve Widdell could have returned home, made the call to Deakin, and then driven to Brighton Dam. But that would have hardly left him any time to ascertain what was wrong at the office. And if there was something wrong at the office, driving back home to call Deakin didn't make sense, nor did driving to Brighton Dam. So, Ellis had initiated his quiet check into how Widdell had died.

By noon he realized he wasn't getting anywhere. While everyone had heard of Widdell's accident, no one he talked to remembered seeing Widdell or his car. Ellis drove doggedly around the outskirts of the town. He parked and went around knocking on doors. Someone must have seen something, he thought. Even in the small hours of the morning, he couldn't believe Steve Widdell had driven into Brighton Dam unnoticed.

He hadn't.

Fairland Briggs, who runs a store on Highland Road, and his wife had been baby-sitting for their grandchildren the night of February 6. Their daughter Rosalie and her husband Jim had not returned till after one, and Briggs and his wife were driving home when the car had begun to cough and splutter and finally stop. Fairland had spent an hour cleaning the carburetor, and afterward they were driving slowly along a twisting section of road when two speeding cars had passed them, bumper to bumper. The lead car had been a Buick Riviera, and looking at Ellis's picture, Fairland Briggs believed it was the one that had crashed. He was prepared to swear the two cars were racing, and he'd nearly clipped the second car as he'd pulled to the center of the road to negotiate a curve. He remembered the second car had broadsided around the bend. It was a green Cougar, like his son's. What's more, he remembered the number, or enough of it, for Ellis to make a trace. The Cougar had Virginia plates, the last two digits nine and eight, the first two letters S and L.

79

In Washington Loren sat on the top floor of the Widdell offices going through the mug shots with Cleary. They'd been through it three times already, and once or twice Cleary had thought he'd recognized someone, only to shake his head sadly on reconsideration, saying he couldn't be sure. The fourth time, Loren had cut a piece of paper in the shape of the moustache, colored it to look like hair, and had Cleary go through the register again, placing the moustache over each face.

Loren was beginning to think Cleary had only imagined he'd seen the man before, or that he'd seen him somewhere away from work, when Cleary said, "I think that's him."

She looked down at a heavily built, clean-shaven man with a receding chin and a drooping lower lip.

"That's him," Cleary repeated, pressing the moustache onto the face and staring at it. "His name's Abe Makram, and I taught him computer maintenance. Of course, the service-man was a lot heavier and . . ." Cleary picked up a pencil and sketched in sideburns and longer hair. "With a little more weight, that could be the service engineer," he announced.

"You're sure?"

Cleary didn't bother to look at the photograph again. "This time I'm sure."

Loren took the details off the register and the personnel file. Abe Makram had worked at Widdell Associates for three years, during which he'd familiarized himself with all the technical aspects of Widdell's business. Makram had left six months ago and given no reason for leaving. He'd left no forwarding address, nor had there been any subsequent requests for references. All she could do, Loren decided, was take the information back to Fairmont and wait for Ellis.

80

Still in Brighton Dam, Ellis was just finishing his lunch at a diner when the uniformed figure of Captain Rogers eased itself onto the stool next to him. "I'll have a coffee on my friend's account," he said to the waitress, and turned his sunglasses on to Ellis. "Hear you've been wandering around showing pictures and asking questions," he drawled.

"That's right," Ellis said. "Didn't want to trouble you. Didn't think you'd want to traipse around town showing pictures."

"Should've asked. Could've got it all done a whole lot faster."

The waitress put Rogers's coffee on the counter. "Find anything?" he asked.

"I think so."

"Got a message for you," Rogers said. "Call home."

"Home!" Ellis's heart jumped uncomfortably. Something had happened to Loren!

"Your office," Rogers said. "In Langley. Your boss, Jim Colson, wants to talk to you."

"Colson's not—" Ellis wondered how Colson had known where he was.

"He seemed to think it was important," Rogers said. "Wanted me to tell you there'd been some changes." Rogers smiled thinly. "Also wanted us to make sure you didn't leave Brighton Dam without calling him." Rogers patted his holster and slurped down his coffee.

Ellis slid off the stool, walked to the pay phones and dialed. Jim Colson came on the line immediately. "Drew, I'm so pleased you called. How are you?" He sounded genuinely interested and pleased to hear from Ellis.

"How did you know where I was?" Ellis asked.

"I knew sooner or later you'd have to get back to Widdell, that sooner or later you'd turn up in Brighton Dam."

"Takes one Agency man to find another. Why d'you want to talk to me?"

"I want a report on your investigation. Dammit all, Drew, I can't have you running about masquerading as an OCI agent and investigating heaven knows what without any effective controls or responsibility."

"I have authority from Theo."

"That authority was unofficial and is no longer valid. Theo's dead, Drew, and I'm in charge now. I don't play deniable games, and I don't set up private arrangements. So if you want to stay on the case, you get your authority from me. And before I give you any authority, I need to know what you've been doing. Which is why I want you back here right away. And bring Professor Eastman with you."

"And what happens when I do?"

"That depends on what you have to tell me."

Ellis decided he wouldn't go in, and certainly wouldn't take Loren in. Whether Colson knew it or not, the OCI was penetrated, and going to Langley could set them both up. He said, "And what if I don't come in, Jim? What if I tell you I'm a private citizen doing this on my own, that I don't need your authority and you don't need my report."

"That would be very stupid," Colson said. "Because you would force me to have you brought in. I guess you should know that I saw the president this morning. This case is no longer Theo's. It's mine."

"Then I strongly advise you to run this case exactly as Theo would have."

"No, Drew. Theo handled this case wrongly. He should have run it openly and in-house. He should never have got you involved on a personal basis."

"A personal basis is all I'm prepared to work on," Ellis said.

"I won't have that," Colson said. "As far as I'm concerned, everything's got to be in-house and aboveboard."

"In that case, I'm out," Ellis said. "I don't have to keep working for the OCI or you."

"And what happens when Zonda gets after you? You're still worried about Zonda, right?"

"Yes."

"Drew, what would you say if I told you that right now you're probably the last thing on Zonda's mind?"

"I'd say you didn't know what you were talking about, Jim. I'd say it was another reason for me not to come in."

"Okay," Colson said. "Don't come in. But do something for me. Go to the address I'm about to give you. It's in Maryland, and for heaven's sake don't attempt to barge in. It's a maximum-security detention center. These are your codes."

Ellis jotted down the codes. "Why do you want me to go there?"

"I want you to meet a Russian defector by the name of Petrovich."

"Defector?" Ellis said, "Since when?"

"Since he stopped working with Zonda," Colson replied.

81

The house in Maryland was surrounded by a park, but separated from it by a high wall and tall gates. All approaches were monitored by surveillance cameras. Ellis drove into the open rectangle outside the gates and stopped.

"Leave the car. Walk up to the gate and identify yourself." Through the bulletproof glass of the guardhouse Ellis saw one of the guards speaking into a microphone, while the attention of a second guard was totally focused on the car.

Ellis got out of the car feeling very vulnerable and exposed, the crunch of the gravel under his feet sounding explosively loud. He stood in front of the gate.

"Walk up to the grill, state your ID and purpose of visit."

The voice came out of a metal speaker set into the concrete gatepost. He said, "Agent Drew Ellis, Eye code 7177. Interview authorization C stroke 11-0-17."

After a few moments the voice grated out of the gatepost. "Return to your car. Open the trunk. Drive up to the guardhouse and stop."

Two guards appeared from behind the house and inspected the car. One of them got in beside Ellis and guided him up the drive to the front steps. Two more uniformed men met him at the top of the steps and took him to a library at the side of the house. Inside, Ellis sat at a large table in the center of the room. A few moments later Petrovich shambled in.

He started when he saw Ellis, attempted to turn and walk away. Then the guards spoke urgently to him, and he came reluctantly and sat opposite Ellis. He said, "I wasn't going to kill you. You must believe that."

"In retrospect," Ellis replied, "I came to that conclusion myself. How long have you been here?"

"Three months. I defected in November last year. I was at another place until three months ago. Then they brought me here."

"Who sent you to Fairmont?" Ellis asked.

"My case officer, Ludovic."

"Is Ludovic his real name or code name?"

"It's the name I know him by."

Code name, Ellis thought. "Why did he send you after me?"

"He said it was a test of my loyalty, a test to convince him that I had really changed sides. It is not an uncommon procedure."

"And did he tell you about Pomarev and the men Zonda killed?"

Petrovich nodded, a helpless and frightened expression in his large eyes. "How else do you think I could find out those things here? But I wasn't to kill you. I was to reveal myself to you, to frighten you, I was to feed you the information about Pomarev and Zonda."

"I might have killed you," Ellis said.

Petrovich shrugged. "It was a chance I had to take." He smiled hesitantly across the table at Ellis. "They told me you weren't a natural killer."

"Who's they?" Ellis asked.

"My case officer, Ludovic."

"You've said that before. Who else was there?"

"Your controller, Theo Goddard."

Ellis nodded. But to make sure, he said, "Describe him."

"A tall man in his sixties, square-lensed glasses, hair parted from the middle."

"You could have gotten that description anywhere."

"He pats his pockets from time to time, as if looking for

cigarettes, and he smells of cow's milk." Petrovich looked mournfully at Ellis. "Why should I lie?"

Why indeed, Ellis thought.

Petrovich leaned across the table. Droplets of perspiration gleamed on his forehead. He cleared his throat and said hoarsely, "Let me tell you something, my friend, this was not the first time I've seen Theo Goddard. Three years ago, a month before you shot Zonda, I saw him in Berlin."

"That's absurd!" Ellis's mind raced. In all the time he'd been running the Lotus network, Theo had only visited Berlin once, and that had been four years ago, not three. "What was Theo doing in Berlin?"

"Meeting Boris Pomarev." Quickly, before Ellis could interrupt, Petrovich said, "I accompanied Pomarev to that meeting. I sat at the table next to them. I heard what they said. Pomarev was under pressure from Simenon, and in order to restore himself and be in a position to take the next step, he needed a coup of some kind. He wanted to capture the Lotus network."

Ellis's heart was pounding madly in his chest, the collar of his shirt damp with sweat. His throat was so dry, he fought to get out the word: "And?"

"And Goddard promised to arrange it."

"You're lying! I don't believe you!" Ellis shouted, coming halfway out of his chair. "Goddard had no reason to betray Lotus!"

Petrovich cowered in his chair. "What I have told you is the truth, comrade. Why should I lie?" Petrovich looked pained and frightened and slightly relieved.

Ellis stared at him. The only reason Petrovich would lie was that he was now being persuaded to create a legend. But why create a legend about Theo after he was dead? Ellis thrust his head into his hands. He couldn't believe Theo had betrayed him, betrayed Lotus, that Theo had had Emma killed. *Darling, they weren't taken, they were betrayed! Darling, I know who!* The words cut through his brain like a laser. "Emma," Ellis asked hollowly. "Was that why she was killed?"

Slowly Petrovich nodded.

Theo, Ellis thought—it couldn't be Theo! Why would Theo betray Lotus, betray him? But he had! Petrovich had just given him the proof!

* * *

Ellis didn't know how long he'd been sitting there when he felt a hand on his shoulder. He opened his eyes. Colson was standing behind him, looking down at him sympathetically. "I'm sorry it had to be like this, Drew," he said. "I really am."

Ellis stared at him dry-eyed. "I can't believe Theo was behind the destruction of Lotus."

"To be honest, neither could we."

"How long have you known?" His body felt heavy with hopelessness, his voice was toneless with despair.

"About a week. Petrovich recognized Theo when they met to talk about you. He carried out Theo's instructions to ingratiate himself with us. Then, when he heard of Theo's death, he made a request to bypass his case officer and talk to someone independent. That was me. He told me how Theo had destroyed Lotus and how he had set you up."

"But why?" Ellis demanded. "Why? And if Theo was on the same side as Pomarev, why did he go to such lengths to bring me back to work against Pomarev now?"

Colson's grip on his shoulder tightened. "Thieves sometimes fall out, he said."

He came around the table and sat down. He had coffee brought in.

Ellis said, "Theo was right about Pomarev running a conspiracy in America, about Zonda killing Amory and Dick Schaffer."

Colson looked steadily at him. "I don't know that. I don't have Theo's files on the subject."

Ellis said, "I have the file. And there is no doubt that Pomarev and Zonda are in America, that Zonda killed Amory and Schaffer, and that they are concerned with the theft of Widdell's computer tapes."

"I want to see that file," Colson replied. "And I want a detailed report of your investigation so far. I want both of them today. I want you to come with me to Langley now and write your report."

"Not Langley," Ellis said. "You have a mole in the office, Jim."

"Did Theo tell you that?"

"Yes. And it's been confirmed by the killings of Yefimovich, Jeff Unsworth, and Theo."

Colson stared at Ellis thoughtfully.

"I don't want to take any chances till the report's finished," Ellis said.

"How will you do your report?"

"I'll check into a hotel in Washington, get myself a typewriter, and courier the report to you in Langley the moment I'm through."

"We'll need to talk about your report," Colson said.

"I'll come in after you've read it and I've collected Theo's file."

Colson stroked his chin, still thinking. "All right, Drew, but I want the report and Theo's file tonight."

"You'll have them." Ellis got to his feet. "I'll call you the moment I'm through."

Colson got to his feet. "Do that." He put an arm on Ellis's shoulder. "And once again, sorry about Theo."

82

Ellis had Langley put a trace on the Cougar, then spent the rest of the afternoon laboriously writing his report in the hotel room he always used while in Washington on Agency business. The report was nine legal pages long, and when he finished he photocopied it at a store down the street. He sent one copy by Agency courier to Colson and retained the other.

It was nearly seven when he returned home to find an anxious Loren waiting for him. He told her what had happened and that he would have to go back.

"You're sure you can trust this Colson?" she asked.

"I think so. We trained together. We've worked together. Jim's no Red agent."

She'd made a light dinner, and while they ate told him about Makram and that she'd checked his last two addresses. Like Vassilos, Makram had moved without leaving a forwarding address, and there hadn't been any magazine subscriptions for her to check. She'd also spoken to Sara Widdell. Two weeks before he died, her husband had dined with someone

who'd offered twelve million dollars for his system. Widdell
had turned the man down.

"Perhaps he decided to steal what he couldn't buy,"
Loren said, and told Ellis that if he loaned her his photos of
Widdell, she would spend the next day checking out restau-
rants in Georgetown.

Ellis gave her the photos, got Theo's file, and drove back
to Washington.

Shortly after nine an Agency limousine collected him
from the hotel and took him to Langley. Two uniformed
guards met him at the entrance and escorted him to Colson's
office. Colson was in shirt-sleeves, his fair hair tousled, his
boyish blue eyes faintly reddened. "Come in Drew, come in."
He waved graciously. "Take a pew."

When Ellis was seated, Colson said, "You've done an
excellent job and your report's first class. He looked directly
at Ellis. "But I'm going to have to ask you to step down."

Ellis studied Colson's face carefully. There was no guile
in it. "If I've done such a good job, why?"

"Because I don't think the way to solve this case is to
pussyfoot around the way Theo was. I believe it's more time
consuming, and potentially more prejudicial to the office, to
go around looking for Widdell's computer system than to find
Zonda and break him.

"Finding Zonda is a routine job calling for legwork and
manpower rather than the intellectual or investigative resources. It's too big a job for one man, and frankly, it would
be a waste of time for you to participate in a manhunt."

"I could at least help," Ellis said. "I know what Zonda
looks like."

Colson shook his head. "I couldn't let you do that. The
fact is, you were separated from the service because of what
your file describes as an obsessional instability concerning
Zonda. With that on record, it's more than my career is
worth to let you participate in a hunt for him. Just imagine
the repercussions if you found each other, if one of you killed
the other. No, Drew, with the best will in the world, I've got
to take you off the case."

Ellis said, "Things have changed since, Jim. I no longer
want to kill Zonda. All I want to do is bring him to justice,
not take revenge."

"I believe you," Colson said, quickly. "But I cannot

ignore the record. If you were in my place, you'd do exactly what I'm doing."

"Except I wouldn't go after Zonda. I think going after the system is better."

"If we do it that way," Colson replied, "we get closer to investigating the candidates—and risk revealing our involvement—and we'd also rely too much on Professor Eastman. What if the codes have been changed, or if Professor Eastman doesn't recognize the system? After all, she last worked with Widdell ten years go. I think we're better off going after Zonda, Drew. Honestly, I do." Colson added, "We won't be needing Professor Eastman. Could you see that she returns safely to Toronto and let me have a note on her expenses."

So that was it, Ellis thought. Good-bye Agency. Good-bye Loren. Then he remembered how Theo had died and said, "You can't run it from here, Jim. You've got a leak that killed both Theo and Yefimovich. There's no way you can run this operation in-house without the opposition knowing. Whether you like it or not, you've been penetrated."

Colson blinked rapidly. There was a moment of pallor under his usually healthy ruddiness. "There's no evidence to show that Theo or Yefimovich were betrayed by us," he said.

"Evidence? Why don't you simply look at the facts! Only half a dozen people knew Yefimovich was coming to America, and Yefimovich got killed. Only half a dozen people knew Theo was going to Toronto, and Theo got killed. Come off it, Jim. There's a mole in the office!"

"There must be some other explanation."

"What?"

Colson tugged at his lower lip before replying. "The Russians could have tagged Yefimovich in Moscow. And we have no evidence that Theo's death is linked to Yefimovich or this case. In fact, all the evidence so far points to a local hit. Theo worked in Toronto and Ottawa immediately after the war, and right now the RCMP is checking that angle."

Ellis stared at Colson. Was he denying the existence of a mole because it was an embarrassment to a new director? he wondered, or was there something else? "Who's taking over the case?" Ellis asked.

Colson smiled sadly. "A team, Drew. I'm putting in a whole team to replace you."

83

All the way from Langley he wrestled with his disappointment. He'd wanted to finish the case. He'd wanted to ensure that he and Loren were safe, and also wanted to spend more time with Loren. But now it was over. Finished. All that was left was to follow procedure for the last time, hand over his typewriter, carbons, and page notes, drive back and tell Loren.

The hotel wasn't the last word in luxury. But it was anonymous and it had memories. An agent's home away from home. His room was the last before the corridor made a forty-five degree turn past four more rooms. He slid the key into the lock.

The noise of the lock turning almost drowned the slight hiss above his head. Something light and soft brushed his nose. Gasping as the thin wire tightened about his neck, he pushed his elbows out but they hit nothing. He felt blood spurt around his neck as the savage pull of the wire threatened to decapitate him. He rose to his toes and his shoulders crashed into a body as he leaned backward to ease the pressure on his neck.

He was choking. His collar felt like a band of fire. There was no use pulling at the wire. He wouldn't be able to get his fingers underneath it, and if he did, they'd only be severed. He leaned his weight against his assailant, pretending to slump. His pulse pounded in his ears and the air trapped in his lungs threatened to explode.

Over the frantic drumming in his ears, he heard the sob of his assailant's indrawn breath, and he smelled something... ancient and musty, mingled with stale, harsh tobacco and sweat. It was the sort of body smell he imagined Zonda would have.

Zonda! He could not allow himself to be killed by Zonda! Not now! There were desperate gurgling noises in his throat, and the pulse in his head was threatening to drum him senseless. Remembering he had shot Zonda in the knee, he swung his foot out and planted it firmly on the man's instep.

The man wriggled against him. The wire continued to saw at his throat, sending sharp droplets of pain like spilled acid across his neck.

He kicked his heel into the assailant's shin, slammed it down into the instep again, and the man screamed with pain but held on. Ellis raised his foot again, but this time swung it outside the line of the man's body. He felt the man raise his left foot in anticipation of the crushing blow to his instep, felt him shake as he stood unbalanced...then Ellis swung his foot sideways, sweeping the man's ankle away.

The assailant's hands flew apart momentarily and Ellis pulled forward, breaking free. He turned to see the man struggling for balance, and Ellis reached for his shoulders.

The assailant kicked out furiously, and the flying foot caught Ellis in the groin. An excruciating, nerve-twisting pain ballooned up into his kidneys. His stomach wrenched and he felt himself folding over. He staggered forward on legs like damp rope, bent double, hunching his shoulders up to his head, ducking and weaving instinctively like a boxer.

He spun as the man pushed past him, heard the footsteps, still uneven, stutter down the stairs. Ellis lumbered after him, past the elevator, and into the stairwell. But he was too late; the man was already two floors down, a dark-suited figure limping furiously.

Ellis staggered back to his room, certain now that his assailant had been Zonda. He lurched to his bathroom. His neck was bleeding, his collar and shirt stained with blood, but the cut wasn't deep and did not entirely circumscribe his neck. He removed his jacket and shirt, washed himself, took antiseptic from the first-aid kit in the bathroom locker, cleaned the cuts and taped them over. Turning his coat collar up over the soiled shirt, he went back to the bedroom. Zonda had known where he was!

Had he been traced, or had the leak come from the OCI? From Colson? He put away the thought. He had known Jim Colson for as long as he'd been at the Agency. Jim Colson's field record was as successful as his own. Jim Colson was no Communist infiltrator. But if not Jim, who?

Nearly everyone at OCI knew agents who used the

hotel, he thought. There was the driver of the limousine, the couriers, the Agency staff that dispatched them, the persons who'd assigned his code number and entered it into the rota books, anyone who accessed the books—the list was endless, and all knew he was at the hotel. Any one of them could have betrayed him.

If he'd still been in service, his mandatory next step would be to inform the Agency. But he was no longer in service. In any ease, what would Colson do if he told the Agency?

The phone rang. Ellis hesitated. Could it be the Russians checking to see if Zonda had succeeded? Or a check from a second killer? Or the mole within the Agency? Or merely someone complaining about the noise. He picked up the phone.

"Mr. Ellis?"

"Who's this?"

"My name is Towson. I'm sorry to call you so late. I believe you left a request for a motor-vehicle trace earlier this afternoon."

It was the Agency! Ellis couldn't believe it. "That's right," he said cautiously.

"Could I have your authorization number, sir?"

It was incredible. He was off the case but his codes hadn't been cancelled. Ellis gave him the code.

"Thank you, sir," Towson said politely. "I'm sorry we didn't get back to you earlier. When I came on duty half an hour ago, I found that for some reason your request had been overlooked. So I got the Bureau of Motor Vehicles to XPD it."

"Good man," Ellis said. "I shall remember this."

"We try to be of service, sir." He gave Ellis the registration details and descriptions of sixteen Cougars registered in Virginia with the letters S and L and the digits nine and eight. Ellis started to shake as he read the list. Only one of the sixteen cars was green and had been registered in the past year. The green Cougar that had pushed Steve Widdell off the road was registered to the Frederick Corporation, a proprietary company of the CIA!

84

Zonda tottered through the darkened streets toward his car as fast as his damaged knee would let him. His knee hurt and his hands and shoulders ached from the effort he'd made to garrot the American agent.

If he'd used a gun, the American would be dead. He was better with a gun than a garotte, and he'd told Pomarev that. But Pomarev had insisted the agent be garotted. The agent had worked in Europe, and Pomarev had wanted the investigators to think that his murder was linked to his previous activities there. Some hope! The agent was still alive, and would have been dead if Pomarev had only let him use a gun.

Zonda was getting tired of Pomarev. While grateful for making him operational again, since he'd come to America he'd become nothing more than Pomarev's gofer. Go here. Do that. Meet me at Dino's. Use the Datsun, not the Volvo. Kill that man. Kill this man. Kill in precisely this way, at this time, in this place. He was no longer a professional but a mechanic. For him the fascinating thing about his work had always been the planning, not the actual act itself. And now, despite the fact that he'd killed more people on this assignment than he had in the year before he'd retired, there was no magic to it anymore. Anyone with a strong nerve and a stomach for blood could do what he was doing. Pomarev needed a butcher, he thought, not an assassin.

With relief he saw his car where he'd left it. He limped up to it and opened the door. Because of the ragged sound of his own breathing, he did not hear the men till it was too late. Nor because of his fatigue were his reactions fast enough. He heard the whir of the blackjack a split second before it hit him.

Forcing himself to turn, he glimpsed the three men and raised his tired arms in desperation. But they were no defense against the rain of blows that broke through his guard

and smashed into his stomach and kidneys while the blackjack swung mercilessly at his head. Muggers! How ironic for
the great Zonda to be mugged. He slumped against the car.
The blows battering him into unconsciousness.

85

From a phone booth near the hotel Ellis called Loren.
Ignoring the surprise and alarm in her voice, he told her to
leave at once, taking only money, changes of clothes for both
of them, and the gun and to meet him at the Hearns Motel
past junction 19 of the Beltway.

An hour later he saw her edge the rented Chevy past the
motel office and hestitantly pull to a stop beside the Porsche.
He led her into the room. She gasped as she saw his blood
stained collar.

"Darling, what—"

"Relax, it's over for now." He lay down on one of the beds
and began telling her what had happened with Colson and at
the hotel afterward. "The Agency betrayed me to Zonda," he
said, "and I suspect that the Agency is involved with the
KGB in the theft of Widdell's system."

"You could have died," she said in a monotone.

"I wouldn't let them kill me." He took her hand and pulled
her down beside him on the bed. "Not now, when I've found
you." He stroked the hair at the nape of her neck. "We're
caught in the middle," he explained gently. "Right now we've
no one to turn to and nowhere to run. Even if Colson finds
Zonda, the traitors within the Agency might stop Jim the way
they stopped Theo, and then go on with whatever the KGB is
planning."

"What do we do, Drew?" she asked, staring at the ceiling.
"We won't be able to keep on living like this."

"It shouldn't be long," he said confidently. From now on
they would stay in motels, moving to a different one each
night, and tomorrow he would contact the Frederick Corporation to see how to tie them in with Widdell. "Everything

we do, everything we find out, brings us closer to the truth,"
he said. "And once we know that, we can stop them."

She sighed. "I wish I could feel so positive." She pulled
herself up on the bed and looked at him. "How badly are you
hurt?"

"Not badly at all. It's a superficial cut, that's all." He drew
her back down beside him. "I'm sorry it's turning out like
this. I wish everything could be simpler and safer."

Her fingers played with the hair on his chest. "You're doing
the best you can, my love." Suddenly she sat up and kissed
his chest, taking his right nipple inside her lips. Her hand
reached down between his legs. He lay back and ran his
hands over her head and body. After a while she said softly,
"Tomorrow I'm going to try and find the restaurant where
Steve was offered twelve million."

He thought that might be dangerous, then realized it was
no more dangerous than sitting in a motel room waiting for
him. Full of a sudden, frantic desperation, he pulled her
head to his and kissed her on the mouth. The length of her
body pressed against him, her breasts and belly soft and
invitingly warm. Quickly he sat up and slipped out of his
clothes, hearing the soft rustle as she threw her clothes by
the bed. He pulled her naked body to him, reached between
her legs and touched her. Her mouth opened to receive his.
Her body opened. He was surrounded by her molten moist-
ness, and the comfort was splendid.

86

March 1, 1988

Ellis paced the motel room, thinking. Earlier that morning, with a lingering kiss and an admonition to be careful,
Loren had left to look for the restaurant in which Widdell had
been offered the money. Ellis picked up the phone and dialed.

"The Frederick Corporation, good morning. How can I
help you?"

Ellis lowered his voice into a tobacco-strained rasp. "Hi, honey, who's the wise guy in your setup running the green Cougar?"

"I'm sorry, I can't give you that information, caller. Who are you?"

"The motor pool, honey, over at Big El. Tell me, what is this guy doing with the Cougar? I've got bills here for a recon engine for it and two gearboxes! Is he going into business for himself or something?"

"I don't know, but I can't tell—"

"He should never have ordered them in the first place, you know that. Regulations clearly state that kind of expenditure has got to be passed by us first. And that car doesn't need no reconditioned engine. It's only six months old! And as for two gearboxes—this guy must be on the make or something."

"I'm sure Mr. Karowitz will be able to explain everything," the girl said. "Who shall—"

"So his name's Karowitz is it? Does he have a handle to it?"

"Yes. Mike. If you give me your name and extension I'll have him—"

"No need, hon. I'm going out right now testing one of those hot-rod Buick Regals we've lifted from the FBI. Why don't I call this Karowitz soon as I get back?" Without giving the girl time to reply, Ellis put the phone down.

An hour later he called back. He recognized the girl's voice. "Hi hon, those Buicks are a gas. Would you believe it, one fifty an hour! You ever been at that speed, hon?"

"Never," the girl breathed. "One hundred fifty miles and hour. . . where do you do it?"

"We've got our own test track. If you're very nice to me, I'll take you out there one day and show you what it's like to hit one fifty on the straight. Is Karowitz in?"

"Sure. I'll put you through."

"I won't forget about the test track."

Moments later a deep voice said, "Mike Karowitz. What's all this shit about—"

"Reconditioned engines. I've got a bill here, $1792 including tax and an order dated February sixth. You had the car the sixth of February, did you?"

"Yeah, sure. But look—"

"Mike, you're in trouble."

"For fuck sake, man, I didn't order any reconditioned engines! That goddamn car's only six months old!"

"I'm not talking about reconditioned engines, Mike. I'm talking about murder!"

"Mur—What the hell? Who are you?"

"For the present, a friend. Don't hang up on me, Mike. I'm looking into the death of Steve Widdell."

"Go fuck yourself, man. I don't know any Steve Widdell."

"I've got witnesses, and I've got paint scrapings of the Cougar from Widdell's car."

"Who are you?"

"I work for the same people you do. Only my people didn't want Steve Widdell killed. You got that? My people are very angry that Steve Widdell was killed and they're going to do something about it. Starting with you."

"I don't know nothing—"

"You're going to be hamburger meat in a very small sandwich, Mike. I think we should meet and talk. I think I can fix something for you and your partner."

"You go to hell!" Karowitz shouted.

"Sure. And while I'm doing that, you just work out who gave me your name."

"What the fuck are you talking about?"

"Work it out for yourself, Mike. There's a lot of very frightened people standing right behind you. And one of them's going to talk, even if you won't. One of them's going to tell us how the two of you killed Widdell, put him in his car, and drove him off the road. And he's going to tell us why."

"You're full of shit," Karowitz grunted. "You know nothing!"

"It's simple when you put the pieces together, Mike. Widdell was murdered. You and the other guy did it. You were carrying out what you thought were orders. Except those orders were contaminated. My people want to find out who ordered you to do it. That's all."

"I got nothing to say to you," Karowitz growled.

"You have to talk to me," Ellis said. "I'm all there is between you and a rap for murder one. Judges these days don't accept carrying out orders as a valid defense, Mike. If you're found guilty, it's life."

"No one'll believe you," Karowitz replied belligerently.

"You want to try me on that? You want me to take the evidence I have, the paint and the witness, to the FBI? You think after I've done that someone's going to stand up and say, 'Don't hang Mike Karowitz. I'm the one who ordered him to do it.' You really think someone's going to do that, do you, Mike?"

"You're talking nonsense," Karowitz said. "You're trying to—"

Ellis asked softly, "You got written authority for what you did?"

In the silence that followed, Ellis felt he could hear Karowitz thinking, that he could feel Karowitz's throat going dry. "And if I talk to you, what?"

"We'll make a deal. My people aren't interested in you. They're interested in the people who gave you unsigned orders."

"And if we meet, what guarantees do I have?"

"None. Except you've got a damned sight better chance of surviving than you do now."

Cautiously Karowitz said, "I think I want to take a look at you, feller. Where do you want to meet?"

"I'll call you in an hour. And I want to see both of you. You and your partner."

"What if he doesn't want to come?"

"Convince him," Ellis said. "Your life depends on it."

87

If there was anything more clumsy or more frightening than one terrified Russian, Simenon thought, it was three terrified Russians. The three men he'd sent after Zonda had brought the assassin back, senseless and, in the opinion of the embassy doctor, if not for the fortunate thickness of his skull and the robustness of his constitution, beyond salvage. The purple-faced, sore-bodied killer woke groggily, vomited, and went to sleep again. When he woke the second time, he stared wonderingly around the room and asked, "Where the fuck am I?"

Zonda's head hurt less than his body. The room's only other occupant was a granite-faced man in his late fifties, reading *Novosti*. He looked up as Zonda moved, and asked, "How do you feel?"

Zonda stretched exploratively. "I'll be okay. What happened? And where am I?"

Simenon said, "There was a mistake. I wanted to talk to you and sent some of our people, who, I'm afraid, were overawed by your reputation and became overenthusiastic." His face set into a rigid smile. "The men are being returned home forthwith. And adequate compensation will be made for your pain and discomfort."

Zonda lay back on the pillows. He was with Russians, so presumably he was in a safe house or in the embassy. His companion looked like top KGB brass. His face was vaguely familiar. And then the man introduced himself.

"I'm Deputy Director Simenon."

Fuck your mother, Zonda thought. Deputy directors of the KGB were persons you crossed the road to avoid. What could a deputy director want with him? He struggled to sit up. His body felt like a large, single bruise. "Why did you want to see me?"

"I wanted to offer you a job. The Foreign Intelligence School is looking for someone with your experience to select and train recruits for Department 5. The post is normally held till retirement age, and while it calls for considerable field experience, requires only moderate physical activity. It carries an entitlement to an annual holiday of three weeks and the use of a villa on the Black Sea, a weekend dacha at Kuntsevo, the use of KGB stores, and foreign exchange and travel permits for holidays abroad once every two years. I think it is a post you should accept."

"I would like to," Zonda said. "But I am currently seconded to the deputy director of the Political Service."

"Ah, yes," Simenon said. "How do you get on with our friend Pomarev?" He smiled and added, "You can tell me the truth. You see, if am to negotiate your release for this post, I shall have to know everthing you are doing for Comrade Pomarev."

88

Loren was getting tired of the sight, and more important, the smell of restaurants. On the basis that someone with twelve million dollars to spare would eat only at the most expensive places, she visited a number of elegant establishments, some aloof, some politely helpful, and some closed. On the basis that someone with twelve million dollars might have special tastes, she called on some of the more avant-garde establishments, where she was greeted with surprise, skepticism, rudeness, or the offer of a drink. But no one recognized Steve Widdell's photograph, and no one could remember serving him any night of the week.

Until she got to Ruggeiro's, that is. Tony Ruggeiro immediately recognized Steve Widdell. "He was one of my best customers, signora, a very lovely man."

Loren asked, "Do you remember when he last dined here?"

"That would have been about the end of January. He came here with Mrs. Widdell. And then, before that, there was the private room—that was the night he dined with Mr. Cas Hardinger."

Cas Hardinger! Twelve million dollars! Loren couldn't wait to tell Ellis.

89

Ellis thought Karowitz would either play it straight or would inform the Agency. If he informed the Agency, they would use the meeting to set a trap. Which was exactly what

Ellis would have done if Widdell had been his operation. So he had to plan to dispose of an Agency back-up, a second car with two or three men.

He concentrated on planning. The Cougar was his only means of recognition. Which meant the meeting had to be in a parking lot, because parking lots were open and any back-up could be easily spotted. He'd have to use an underground lot, which would disrupt any radio communication between Karowitz and a back-up team.

Ellis thought for a while about locations. Then he checked out of the motel and drove to the National Sheraton. He'd stayed there on his service visits to Washington and knew the hotel's parking lot, burrowed deep underground, had only a single entrance and exit. He drove three floors down along sharply angled ramps to the lowest level of the lot, parked and took the elevator to the lobby.

The lobby was hushed, with its usual quota of strolling guests and attentive, brown-uniformed bellboys. Ellis used a phone near the reception desk to call Karowitz. "I cut this line in thirty seconds," he began.

"Yes, but—"

"No buts. Is your friend coming with you?"

"Yes."

"What's your friend's name?"

"What? Oh, uh, Tony Ulner."

"Right. I want Ulner with you all the time. And I want you to bring the Cougar. I don't want any followers, or anyone else monitoring the meeting. I'll be watching you from the time you leave your office, so don't try anything clever. You breach any of these conditions, and we don't meet."

"Okay, okay, I hear you."

"Fine. Then leave now. Drive to East Arlington and go south on Columbia Pike. Past the Navy Annex and the Sheraton you'll come to an intersection with Scott Street. Four blocks beyond that you'll come to a shopping mall with a pizza parlor called Perfect Pizza. Park in the mall. Go in the pizza parlor and have a pizza."

"Sure," Karowitz said. "Any particular kind?"

Ellis couldn't make out if Karowitz was being cocky or resentful, and decided it was too late to matter. "I recommend the Four Seasons," he said. "Now repeat what I told you."

"Columbia Pike, Scott Street, park inside the mall, have a Four Seasons pizza at Perfect Pizza."

"What else?"

"I bring the Cougar and my friend. We tell no one about the meeting and make sure we aren't followed."

"Good. You try anything, and both of you will be talking to the FBI."

"Don't worry, scout. We aren't going to try anything."

The mall he'd told Karowitz about was only a few minutes away. Ellis drove there, parked, slid down in the passenger seat and waited. Sometime later a green Cougar turned smoothly into the parking lot. There were two men in it, and its license number was the one he had checked out with Towson. Engine burbling throatily, the car drove quickly past him and parked. Karowitz and Ulner got out and looked slowly around the lot. They were both very big and very solid looking. Professional sandbaggers, Ellis thought.

Ellis cringed as their coldly appraising gaze swept first over his car then carefully over the rest of the lot. Both men gave almost imperceptible shrugs, turned and walked through the lot to the pizza parlor. Ellis waited. Four minutes later, when no one had yet followed them into the lot, Ellis eased himself upright, started his car, and drove quickly back to the Sheraton.

Even though it looked as if Karowitz might be on the level, Ellis decided he couldn't take any chances. The lowest level of the car park was still partly empty, and he parked next to the elevator, at the end of a row of four empty spaces. Taking note of the bay number, he hurried up to the lobby, called the pizza parlor and asked for Karowitz. "You've got four minutes to finish your pizzas, pay your bill, and get over to bay S163 in the Sheraton parking lot."

"Four minutes. Hell, man—"

"You'll be there with Ulner, and you'll park the Cougar nose in. Then I want you and Ulner to get out of the car and stand beside each other on the right side of the car, facing away from the car. You got that?"

"Sure. We'll be there looking like a pair of Siamese twins," Karowitz said.

Ellis slammed down the phone, raced downstairs, and moved his car away from S163. In precisely four minutes the

Cougar nosed in and parked. Fifteen seconds later Karowitz
and Ulner were standing side by side on the right of the car,
staring at the door to the elevators. Ellis opened the door and
stepped out, holding the Colt.

Karowitz and Ulner turned to watch him as he backed
along the wall enclosing the shaft. "Okay," Ellis said, coming
to a halt, "talk, and talk fast. Who have you told about this
meeting? Who's following you?"

"You didn't want us to tell anyone," the man Ellis
thought was Karowitz said. "And no, we weren't followed."

"Good. Now who put you up to killing Steve Widdell?"

"Who the fuck are you?" Ulner's snarl was low and
angry.

"My name's Drew Ellis."

"You know nothing from nothing," Ulner said.

"I know enough to put you both away for a very long
time. Now tell me who and tell me why. Otherwise get back
into your car and go. And I promise you before you reach
Langley, you'll be arrested."

"You're bluffing." Ulner said.

Karowitz asked, "How do we know we can trust you?"

"Because I'm one of you," Ellis said. He shoved the Colt
under his belt, delved in a pants pocket, and held up his
cancelled OCI ID. "Because I've been where you've been.
Because, like you, I've been used." He could see interest
replacing the veiled hostility in the two men's faces. He said,
"Hell, take a good look at me. You think I'm old enough to take
retirement?" He leaned forward, pulling his hair back from his
scalp, showing them where Zonda's bullet had gouged into it.
"That's how they retired me, folks. You want the same?"

"What the hell did you do?" Ulner asked.

"I obeyed orders, just like you. It was a different place,
but the principles were the same. I got mixed up with the
Russkis and I did too much. When what I did got embarrassing,
they tried to get rid of me. Just like they'll do to you."

"If you want us to believe that, you'll have to be more
specific," Ulner said.

That was just how he would have put it, Ellis thought.
He was beginning to like Ulner. He said, "There's no time for
that now. If you want to find out what happened, you'll have
to check it out. Most of it is on record. Now tell me about
Widdell."

Both men exchanged rapid glances and remained silent.

Ellis wondered if they were stalling. He said, "Steve Widdell wasn't the only one who was murdered, you know. Two other people have also been murdered, Lucas Amory and Dick Schaffer. They were the only other people who knew Widdell's codes. And it was Widdell's codes your people wanted, wasn't it?"

Karowitz said, "Go on."

"The only difference between the death of Widdell and the deaths of Amory and Schaffer was that they were killed by the Russians!"

Shock, disbelief, and amazement flickered in quick succession across the men's faces. Ulner said softly, "I don't believe you, Ellis. The Russians have nothing to do with this."

"We have conclusive evidence of their involvement," Ellis said. "Amory and Schaffer were killed by a professional Russian killer known as Zonda."

"I've heard of Zonda," Karowitz said. "But I'm—"

"That's why you guys had better talk," Ellis interrupted. "You're in way over your heads. You might well be working for the other side."

"No," Karowitz burst out. "You're trying to frighten us."

"It's too late for that," Ellis said. "You can talk or you can leave. But once you move out of here, you've forfeited your last chance. You're finished, both of you. Now tell me who put you on to Widdell."

Karowitz and Ulner exchanged glances. Karowitz said, "And if we talk, what guarantees can you give?"

"Nothing, except that I'll do my best for you. Which is a hell of a lot more that you've got right now."

Karowitz said, "We work for a separate division of the Agency. It's called Bildeberg."

"I've never heard of it," Ellis said.

"Few people have. It's very secret."

The background squeal of tires on the ramp above rose to a sudden, shrilling scream. There was the harsh roar of a straining engine accompanied by the dull thwack of air being parted by something solid traveling very fast. Karowitz and Ulner both looked at Ellis. In unison they shouted, "Move!"

There was a blue blur behind the two men, a shrill yelp as wheels momentarily locked. As he jumped, Ellis glimpsed a blue car with shadowy figures in the rear seat and the thin, gleaming barrels of automatic rifles protruding from the rear windows. Muzzles flashed. The confined space was filled with the deafening chatter of automatic fire. Ellis felt something burn his chest as he landed on his shoulder, between the front bumper of the Cougar and the boundary wall. Blast, flash, roar! Bullets ricocheted off concrete and metal and thwacked into flesh with the sound of axes hitting wood. From beneath the car's wheels Ellis saw Ulner and Karowitz stretched out on the floor, blood pimpling from the holes in their backs and trickling over their outstretched arms. He took out the Colt and crawled around the Cougar. The roar of engines and the scream of tires filled his ears. The car had turned and was coming back. He leaned around the wing of the Cougar and fired.

The gun bucked in his hand and the windshield of the onrushing car shattered. It snaked wildly, and for a terrifying second Ellis thought it would smash into the Cougar. Then the driver pulled the wheel around and straightened it before braking hard for the turn onto the ramps.

Ellis moved out of the cover of the car, aiming at the shadowy figures at the back. The car slewed sideways as he fired, then charged up the ramp. He ran back to the boundary wall and fired two shots at the shrieking tires above him, heard them ricochet off the concrete, heard the shrill of the tires grow fainter.

He rushed over to the fallen men. Both lay on their faces, their arms spread out, their backs cruelly punctured by the hail of fire. Ellis placed the back of his hand in front of Karowitz's mouth, felt for the pulse at the throat.

Nothing.

He moved across to Ulner. Blood was trickling from his mouth. His eyes were open. They focused on Ellis. The lips moved. "Bastards."

"Take it easy," Ellis said. "I'll get help."

"No. Wait."

Ellis picked up Ulner's wrist, knelt and waited. Ulner's pulse was irregular and his skin was clammy. His cheeks and forehead were covered with a pasty sweat.

Ulner's lips moved again. "Swear to me you're real."

"I'm real," Ellis said. "I swear that."

"This was supposed . . . to . . . be you." Ulner coughed. "The bastards turned the tables on us."

"Who?"

"The Agency. We were working for a subsection called Bildeberg. . . . They wanted . . . Widdell's system. We . . . tortured him for the codes. He died. . . . We . . . faked . . . accident."

Ulner's pulse was growing ragged. He was going fast. "Who is Bildeberg?"

"I—I wish—"

"Names," Ellis said urgently. "I want names."

"Courtney . . . he's the head honcho. There's others . . . an intelligence conduit. There's also—" Ulner's head rolled slightly. His mouth sagged open and his eyes took on the texture of iced-over pools. Ellis felt the faint throbbing beneath his finger cease.

"Ulner," he said, "you can't die on me! Not yet. Ulner, tell me who runs Bildeberg!" He leaned forward and tried to turn Ulner onto his back, felt pain in his chest as if a knife had been inserted into his ribs, felt the wetness against his own chest, gasped and nearly fell over Ulner.

90

Ellis staggered back to the car, then opened his jacket and looked. He'd been hit by a bullet, and the wound—a seeping, blood-filled hole—was soaking the entire left side of his clothing. He took out his handkerchief and wedged it against the wound. He had to find somewhere to rest before the shock wore off and the pain became intolerable; he had to find somewhere to hide before he bled to death.

Going to a hospital with a gunshot wound was impossible. Going to the Agency, equally so. Where could he find someone who would understand and believe him, someone who would not be intimidated? Think, for Heaven's sake, think! he told himself. You've spent all your adult life in intelligence. There must be someone you could go to with a bullet in your belly and say don't ask any questions but please help me because I'm your friend!

Friend! The only friend he had was Patrick Morell. Ellis drove slowly, looking for a phone booth. Finding one, he dialed the church and got through to Patrick. "It's Drew," he said. "I need help. I'm hurt and I need somewhere to rest."

"Can you make it here?"

"I think so."

"How long will you be?"

"Give me half an hour."

"Come to the house," Patrick said. "I'll be waiting for you."

It was that simple, Ellis thought. Or was it? Had Patrick's phone been bugged? Was there an Agency alert for him? Had the Agency expected him to call Patrick? He was becoming paranoid. No one could have anticipated he would call Patrick. But what if they had put a check on all his contacts. Paranoia! The wound was beginning to hurt, and he was starting to feel light-headed. He pressed the handkerchief harder against his side and forced himself to concentrate on traffic. He couldn't pass out now, not when help was so close.

Patrick lived in a small bungalow behind the low-roofed, modern-looking church. His car was parked in the driveway outside the garage. Ellis stopped behind it, and pressing the handkerchief to his side, stumbled up the wooden steps of the porch.

Almost immediately the front door opened. Ellis saw Patrick framed in the opening, then he was reaching out, helping Ellis in, holding him as they walked down a short corridor into a living room, where Patrick helped him onto a sofa.

Ellis said, "First thing, could you—"

"First thing, I'd better get you a doctor," Patrick said.

"It's a bullet wound," Ellis said. "There can be no—"

"There won't be." Patrick walked briskly from the room.

Ellis slumped against the side of the sofa and closed his eyes. When he came to, the doctor, a pleasantly open-faced young man with comfortingly warm hands, was examining him on Patrick's bed. He dressed Ellis's wound and gave him some painkillers. The bullet had chipped a rib on the way out, he explained, but caused no other damage. Ellis was suffering from shock and loss of blood, and would be okay in a couple of days if he rested.

"Of course, you'll stay here," Patrick said. "So that I can make sure you'll rest."

Ellis forced a grin. "Thanks. But there's some things I ought to tell you."

"Later," Patrick said. "You're slurring, and right now you need to rest." Gently he pushed Ellis back on the bed.

Ellis told Patrick he was due to meet Loren at the Best Western Ambassador Inn on the Beltway at five o'clock.

"You aren't going anywhere," Patrick said firmly. "But I'm putting on my best dog collar, taking your car, and going to collect her."

91

Later that evening, over bowls of minestrone and platefuls of spaghetti, Loren told the men what she'd discovered, and Ellis told her and Patrick everything that had happened.

Patrick's face clouded. "This is heavy stuff, Drew, and there isn't a lot you can do about it. You can't take much more of this."

"So who do we take it to?" Loren asked.

"The Agency or the FBI."

"The Agency is out," Ellis said quickly. "The OCI is penetrated, and Theo, Yefimovich, and Jeff Unsworth all died because they were betrayed."

"What about another division in the Agency?" Patrick asked.

"Karowitz and Ulner worked for another division," Ellis replied. "We don't know how far the corruption spreads. We have no way of knowing if the person we go to isn't already connected with Bildeberg."

"Let's take it to the FBI," Patrick said. "They'd love a chance of investigating the Agency."

"But how do they investigate the Agency without talking to someone within the Agency? And how do we know that person is clear? Theo's death was organized by someone on the side. If the FBI talk to the wrong people, that could happen to us."

"And how do we persuade them to believe us?" Loren asked. "All we have so far is a theory about the deaths of Amory and Widdell, a theory that their deaths are connected to those of Goddard, Yefimovich, and Unsworth. We have no hard evidence of anything. And if the OCI wants to cover up the connection, all they have to do is produce Drew's file and say he's got Zonda on the brain."

"So what do we do?" Ellis asked.

"We do it ourselves," Patrick replied.

"Ourselves! Look, Patrick, I'm not involving you in this any further. You've already done more than enough and run too many risks."

"Stopping men like Pomarev is God's business," Patrick said. "Have you thought what sort of a country we'll have if our president is controlled by Communists? Are you aware what they have done to religions everywhere?" Patrick shook his head. "If you two are the only allies I have, so be it."

"But we still need a plan," Ellis pointed out.

"That's simple enough. First of all let's find out who or what Bildeberg is. Then let's go after Cas Hardinger. Let's ask him if he did offer Widdell twelve million dollars, and find out if he's connected to Bildeberg. Loren and I can start some preliminary research now, and you can join in as soon as you're better."

Ellis asked, "Have you considered that this could get violent?"

"Yes. That isn't a problem. I can take care of myself."

Ellis moved stiffly and pointed to his chest. "There could be more shooting."

"I have a gun." Patrick unlocked a cupboard and took out a Colt automatic. "Pray God I never have to use it."

92

March 3, 1988

For two days while Ellis rested, they tried to work out who or what Bildeberg was. Discreet inquiries to contacts at the Agency brought no response. A guarded phonecall to Graydon had the same result. Reference books from the small library farther up the street only informed them that Bildeberg was a town in what was now East Germany. In desperation Loren turned to the telephone directory.

And found it.

The Bildeberg Institute as large as life, with offices near Georgetown University.

Loren went there and looked at a mock neo-Palladian building. She watched people go in and out, some old, some young, all academic and scholarly. She went in and asked what the institute did. It provided economic intelligence, she was told, and was given a brochure which showed a list of trustees that looked like a list from *Who's Who*. The Bildeberg Institute couldn't have anything to do with the Agency, Ellis decided: the Bildeberg Institute couldn't have anything to do with manipulating the election of a president. Except the head honcho, patriot, and intimate of at least four presidents was named Courtney.

93

The library was a richly comfortable room bathed in light that slanted through the tall windows. As Ellis walked stiffly to the halfway point between the door and the desk, the trim, well-tailored figure of Ambassador Courtney advanced toward him.

That morning, through Tom Graydon, Ellis had arranged a sterile phone call to the ambassador and asked to see him as soon as possible. The ambassador had sounded hesitant until Ellis had said the matter concerned Bildeberg and couldn't wait. "If it can't wait, I suppose I'd better see you today," Courtney had mused aloud, and asked Ellis to see him at two.

The ambassador was a small, sharp-featured man with wiry gray curls encircling his head like a halo. His eyes brimmed with intelligence and warmth, and his handshake was crisp and firm. "It is so good of you to come, Mr. Ellis. I hope you had no trouble finding us."

"It is good of you to see me at such short notice, Mr. Ambassador."

When the two of them were seated, Courtney said, "You wanted to see me about Bildeberg."

"Yes," Ellis replied. "I work for the Office of Counter Intelligence and am currently investigating the murder of Steve Widdell and the theft of his computer system."

Ellis added, "Two days ago two men, Mike Karowitz and Tony Ulner, were shot and killed. Karowitz worked for the Frederick Corporation, which is an Agency undercover corporation. I believe the two men were killed to prevent them from talking to me. I was shot too."

"My dear fellow, how terrible. Are you sufficiently recovered now?"

Ellis ignored the ambassador's question and went on. "Before he died, Tony Ulner told me he'd been working for a special CIA section called Bildeberg, which was responsible for the accidental death of Widdell and the theft of his tapes."

"And because of the name Bildeberg, you have come to me." Courtney leaned back, smiling, and crossed his legs neatly. "Let me tell you first of all, we have nothing to do with the CIA."

Courtney poured coffee, tea for Ellis, and offered sandwiches. He said, "Our Bildeberg was formed during the Depression by men of goodwill to help where government was not able to. It was originally thought that once the depression ended, the need for the organization would also end. But that proved not to be the case. There are always needs in our society that a government cannot see or completely fulfill."

"What kinds of needs?" Ellis asked.

"The elimination of poverty, the spread of education, the advancement of science. These are the areas in which Bildeberg renders specific help. It funds charities. It offers scholarships. It endows chairs of learning. It has devoted considerable resources to the spread of computer literacy, the development of genetic biology, and the advancement of ergonomic design. I personally am concerned with the geopolitical aspects of Bildeberg, the reduction of tension between East and West, the creation of a dialogue between the First World and the Third. Do you realize, Mr. Ellis, that in thirty years time nearly a third of the population in the underdeveloped countries will be starving?"

"How is Bildeberg financed?" Ellis asked.

Courtney smiled. "I see what you're getting at. No, Bildeberg is not funded overtly or covertly by the CIA. The source of Bildeberg's income is the sizable trust fund created many years ago when Bildeberg was founded, donations, and payment for the work we do in providing economic intelligence."

"So what has Bildeberg to do with the death of Steve Widdell?"

"Nothing, Mr. Ellis." Courtney gave a delicate shrug. "I do not know either of your informants, so I cannot tell you why they spoke of Bildeberg."

"Has Bildeberg any political connection with the Agency?" The ambassador shook his head slowly in mild disapproval. "Bildeberg isn't a political organization, Mr. Ellis. Some of its members, through choice or duty, are concerned with politics or are employees of the Agency. But their only use to Bildeberg is in their private capacity."

Ellis said, "Before he died, Ulner mentioned your name in connection with Bildeberg."

"My name?" Courtney's eyebrows arched. "Are you sure of that, Mr. Ellis? After all, Mr. Ulner was dying, and both of you were subject to considerable stress. Was it possible that you did not correctly hear what Mr. Ulner was telling you?"

"I heard what I heard," Ellis said. "Was Ulner working for you?"

"No." The ambassador smiled and shook his head. "No. Mr. Ulner was not working for our Bildeberg."

"You mean to say..." Ellis couldn't believe the simple evasiveness of the ambassador's answer. "You're telling me that—"

"It is the only possible answer," Courtney said. "You see, our Bildeberg is composed of men like me, old men with little physical fire or love of physical violence left in them. We would not dream of shooting at young men like you." Smiling, the ambassador got to his feet. "I'm sorry I cannot be of more help, Mr. Ellis. Perhaps if you ask among your colleagues at the Agency, you might find their Bildeberg."

Without quite being aware of how he got there, Ellis found himself at the door of the library. As if by some invisible signal, the attendant opened the door and held out Ellis's coat to him.

94

The wires connected to the microphone in her panties itched, and the tape holding the wires pulled irritatingly at the tiny hairs below her navel. Loren forced herself to sit still and concentrate on what Cas Hardinger was saying.

They had decided that while Ellis saw Ambassador Courtney, Loren, who'd once worked on a high school paper,

should talk to Cas Hardinger using the cover of a journalist
ostensibly working on a story of Corporate Takeovers. Patrick
had a friend on the *Washington Globe* who had fixed the
documentation and the appointment, and Ellis had procured
the taping equipment. "Don't worry about a thing," Patrick's
friend had advised Loren. "Simply ask the same questions
you normally would, except be a lot ruder and a lot more
aggressive."

Which wasn't easy with an itching crotch and a fluttering
heart, and being wired to Patrick somewhere outside the
MatCir Building, hoping he could hear her and would be
able to intervene if anything went wrong.

Hardinger was small and testy, with eyes like flashing
electric signs and a nose you could slice bread with. "Yes,
Miss West," he was saying, "I did have dinner with Steve
Widdell on the twenty-first of January, and I did offer to
purchase his computer system."

"For twelve million dollars?"

"Plus stock options and profit shares." Hardinger appeared to force himself to sit still for a moment. "Unfortunately, before the deal could be finalized, Steve Widdell
died."

"So Steve Widdell accepted your offer?"

Hardinger's eyes flashed. "Yes." His narrow mouth coiled.
"It isn't every day one gets offered twelve million dollars."

"Would you say you were paying Widdell more than the
market price?"

"Let's say I was paying Widdell what his system was
worth to me."

"But more than the market price?" Loren insisted.

Hardinger's eyes swept angrily over her and darted
away. "What I was buying was Widdell's market research and
polling expertise. It is expertise my companies spend a lot of
money purchasing. I thought it would be commercially ad-
vantageous to own the company best capable of providing
such expertise, and my offer was based on the worth of that
purchase to my corporation, and not on any outside valuation."

"What about the political aspects of Widdell's system?"

"What about them?"

"What did you intend to do with them?"

"As I understood it, Widdell's so-called political system
was simply an application of polling and market research

techniques to elections. My view is that those techniques are more profitably confined to industry."

"So you had no interest in the political aspects of Widdell's system?"

Hardinger's smile was only a molar away from a snarl. "I am a businessman, Miss West, not a politician."

"Of course. Do you know of an organization called Bildeberg?"

"No," Hardinger said, firmly and forthrightly. "I do not."

95

After Ellis left, Courtney gave instructions that he was not to be disturbed and drew the curtains in the library, shutting out the brilliant day. He had a need to think, and for what he needed to think about, darkness was better.

Many years ago, when Bildeberg had been founded, the object of the society had been service to the community and the people; and over the years Bildeberg had indeed made opportunity available to people of talent, provided welfare for those who deserved it, educated those who would profit most by it. Over the years, too, Bildeberg had grown. It had become more powerful and more influential, and with that growth had come an erosion of the soul. The only thing binding the people who comprised Bildeberg today was unlimited ambition, a love of power, and a fascination with manipulation. Bildeberg was no longer the caring organization of sixty years ago. The core of the organization was gone; it had no center of the spirit, only a center of power.

And that had been his fault as much as anyone else's, Courtney reflected. He had participated in and presided over the erosion of Bildeberg's essential values. What had begun with minor compromises and temporary accommodations, had grown to exceptions of principle, to opportunism and expediency, to . . . to murder and treason!

He should never have given his approval to the seizure of Widdell's system he told himself. But what alternative had there been? They had to take the system. And the other members would have done it whether Courtney had agreed with them or not.

That final compromise of principle, as well as attaining the right objectives through the wrong means, had brought about the present moral impasse. What had happened to belief in oneself and in one's God, the beliefs that had underpinned not only the original members of Bildeberg but the founders of the nation?

Gone, he thought, all gone. Morality had been replaced by expediency, patriotism by treachery, the enrichment of life by slaughter. He stared into space. They were lost men, dominated by greed, fear, and the lust for power. And Bildeberg—his Bildeberg—had murdered on a massive scale! Bildeberg was conspiring with Russians to elect a KGB candidate to the presidency! Bildeberg—his Bildeberg—had committed treason!

He could not allow it to go on. Somehow, the men of Bildeberg had to be stopped—but without compromising the name of Bildeberg. Which meant the individuals had to be stopped. He picked up his private phone and dialed the number through which Drew Ellis had made contact. He would use that young man to stop Bildeberg. At the appropriate time.

96

March 5, 1988

His side still hurt. Ellis parked outside the Holiday Inn and went into the coffee shop. Patrick had gone through the Bildeberg brochures Loren had brought back and had the bright idea of checking if Jonathan Bradley, Bildeberg's research director and resident computer genius, had ever visited Widdell. A brief conversation with Pat Cleary had confirmed that Bradley had visited not once, but four times, and that on each visit he'd spent a considerable amount of time finding out everything he could about the system.

"Let's talk to him," Patrick had said, which was why earlier that afternoon Ellis had called Bradley and told him he had a message from Hardinger concerning Bildeberg that was so important it could only be delivered face to face. Ellis had insisted that Bradley contact no one and meet him right away.

He recognized Bradley from the brochure picture, noting that Bradley was heavier and not as boyish as he'd been depicted. "I must say, this is most irregular," Bradley protested as Ellis joined him. Ellis noted he rubbed his palms and fingers along the front of his thighs, and that his forehead had just been wiped dry. "Cas Hardinger must know we do not meet with third parties like this."

Ellis said, "Outsiders know of your involvement with the Widdell tapes."

Bradley paled. "What outsiders?"

"Me," Ellis said.

Bradley stared at him perplexedly. "And you've been talking to Hardinger?"

"Friends of mine have."

"So what's any of this got to do with me?"

"Steve Widdell was murdered," Ellis said. "I think you are an accessory to his death."

"Ridiculous! I had nothing to do with Widdell's dea—" Bradley's mouth froze in mid-phrase. With a conscious effort, he closed it. "Who the hell are you? You're not one of Hardinger's people. Who are you?"

Ellis flashed his ID. "Office of Counter Intelligence," he said quickly, putting the card away. "We're looking into Widdell's death."

"Office of Counter Intelligence, what's that? A branch of the FBI?"

"No," Ellis said. "Worse than that. We handle things the FBI can't handle. We settle things in a way the FBI won't. So tell me about Widdell's death. Tell me about your visits to Widdell's office and what you did with the tapes."

Bradley stared angrily at Ellis before dabbing at his forehead again and looking away. His jaw muscles moved as if he were biting down on a nut.

Ellis asked, "Where are the tapes now?"

Bradley swung his head around furiously. "Go to hell!" he cried. "I'll be damned before I tell you anything." He jumped to his feet. Ellis tried to rise with him, but his side wrenched. Bradley backed away from the table, pulling the raincoat he had placed on the back of his chair over his arm.

"Wait!" Ellis shouted.

"You wait, goddamn you! You stay away from me!"

Ellis stopped in horror. From underneath his raincoat Bradley had drawn a gun. Sweating furiously, Bradley backed fearfully away from him. As he reached the corridor outside the coffee shop, he threw the raincoat over the gun, turned, and ran.

Ellis sat down slowly. From the table beside the door Patrick Morell put down his newspaper and walked over. "Three down," he said, "Now let's wait for reactions." He patted his pocket. "That was close. For a split-second there I thought I was going to have to shoot him."

97

Later that evening, summoned by an urgent call from Jonathan Bradley, the executive committee of Bildeberg met. The four other members seated themselves and listened attentively while Jonathan Bradley recounted what had happened at the Holiday Inn that afternoon. He finished breathlessly; recounting what had happened made his heart pound uncomfortably.

Cas Hardinger said, "Yesterday I was interviewed by a woman named Loren West who said she was from the *Washington Globe*. Her only interest in talking to me was to find out about my dinner with Steve Widdell and my connection with Bildeberg. After Jonathan told me what had happened to him, I checked with the *Globe*, which denied both the existence of a Miss West on their reporting staff and sending *anyone* to interview me." He looked directly at Colson. "You're our chief of security, Jim. Tell us who's looking for us and why?"

Colson said, "Drew Ellis is a former agent whose connection with the OCI was severed two years ago because of emotional instability. A few weeks ago Ellis was unofficially brought back into the OCI by Theo Goddard to find Widdell's system."

"Why didn't you kill him the same time as Goddard?'" Hardinger asked.

"Because I didn't know he was with Goddard. Afterward, when I found he was on the case, I let him run till I could find out how much he knew. When I did, I sent Zonda after him. Zonda failed, and Ellis went into hiding. Somehow he traced Karowitz and Ulner and forced them to meet with him. Karowitz asked me for advice, and I sent him to the meeting followed by a team that should have taken out all three of them. Karowitz and Ulner were killed, but Ellis escaped and went into hiding."

"Who's the woman?" Bradley asked.

"Loren Eastman, a computer scientist who once worked with Widdell and was recruited by Theo Goddard to help locate and identify Widdell's system. She's been working with Ellis since Goddard's death."

"Can she identify Widdell's system?" Bradley asked.

"I don't know."

"I thought you told us that with Goddard's death all investigation would cease," Hardinger said accusingly.

"All official investigation has ceased," Colson replied. "Ellis is unofficial."

"And highly dangerous. What are you going to do about him, Jim?"

"What would the executive committee of Bildeberg like me to do?"

"That's obvious," Hardinger said. "Both Ellis and the woman know too much. They will have to be eliminated."

"Or diverted," Ambassador Courtney murmured.

"It's too late for that," Cas Hardinger snapped. "They're on to Jonathan and they're on to me. It's only a question of time before they know everything. I vote for their liquidation."

"No!" Courtney cried. "We cannot murder simply to hide our crimes. Both these people must be dirverted." He looked appealingly at Colson. "Surely you must know a way of doing that."

Slowly Colson said, "I have known Drew Ellis a long time. We trained together, we worked on parallel assignments in Europe, we were stationed in Germany at the same time. He is ambitious, tenacious, and stubborn. The only way he can be stopped is by a bullet." He leaned forward so his face was in the light. "Drew Ellis is too dangerous," Colson said. "I say he has to be killed."

98

"The men of Bildeberg have decided to kill you!" Ellis felt his blood run cold as he heard Ambassador Courtney's voice. "You must get out! You must disappear!"

"Damn you, I won't."

"But you must!" Courtney's voice was hardly more than a whisper, as if afraid that he'd be overheard in his own house.

"Why are you warning me?" Ellis asked.

"Because there must be no more bloodshed."

"Running won't help. They will only find me. The only way to save myself is to stay and fight them."

"You don't know what you're saying. You cannot stop them. They're much too powerful for any man."

"If I knew who they were, it would help . . . anything would help."

The ambassador went silent. The first call had come twenty minutes earlier, after one A.M., Patrick had answered and told him his sterile contact had been reversed and that Ambassador Courtney wanted to get in touch with him. "Not here," Ellis had said, urgently.

"You can always call him from here," Patrick replied.

When he'd gone downstairs and called, Courtney said, "You're asking a lot. You're taking on a lot. You'll never succeed."

"If I had your help, I could at least try. Who knows what might happen then. And if I don't try, who can?"

Courtney asked, "Can you come here?"

Ellis suspected a trap. "No. That would be too dangerous. Your place could be under observation. You come here."

"Where's that?"

Not Patrick's, Ellis thought—somewhere else, where

243

they would not attract notice and where he could set up a discreet preliminary observation; somewhere easily accessible and with more than one exit. He remembered a shopping mall in the center of Chesterbrook, the shops closed now, but the lot still illuminated with neon signs and exterior lighting. The ideal place: deserted, well-lit, and with easy entrance and exit. He told Courtney to be there in half an hour and to come alone.

"I couldn't do that," Courtney protested. "I haven't driven a car for twenty years."

"Nothing much has changed since then."

"Places have changed," the ambassador said. "I don't know places the way I used to, or routes. I might never get to you."

That sounded logical. Ellis sighed and asked, "Is your driver to be trusted?"

"Yes. He's been with me twelve years."

"I'll see you both, then," Ellis said. "But I warn you. If you—"

"Mr. Ellis," Courtney said. "I am too old to be frightened by physical threats. You have my word this is not a trap."

"I'll see you, then." Ellis put the phone down. This time he didn't feel the ambassador was lying.

99

Nothing moved in the mall. Ellis checked the controls on the tape recorder he'd procured for Patrick and Loren, rechecked the tape. Ten minutes later a black Lincoln edged across the parking lot, slowed hesitantly by the brightly lit but empty Safeway and stopped.

Ellis waited. Cars swept past on Main Street, but there was no sign of any following vehicle. Ellis got out of the car—gun in one hand, tape recorder in the other—and ran quickly across to the Lincoln. It wasn't a trap, Ellis decided. He sidled along the side of the Lincoln and tapped on the passenger window.

Courtney and the driver both started. As the driver turned, Ellis could see he clutched a small pistol to his chest. Courtney opened the door.

"Out" Ellis said. "We talk in my car. Yours is too conspicuous."

Courtney said, "This car would be safer. It is fitted with bullet-proof glass and a reinforced metal skin."

"All right," Ellis said. "But we'll have to keep moving. Ask your driver to wait in my car. You get into the front passenger seat of yours. I'll drive."

Courtney hesitated for a moment, then did as he was asked. Ellis took the driver's spot, eased the Lincoln into gear and drove it slowly, without lights around the mall. "Please be careful, Mr. Ellis," Courtney said. "This vehicle is Lloyd's pride and joy."

Ellis placed the cassette recorder between them and switched it on. "I am going to record everything you say," he told Courtney. "If there is anything too sensitive to be recorded, press this switch here." He placed his finger on the pause button.

Courtney looked down. "What will you do with the recording?"

"Use it to recall what you've said. Use it as evidence of what you've said." Ellis reached down, switched on the recorder, pressed the play and record buttons. He said, "This tape is being prepared by Drew Ellis, former OCI agent, ID number 70930, at approximately two-thirty A.M. on Sunday, March sixth. This tape is a record of a meeting with Ambassador Whillan Courtney, presently head of the Bildeberg Institute. The meeting is being held at the ambassador's request. The ambassador and I are meeting at a shopping mall in Chesterbrook, Virginia, and this interview is being conducted in the ambassador's car. The ambassador and I are the only parties present." Ellis turned to Courtney. "Tell me about Bildeberg. Start with a recap of what you told me yesterday."

"I'll start with a brief history," Ambassador Courtney said. "Bildeberg was founded in the Depression by a man of goodwill, Jacob Landau, a German who had emigrated to America and founded one of the country's largest, most successful and conservative banks. A wise man, Landau had foreseen the Depression and had taken steps to protect himself and his colleagues against it, steps that left him and his clients not only protected, but in a position to make vast sums of money.

"Landau, who was a deeply religious and caring man, felt it was wrong to profit from the misfortunes of others. So gathering certain of his clients, he formed Bildeberg, named after the place where he was born, to help end the Depression and do what they could to remedy the failure of governments.

"When that crash came, the government was as much to blame as anyone. They had ignored the signals, had ignored the warnings, had taken the easy way out and believed the boom would go on forever."

"So Bildeberg is something more than just a charitable organization?"

"Yes," Courtney said. "Bildeberg has always tried to ensure that governments do not repeat the follies of the past, that 1929 does not happen again." He placed a thin hand on Ellis's arm. "And it is happening again. It is happening now. Look, for example, at the deficits the government builds, deficits that would be in trillions by the end of the century. Look at the irresponsible lending the government does nothing to stop. Look at the waste and inefficiency the government allows in every sphere of its operations. Believe me, my friend, governments, too, need watching, and need guiding."

"And controlling?" Ellis asked.

"Influencing is a word we prefer to use."

"With Widdell's system you could control the electoral process," Ellis said. "And if you control the electoral process, you control the government."

"That is something I have long considered," Courtney said gravely.

They circled past the point where Ellis had joined the ambassador. Ellis glimpsed Lloyd, Courtney's driver, seated upright behind the wheel of his car.

"When I was at Cornell," Courtney continued, "I paid great attention to the works of Plato. I agree with Plato that the best, the most efficient, the most humane government is a benevolent dictatorship."

"Except who decides what is benevolent?" Ellis asked. "Who decides who will be the dictator?"

"Who shall guard the guards themselves?" Courtney said with a sad smile. "That is a question that has also concerned me, but in the abstract. I had always thought the men of Bildeberg were benevolent. I had always thought the goodness of the men of Bildeberg entitled them to lead. Until now." He paused. His face was gray. There was a light patina of sweat on his broad forehead. "All power corrupts," he said hoarsely. "The men of Bildeberg have been corrupted. Not absolutely, because their power is not yet absolute. But corrupt enough that I now seek to ensure that the power of Bildeberg will never be absolute."

They drove around the far side of the lot. "When the decision to acquire Widdell's system was first taken," the ambassador continued, "it was essentially a defensive measure. If the system was as infallible as we had been led to believe, it was better that we controlled it rather than others."

Ellis skirted the potholes. There were fewer stores on this side of the mall and the lot was darker. "We used that argument as our justification to obtain Widdell's system at any cost." The ambassador's tone was heavy with regret. "At any cost, including murder! Including treachery!" Courtney pressed his hands to his face. "The men of Bildeberg have allied themselves with the Russians!"

"The Russians!" Ellis's hands jerked, making the car sway out of its gentle turn. Quickly he corrected the skid.

The ambassador seemed not to notice. "Yes. The Russians. You see, by the time we got to Widdell, the Russians had already stolen his system. So an alliance was struck. The men of Bildeberg and certain Russians will control the presidency of the United States, and through the control of that presidency, influence the outcome of events in both America and Russia!" Courtney slumped in his car seat. "The world as we know it will be controlled by a coalition of Bildeberg and the KGB!"

Ellis turned the car toward the brighter side of the mall. He could make out his own car in the lights from the windows of the Safeway. "What Russians?" he asked. "And who are the men of Bildeberg?"

"The Russians are led by a KGB agent, Boris Pomarev. Bildeberg paid him two million dollars for Widdell's system and agreed to replace our presidential nominee with his. Do you follow me, my friend? Bildeberg is working with the Russians to elect a KGB candidate!"

"Who is your candidate?" Ellis asked.

"Senator Kevin Anderson."

A horn blared in a long, single, continuous note. The sound came from his car. In the reflected light of the shop windows, Ellis saw a figure slumped over the wheel and shapes moving beside his car. The darkness flamed as a shot whined off the bullet-proof skin of the Lincoln.

Ellis turned on the headlights. A blazing white beam of light leaped across the tarmac, illuminating the chauffeur, slumped over the wheel of the car, and two men with drawn guns crouched beside it. Beyond his car another car had drawn up. Quickly Ellis turned off the lights. The curtain of darkness that followed was like a physical force. Ellis wheeled the car into a skidding turn, his mind recognizing as he did so the image of a man standing up beyond the cars, hurling something.

He heard rather than saw the metal object bounce on the road in front of the car, heard a thump against the front bumper that grew into a mushrooming explosion of sound and light that thundered against his eardrums and blinded him with its flaming orange flare. He felt the car rise like a skittish pony and its steering twist limply in his hands. There was the sound of dragging metal. The flaming hood rushed toward gleaming walls, and Ellis's body was smashed against the car door. The thump of the car hitting the curb threw him forward against the windshield. Then the wall was crumpling the hood, pressing it into the windshield, grinding, crunching, crackling—

Silence!

100

Ellis lay slumped in the silence. The right side of the car, which had taken the full blast of the grenade and the impact into the wall, was a crumpled, smoking ruin. Courtney was stretched half out of the windshield, his body curled, hands spread out to the fire. Ellis's side hurt. There was a trickle of blood down his forehead. He tried to move and couldn't.

From behind him he heard shots, felt the car vibrate

from the impact of high-velocity bullets. He couldn't move. He wouldn't move. It was useless. It was over. There were more shots. The hoarse roar of a car engine. Shouts. Lights. Someone was beating at his door. "Drew, are you all right?" Patrick!

Patrick was standing outside the car, pulling at the door. "Drew, are you okay?"

Ellis nodded and tried to move.

"Hang on. Let me unfasten your seat belt."

Patrick unfastened it and yanked at the door. It groaned but did not move. "For Heaven's sake, give me a hand! This whole thing's going to go up at any moment! Hurry!"

The urgency in Patrick's tone forced Ellis to move. He leaned against the door and pushed. The door groaned again and again remained rigid. He could feel the heat of the flames leaping along the fender. He pressed his shoulder to the door and pushed again. Groan. Again. Groan. Again. A white-faced Patrick tugged frantically at the door. Ellis cannoned his shoulder into it. The door moved. But not enough. Once more. The groan became a grating squawk. Again. It moved a whole three inches! Once more! Twice more! The door twisted open. Ellis wriggled through the gap, stood up, made a run around the car to Courtney.

"Leave him!" Patrick cried. "He's dead."

Ellis turned to look at the blood-streaked face of the ambassador, the flames already licking at those wiry strands of hair; those eyes, once so bright with intelligence, forever closed.

Ellis reached into the car for the tape recorder, pulled it through the window, turned and ran.

101

For the third time they listened to the tape of Ellis's conversation with Courtney. "The only problem," Ellis said, switching off the recorder, "is that it's no longer evidence. Without Courtney's corroboration, it's useless in a court of law, or as a means of convincing anyone else."

Loren set more coffee in front of them as they watched an early morning news report on Courtney's death. Against a backdrop of the charred Lincoln piled into the supermarket wall, a serious-faced newscaster reported that shortly after two-thirty that morning, former Ambassador Willan Courtney had been assassinated by a terrorist bomb planted in his car. There was no indication of who the terrorists were or what the ambassador had been doing in a deserted shopping mall at that time.

"Another cover-up," Ellis said despondently as a weather forecast replaced the news story. "Courtney's death is going to be swept under the carpet." He was beginning to feel desperate and frustrated. He'd gotten so close to the truth, and it had been taken away from him.

"But we have to go on," Patrick encouraged. "Why don't we confront Anderson with the tape?"

"How do we get to him?" Ellis wished he didn't feel so despondent.

"We could start by sending him a copy of the tape. For his ears only. Then we confront him and force him to talk."

Almost by coincidence, Senator Andersons' face filled the television screen while an excited reporter's voice-over announced, "We have just heard from South Carolina that Senator Kevin Anderson has withdrawn from the presidential primary campaign. Carl Boothby is in the senator's South Carolina campaign office right now, and we'll be going to Carl for an interview with Senator Anderson as soon as possible."

"Anderson's resigned!" Loren cried. "That's impossible. He's Bildeberg's man."

"Not anymore," Patrick said. He held out his cup for more coffee, then focused his attention on the screen again.

Five minutes later a haggard and distracted-looking Kevin Anderson appeared before the cameras and announced he was resigning on medical advice. He had a pulmonary condition that made his advisors doubt if he could stand the strain of full-scale primary and presidential campaigns.

"Another victim of the increased number of primaries," Patrick said, just as a reporter asked Anderson if his retirement had anything to do with the death of his close friend, Ambassador Whillan Courtney.

Anderson paled visibly before he said it had not. With a flash of his old bombast, he added that the foul murder of one of the most honorable men in American public life had shocked, outraged, and deeply grieved him, but had nothing to do with his retirement from the presidential campaign. The program switched to a shooting in Rexdale and traffic news.

"Anderson's lying," Ellis said. "Something about Courtney's death scared him. I bet you he's physically fit as anyone else who's spent thirty years in politics."

"So what do we do now?" Loren asked.

"Go after the other candidates," Patrick said.

"You mean check out all ten of them? That's a year's work!"

"Not all ten." Patrick smiled. "Just three. Taylor, Crane, and Milovan."

"Why those three?" Loren asked.

"Because as things stand now, one of those three is going to be the next president—"

"And we're only interested in winners," Ellis finished.

"We're interested in making sure the man who stole Widdell's system doesn't become president," Patrick said. "We're specifically interested in the backgrounds of these men," Patrick continued. "We know that Courtney said Anderson was Bildeberg's choice for president. But Courtney wasn't the only one making that decision. I'll bet that when the board of directors went in with Pomarev, they must have switched to another candidate—Pomarev's candidate. My guess is that somewhere in that candidate's background there's a Soviet connection. Something in his childhood, perhaps, a political affiliation at university, something that ties him to Pomarev and the Russians."

"We're looking mainly at childhoods then?" Loren asked.

"Mainly, but not exclusively," Ellis replied. "Most of the candidates' adult lives have been lived in the public eye, and a Red connection would have been picked up by now. We should examine their lives before they became public figures."

"If you like, I could start with Senator Crane," Loren offered. "Senator Crane's mother is on Dean Stockwell's campaign list, and he knows her quite well."

Ellis said, "I'll take Milovan. With his Russian background, his standing among the emigré community, he's the most likely one. He probably still has family in Russia."

Patrick smiled. "That leaves me with Vice President

Taylor. Let's get moving right away. Illinois is in ten days."

102

March 7–8, 1988

Pastor Patrick Morell spent the next two days checking up on Vice President Bradley Taylor. Nowhere did he find even a hint of Communist allegiance. Born into a wealthy political family—Taylor's father had been a U.S. senator—he had gone to the most reputable prep schools and become a Yale baseball captain and a Phi Beta Kappa. He'd volunteered in World War II and flown fighter planes in the Pacific. Before going into politics, he'd cofounded a major investment banking company.

Patrician and slightly aloof, he'd lacked popular appeal, though in running for the Senate three times, he'd won twice. The party, however, had recognized his administrative talent, just as successive presidents had recognized his natural flair for diplomacy. He'd been chairman of the national committee, U.S. ambassador to France, a special envoy to the United Nations, and chairman of the president's intelligence committee. He'd been one of the few people bold enough to tell President Nixon he should resign for the good of the country.

His Senate record had been right of center. He had supported Vietnam, opposed much of the early civil rights legislation and the nuclear test-ban treaty. As vice president he'd been against the SALT treaty and for the Star Wars program, and on a recent visit to Moscow he'd had a public and coldly polite disagreement with the Soviet foreign minister.

Not even the vestige of a KGB candidate there, Patrick concluded. In fact, after its present occupant, Bradley Taylor was probably the last man the Russians would want in the White House.

103

In New York Ellis sat on a pile of milk crates in Milovan's Grocery, watching Mikhail Milovan slice bacon and check out goods. A small man, Milovan had a paunch curving out under his apron, a shock of gray hair, wire-rimmed glasses and a handsome moustache. Between customers he talked. "Afram used to sit right there and do his homework. Then he used to help me with the account books, unless he had a game. He was football and baseball captain at St. Peter's, you know, and could have made the Dodgers, but there you go. He wanted to do other things."

"Would you have liked him to become a baseball player?"

"Yeah. Think of all those free tickets." Milovan grinned. "Free tickets is all." He approached Ellis, wiping his hands on the front of his apron. "No, I prefer my son to be doing what he likes doing, being governor. You know, the night he was elected, he called me and his mama up to the platform. This is my dad, he said, he makes the best bagels in the whole state, and he gave my address right there on television, like it was a commercial."

"Does it affect you, having a governor for a son?"

"At first it did. There were some people who just came to look and say, I bought my salami from the governor's dad. But that passes. Now people come here because they like the salami. If I serve bad salami, governor or no governor, they go somewhere else."

"Didn't you want your son to take over the business from you?"

"No, this is hard work. On your feet all the time, sixteen, seventeen hours a day, and at the end of the day what have you done? Sold a little this, bought a little that, made a little money. Far better to be a doctor or a governor or a baseball player. In any case, this place would be too small for my son. He thinks too big. He has to get out and stretch."

"Did he always like politics?"

"Oh, sure. He always liked debating, and arranging things for people to do. That's what politicians do, right? Talk and fix things."

"You think he'll make president?"

"I hope so. He'll be the best goddamn president this country's ever had."

"And you don't think being Russian would be a disadvantage?"

"Russian? Who's talking Russian? My son's as much a goddamn American as you are."

104

A sudden spell of mild weather had brought spring early to Camden, and as she drove out of the town, Loren could see the fields were lush and green and the hedgerows bright with spring flowers. Dean Stockwell had not only arranged for her to meet Mrs. Eleanor Follet-Crane, the senator's mother, but he had devised a cover story. As part of its course in American government, the university was conducting a survey into the backgrounds of presidential candidates, so that scholars of the future would be able to determine the qualities and characteristics that made a man president.

The magnificent Crane house was outside Camden, where the senator was born. The house was lined with porches and balconies and built on a bluff overlooking both the road and the sea. An elderly butler appeared on the front porch and led her to the side of the house, where Mrs. Crane waited under a golf umbrella, reading a biography of Thomas Jefferson.

She was a trim, formally dressed figure in a smart green skirt, with a cashmere shawl around her shoulders. There was a brittleness about her, and a sense of precision. Before putting away the book, she inserted a bookmark between the pages.

"So you're going to write a book about my son?" Mrs. Crane spoke with a cut-glass brilliance. She was over seventy,

Loren reckoned, her face and hands heavily lined, and covered with brown liver spots. Her eyes were a startlingly clear blue.

"I am researching a monograph for the university," Loren corrected. "It is part of a much larger study to ascertain the characteristics and qualities of successful presidential candidates. The work will not be completed for many years, but we will be publishing interim reports after every presidential election." She smiled and added, "I believe the next report will be mainly concerned with your son. I believe your son will be the next president of the United States."

Mrs. Crane gave a frosty smile. "I hope and believe that too. It's what his father would have wanted."

Loren studied the frail figure in the chair opposite her. It was difficult to believe that fifty years ago this prim precise old lady had scandalized New England high society when she'd run away and married Frank Crane, who'd been born Franco Carmini, the only son of Salvatore Carmini, who had throughout prohibition kept many of those same high society cellars awash with first quality bourbon, gin, fine French wines, and twelve-year-old scotch.

"Does the senator inherit his political ambition from his father, then?" Loren asked.

"Good Lord, no!" Mrs. Crane laughed easily. It was a pleasant laugh. Loren warmed to it. "My husband Frank had no interest in politics and no liking for politicians. 'Turds,' he used to call them, 'turds, Eleanor *mi amore*,' he used to say, 'who we must either buy or fawn upon, and in any case live with.'"

Loren relished the old lady's imitation of her husband's heavy Italian accent. She'd been told that it was the Carmini money that had made old Thurston Follet finally reconcile himself to his daughter's marriage, that after generations of reckless living the Follets had been down to their last hundred thousand or so, and that this magnificent and much loved family home had been about to be sold. Loren wondered if there was any truth in the legend that upon his acceptance into the Follet family, Franco Carmini/Crane had sealed the pact by giving Thurston Follet the deed to this house.

"But even a turd can bring status, if he is a senator, or a president," Mrs. Crane continued. She flashed a bright smile.

"You've heard, no doubt, how I eloped with the son of the family bootlegger?"

Loren nodded.

"Frank was no bootlegger," she said. "He was too damned straight." She told Loren that Frank Crane had made his money in real estate and the financing of wartime industry. "But however squeaky clean he was, however many works of art he bought or universities he endowed, my husband was never really accepted by people like my father. Just think of the difference." She smiled and added, "If his son had been president, or even a senator... pity Frank couldn't live to see this."

Loren asked about the senator's childhood.

"It was normal," Mrs. Crane said, "if you could call being the son of one of the wealthiest men in America normal. If you want to know the truth," she confided, "I think we spoiled him terribly." She told Loren that she hadn't been able to have another child, and Frank, Jr. had been their baby for much too long. In school his academic record had been about average and he'd been good at games, particularly football. He'd grown up a pleasant, spoiled and rather dissolute youth, devoid of ambition. "What else could you expect," Mrs. Crane asked, "from someone who inherited a trust fund of five million dollars at twenty-one? I've always believed that was why he got such a poor degree in Law at Yale, not the women, drink, and parties."

Loren asked, "When did he become interested in politics?"

"After that terrible war in Vietnam."

The story of Frank, Jr. being drafted into a war he didn't believe in, his capture, harrowing imprisonment, and daring escape with five members of his platoon, was popular history and figured prominently in his subsequent election to congress and later to the senate.

"He seemed to have learned from the experience," Mrs. Crane said. "And changed for the better. When he came back, he had a purpose. He used to tell me, 'We are here for a short time only, and we must use that time to make the world a better place.'"

Loren thought the senator's biography reflected that change. After his return from the war, he'd become a congressman, then senator three times, and deputy chairman of the National Committee, a vibrant spokesman on unemployment, the underprivileged, alternative sources of energy, and the necessity to curb the arms race. And now, Loren thought, he was about to make history.

105

In Paul Gray's lapel was a gold pin with the figure 45 that had been given him when he'd retired as head of St. Peter's. He smiled. "Even if I didn't remember Afram Milovan, I would now. I recall there was always something of the bantam cock about him. He was easily roused and could get quite ferocious. He once hit a baseball catcher who'd called him a lousy Polack, completely forgetting that the catcher was still wearing his mask." Paul Gray smiled at the memory, and poured Ellis a second cup of coffee.

"Was he always getting into fights?" Ellis asked.

Paul Gray sipped his coffee. "No. Not always. Only when he was pushed. Mainly, I remember he was a very serious boy, quite studious, without much of a sense of humor. His big passion was debating."

"And his politics?"

"Oh, yes, there was always that." Paul Gray wandered to a corner of the room, selected one yearbook from a row, opened it and showed it to Ellis. Afram Milovan had listed his ambition as being mayor of Brighton Beach.

106

For the next two days Loren remained in Camden, talking to friends, former teachers, campaign workers, the senator's local staff, and the men Frank Crane had brought out of Vietnam. Almost as if it had been rehearsed, everyone confirmed Mrs. Crane's story. A spoiled, immature, and slightly dissolute adolescent had been purified by his experience of a hated war and transformed himself into a good, warm, public-spirited human being. Without exception everyone loved and believed in Senator Frank Crane and wanted him to be president.

On the second morning the local cable TV station interviewed Loren about her book. It was a painless experience affected only by the unnerving effect of being recognized by people she'd never met before. This was what celebrities had to live with, she thought, after being greeted with a cheery "Hi, Loren!" by the garage owner who'd sold the young Frank Crane his first car, and a wondering "Haven't we met somewhere before?" by the proprietor of the drugstore where the future senator used to hang loose, pretending to be James Dean.

She returned to the hotel around lunchtime, feeling watched and with her face set in a hesitant smile of greeting. She would return to Washington after lunch, she decided. She'd done all she could in Camden, and as far as Senator Frank Crane's early life was concerned, all was sweetness, light, and love.

She'd just finished packing when the phone rang. "Loren Eastman?" The voice was a low-pitched whisper.

"Yes. Who are you?"

"I saw you on television this morning."

Oh, dear, she hadn't really expected crank calls. She moved to put the phone down.

"You're being bullshitted like the rest of them," the voice whispered urgently. "Frank Crane was no hero! Frank Crane was a collaborator!"

"Who are you?" Loren asked again. "How do you know this?"

"I was captured with Frank Crane in Vietnam," the voice said. "The name's Savona, Ted Savona. You can look it up in the records. I am the only one who didn't get a citation."

"Where are you, Mr. Savona? When can we meet?"

"You know the Tulsane Trailer Park?"

"I'll find it."

"Be there in half an hour." The husky whisper ended with a sharp click.

107

"Sure," Francis Crowell said. "Milovan would have made a great trial lawyer, if he'd stuck to the law instead of going into politics." He was a man in his early fifties, with a pleasant, open face, tousled hair, a pronounced jaw, and a large smile. "The thing about trials," Crowell continued, "is that preparation pays off. And I've never known anyone to prepare more thoroughly than Afram."

"Even though he was into politics at the time?"

"No, he wasn't into politics when he joined here," Crowell said. "He was concerned with righting wrongs and earning money. He'd just gotten married, you see, and wanted to start a family. The politics came later."

Ten years later, Ellis recalled. "The Corona case?" he asked.

"Yes." The Corona case had involved a group of blue-collar, Italian families who had fought the city council which had been trying to tear down their homes to build a new and prestigious office. Milovan had fought the case in the courts and on the streets. His victory had brought him to the notice of Governor Richard Kofax, who had persuaded him to run for mayor.

"If not for the Corona case, he'd still be a trial lawyer," Crowell said.

108

The Tulsane Trailer Park was four miles out of Camden on a brown esplanade by the sea. A wooden sign fringed with

plastic seashells and ringed with light bulbs announced it.
Loren bounced down a dirt road to a wood-framed office. As
she walked up to it, a sun-browned man with parched-looking
skin and crepey neck came onto the porch. He wore a dark
brown uniform shirt and trousers and above his vest pocket a
little red badge that read, *Supervisor.*

"I'm looking for Ted Savona," Loren said.

The supervisor shook his head. "No Ted Savona here, miss."

"You have a register of people staying here?"

"Sure, but I have no need to look at it. I know everyone
who's here. And there's no Ted Savona."

"I'd like to see your register, if I may."

"You sure you want to do that?" The supervisor scratched
his head and looked perplexed. "I know who's in my camp
and who ain't. And most people around here take my word."

Loren tried a smile. "I take your word too. But mistakes
happen."

"Not with Ted Savona," the supervisor muttered. "I'd
know if Ted Savona was in my camp. You know something, I
wouldn't let him into my camp. The man's crazy. Drunk most
of the time, calling people names, shooting off his forty-five.
No, ma'am. There's no Ted Savona in my camp."

Loren said, 'I'd still like to see the register."

The office door opened and Luther Waverley came out.
Waverley was one of Senator Crane's assistants and had been
captured with Crane. He'd shown Loren around the local
campaign headquarters and introduced her to some of the
people who'd known Frank Crane as a teenager. "Hi, there,
Miss Eastman," he called. "What brings you out here?"

"I'm looking for someone called Ted Savona."

"Ted Savona? What d'you want with him?" He walked
past the supervisor and stood in front of her, big, burly,
smooth-faced, and smiling.

Loren felt uneasy. Behind Waverley's smile she sensed
the faintest hint of menace. "He called me at the hotel and
wanted to meet me here."

"Here?" Waverley burst out laughing. "If Ted Savona
sets a foot on this property, Jethro will be applying the sole of
his boot to the seat of Savona's pants, won't you, Jethro? Ted
Savona's crazy," he said. "He's been crazy ever since the
senator brought him out of 'Nam."

"So you know him?"

Waverley grinned. "Everyone does, ma'am." The grin faded. "But yes, Ted was captured with us. But I'm afraid he never made it out with us. He chose to stay behind, and I think it just got to him afterward. He's crazy as a three-speed roller skate." He took Loren's arm. "You've got no truck with people like Ted Savona, ma'am."

Loren pulled her arm free. "I'd still like to check," she said.

"Sure. Go ahead. Show her the register, Jethro."

Jethro did. There was no Ted Savona registered there that day, that week, or throughout the whole of the preceding month.

"You see, ma'am," Waverley said, walking her back to her car. "Man's crazy. Always phoning up people and sending them to Jethro's camp. Man doesn't like Jethro, you see. Man's crazy. You shouldn't talk to him or listen to him."

"Doesn't look as if I'll get a chance to," Loren said. "I go back home this afternoon." He opened the car door for her. "What are you doing here?" she asked.

"Checking voter registrations, ma'am. We need to get as many people registered as we can. After all, don't we all want to see the senator make president?"

109

Former governor Richard Kofax was a rotund, almost clerical looking man, with a round chin, a pert nose, and rimless glasses. "Yes, I remember Afram's first speeches," he said. "It was like he was in a courtroom. And if someone heckled him, he got thrown. I mean, he was great in a television debate, but we didn't have television debates in those days, we were out on the street and we expected the other side to heckle."

Kofax smiled. "But he learned quickly. By the time the campaign was finished, you never saw a quicker, more smooth-talking political animal than Afram Milovan."

"What do you think of him as president?"

"I think he'll make a damn good president."

"And his Russian background?"

"Young man," former governor Kofax protested volubly, "this is America!"

110

They each returned to Patrick's retreat house that evening, Patrick bringing two bags full of Chinese takeout food he'd picked up on his way from church.

"Taylor's clean," he announced after he'd set a table and laid out the food. "Though, mind you, he may not make president." He told them that in Florida, Alabama, and Georgia, Vice President Taylor had lost heavily to Senator Crane.

"And the KGB candidate isn't Crane," Loren said. "Crane's a war hero. He saved not only himself, but his men from the Viet Cong. They'd all been ill treated by the Viet Cong, and they loath communism. And despite marrying the family bootlegger, his mother's so blue-blooded she could be American royalty."

Ellis said, "Even though he's Russian, it's not Milovan." He told them how Milovan's childhood had been that of just another poor, ambitious, immigrant kid, that Milovan had worked hard, had genuine ideals, and like most immigrants who'd made good, believed fervently in the American way of life.

On television, Jay Emerson III, a heavy-shouldered man with a thick-jawed, bullfrog face and horn-rim glasses, was being interviewed about the results of the southern primaries. "I don't remember such massive support for a candidate since President Donnelly swept the South on his way to the the White House," he was saying. "What I think is most significant about Senator Crane's victories is not their number, but the proportion of the vote he collected. That doesn't augur at all well for Vice President Taylor, and come the conventions, I believe we are going to see Crane as the candidate."

An off-screen voice asked, "Do you think that Senator Crane could be our next president?"

Jay Emerson III permitted himself the shadow of a smile. "It's a long way from the primaries to the presidency, but if Senator Crane keeps repeating the results he's had here today, and if the opposing party keeps on sending out the conflicting signals I believe they have sent out in the South, then Senator Crane has an excellent chance of becoming our next president."

"There's something I haven't told you about Senator Crane," Loren said. Watching the TV screen, she recounted the call from Savona and her visit to the trailer park.

"Interesting," Ellis said. He looked at the television screen, where the face of Jay Emerson III had been replaced by that of a smiling Senator Crane. "Why don't we recheck the senator's war record . . ."

"And trace Savona," Patrick said.

111

March 10, 1988

The Veteran's Bureau clerk was bearded and built like a wrestler, his long hair pulled back and tied behind his head with a bandana. Patrick said, "I don't expect you to give me his address, but I want to get in touch with Ted Savona." He gave the clerk Savona's unit and number. Earlier that morning he had checked with Records and confirmed that Savona had been captured with Senator Crane and was the only member of the company to have elected to remain behind.

"You expect right," the clerk said. Patrick saw he was in a wheelchair and that his legs were amputated above the knee.

"It is important he contacts me," Patrick said.

The clerk looked at him indifferently. Patrick thought that after the trauma of Vietnam, nothing could really be important. He said, "It's not my crisis, it's his. It has to do with what he wants to tell the girl who was on television in

Camden, about Senator Crane. If he contacts this number, he
can get in touch with her. Her name's Loren Eastman. Tell
him she went to the Tulsane Trailer park, as he asked, but he
wasn't there."

The clerk finished scribbling a note and looked at the
phone number Patrick gave him. "Is this urgent?"

"I think it is, but only Savona knows exactly how urgent.
He's the one who wanted to talk to Loren Eastman."

"About Senator Crane?"

"That's right."

"The same sonofabitch who's running for president?"

"Right again. Don't you like Senator Crane?"

"I think he's an asshole. I think all officers are assholes."
The clerk looked at the message again. "Savona wanted to
work on the senator's campaign?"

"I don't think so. I think Savona wanted to stop the
senator from running."

The clerk stared into Patrick's face. "Tell you what, I'll
give him your message, if I see him."

Patrick said, "Look, you aren't the only one who was
hurt. I was there too."

The clerk wheeled his bulk to a filing cabinet at the rear
of his office, balanced a box file on his thighs, and heaved
himself back to the desk. He opened the box file. "And just in
case I don't see him, he lives out by Occoquan Creek." He
scribbled an address.

Patrick looked at the piece of paper. "No phone?"

"No." The clerk stared thoughtfully at Patrick for a
moment. "If you're going to see Savona, be careful. He's
unpredictable and doesn't like visitors."

112

March 11, 1988

The part of Occoquan Creek where Savona lived consisted
of small farms interspersed with marshland. There was a fetid

salt smell about the place, and they had to ask twice before they found the clearing where Savona's shanty stood, fronted by a broken wooden gate and a sagging timber sign. The house was surrounded by trees, thick vines and undergrowth.

Drew climbed out of the car and called, "Anybody home?"

There was no answer. He and Loren went to the front porch. The metal door was locked and the screened windows shut. There was no bell or door knocker. Ellis pounded on the door with his fist. "Mr. Savona, are you there? Ted, could we talk with you?"

Loren walked around the side of the house, put her hand on the radiator of the muddy truck jacked there. "The engine's cold," she reported.

Ellis knocked again. He heard the whiz of the shot a split-second before it ricocheted off the door and careened away, whining. Instantly he flung himself to the floor, looked up and saw Loren still erect and shouted, "Down!" She quickly lay down beside him.

Ellis raised his head and looked. There was nothing except trees and silence. The place where the bullet had hit the door was chipped. "Whoever you are," he shouted, "we mean no harm! We're looking for Ted Savona."

A man's voice called, "Get to your feet. Get your hands in the air. Come down off the porch."

Ellis got to his feet slowly and stood up, his hands in the air, and waited while Loren followed his example. They went down the steps and stood before the house, feeling vulnerable and exposed.

"What d'you want?"

The voice came from a clump of trees a little to their left. Not that the knowledge did them much good, Drew thought wryly. Even if he had his gun out, he couldn't pinpoint his target in that tangle of leaves and bushes. He shouted, "Are you Ted Savona? My name's Drew Ellis, and this is Loren Eastman. You wanted to talk to Miss Eastman a couple of days ago, remember?"

After a few minutes a lanky broad-shouldered man emerged from the trees immediately in front of them, carrying an automatic rifle. He wore a combat jacket over an open shirt, with faded jeans tucked into calf-high boots. His hair was pulled behind his head and tied with a bandana. His long, lean face was unshaven. His pale eyes studied them carefully. "Show me some identification, slowly, one at a time. You first, Ellis."

Ellis pulled out his OCI ID and showed it. Loren pulled out her driver's license.

He squinted at the documents, then nodded. "How did you find me here?"

"We asked around. Someone else who wasn't too fond of Senator Crane told us." Ellis gestured with his head. "Why all the protection, metal doors, metal screens?"

"Burglars."

"Mortise locks would be more effective against burglars than metal screens, Mr. Savona. Who d'you think is going to shoot you?"

Savona's pale eyes blazed momentarily. "Why don't you mind your own fucking business," he snapped.

Ellis said, "Maybe we could arrange better protection than this. We can find you a place with round the clock guards till the elections are over."

"I'd need more than that," Savona replied, "I'd need the kind of protection you give informers. A new identity, a new start, that sort of thing."

"That can also be arranged, if what you said was important enough."

"It's fucking important," Savona said. He lowered the gun, came up the steps, unlocked the cabin and waved them in.

The inside was sparse—a bed, a table, two chairs, two cupboards for clothes and provisions, boxes of ammunition, and three more guns. Savona made them coffee, took out a tin and rolled himself a cigarette. He told them he'd waited for Loren near the trailer park until he'd seen Luther Waverley drive up with some of Crane's workers. "They'd have killed me if they found me," he said hoarsely, and added that he believed his phone call to Loren had been intercepted. Savona alternated gulps of coffee with long drags at his cigarette. "I'm going to tell you the truth about Crane—the senator," he said, giving them a broken smile, "now that he's going to be president and all." His eyes filled with a sudden, bright intensity. "It didn't happen like they say it did."

"What didn't happen?" Loren asked softly.

"The capture by a company of gooks, the gallant battle,

the six months of daily torture in prison camp, the daring escape."

"Are you saying none of it happened?" Ellis asked.

Savona lifted the cigarette to his lips and smiled crookedly. His fingers were scarred, the nails short and rimmed with dirt. "Oh, it happened all right, or some of it did, but none of it happened the way they tell it now. For a start, we were not staked out at a camp, we were on patrol. Only we weren't patrolling, get me? We were laying down without anyone on watch, stoned out of our fucking minds. It was the lieutenant's— that's senator to you—birthday. And when they came, we didn't fire a fucking shot."

"According to the published story," Loren said, "four of your buddies were killed resisting the Viet Cong."

"Not so." Savona shook his head vehemently. "The men who died did so on the way to our first camp." His hands shook a little as he lit another cigarette. "We were marched for something like ten days to this stockade . . . forced marches, mainly at night, with very little food or water. Those little slit-eyed bastards were contemptuous of us. They used to beat the hell out of anyone who fell behind or slowed down. The four men who died were beaten to death."

Savona pulled deeply at his cigarette, a faraway expression in his eyes. "At camp it was standard procedure to break the newcomers, so we'd know who was boss. The first few days they beat us up regularly, with anything they had—fists, boots, bamboos, you name it, they used it. They'd play little games, like forcing us to stand anytime they entered the room where we were kept—not easy if someone had just kicked the shit out of you and your hands were tied behind your back. Sometimes, for the hell of it, two of them would pull the ropes so tight you could hear your heart pounding in your head as it tried to pump blood into your hands and feet. Ten minutes of that—" Savona abruptly stopped talking and stared into space. His cigarette went out. After a while he lit another cigarette and continued. "Crane got it worst because he was an officer. Then one day—maybe a week, ten days after we'd been at the camp—this Russian came. The beatings and the torture lessened and then stopped. A few days later we were given a little extra food. And in the evenings, after dinner the Russian started sending for Crane.

"At first we thought Crane was being brutalized as part of

some after-dinner entertainment. But that wasn't the way it was. When he was brought back, he'd usually been fed, and once or twice he even smelled of beer. For the rest of the time we were in the camp, I don't believe Crane was beaten.

"After a few weeks the Russian went away. But the gooks continued to treat us okay. We fit in to the routine of the camp. Then, about four months later, the Russian returned. The first night he came back, Crane was taken to his quarters, and came back belching and full of beer.

"Two weeks later Crane suggested we make a break for it. He said he'd lulled the Russian into false confidence, that he wanted to take the survivors of his platoon back. It was a crazy idea then—we had no maps and no idea of where to go. And we knew that if we were captured, what we'd already been through would feel like a picnic. But Crane insisted, and Luther and the others agreed. I did too."

There was sweat on Savona's forehead. "Two nights before we made our break, I hear Crane talking to the Russian. The Russian was describing the route we should take, the VC patrols we should avoid. I thought, at the time, the Russian was planning the escape so he could have the kudos of recapturing us. I feigned illness, which wasn't difficult, and stayed."

Savona ground out his cigarette and lit another. "But that wasn't what the Russian wanted. The Russian *allowed* Crane to get away."

"Why would he do that?" Ellis asked.

Savona stubbed out his cigarette and grinned. "I'm saying Crane's escape was fixed. The Russians wanted him to be a hero."

"Why—" Loren asked, and realized she knew the answer. "Do you know who this Russian was?"

"Yes. His name was Pomarev."

Loren and Ellis stared at each other. Then Loren asked, "So why tell us this?"

Savona gave her a twisted smile. "Why d'you think?" He looked slowly around the cabin, his gaze moving from the metal shutters to the rifles and the boxes of ammunition. "If Crane becomes president, they can't afford to let me live.'

"You'd better come in with us and make a proper statement," Ellis said. "Then we can arrange protection for you." He gestured at the cabin. "Much better than this."

"I ain't leavin' this place," Savona said. "I'm not leaving my guns."

"They won't be enough if Crane really wants you. You're going to need more than this."

"I ain't going nowhere," Savona said.

The grenade, lobbed with unerring accuracy, rolled through the door. For a moment the three of them stared at it, then Ellis grabbed Loren and hurled her to the back of the cabin. The explosion was deafening. They were flung against the far wall. The cabin thundered and shook. Wood, metal, and shards of glass flew through the air. Flame caught and erupted. A large hole appeared in the wall. Ellis felt the cabin crumble.

Savona, or a part of Savona, was lying blown across the bed, his camouflage jacket charred, his face and beard bloodstained. Timbers cracked and fell. Ellis pulled Loren toward a narrowing opening in the back wall, held a timber as she squeezed through, followed her into the clear air outside and began to run.

Behind them smoke and flames belched into the air. They pushed through the undergrowth till they reached the river. The cabin burned, and there was a horrible silence. Ellis drew his gun and waited. No one came.

After what seemed an eternity, Loren asked, "What do we do now?" Her voice scratched, like stone scraping on glass.

"We get back," Ellis said. "And we have to stop Crane."

113

"It looks like the attack was carried out by professionals," Patrick said. "And from the use of grenades, most likely Vietnam vets."

"Crane's buddies," Ellis said. They were back in the retreat house, analyzing what had happened with Savona.

"How did they locate him?" Loren asked.

Patrick said, "I suppose Crane's people were alerted after your visit to Tulsane and set out to find Savona. They were vets, remember, and could have gotten the address far more easily than I did."

"If Crane is the KGB candidate, how do we prove it?" Ellis asked.

"Simple," Loren said. "Let me examine his computers."

"Difficult," Patrick said.

"Virtually impossible," Ellis said.

They stared at each other.

"Unless," Ellis said, "I could rustle up a fake Department of Industry ID and some clothes befitting a civil service matron."

"Matron!" Loren exclaimed.

Patrick said, "There are some clothes left over from the church play... We did 'The Cocktail Party'"

"Very progressive," Ellis said. "Did you keep any dowdy clothes?"

114

March 12, 1988

Senator Crane's campaign headquarters were the top three floors of a building on Neal Place easily identifiable by the wide blue banners spread across the face of the building and windows plastered with posters. Past the guarded entrance earnest young people, neatly dressed in suits and skirts and wearing blue lapel buttons, moved with certainty. Through an open door Loren saw a number of people seated around a long table piled with envelopes, campaign packages, and letters. No one hanging round the soda machines or water coolers, she thought, as a ponytailed girl came out from behind a door marked PRESS and told Loren that everyone was in Illinois.

"Oh, dear," Loren said, and blinked behind the pink horn-rimmed glasses Patrick had gotten for her, together with the calf-length skirt, pink cardigan, thick stockings, and flat-heeled shoes. "I'm from the Department of Industry." She opened the battered briefcase Patrick had provided and showed the girl a creased and stained ID. "I've come to inspect the computers."

"Inspect?"

"Yes. It's a statistical requirement."

"Can't you come some other time? Mr. Melkonian is in Illinois."

"I don't have to see Mr. Melkonian," Loren said. "I just need to look at the computers and have some simple questions answered."

The girl chewed her lip. "Hang on. I'll ask David Manners if he'll see you."

Three minutes later a rumple-suited figure with an affable smile and thick-lensed glasses came in and asked what he could do for her.

Loren told him her name was Carrithers and she was from the Department of Industry, which was running a survey on the electoral use of computers. Senator Crane's was the third office she'd called on that day.

She should have made an appointment, Manners chided. Everyone was always busy during elections and—

Loren appologized. She wouldn't take long, and the questions were so trivial that the department felt an appointment was unnecessary. They were not interested in the kind of data that was stored on the computers, but simply wanted to know what kind of computers were used, their capacity, duration of use, that sort of thing. She said Manners could refuse to answer any question he didn't like.

He asked her to follow him upstairs. She was lucky, he told her, because right now things were quiet. But in an hour, when Mr. Melkonian was back from Illinois, the whole place would be jumping.

On the top floor three rooms had been set aside for Crane's polling division. In one of them three technicians sat watching two VAX computers; in another three paper-covered desks were crammed end to end; and in the last she saw rows of chairs and tables, which Manners explained were for those on the research staff who spent most of their time in the field and only came into the office to file their reports.

He walked Loren through his office and showed her the computers. Loren asked him about memory capacity, duration of use, and how the system worked.

Manners said, "Our basic data consists of historical voting records and demographic data such as age, sex, race, religion, and economic status. We keep these records as up-to-date as possible, because they are the constant against which we check our samples of voter attitudes. That is what the people in the next room are doing—updating basic data and sampling voter attitudes."

"How accurate are your samples?"

"Very accurate. For instance, if 600 people are asked if they would vote for Senator Crane or Vice President Taylor, 570 of those replies will be accurate to within three percent. That means that if our sample said fifty-six percent would vote for the senator, the senator would in all likelihood receive between fifty-three and fifty-nine percent of the vote."

"And you have the same accuracy with regard to voters attitudes on, say, abortion?"

"Yes. Each reply is cross-checked against the voters demographic profile and overall voting records. We are confident of an error factor of less than three percent."

"And what do you do with this information?"

"If we know how a particular state or group of voters feels about abortion, we moderate the candidate's views accordingly."

"Regardless of the candidate's own views?"

"The candidate's views are also a factor we take into account."

"Do you have a system of control codes?" Loren asked.

Manners nodded. "Doesn't everyone?"

Loren asked, "Could you pull up some data for me? Anything at all. I just want to say I saw the system working."

"Sure." Manners led her to a terminal across the room and punched some keys. A voting list for a particular county filled the screen.

"Fascinating," Loren said. She sidled between Manners and the terminal and punched the keys in rapid succession, counted three and hit \. There was a moment's silence. Then, as if practicing on a mistuned flute, the terminal played the opening bars of "As Time Goes By."

"Hey," Manners said. "How did you do that?"

"Simple." Loren choked. Suddenly her eyes were filled with tears. "If only I could remember how."

Manners stared at her. "You all right, Miss Carrithers?"

Loren blinked back the tears. "Yes. It's these glasses. It's a new prescription and sometimes looking at a computer screen makes my eyes tear."

"I have the same problem sometimes." Manners said sympathetically. "Except I find the screen blurring."

Loren pulled off the glasses and dabbed at her eyes with a Kleenex. Ten years ago that code had been a private joke between Steve Widdell and his staff, after he'd discovered that all of them were mad about *Casablanca*. She tried to keep her hand from trembling. She had found Widdell's system.

A man burst into the room holding a briefcase. "David, David, where the hell have you been? I've been looking everywhere for you."

Manners surveyed the intruder coolly. "I've been right here, Mr. Melkonian. You're back from Illinois early."

"Yes. I got an earlier flight because there's something I want rushed through. Can you come into my office right away?" He looked curiously at Loren.

Manners said, "This is Miss Carrithers. She's from the Department of Industry. She's doing a survey on the electoral use of computers."

"A government survey of computers." Melkonian gave her a nervous smile. "It smells of Big Brother."

"No," Loren said, trying not to look too obviously at him. "It's just a survey." Melkonian was shaped like an overweight penguin, with large, rounded shoulders and a belly that ballooned over the narrow belt that held up his prefaded jeans. The last time Loren had seen that face had been in Steve Widdell's offices, looking through photographs of past employees when Pat Cleary had identified Abe Makram.

"What's wrong, miss? You look ill?"

Loren realized she was trembling. "It's nothing," she whispered. "Nothing. Just my glasses. Wrong prescription."

"Can I get you some water? Would you like to rest?"

"No, no. I'll be all right once I get outside. Once I get some fresh air." She brushed past Makram and Manners and hurried unsteadily to the door.

115

Ellis said, "We have to create a confrontation with Crane."

Patrick shook his head. "That may give you a lot of satisfaction, but it is not going to give us the proof we need to stop him."

"What about the computer system?" Loren asked. "Crane is using Widdell's computer system?"

"The system isn't Crane's, but Makram's," Patrick said. "And in any case, can you prove that Makram also didn't insert a code to make his computers whistle?"

"The same tune!" Loren cried. "Come on Patrick! What do you expect?"

Patrick waved a hand placatingly. "I know," he said, "I know. And that is the essence of our problem. We know the KGB and Bildeberg are working together, and we believe that KGB candidate to be Senator Crane. Our only evidence is a tape recording by a man now dead, the story of a member of Crane's platoon—now also dead—a computer system which is not Crane's, the existence of an organization called Bildeberg, and the murders of Steve Widdell, Lucas Amory, and Dick Schaffer—none of which can be directly connected to Crane."

"We don't have time to get any more proof," Ellis said. "Illinois is in four days. After that Crane will be even more difficult to dislodge, and will have made himself more powerful allies. We've got to do something now"

"Like what?"

"We must get Crane to withdraw. And we do that by threatening him with the evidence we have. The media doesn't need as much evidence as a court of law."

Slowly Patrick shook his head. "I guess it's worth a try."

Ellis walked across to the phone and called Crane's campaign headquarters in Illinois. The senator was out at a meeting. Ellis spoke to Luther Waverley. "My name's Drew

Ellis. I'm a former OCI agent. I was with Ted Savona when he died. Tell the senator I know exactly what happened in 'Nam. Tell him I know about his computer system and his relationship with Boris Pomarev. Tell him that unless he arranges to meet and talk to me in the next few hours, I'm going public with everything that I know." He gave Waverley a phone number and put down the receiver.

An hour later Crane called. "Mr. Ellis, let me say first of all that the only reason I am calling you is to tell you that my prisoner of war record has been most carefully investigated and that record is totally contrary to the lies spread by a former member of my unit who was mentally unbalanced. Secondly, I want to warn you that if your preposterous allegations are repeated, I will bring an action against you for damages so substantial that two lifetimes will not be enough for you to pay them off."

"Savona was saner than you," Ellis said. "And Savona was murdered. Few people will believe that's simply coincidence. Besides, your computer system is a dead ringer for one that was stolen from Steve Widdell by a KGB agent called Boris Pomarev. Ambassador Courtney told me all about that in a recorded conversation I had with him before he died."

"The computer system isn't mine," Crane protested. "It's something I've hired."

"From Mr. Melkonian," Ellis said, "also known as Abe Makram, who once worked for Steve Widdell and helped Pomarev steal his system."

"I don't investigate the lives of everyone I do business with," Crane replied.

"Of course not," Ellis said. "You'll have lots of time to explain that to the press."

Crane asked, "Mr. Ellis, what evidence do you have of these allegations?"

"I told you. A tape recording of my conversation with Ambassador Courtney, the records of my investigation into the theft of Steve Widdell's computer system, and the deaths of Steve Widdell and his former associates, Lucas Amory, and Dick Schaffer."

There was a long silence before Crane asked, "Are you prepared to show me this evidence?"

"Yes. Provided we can meet quickly and alone."

"Agreed."

"Good. Eleven o'clock tomorrow morning at my house."
Ellis gave Crane directions. "You will park your car on the
driveway in front of the house and get out of it. On the lawn
outside you will see two chairs underneath an apple tree. You
will sit in the chair facing the tree."

"Mr. Ellis, are you sure this charade is necessary?"

"Very," Ellis said. "Both our lives could depend on it."

116

March 13, 1988

Early the next morning Ellis drove home with Patrick
and Loren. They jogged slowly through the woods, and
satisfied there were no intruders or ambushes, returned to
the house. With muted good-byes, Patrick and Loren left.

The house felt strangely alien as Ellis changed into
running shoes and his brown Goretex running suit. He
checked the cassette recorder and the magazine of the Beretta, collected binoculars, a hunting knife, and a spare clip of
ammunition, and went to the spot Petrovich had used, to
wait.

Crane's white Cadillac Seville was startlingly obvious as
it undulated over the earthen track, little puffs of dust rising
around the rims of its white-walled tires. Ellis peered at it
through his binoculars. Crane was driving—a burly man in a
pale blue suit, with short blond hair parted neatly to the side,
slightly protuberant blue eyes, a pensive expression of calm.
He drove to the front of the house, got out of the car, and sat
in the chair Ellis had placed beneath the apple tree. Ellis got
to his feet and loped down the hillside.

When he was level with the house, he called, "Crane,
I'm coming out now. I want you to sit where you are and to
place your palms flat on the tops of your thighs."

Crane stared resentfully at the trees but did as he was
told.

Ellis walked into the clearing, gun held loosely in one

hand, tape recorder biting into his chest. The morning was too warm for Goretex, his body covered in a light sweat. "Let me tell you what I know," he began. "Before he died, Ambassador Courtney told me everything about Bildeberg, how it was founded, how it went after Widdell's system, how it came to an arrangement with the Russians, how Bildeberg's own candidate was replaced by one favored by Boris Pomarev.

"I know you have Widdell's system, stolen by Pomarev with the help of your chief pollster, Melkonian, who is also known as Abe Makram. And I know what happened between you and Pomarev in Vietnam." He patted the recorder. "I have a recording here of my conversation with Ambassador Courtney. I also have copies of a report submitted to the Office of Counter Intelligence covering all the other matters, including the sworn affidavits of Loren Eastman and myself of our meeting with Ted Savona. If we do not reach agreement now, it is my intention to deliver all this evidence to the media."

Crane glared at him. "I could sue you for libel."

"Perhaps you could. But even if you succeed, it will be too late. You'll never make president."

Crane swallowed. "What do you want?"

"First of all I want you to withdraw from the presidential primaries. Then I want you to tell me who else is in Bildeberg. I want to know who Bildeberg's Agency contact is, and who in the Agency works with Bildeberg."

"And presumably you will want them to withdraw from whatever they are doing?"

"Withdrawal may not be enough," Ellis said.

Crane sighed. He was bigger and more florid than his publicity photographs. His skin was rougher, and his camera smile successfully hid the mean curve of his mouth. He said, "Why don't you sit down, Mr. Ellis, and let's talk sensibly."

Ellis walked to the apple tree and leaned his back against it.

"First of all," Crane said, "there's as little point in my telling you who I know in Bildeberg as there is in your attempting to divert them. Bildeberg is a living, growing organism. It stretches through many communities and countries. You take out one member, and another replaces him. You take out one section, another replaces it. If you devoted the rest of your life to the task, you still would not finish off Bildeberg.

"Secondly, neither the objectives of Bildeberg nor those of Boris Pomarev and his Russian friends, are hostile to America, or Russia. The coalition we seek through the control of the presidency will usher in a new era of peace and prosperity. What we seek, Mr. Ellis, is a rapprochement between this country and Russia, a rapprochement that will bring an end to the state of muted hostility that presently exists, a rapprochement that will end the reckless and futile expenditure of resources on arms, a rapprochement that will eliminate the risk of nuclear war and bring true peace in our time." Crane stopped and looked around as if expecting applause.

"How do you mean to achieve this?" Ellis asked.

"Quite simply, through a shared control not only of the presidency, but of the Politburo. You see, Mr. Ellis, Pomarev's participation in Bildeberg has a reverse effect. It makes him one of the most powerful men in Russia, and through Pomarev and men like him, we will control the Kremlin."

Men like Pomarev and Crane would never use that control for the benefit of others, Ellis thought. They were evil men, killers and accessories to murder, ruthless men, thieves without moral scruples of any kind, men whose only god was personal ambition. Men like Crane and Pomarev and Hardinger would only use such control to expand their own power and benefit themselves.

As if to confirm that, Crane said, "Underpinning this structure will be a vast new Russo-American economic combine, bigger and more powerful than any economic unit the world has ever known. You, too, could be part of this new world, Mr. Ellis. All it takes is a little courage, now."

And afterward, Ellis thought, all it would take was a bullet in the back of the neck. He said, "No, Senator. I'm not buying that."

"I implore you," Crane said passionately, "please accept my word. Our objects are peace and prosperity for all. I personally would never do anything that would hurt my country. Like you, Mr. Ellis, I have put my life at the service of my country."

Ellis shook his head. "You'll have to do a whole lot better than that, Senator. I neither trust you or believe you. And I don't trust Boris Pomarev either."

Crane sighed. "I see that convincing you is going to take more time than we have." His mouth twisted. "Let me put it another way. How much do you want for your information and your silence? I am authorized to offer you any amount within reason that will buy the silence of you and your colleagues." He stared hopefully at Ellis. "Say a quarter of a million dollars . . . ? Each?"

"No, Mr. Crane."

"Half a million dollars each?"

"No. We are not for sale."

"There's more. You can have what you want. My offer is underwritten by Cas Hardinger. You know of Cas Hardinger?"

"And his involvement with Bildeberg, yes."

"So don't be foolish, Mr. Ellis. Take what is offered. Go away and live happily." He reached into his pocket and held out a piece of paper. "Write whatever figure you want."

Ellis stared at the paper. It was a check drawn on the Chase Manhattan Bank and signed by Cas Hardinger. The amount was left blank. Ellis reached forward. He heard the whir of a bullet in the air between him and Crane, followed by the deep roar of a high-powered rifle. He hurled himself to the ground and twisted into the narrow shelter afforded by the apple tree.

Ellis looked over his shoulder at Crane, still seated comfortably, hands hovering in front of his jacket. Crane hadn't intended paying him any money. Crane had simply sprung a trap, and right now he was trapped between a gunman and Crane.

A second shot thundered out, snapping into the tree by his chest. Ellis turned sideways and rested his shoulder against the tree. He pointed his gun at Crane. A third shot crashed out, high and to his left. Ellis cocked his gun. "Go on," he shouted at Crane. "Get the hell out before I kill you."

Crane took one look at the cocked gun and hurried over to the Cadillac. Ellis kept him covered until he got into it, wheeled the car around, and drove away. Ellis watched the car go. The paper had been the signal for the unseen gunman to fire. But how had a gunman got there? How had a gunman known?

Ellis risked a look around the trunk of the tree. The shots had come from the knoll behind the house. Unbuckling the tape recorder, he sat in a sprinter's crouch and waited, feeling the muscles of his thighs and calf tense. He focused all his attention on the woods at the edge of the lawn. Three,

two, one . . . He felt his muscles tremble, his stomach tighten
as if on a drawstring. Go!

He exploded into a sprint. His wheeling legs pounded
the earth. Grass blurred under his feet. A shot rang out. He
swerved. A second shot. He rose into the air, flying forward,
arms folded in front of his face, landing on bent arms and
knees, sliding on dead leaves, swiveling sideways and rolling
into the forest. Safe!

He rolled till he was sure he was sheltered by the trees,
then turned on his face and crawled. He would make for the
knoll from the side, dragging slowly through the undergrowth, sitting up cautiously when he believed he was out of
sight.

No one fired.

He stood up. Still no shooting. He darted across the trail
and plunged into the woods on the farther side, running
lightly, gun held loosely in his right hand. He would climb
out of the dip under cover of the forest, go up the side of the
knoll. It was only near the top that he would have to be
cautious. That was where the trees ended and there was no
cover.

He began his climb. As far as he could see, nothing was
moving on the knoll. The gunman might have come down the
side of the hill, but then it occurred to him that he wasn't on
a trail, so how would the gunman know where to come?

Ellis ran on. He could see the dappled sunshine beyond
the trees. He slowed momentarily, searching the undergrowth for any sign of movement. Out of the undergrowth
almost directly in front of him a woman stepped out. Emma!

He had only a split second to register the vision of
Emma standing in front of him, arms held out toward him in
the position he had taught her, hands clasped tightly around
the butt of a gun.

"Emma! No!" He tried to bring his gun hand up, but it
was weighted with lead. "Emma! It's—" The gun belched
flame. Ellis felt the bullet catch him high on the chest, felt
himself rise through the air on legs that were suddenly
weightless, felt himself float downward as Emma's gun followed
the trajectory of his fall.

It wasn't Emma! Emma was DEAD!

Ellis hit the ground and rolled on the soft leaves. Emma
lowered her gun, revealing the lower part of her face. It was

not Emma, it was definitely not Emma! It was someone repeating Goddard's ploy with Petrovich, someone who'd had access to his file! Ellis raised his gun and fired.

The bullet drove into the middle of her chest above her lowered gun. He saw the shock in her eyes and the way the light suddenly went out of them as, hands unclasping, knees folding, she crumpled onto the muddy earth. Ellis couldn't move, didn't want to move. It was peaceful lying on his back staring at the patterns the trees made against the gray sky. Peaceful, quiet, listening to gentle rustlings and the pounding of his heart. He had killed Emma. No it wasn't Emma. It was—

There was another sound, slow, deliberate, repeated. The gunman had placed the girl on one side of the knoll and gone scouting down the other. Now he'd heard the sound of the shots and returned. Ellis closed a nerveless hand around the butt of his gun and turned his head toward the gentle sound of movement.

Through a gray mist Ellis could hear footsteps getting closer. He closed his eyes tightly then opened them. The footsteps were closer. The mist had cleared. Suede cavalry boots were advancing over the leaves toward him, brown trouser legs pressed against the drooping barrel of a Winchester. He lay very still, moving his eyes up the legs, up the gun barrel.

"I'm sorry, Drew."

It was Jim Colson! Colson was Bildeberg's Agency contact! In one final desperate second everything fell into place. Colson was part of Bildeberg. Colson had worked with Pomarev in Berlin to further the objectives of Bildeberg. Colson had betrayed Lotus to protect Pomarev, and it was to protect Colson that Pomarev had had Zonda kill Emma! *Darling, liebchen, they weren't taken, they were betrayed! Darling, I know who!*

And when Theo had begun to investigate the deaths of Amory and Widdell, when Theo's investigation had drawn close to Bildeberg, Colson had killed Theo. And used Petrovich after Theo's murder to make Ellis reveal what he knew. And when he'd known, had attempted to have Ellis killed in the hotel. Crane must have told him of their meeting, and Colson had come to kill him, bringing a fake Emma to shock him into temporary immobility. Jim, Ellis thought. Why did you? How could you?

Colson was looking down at him, his blue eyes pitiless. "I can't let you stop us, Drew. You must understand that. You must understand that more is at stake than your life or mine. We must think of children and future generations, we must preserve America for them. I am—"

Ellis pulled the gun around and fired.

Colson jerked, setting off the Winchester, then staggered backward, looking in surprise at the bloody red stain that had blossomed across his chest. "No," he gasped. "You wouldn't . . . you couldn't. . . ." Colson sank to his knees. "Drew, my fr—" He slumped forward, looking for a moment as if he were throwing himself down in worship. Then his arms crumpled and he sagged sideways, his open eyes staring into Ellis's.

117

His chest tightly strapped, the pain dulled by drugs, Ellis lay listening as Patrick told him how they'd raced back to the house at the sound of the shots and found him in the clearing beside Colson. They'd pulled him away, brought him back to Patrick's retreat house and sent for the same doctor who'd treated him before.

The doctor said Ellis was lucky the bullet had been diverted by the zipper of his running suit. Its velocity, however, had the effect of driving a narrow metal wedge into his sternum, chipping a bone and rendering him almost unconscious. The doctor had insisted Ellis rest and move as little as possible for the next few days. The way he felt now, Ellis hoped he'd never have to move again.

"I'm sorry we let Colson get into the woods," Patrick said. "We should have been more thorough."

"It was a big area to cover with just the two of you," Ellis replied. He thought, I have killed twice. Christ have mercy on me. I have sinned. I didn't want to do it. It was forced on me. Through my fault, he muttered silently, through my most grievous fault. Forgive us our trespasses.

"You did the right thing," Patrick said firmly. "You did the only thing you could do. Nowhere in the bible does it say that you have to sacrifice your life for the sake of evil. And Colson was an evil man." He checked the bandages on Ellis's chest. "Because of the deaths, I had to go outside." His hand tightened on Ellis's as Ellis started. "Don't worry. I took it to a pristine source—Sid Rayburn, the president's attorney, and then," Patrick smiled softly, "President Donnelly himself.

"Donnelly had me meet with a special section of the FBI, which, pending talking to you, has sanitized the recent deaths. They've also taken care of the doctor's report. And everyone agrees that the best way to stop Crane is by giving the evidence we have to the media. I've arranged for my friends on the *Globe* to examine the evidence tomorrow and meet with you."

"What about the others?" Ellis asked. "Hardinger... Bradley?"

"The FBI is currently checking into Bradley's professorships. I think he's going to have a hard time getting an important job again. And as far as Hardinger is concerned, it seems the FBI fraud squad wants to talk to him about tax irregularities and certain illegal share deals he's made." Patrick shrugged. "It seems that even if Bildeberg's plan succeeded, Hardinger would not have benefited from it."

"What about Makram?"

"The FBI is checking him out. They think he could be a deep-cover KGB agent using the identity of a dead person or a Russian emigré. With a bit of luck they'll get him before the Crane story blows. And best of all, the FBI has got some very interesting information regarding Pomarev. It seems a note was delivered to the home of the director yesterday, written in Russian on KGB notepaper. It was unsigned and bore no fingerprints, but in the view of the FBI experts who examined it, the paper comes from the office of KGB Deputy Director Vladimir Simenon.

"The note says that Pomarev's operation in the USA is not sanctioned by the KGB, that the KGB is opposed to the aims of that operation and to the people behind Pomarev. It goes on to say that Pomarev is a traitor, that they have evidence he was paid two million dollars to join with Bildeberg, among whose members were Whillan Courtney, Senator Anderson, Jim Colson and Cas Hardinger. It says that Pomarev worked together with Colson in Berlin to further the objectives of Bildeberg, which were in direct opposition to those of Russia and America. Apparently, Pomarev's involvement was discovered by the KGB, but before they could get the necessary proof, he broke up the Lotus network, was promoted to the deputy directorship of Service A, and was thereby able to put himself beyond the reach of the investigation."

Emma, Ellis thought resignedly. Poor, dear Emma. He said, "Simenon is the director of the KGB. What is he doing about this?"

"He says that he has taken certain steps to prevent Pomarev's plan from succeeding. He doesn't say what those steps are." The phone rang. "That'll be for me." Patrick picked it up. "Yes? Just one moment." He held the receiver out to Loren. "For you."

Loren frowned nervously as she held the receiver to her ear. "Hello. Who is it?" Her voice tightened as she said, "Yes, this is Loren Eastman." Her face went white and tears came to her eyes. She said, "Yes, yes, of course I will." They all heard the snap as the receiver at the other end was replaced. Loren remained staring into space, receiver held to her ear, tears rolling unheeded down her cheeks.

"What is it?" Ellis and Patrick asked in unison.

She looked at them numbly. "It's Marty," she said. "He's been kidnapped by Pomarev and Zonda!"

"Oh, God help us!" Patrick put his arms around her shoulders. "What exactly did Pomarev say?"

"He said if I wanted Marty back alive, I had to be at my home in Toronto by noon tomorrow. I was to bring Ellis with me, together with every shred of evidence we've collected. He said that if there was any attempt to inform the media about Crane, if I did not do exactly as he said—or if I made any attempt to inform the authorities—he would have Zonda shoot Marty."

"He can't," Patrick replied quickly. "You won't . . . Ellis can't travel. Don't worry about a thing, Loren. We'll get the FBI and the RCMP—"

"We can't let a child die over this," Ellis said.

Patrick frowned. "There isn't a lot we can do. We should leave this one to the authorities. They have greater experience and greater facilities in these things."

"Pomarev wants Loren and me. It would be safer to do

as he says. We cannot sacrifice a little boy's life over this."

Patrick stared at him. After a while he said, "Drew, I know what you're planning. Don't do it. You're too ill to make it work."

"It can work," Ellis said fiercely. "'It will have to work." He took the phone and held it out to Loren. "Call your husband and find out if it's true. Impress upon him that he should do absolutely nothing. Tell him you have everything under control."

Loren looked at him. "But—but—"

"Do it," Ellis snapped. "Patrick and I have an idea." Patrick took Ellis' hand and began to pray.

118

March 14, 1988

Loren's house in Toronto had been shut up for two weeks and the air inside smelled stale. Ellis and Loren waited in the downstairs living room for the phone to ring. Outside the sun shone from a cloudless sky. The shreds of snow that had lined the pavements on Ellis's last visit had disappeared.

According to Loren's former husband, the kidnapping had been effected very smoothly. There'd been no violence, no forced entries. One moment the child had been playing in the backyard, the next moment, like an errant cloud, gone. They'd only realized his disappearance and contacted the police moments before Loren had called. Tredigar had been furious at having to call them off, ending the conversation by shouting, "I don't know what you think you're doing, but he's my child as well as yours!"

Which had been one more weight to add to the burden of guilt and responsibility Loren already carried. For the thousandth time she asked Ellis, "Do you think Marty will be all right?"

"Yes," Ellis replied patiently. "They won't do anything to

him while we have the evidence they want." He didn't tell her that everything would happen afterward, that Pomarev had to eliminate them as well as the evidence.

The phone rang. Though they'd both been willing it and expecting it, they both started in surprise. Loren picked it up, going suddenly pale and dry-mouthed. "Yes," she said hoarsely.

Ellis leaned in front of her and caught her eye. Loren nodded. He took the phone from her. "Pomarev, this is Ellis... Yes, we're here in Toronto exactly as you ordered... Since you checked us out at the airport, you know we're alone. But there's one thing: We didn't bring the evidence you wanted."

"I warn you, Mr. Ellis," Pomarev said, "don't play games with me or with the life of this child. You know who and how many times Zonda has killed before."

"And how many kinds of a fool do you think I am to bring the evidence to a location known to you without any kind of protection?" Ellis replied. "No, Mr. Pomarev, if this exchange is going ahead, then it must be on mutually agreed terms. And the first of those terms is that we must not be placed in a position where we could be compelled to surrender the evidence without you returning the child to us unharmed."

"I am a man of my word, Mr. Ellis. And why should I harm a little boy if I already have what I want?"

"Nevertheless, this is how the exchange is being done," Ellis said. "The evidence is being flown over separately by a courier. When it arrives in Toronto, I will let you know. Then you will let us know where to meet. At the meeting you will produce the child, unharmed. Then we shall give you the evidence you require."

After a short pause, Pomarev said, "That seems fair. As long as you deliver all the evidence, Mr. Ellis—tapes, copies, everything."

"That I will," Ellis said. "As further protection, the case containing the evidence will be locked and wired, the combination known only to me. Any attempt to force the case will not only destroy the evidence, it will destroy everyone in the room with it."

"Mr. Ellis, I am a man of my word. Such measures are unnecessary."

"They have already been taken. When we know the

child is safe, I will open the case in your presence and you can check to see if you have all the evidence you need. Because the mechanism cannot be safely activated a second time, there will be no prior examination of the case."

Again the short pause before Pomarev said, "Agreed. I congratulate you on your thoroughness."

"Fine, where do we meet?"

"I will call you back when you have the evidence."

"Do you have a number where you can be reached?"

"No," Pomarev said. "Don't call me, Mr. Ellis. I'll call you."

Twenty minutes later he did. "Mr. Ellis, has your courier arrived?"

"Yes."

"How long will it take you to collect the evidence?"

"Five minutes."

"Are you ready to leave right away?"

"Yes."

"Good. Now, write this down. Go north on Don Mills Road until you come to the intersection with Lawrence. Go west on Lawrence and turn into the first shopping mall you see, which will be on your left. Just inside the entrance you will find three pay phones. Be at the middle phone in seventeen minutes." He put the phone down.

Ellis chained the briefcase containing the evidence to his wrist and gave Loren Pomarev's directions. They were at the shopping mall in twelve minutes.

119

An hour later they were still traveling. Using a series of pay phones, Pomarev had moved them west, then north, and now they were traveling east, a journey designed not only to reveal any followers, but to wear them out with anxiety and monotonous effort. Ellis's chest hurt, and the constant stopping, starting, and darting into phone booths made him feel tired and ill.

They drove east, along the northern border of the city. Pomarev's next call was made to a small shopping mall, and the one after that was only four minutes away, behind a gas station. Loren looked wan and tense when she returned. "It's the last one," she said, throwing herself behind the wheel of the Volkswagen. "He wants us to go to the end of Brimley Road and stop."

The street was bordered by a lengthy development of suburban houses, then by two vast fields. It ended amidst a partially constructed housing development, with parked bulldozers ahead. Loren stopped the car, and Ellis saw Zonda walk out of an unfinished house behind them, stop halfway across the road and beckon. They got out and walked toward him.

Zonda was bigger than he remembered, with flat, Slavic cheeks behind that curving mustache and sea-mist eyes. The scar beneath his lower lip was vivid. His face betrayed a faint glimmer of interest as he looked over at Ellis. Then he stood aside, motioned them to precede him up the boarded driveway into the unfinished house.

The windows were flecked with white paint, the interior dusty and uncarpeted. Pomarev stood by a curving stairway just beyond the entrance, the politeness of his smile eradicated by the long barreled Sturm-Ruger in his hand. He stepped back and pointed to a door behind him. "We go down there."

Ellis stopped. "First the child," he said.

"He will be brought to you." Pomarev lifted his head and called out in Russian. A door of one of the bedrooms above them opened and a woman came onto the balcony, holding Marty.

"Baby!" Loren strained toward him, but Pomarev stood firmly by the stairway, his gun focused on them.

"You shall have him very soon, Professor Eastman. Now let's go downstairs and finish our business."

"No," Loren said. "I want Marty with me."

Above them Marty was wrestling with the woman and crying out "Mommy! I want to go to my mommy!"

Again Pomarev said something in Russian and the woman released the boy, who bounded down the stairs past Pomarev and into Loren's arms. "Don't worry, darling, Mommy's here, everything will be all right." She straightened up carrying him and smiling, following Pomarev down another flight of stairs, Ellis by her side.

They entered a vast basement room that spread the length of the house, its walls unfinished, timbers and foundations exposed. Four electric bulbs cast a shadowy illumination. The killing ground, thought Ellis, where packed earth and concrete would muffle the sound of shots and cries of anguish. He forced himself to concentrate on his task. Everything depended on him now, how swiftly and efficiently he could move. Pomarev was standing in front of him; Loren and the child beside him; Zonda, who had followed them downstairs, one foot on the stairs. It was the worst conceivable position, Ellis thought. He'd have to attack in opposite directions. But too late for regrets now. Too late for anything, especially if he got it wrong.

"You have the child," Pomarev said. "Now deactivate the briefcase and open it."

Ellis closed his eyes for a moment, said a silent prayer: Not my will, O Lord, but thine be done. Deliberately, he unlocked the case from his wrist. Though Zonda was the more lethal, he'd have to start with Pomarev, who had the drawn gun. Turning away so his shadow fell over the case and his body shielded it from both Pomarev and Zonda, Ellis knelt and unlocked the combination. He gripped the lid of the case with his left hand and slipped his right beneath it. His searching fingers coiled around the butt of the Colt.

"Ellis! What are you doing?"

Pomarev! He had to act now! He swivelled, hurling the case at Pomarev. The case struck Pomarev in the face and shoulder, knocking the gun out of his hand. Good. That was more luck than he'd thought he had. He came upright, fighting the pain in his chest, Colt clutched in his hand.

"No, Drew, no!" Suddenly Loren and the boy were between him and Pomarev.

Then a swinging arm cast Loren aside, a fist struck Ellis in the plexus, and a vast circle of pain imploded, spread, spiraled. The air sucked out of him in a giant vacuum. His legs went limp and he staggered for balance. Tears streamed from his eyes. The gun slipped from his nerveless fingers and clanged to the floor.

He had to move! Had to! He twisted his body, moved his shoulder out at Pomarev, saw the gun at his feet, let his knees go, fell over it.

Pomarev was on him immediately, hands tearing at his

shoulders, forcing Ellis onto his back. Ellis's palm swept the floor. He beat at it with his elbow. Felt under him and closed his fingers around the gun butt.

A second chance! Pomarev saw what he was doing and moved quickly. His hand snaked forward and pinned Ellis's wrist. "Shoot them," he called over Ellis's head. "Shoot them all!"

Zonda had moved into the room, gun drawn and pointing down. Ellis knew this was it. There was no way Zonda would miss at that range. He was going to die.

He let his eyes wander up the hollow of the barrel, saw the gun cocked and the safety catch off, saw Zonda's finger curve against the trigger.

Oh God, forgive my sins. Accept my spirit.

Zonda's finger moved, the muzzle flashed and the sound of the shot filled the room. Ellis felt nothing. Zonda had missed—but Zonda couldn't miss at that range. A thick wetness fell across his face. He was dying, too numb from shock to feel anything. He was—

Pomarev slumped forward onto him, his bloody head pressed to Ellis's face.

120

Slowly Ellis pushed Pomarev away and sat up. Zonda's gun moved to cover him. "Take the woman and child and go," Zonda said. "Everything is finished."

Ellis looked across at Pomarev. "Why?" he asked.

"It is an internal matter," Zonda said. "He was a traitor. What he was doing here did not have the sanction of the KGB."

"Nor of Vladimir Simenon?"

Zonda stared at him for a moment before he said, "Yes."

121

They drove back to Loren's, Ellis painfully, Loren hugging Marty, who, with the unpredictability of children, fell sound asleep. Ellis called Patrick and told him what had happened, told him they'd not been seen or heard and that a body squad could probably clear everything up.

Patrick took ten minutes to talk to the FBI and organize the squad, then told Ellis that soon after receiving a phone call from the *Globe*, Crane had withdrawn, that Makram had fled, and that Hardinger had been arrested on charges of tax fraud and insider trading. "You can come home now, Drew," he said. "It's all over. There are lots of people who want to talk to you in Washington and shake your hand."

"Yes," Ellis said, with a sense of gnawing emptiness.

"The Bureau's very impressed with you. They even want to offer you a job."

"Thanks but no thanks," Ellis said. "I'll call you as soon as I get back to Washington." He put the phone down and told Loren, "It's over now. You'll be safe. The kid'll be safe."

She reached up and touched his face. "And what about you?"

"I don't know." This is the end he thought. It was over. Finished.

She said, "You could stay here awhile, if you wanted to. That way we could get to know each other better. Marty too."

He looked from Loren to the sleeping child and back again. He thought: to begin again is a privilege given to few. He reached forward and took her hand.

ABOUT THE AUTHOR

OWEN SELA, who makes his home in London, England, is a prolific author. His first success was the thriller *Exchange of Eagles*. Since then he has written a number of fast-paced novels of espionage including *Kremlin Control*, *The Skorpion Dossier* and now, *The KGB Candidate*. Currently Mr. Sela is hard at work on a panoramic historical novel set in early India.

A Thrilling Development
from